Praise for *Thy Neighbor* by Norah Vincent

"There are no more secrets, as *Thy Neighbor* so artfully demonstrates, and we know so much that it's bound to kill someone, and deaden us. Worse, we're beyond being redeemed by a rain squall and a renewed appreciation for the miracle of being alive. That's the heartbreaking truth at the heart of Norah Vincent's dark funny debut novel." —*The Millions*

"Explores the boundaries of parent-child relationships, love, privacy, criminality, abuse, and normalcy . . . Pretty intense."
—*The Buffalo News*

"Filled with the darkest sides of the human capacity for cruelty, Vincent's fiction debut is no forgettable beach read. Instead, she presents a slicing examination of the bonds between families, neighbors, and strangers in a way that will have readers wondering about the secrets on their own streets." —*Booklist*

"Missing *Thy Neighbor* could be a crime. . . . When [Vincent lets us see what Nick is seeing] it's hard to look away and it's hard to feel sorry for Nick anymore. That he's a voyeur becomes as reprehensible as what he sees and what happens is a big surprise." —*The Washington Blade*

"This first novel is an absorbing psychological mystery. . . . The depiction of depraved excesses, along with some of the neighbors' more bizarre behavior, provides a vivid and warped background as the novel delves into the characters' motivations and emotions with empathy and acuity."
—*Library Journal*

PENGUIN BOOKS

THY NEIGHBOR

Norah Vincent was born in Detroit, Michigan, in 1968. Formerly an op-ed columnist for the *Los Angeles Times*, she is the author of two previous works of nonfiction, the *New York Times* bestseller *Self-Made Man: One Woman's Year Disguised as a Man* and *Voluntary Madness: Lost and Found in the Mental Healthcare System*. She lives in New York City.

Norah Vincent | *Thy Neighbor*

Penguin Books

PENGUIN BOOKS
Published by the Penguin Group
Penguin Group (USA) Inc., 375 Hudson Street,
New York, New York 10014, USA

USA | Canada | UK | Ireland | Australia | New Zealand | India | South Africa | China
Penguin Books Ltd, Registered Offices: 80 Strand, London WC2R oRL, England
For more information about the Penguin Group visit penguin.com

First published in the United States of America by Viking Penguin,
a member of Penguin Group (USA) Inc., 2012
Published in Penguin Books 2013

Grateful acknowledgment is made for permission to reprint excerpts from the following copyrighted works:
"As I Walked Out One Evening" from *Collected Poems of W. H. Auden.* Copyright 1940 and renewed 1968 by
    W. H. Auden. Used by permission of Random House, Inc.
"The Silken Tent" from *The Poetry of Robert Frost*, edited by Edward Connery Lathem. Copyright © 1969 by
    Henry Holt and Company. Copyright © 1942 by Robert Frost. Copyright © 1970 by Lesley Frost Ballantine.
    Reprinted by permission of Henry Holt and Company, LLC.

THE LIBRARY OF CONGRESS HAS CATALOGED THE HARDCOVER EDITION AS FOLLOWS:
Vincent, Norah.
    Thy neighbor / Norah Vincent.
    p. cm.
    ISBN 978-0-670-02374-5 (hc.)
    ISBN 978-0-14-312366-8 (pbk.)
    1. Parents—Death—Fiction.   2. Voyeurism—Fiction.   3. Psychological fiction.   I. Title.
    PS3622.I536T48 2012
    813'.6—dc23   2011043907

Printed in the United States of America
10 9 8 7 6 5 4 3 2 1

Designed by Carla Bolte • Set in Warnock Light with Metro Office

This is a work of fiction. Names, characters, places, and incidents either are the product of the author's imagination or are used fictitiously, and any resemblance to actual persons, living or dead, business establishments,
events, or locales is entirely coincidental.

O stand, stand at the window
As the tears scald and start;
You shall love your crooked neighbour
With your crooked heart.

—W. H. Auden

Thy Neighbor

A suburban neighborhood at night is like a body on a surgeon's table.
Defenseless.
Out cold.
Yet also palpably alive and beckoning.
Flirtatiously inert.
As if waiting.
As if asking for something to be done.
It lies there, like a living, sleeping creature in the dark.
Shallow breath and loose appendages.
All its houses spread apart.
So infinitely still.
But wide open.
Splayed.
As if each wall had rolled up with the waning of the day,
And each lawn, each drive unfurled itself.
A tongue of silent invitation.
The hurt is unmistakable.
The wound in a place of rest.
Is vulnerable.
A tender, tender bruise is peace.
And quiet speaks.
Here I am. Here I am.
Hiding.
Over here.
Now over there.
Again here.
I hear you.
Taunting.
I feel you.
Imply consent.
You, so animate, inanimate,

Sprawling in the bounds of your serpentine streets,
Your painted boxes all arranged
In rows and skirts of foliage,
Indiscreetly shield each dear, dear nesting thing.
You possess me.
And so I you.
I possess this quiet place and all its houses.
At night, I am the dream of stealth
To all my silenced people.
A sort of god, unknown,
But half believed in.
I am he who wakes while all are sleeping.
Watches while they wake.

1

I found that little ode to psychopathology this past Monday afternoon crumpled in the wastebasket by my desk. It was strange to have found it there, I grant you, or even to have noticed it at all, since I don't make a habit of pawing through my trash.

But this particular item, on this particular day, couldn't help but catch my eye. It was written on pink paper, for one, which I could see especially well because that wastebasket is made of metal mesh and because, as on this occasion, it is almost always empty. Or empty of paper, anyway.

I never do any work by hand. I write on the computer, and when I do make the minimum payment on my bills, always several months late, I do it paperlessly on the Web.

That basket's a prop more than anything, the kind of design-challenged bachelor's IKEA accessory you're supposed to have in any respectable writer's sanctum, and if you're a real *guy* guy, the place where you repeatedly shoot and miss idle baskets with your college hacky sack while balanced on the hind legs of your desk chair, dredging up your bright ideas.

But I'm not a real *guy* guy, so I wouldn't know. I'm just a hired clown covering for a nerd.

The sad truth about my wastebasket is that I've heaved more vomit into it than toys or paper. The mesh is surprisingly retentive, you'll be relieved to hear, and a snap to clean with a garden hose.

More often than not, that stout receptacle is the first thing I see when I wake, or the first thing I hug and plunge my head into, depending on how hard the clown was covering the night before—specifically, how many times he yelled "Shots!" (or something equally adolescent) down the whole length of the bar before someone in a position of authority forcibly retired him for the night.

I sleep on the couch in my study a lot more often than I sleep in my bed, because I usually can't make it up the stairs.

And so it was on Monday, when I woke to find the strange pink bile-flecked piece of origami perched on a slick of Jameson like some oblivious flamingo sunning itself on an oil spill.

Pink is not a color I confess to—on paper, anyway. That's a really tired cliché of fragile masculinity, I realize, but there it is. Predictable and true. In that, as in so much else, I'm drearily typical. Not that I haven't gone the other way—I've embraced the macho pastel in the past, and that's more embarrassing to admit. I wore the pale pink polo for a semester in college, to show I wasn't afraid, and I swore more colorfully then, too, about all the pinkest parts of the female anatomy, just in case there was any doubt.

But there has always been doubt. How could there not be doubt when this person, this image that is me, is not organic? Not grown out of the common ground and the consensus of culture into solid, conforming meat that is exactly what it looks like: a dude.

I am not that.

I was never that. I was a child built by committee, and then a man by osmosis.

I'm a plastic cast of put-on, pumped-up, artificial dude*ness* at best, that bears absolutely no resemblance to the freak show insect-boy beneath. I look like I stepped out of a catalog, because I did. I memorized myself from movies and men's magazines.

I'm not a person. I'm a facsimile. As far from myself as the antipodes, and—big surprise coming here—I drink to cover the distance.

My teenage years were ones of vengeful transformation.

In the mirror, as I watched myself grow into the sculpture of my parents' good genes, and out in the world, where I saw the pagan beauty of my face begin to wield its power over other people, men and women, I learned that I could use my looks as a glare to hide the drab and charmless grub that lived behind my eyes.

At seventeen I was lean and six foot three, a specimen in the making. I didn't have to try. But by thirty I was tired and showing the drink, a breaking man with too much vanity and time on his hands. And so I did what idle, vain men do. I took supplements. And I joined a gym, flexing and ripping my besotted flesh six times a week until I got the body that only banned substances can build.

And here I stand, at thirty-four, a perfect fake, the botched product of one of those boys' preparatory boarding schools where dishevel-haired, smooth-cheeked yachting models are bred, acquire their torsos on the swim team, and have been wearing designer loafers without socks since they were shitting themselves raw.

I may not be one of the boys at heart, but I do a damned good impression all the same. I've had years of practice, and I dress the part. Business casual, of course. The uniform for every middle-class white American male from six to sixty. Khakis and a button-down. A polo and cargo shorts in summer. Done.

Workers of the world. We might as well be wearing burlap gray pajamas, marching every day to our salt mines of finance and information technology, hurrying home fully cocked (pharmaceutically, if necessary) to pound our Pixy Stick wives into fruition so that when the next replica pops out we'll be waiting at the door of the womb ready with the slip-ons, quipping to our, and only our, infinite delight, "If the shoe fits . . ."

Jesus. Shoot me now.

That's my pedigree, but not, I hope, my fate. So far, I have eluded the wife and family, as well as the white-collar white slavery on the trading floor, or the soul-sucking dronery of the corner office P and L.

I work at home, or pretend to, and on my own creaturely schedule. I sleep late, and I stay up late. In winter I barely see the light of day. When most people are getting up, I'm just going to bed, and when they're picking up their kids for soccer practice or propping their eyes open with triple shots of McSpresso to make it through the four p.m. fit of narcolepsy at Shiteco, I'm just having my blissful waking piss.

I spend the early evening putting myself back together from the night before—DayQuil, Nicorette, Gatorade—so that I can make a college stab at writing whatever book review or snarky think piece I've been assigned that month. I say month, because there really isn't enough work to tally on a weekly basis, and most of it's long-deadline, loose-ended, sidebar pap that a frisky summer intern could bang out stoned.

I give my so-called job my over-the-counter all for as long as I can stand it—usually twenty minutes max—and then I turn to this virtual notebook instead, because it's the only place in the world where I can hide my third-rate mind and my shameless shame and exhibit them at the same time. Yell it all into the void for safekeeping, where it does and does not exist. I do this every day, usually for an hour or two, or for as long as it takes for Dave to interrupt me.

That is Dave's entire function: to interrupt. And subsequently, to distract. He does this very well, and that is the only reason why I allow him over the threshold.

Dave is somewhere around my age, a year or two older. He told me once, but I can't remember and can't be bothered to ask. Our dads played golf together, so I've known him off and on for most of my life. We drink together at least three nights a week and drive each other crawling into the vomitorium at dawn because neither of us can resist the taunt—"pussy"—when the phrase "I think I've had enough" or something similarly bleary and cautionary burbles up from one or the other of us far too late in the evening.

We're both still emasculated enough by our late fathers and our failures to think that liver damage and venereal disease are veritable measures of a man's worth, and we behave accordingly.

We sit. We drink. We rail and rhapsodize about cunt, and we are generally such a shameful waste of plasma that we dishonor even the furniture.

Dave runs his dad's vending machine business the way all reluctant sons pursue the foisted inheritances of untimely death, with resentful passivity and a well-nursed conviction that he was meant for something better.

His dad dropped dead at fifty-two one afternoon on the racquetball court when Dave was just out of college, and Dave was left to salvage the family's misfortune so that his younger sister, Sylvia, then a junior in high school, could go to college herself, and his mother, Kitty, who is everything her name implies, could go on living in the kept, cosmetic style to which she had become accustomed.

So ended Dave's promising career as a fashion photographer and jet-set seducer of women, or whatever the fuck it was he thought he was meant for, and so began his real life as paper trail CEO, bibulous wingman, and sedentary misogynist.

He does nothing of any value or importance with his time, unless you count playing a mongoloid Falstaff to my Hal, but he lives very well nonetheless. For appearances' sake, he signs his name to the company financials every quarter, having satisfied himself that he's bilking the IRS out of a respectable six figures and not in turn being fleeced by his proxy, Alex, the stooge he pays far less to run the company than he pays himself not to.

Dave looks like every January man I see at the gym. You know the breed.

The guys my age and up who've been eating too many dollar value meals with their kids and look like gorilla fertility goddesses as a result. They're the New Year's resolutionaries who crowd into health clubs in the first weeks of the year and go through the motions on the ab crunch and the recumbent bike before they come to their senses and realize that it's health care they want, not health.

Thank God they lose heart so quickly, or I would.

Dave is one of their number except that he looks like he's been living in a cave his whole life, which, if you count his home theater, is largely true. His freckled fishbelly flesh is so pale it's blue, and has the consistency of an under-cooked donut. His eyes are as flat and black as a shark's, darting blankly back and forth between silver lids. The pupils are always dilated to the point of nearly obscuring the iris, which is some murky, barely discernable shoe-shine shade of brown that makes you think of death by tobacco.

Dave is a loathsome specimen. Existentially disgusting. Repulsive even to the idea of God. A dead soul in a goblin's body.

Even that is too worthy a description, too loaded with conscience and art. Dave is without either, and whatever made him is, too. He's like something out of a Hieronymus Bosch, but less dignified. A stinking example of all I hold profane. So much so, that I consider it the surest proof of my wretched-ness that I have stooped to make him, or keep him as, my friend. My best friend, if time wasted together is any indication.

Christ, what a mess.

How did I get here? And why do I need the added humiliation of a witness? Living alone and shoestring employed in a three-bedroom house in the suburbs—the house I grew up in, actually—which is now like a mausoleum to the undead, and a terrarium of aggrieved neglect.

On the face of it, this should have turned out better.

I am the scion of well-planned, well-executed privilege, boundless oppor-tunity, first-grade art class affirmation, tennis lessons, test prep, and day camp. I am the proud cum laude recipient of an obscenely overpriced higher education from one of the best small liberal arts colleges in the nation.

So what could be wrong?

A good question.

A very, very good question.

Well, Doctor (*cough*), here's the thing. I am also, as it happens, the beloved only boy of two handsome, cultured, Catholic professionals (one actual, one manqué) who reached middle age in the wrong spirit (a poor pun intended here, I'm afraid), and, *whoops*, killed each other in a drunken row three weeks after I received my dearly bought diploma.

That's right. Killed each other. Dead.

Actually, my father killed my mother, then himself.

This is the tie that binds Dave and me.

Sort of.

Dead dads (and for me, a dead mom and murder-suicide thrown in). Same age at onset of grief, or shock, or developmental arrest, what have you. Both wrecked, aimless sons, and with foisted inheritances to boot. His a business, mine a house. A house, fully paid off, that I can live in practically for free and that, despite its horrored past, I can't bring myself to sell or leave or incinerate.

I'm sorry? What's that?

Depressed? Destroyed? Crushed beneath the boot heel of fate?

Why, yes. I suppose so.

That's the short of it.

I am, to put it limply, a lost boy playing at lost generation because my father blew my mother into the next life with the family .45 and then tasted the muzzle for himself one summer evening while I was off finding myself in the national parks and legal whorehouses of the American Southwest.

Now give me my pills and walk away.

Actually, I don't see a doc.

I get my pills from Tijuana via a stripper friend, Jaz (short for Jazmin—not her real name, I'm guessing), who deals a sideline in pharmaceuticals. She can get me anything, but most of what I want is benzos. Anxiety balms: Valium, Xanax, Klonopin, Ativan, whatever's on the menu. When dosed liberally and taken with magnums of alcohol, they knock me on my face for long enough to mimic sleep.

They're doozies, but they can work in the waking hours, too. With just the barest nip or two of sour mash, they level the quake-rubble topography of my mind and let me coast on the barren plain of sweet amnesia like the kid I once was, taking those first euphoric pedal strokes on my brand-new BMX bike.

Thanks, Dad.

For the bike, the memories, the aftermath. For the genes that, in light of past events, you really have to wonder about.

What am I capable of? Can you be programmed for capability? Culpability? Or is that all in the upbringing? The circumstance? The substance abuse?

Hard to say, really.

I'm fine on the first count at least. Free and clear on the early influence, as I believe I've said. Golden normal child—as far as anyone could tell. Well heeled and well liked. Mom and Pop blameless in the offing. Not even an unwarranted spanking I can bring them up on. Just good, solid provider parenting that foretold nothing of what was to come.

As for circumstance, I'm slipping that second trap consistently. No wife, no bullet. Simple as that, and a staunch rule in this house. No woman is ever around long enough for me to kill her. Or long enough, that is, when I'm untreated and capable of wielding anything heavier than my whiskey-softened cock.

Which brings us to substances. Ordinarily, I'd agree. That's got trouble burned into it as surely as a brand on my ass cheek that says: RUN! Which is why, as a matter of policy, I never drink alone. There's always a crippler in the mix. A mellower, a flattener, a tranquilizing dart blown into selfsame ass cheek by cautionary zookeeper me before I even get the barest hint of a pheromone in the vicinity. No one has seen me blood count sober since I was twenty-one. Not even Dave, though that should go without saying, since no moderately intelligent or humane human being could stand Dave's unadulterated company.

But Dad.

The question of Dad.

That's a tough one. The toughest, and the one I can't resolve.

Why did he do it? And did he pass that reason or loss of reason down to me?

Unknown.

No one heard anything that night. Not a cross word spoken, or not so as it, or they (there must have been more than one word), could be heard reverberating around the neighborhood before the gunshots unquestionably were.

I wish I had that script. I really, really do. God, what an artifact. To know what they said to each other—so civilly, it seems, as not to have been overheard—what they whispered, implied, insinuated that led up to: *Bang.*

The gun going off as a last act.

I've written it a hundred times in my head and crumpled it a hundred times in frustration, just as I, too, have crumpled to the floor in a rough-hewn ball, like the draft in the digital dustbin.

Inadequate, as usual.

I understand nothing but this. Grief is exhausting. To me, it is happening minutely, on a cellular level where I can't console or reach it, but where it reaches me more potently than any other toxin, wending through my liver and my spine and all the way to my extremities like venom that's not kind enough to kill.

Maybe there's a clue. Were they kind words they said to each other that night? A kindness spoken, a kindness done, and silence thereafter?

I can't know.

But I know that they both come to me in the night or the day, or whatever twilight I inhabit without the company of Dave or the static of substances.

Crepuscular visitations.

I wake in the dusk and I am not alone, and for that fingernail of time when I am three parts aware and not yet abusive, they appear.

I rouse to the scent of them.

That is how they come, and only how they come.

There are no apparitions. No banging in the pipes or blurs in the mirrors. Nothing so dramatic.

Just smells. Perfect, spot-on smells, which, I realize now, are the absolute essence of any person, any house, any moment in time. The residue of its uniqueness carried on the air, more intense, more real than any spectral visitation.

I have smelled, for example, the replica of a Saturday winter morning circa 1984, when I was eight and waking late for hockey Little League, lying drowsy in the fug of my down comforter, my whole consciousness focused and filled with the ecstatic prospects of the day. The game, the hot dogs after, the movies late in the afternoon, the sneaking spy game of the house to myself all evening while the babysitter did her nails in front of the TV, and, best of all, another whole day of buffer between Monday math class and me.

All of this emotion, immediate again in my nose, of all places, and so in my mind.

Frying bacon, the sharp, salty, metallic ting of the driveway being cleared, and bittersweet exhaust from the warming car in the garage, the back door opening and closing as Dad dashes in for gulps of creamy sweetened coffee, the cakey egg, vanilla bean of pancake batter, and its caramelized drabs that burn on the skillet, the melting plastic spatula, the brand-new carpet on the stairs, the oily musk of soiled pajamas in a heap on the floor, and the funk in the sleeping cat's coat.

I smell it all as if in memory, but in the present, and I feel it all again so keenly, as if a life lived and a pathway seemingly expired could bend back on itself and return, this instant folded to that instant, the past touching the present, fused in some quantum dimension.

Scent is the truest messenger. A particle and a wave. A waft.

Swift as, sylphish as thought.

As real, and at once unreal, as it ever was.

Ghosts.

I told you there were ghosts. Or was it undead? I said undead. A mausoleum to the undead. And so it is, redolent and rife with them.

They come to me most often as themselves, without context, their scent coiling around me like campfire smoke.

Just as I am coming to, they come to me.

There is the smell of my father's fresh sweat, so sweet and alkaline and inoffensive, like a tuber cracked open raw. There is the smell of his Old Spice shaving soap and the pomade he put in his hair, the loose change in his side pockets, the talc he sprayed on his feet. There is the crisp starch of his cotton dress shirts, and the sere residue of the chemicals that cleaned them, the warmed wool of his dark suits mingling these odors and sending out his signature around him like an aura you could taste.

And so I taste it. Unmistakable. Lurking, unfriendly, the heavy dregs of him accumulate, hanging, moist at first, and then stifling like the after-stench of someone else's shit until I can't stand it any longer. I lurch from the invasion, recoiling back and across, throwing up the window to disburse him, leaning out and gasping for help, or an exorcism of air.

Less often, there is my mother.

She comes, too, in her own time, like a victim, on her knees, low to the ground. I can smell her only when I'm lying down or prostrate in the room, weeping at my most distraught, stooping for the purpose, down on my own knees and hands, dogging the room for her.

She smells of crusted breast milk and saliva. My first months of life. Baking soda and wet stones, copper, zinc, and alloys of the blood in rough congruence with suet and salt water. She rests in all the low lies of this house, as brisk as sea air and as uplifting, fragile yet persistent, clinging to the fabrics of things, and wise. Wise as every inkling and end point after the fact.

She is never here when he is. They only come alone, and separate. Always apart. Which, I presume, is where they must be now. Dead or in transit, whatever that is. And likewise in their missions to me. They move, parallel and passing. Cords of a circle that do not cross. And I am the circle that contains them. Their circle of entrapment and separation. Both. Encompassing but lost, in and of myself, without compass, trudging in a ring, trapped as they are, and trapping.

I do it all again.

And again.

I have been doing it for years.

And I find that I do not remember anything really. Nothing recent. Nothing real. That paper in my basket is mine. The pink piece of paper, a ream or single sheet of which I do not to my knowledge possess. And yet there it is. And the poem written on it is mine, too. Clearly—if a bit more sloppily put down, the letters strangely spaced and sloping, as though written in the dark or, yes, under the influence. But I have no memory of writing it. All its code is foreign to me, even as I hear the echoes of its self-important conflict here, in these lines that I am writing now.

But for whom?

To accomplish what?

To—

Damn it.

There is Dave now.

The reliable fool, ringing the doorbell like a twat, punching his thumb at it peevishly, relentlessly, as if it were one of his candy vendors on the fritz. It chimes its rinky ding-dong arrhythmically, like a spring-loaded atonal bird, or some quaintly calibrated toy being abused by a thoroughly modern brat.

Ding-dong. Ding-Dongdong-Ding-da-dingdong.

Ease off, you shitpile. I'm coming.

2

Monica sits by the bay window and looks out. She does this often after we're done. Just sits there. Staring off. Staring out. Somewhere else. Yet strangely present as well, and satisfied. Or spent. Like she's gotten it out of her system again—whatever it is, and for however long it lasts.

Unlike most women I've slept with, she doesn't want to be cooed to or cuddled after sex. She doesn't want the intimacy that fucking is supposed to have bought, and I'm relieved not to be asked. That's why we stay at it, meeting once or twice a week, impromptu, whenever the mood strikes, having at it rough and raunchy, like a couple of haters, clawing for each other's eyes and missing, or being blocked by a fist, a forearm, a set of teeth. We're both usually banged up afterward. Bites, scratches, scuffs, burns. All the marks of the weapons that were handy, or the obstacles, objects, surfaces we ground on, slid across, slammed against.

I met Monica in early March, three months ago, at the Swan, the suburbasexual hellhole that Dave and I frequent most nights when we have even the remotest intention of getting laid. It's a lounge more than a bar, which in Midwestern terms means they serve a sickly sweet assortment of champagne cocktails and mocktinis so that the leggy legal secretaries and other temporary professionals who go there looking to land their first husbands don't feel they've been had on the cheap.

Meanwhile, the razor-burned bucks in—what else?—business casual can get good and nasty on Jägermeister and Red Bull before they turn their guns on the girls.

The Swan also serves something they have the hayseed pretension to call New American tapas, which means that the iceberg lettuce may have the odd pecan or pomegranate seed drowning in the usual bog of bacon-bitted blue cheese, and the pumpkin vegetable lasagna, gamely disguised with a sprig of wilted parsley and a Zorro drizzle of salad cream, came from the "healthy options" aisle of the freezer section at Kroger.

The cuisine is septic enough that, if you have to eat something, either to soak up the swill or to keep your speech coherent for as long as it takes to get Gloria to give you what you came for, you're well advised to go veggie. I don't doubt that some poor portly middle manager has been paralyzed from the waist down by tainted meat he ate here and never heard from again.

Monica stood out in this crowd at first glance, mostly because you didn't feel you had to take her out back and hose her down to get a sense of what she really looked like. She wasn't wearing makeup, and she was beautiful, just plainly beautiful, standing there, silent and staid, animally alert, an incongruous still point in the hustling throng.

I don't remember what we said to each other that night, if anything. I only remember walking to and opening the bar's front door for us, mechanically and with complete confidence in what was to follow, as if we had been married for twenty years and were leaving a party the way couples do when the desire to go on socializing has been suddenly and powerfully outweighed by the need to be home alone.

What a relief. What a surprising joy. Not to have to eke out the usual pleasantries to a pair of vacant Girl Scout's eyes batting their lashes at you as furiously as they can through the resinous crud that's been applied to them. How refreshingly cool to be just as angry as the other person, and just as loath to varnish the introductions.

I'm almost certain she didn't say a fucking thing, or even indicate. Not as I walked to the door, not as I opened it and looked across the room at her with all that blunt assumption that had no basis in anything but instinct. Not as I waited for her, not as she slid by me, not as I passed behind her into the parking lot, walking five paces behind, watching all her perfect lonely details expose themselves unawares.

She would have felt my eyes on her, unsure, lingering on her scapulae, marking them in tempo, sawing back and forth beneath the skin, pushing out, announcing themselves again and again, a fair warning as she walked, arms swinging freely, hands clenching and unclenching slowly into fists.

Her hair was boyishly short, a cap cropped close enough to show the cowlicks in back, where the soft pelt conformed to a swirl and, under the light, revealed the glints of red in it. The hairline ended in a playful point just left of her spine and a delta of pale down that spread, paler and finer down the nape, and disappeared.

I felt nothing sexual. Except rage. That old thing, boiling up in me and breaking into a rank ammoniac sweat, reeking up to meet her own rage, which itself had been evident from the start, and smelled strongly sour, too, of cat's piss and onions. I would have laughed at this last bit then, or even laughed at it now, but I have too little perspective to wholly scorn the inelegance of our—our what?—our little feral union, call it? Our less than poetic coming together?

Whatever.

The act and the emotion are both trite, even by allusion, and were then. I can't correct that. We reeked and we fucked. What else?

I didn't feel desire, except the desire to do violence to myself by dint of her. I suffocated myself in her, gratifying with another what I had only half accomplished alone, in secret and with self-pity, which was not welcome to me or to her.

For her it wasn't even in the repertoire.

That was Monica. And there was I, being led, because I had no idea what to do with her or anyone like her, going as I had for so long, by gravity of impulse, down; the vertigo gaining in the turns, the spiral closing, faster and farther, heavy to the core with a collapse that never quite occurs.

But almost.

You say it with that reaching inclination in your voice.

Almost.

And you get the torque of it close enough.

On that first night, she sat by the window afterward, nude, and we finally squeaked out a few words, the first of which were just a bad joke.

"What's your name?" I said and laughed.

It was what I wanted to know, and all I could really think to ask at first, maybe because it seemed I knew so much else already without asking. That was an illusion, of course, as it always is—the thinking I knew—but partly true as well, as it also always is. I knew the mood and the implications, but none of the details.

The reverse of what usually happens.

But I also had my hand inside her back, and my thumb and pinky in her sleeves, doing the mirror puppetry of all such encounters, making her up out of cloth, animating in accordance with my need.

She made this easier by saying nothing, giving away nothing but the vague auguries of a confidence trickster.

Belief does all the work.

She could have been anyone. She was anyone, and then became the someone I had scripted for her. The empty actor, filled by an imaginary role, makes it real. But the role is only as real as our categories, like taking a sky full of stars and seeing shapes in them, and then traits, and charts of personality and influence. It was all use and projection, but that is all it ever is, until the gun goes off or the blade goes in, intimate and clean.

Her voice was high and thin when she said her name, as if the sound was coming through a reed from a long way away.

"My name is Monica," she said, still looking out, her face a sketch of shadows turned away. "And yours is Nick Walsh."

There was no bait in the way she said this, but I wouldn't have taken it anyway. I was arrogant enough to presume that everyone at the Swan knew me, if not by name, then by sight and sordid reputation. She could have asked just about anyone and gotten the worst about me by rote.

"Yes," I said. "I'm Nick."

She wasn't coy in pursuing it. She didn't ask me if I wanted to know how she knew me. It didn't matter to either of us, and neither of us was pretending that it did. We didn't say superfluous things. That much had been established already, and it was the best part. No parries. No feints. Only sharp points coming straight on.

Just ask what you want to know and get an answer. Say what's on your mind and take the same back, harsh as it would come. How many people can you do that with? I can't think of one. Even Dave has to be humored with topical avoidance and kept in his sustaining myths like a pot roast trussed with string.

But Monica was just bullish in her quietude, like a T-shirt that says, GO FUCK YOURSELF IF YOU CAN'T TAKE IT, except that she was much too confident to swear or need signage. The announcement made itself in slow moves and few words, and in her dancer's posture, which, to be honest, was just a bit too this side of Mia Farrow unhinged for my taste, but not enough to tear me from the pull of her. There was something creepy there, no doubt, as if she had a plan and was taking her time, or like she knew she could have you killed with a nod, so why hurry? Why even raise your voice? It was weird, but good cult movie weird, and I liked it.

I just did.

It fit into the part of me that no one sees and that the foulmouthed clown in the polo shirt strenuously conceals. With her, I was coming as close as I ever have or can to being myself. Whoever that is.

And ain't that love?

By definition?

Or something like that?

Maybe. But I couldn't have said so.

She had been through way too much already in her young life, or so it seemed, to tolerate romance. Hadn't I? She had a soured view at twenty-something. Long before that, probably.

I didn't ask her how old she was. That was damning frivolous speech, or so her poise implied. If you can't deduce even the obvious, buster, don't advertise your ignorance.

But I did deduce enough. She had those wisps of golden hair all over her belly and her inner thighs and forearms, the ones that line with tiny bubbles in the bath, and turn coarse and black or break off on a girl's thirtieth birthday, so I knew she was well south of that mark.

She also had that soft, forgiving roundness in all her limbs, all the way down to her knuckles, which were plump and barely creased and which, if this weren't worldly Monica we were talking about, you could still almost see clutching a purple pen and writing, "Dear diary."

But that innocence was long gone, or time-lapsed in the past-life portion of her brain, inaccessible to the adult.

So what do you say to someone like that? Seeing the scar tissue and the baby fat both at once, or thinking you do?

You say something tired, of course, but something you actually mean, so it's not a total disaster.

"Are you okay?" I said to her figure in the window, knowing full well that, where it counted most, she wasn't.

She didn't answer.

"Monica?"

"Yes, yes," she said, annoyed. "I'm fine."

"Did I hurt you?"

"Of course not."

There was a long pause, and then, more softly, with kindness in her voice, she said, "I'm glad we met. I'm glad we did this. It's good."

And then she eased herself away from the window and began putting on her clothes. I watched her. Every motion, every choice of garment, and in which order.

She put her socks on first, which I'd never seen anyone do, especially after sex with a stranger, and she sat to do it, very deliberately, raising one foot at a time to the seat of the chair, resting her chin on the bent knee, exposing the cleave of her vulva without modesty or guile. She gathered each sock with her thumbs and forefingers into concertinaed rolls around the toe, then unfurled them gingerly, hunch by hunch, over the arch, around the curve of the heel, and up the bend of the ankle, straightening her leg for the last pull, like a ballerina at the barre.

I loved it that she wore socks, plain black socks that she'd probably bought at a street fair in packs of six. And I loved it that her bra had no underwire or clasp. She slipped it on over her head and slid the stretch cotton over her breasts, untwined the slender straps across her shoulders, and wrestled abruptly into her shirt, a tank, formfitting, flattering, but in no way crude like the hooker halters the sluts wore at the Swan.

Her underwear was as sensible as the rest. Hipsters, white. Probably also bought in packs. Her jeans were loose and worn, hanging low and boyish on her narrow hips and ripped around the hem where they'd dragged on the ground. Her sneakers were black and plain, canvas slip-ons with a white rubber sole.

All simple easy wear. No advertisement for any kind of cool or attitude or need to be seen. Still she was beautiful, and she made you look. The kind of person who could wear a sack and have allure, because the signal was coming from her mind and beaming right to your mind, if you had one, or bouncing off and bewildering the vacuum it found there instead.

It was the same every time we met. The sex that somehow retained the anonymity of the first attempt, but also gained familiarity over time, and then the sitting mostly in silence—we did this, as I did almost everything else, in my study—she at the window, I on the couch watching her or half dozing. And then she would get dressed and go, stopping to put her hand on my shoulder on her way out the door.

She did this each time. Stopped, placed her palm on me, let it rest there for a beat, consolingly, as if she knew I was grieving and wanted me to know that she knew, even if she didn't know what for.

That came to be my favorite part, the part I waited for and needed the most. It meant a thousand times more than anything she could have said, or anything anyone ever had said, about my parents or about me. There was so much care and camaraderie in it, like a curative laying on of hands between the sick and dying.

I never moved when she touched me. I never looked up at her in recognition. I just stared at the place where she had been near the window, or at the weak reflection of her in the window, framed by the doorway and backlit by the light in the hall: her figure, my darker mass below, her arm between us.

We looked like we belonged in this house with the other partial residents. Ghosts at the window between worlds, passing across panes of glass as plays of light and shadow that would shatter with a carelessly tossed stone. I looked at our reflections, and in my head I always said something to her, as if I half believed she could read my thoughts, or receive them through her arm in the flesh.

This time I said, "Tell me," because I knew she was hiding so much. The hidden things were gaining weight with every contact. Her past would make its way into every acquaintance, as mine had, and it would come, as it always had for me, to a breaking point. Either you shared or you turned away.

I didn't want her to turn away, and I knew that this time I couldn't.

I had given up.

When I met Monica I was already too weak with the wear and dissolution of the past thirteen years to do anything but lean passively away and scratch casually at anyone who tried to get under my skin, until they atrophied with neglect and fell off like a scab. But I couldn't do that with Monica, obviously. Because she'd gotten in. Or, more to the point, because she knew something.

That's what infatuation always feels like. Like the other person knows something, or maybe a lot of things that you just have to find out. Things that seem crucial, or meant for you alone, and the whole point of the game is for them to keep the files from you and for you to hack your way in.

Monica was a skilled enigmatist.

Actually, that's not quite right. She was a maze and a puzzle to herself as much as to me. But she made me feel as though I had the encrypted map or the hidden piece that would set it all out in the open and cure her. And the reverse was also true. She seemed to have my missing information, the bit that would finally, mercifully put me down for good.

And that's what I was looking for. Something to finish the goddamned endless purgatorial pause of my stopgap junior-grade life. Something sure enough and with a steady hand that could achieve the desired effect with one blow. I kept Monica around for that.

Whenever, if ever, she got around to it.

3

I was up all night again with Dave. I woke again on the couch.

This time, no puke, and no lunatic notes from myself. Just the usual morning sickness that comes of not having been sick the night before.

My head is like an anvil, and I could swear that my mouth and my asshole have changed places. My entire alimentary canal feels as if it's been scoured with steel wool, sphincter to sphincter.

And so it goes.

Manikin me has stamina if nothing else. We'll give him that. Dedication to the cause of progressive dehydration, cell death, and episodic amnesia. Self-absorption remains intact and growing. Waking suicidal fantasy robust.

It must be getting on toward eight. I've been lying here for hours. Dusk is settling around the window casements and in the corners of the room. I can see from here that Mrs. Bloom's kitchen light is on across the street, and her weak porch light, too. She always turns that on at dusk, and then the kitchen light after, fortifying the house for the long night alone.

In recent years, on winter afternoons, when it got dark early and I would be lying here, as usual, in state, half waking, it became a ritual to look across the street and watch Mrs. Bloom moving around her house turning on lights. Now I wait for it in summer, too, as I have tonight, even if I've been awake for some time.

She turns on a lamp in the upstairs window, a single candle bulb like the ones people put up at Christmas. But she puts it only in that one corner window upstairs, and she keeps it there all year long. Every night it's the last light she puts on, and every morning it's the last light she turns off. On the nights when I haven't passed out, usually when I'm with Monica or I haven't been with Dave, I see her do this just before I go to bed, just as the light is coming up.

I find it calming and reassuring, as if the night watchman has been on duty. The last light going out is his signal that it's safe to sleep.

As a kid, on summer nights around this time, in early June, when my parents put me to bed, I would lie in my room and look out across the street at the line of trees behind the Blooms' house, bulbous black silhouettes against a lilac sky. In their shapes I traced the profile of a sleeping giant lying on his back: Afro hair, short forehead, long nose, chin, chest—even legs that disappeared behind the houses next door and reemerged down the block as upturned feet. In a breeze it looked as if the giant's hair was rustling or his chest was moving up and down, breathing. I imagined that he was there to protect me, and so long as he was asleep, all was well with the world and our piece of it.

The Blooms still lived there then. They've lived here since the development was built nearly fifty years ago. Mr. Bloom died a few years back, and since then Mrs. Bloom has been making her night and morning rounds.

But the candle bulb has been in the window for a lot longer than that. It's been there at least as long as I've been back. I remember seeing it the night of my parents' funeral. For thirteen years or more that bulb has been lit every night and extinguished every morning at dawn.

As for the other lights staying on all night, that started only after Mr. Bloom's death. She must be afraid to sleep in a dark house alone, or she thinks the lights will deter burglars. Then again, maybe she's like me and stays up all night for other reasons, except instead of throwing herself blindly into the bull run of human debauchery, as if she thinks the angel of mercy is in the oncoming traffic, she's reading calmly by lamplight, sipping a glass of sherry and waiting patiently to die with some dignity.

That's how I feel, anyway, dignity or not. And I had my parents for only twenty-one years, a quarter of which I was too young to process or intelligibly record, and another third of which I spent away at school. But the Blooms were married for fifty years, or thereabouts. Maybe more. Fifty fuckin' years. And they were there for all of it.

Ten years in, they had one daughter, Karen, who grew up way too fast and took off pregnant at seventeen or eighteen. Dropped out of high school in her senior year, hooked up with a bad crowd, left, and never came back. Except once, about a year later, to dump the kid she didn't want and couldn't rear. A girl. The Blooms named her Robin and raised her as their daughter. Karen fell off the map until a few years later, when the Blooms got word that she'd died of an overdose in a squat somewhere out east, Baltimore or Philly.

It seems that running away runs in their family, because the Blooms kept Robin only until she was twelve, and then she, too, just disappeared. *Poof.* Gone. Maybe she didn't believe her mother was dead and went to find her. Maybe her father came and took her. Or maybe it was a pedophile with a ladder and some chloroform. No one knows. But that's what the candle bulb in the upstairs window is for, I'm sure. For Robin. A reminder. A vigil. A signal, in case she's out there watching, that says: You're always welcome home.

I hardly knew Robin, or even knew of her. By the time she was four or so I had headed off to boarding school and then college, and by the time I came back she was gone. But by all accounts she was a good kid. Sweet. Reserved. Excellent student. Precocious, actually. Read all the time—poetry especially, and stuff that was way, way above a normal elementary schooler's level. Way above a high schooler's level.

I remember my mom telling me about one particular day when she'd gone out to get the mail—the mailboxes are clustered across the street on an easement of the Blooms' property—and she saw Robin lying out on the Blooms' lawn reading a copy of what looked like *The Inferno.* My mom knew a thing or two about Dante. She had a PhD from Barnard in English lit, and she was a voracious reader all her life, keeping up with trends in academic and trade publishing. She said she remembered having had enough trouble in her time as a TA getting her freshman charges to read *The Inferno*, let alone understand it. But an eleven-year-old? There was no way.

She thought she was seeing things, so she asked Robin if she could have a look at the book. Robin handed it over with a shrug. Sure enough, it was the real deal—and the Pinsky translation no less, in a bilingual edition with the English on one page and the Renaissance Italian on the facing one. Both pages were covered with Robin's childishly looped marginalia.

Mom was very impressed by this.

"Pinsky's is the only English translation that comes close to preserving the delicate terza rima of the original," she exclaimed. "It's subtle and complex, and from what I could see, that kid was getting it. Really getting it. She wasn't just carrying it around for show, scribbling hearts and love doodles in the white spots. She had actually written the word 'TRUST' in capital letters next to the first appearance of Virgil's name."

Amazing girl, I guess. And a tortured one, if that's the reading she was taking refuge in at that age. A really sad story. As sad as my own.

After my parents died and I took over the house, the Blooms were the only people I felt comfortable with. Not that we spent long afternoons together over tea, but now and again, if we were both outside at the same time and happened to see each other—usually it was Mr. Bloom I'd see—we'd stop and talk for a few minutes.

We'd stand in one or the other's driveway, or on the curb near the trash cans and recycling bins that one of us was taking out or bringing in, and we'd talk in that liberating, socially graceless way that people who've lost everything do.

I felt sorry for them. They'd had it rough, losing two girls, and they took it hard—on themselves—as if they'd done something wrong that had made it all turn out so badly. Only they didn't know what that thing was.

I felt a kinship with them, too, because they were the only people I knew who had been through anything remotely as painful and inexplicable as I had.

The Blooms had no more answers than I did, and no more sense of reparation, or expiable fault, which they would have gladly taken as a substitute if it could have brought some relief. But no power can absolve an indiscernible sin. We were like overly conscientious kids in the confessional, feeling the dogmatic heft of human wrongdoing but unable to ferret out our own crimes.

As a seven- or eight-year-old, when I first started going to confession, I often confessed to things I hadn't done—small things, lies, impure thoughts, whatever came to me—because I hadn't actually done anything bad that I could think of, and then I'd cry while receiving absolution, convinced that the black mark was still there on my soul.

But then I was no great student of church teaching. Most of it was lost on me and left me bewildered in ways that made my parents pant and choke with laughter when I asked them about it. For the longest time, I thought the priest was saying Jesus and the twelve *decycles*, and I always wondered why the son of God was riding around with a bunch of clowns. At the time, I earnestly thought of running away with the circus, like it was a good deed I could perform during Lent. I never lived that one down—it was a family joke forever.

But through the veil of humor and confusion, my remorse was real enough. Remorse over something I couldn't understand.

That was the feeling the Blooms and I shared in later life.

After Mr. Bloom died, I never saw Mrs. Bloom, except obscurely, framed in windows, walking through the house and turning those lights on or off. I never rang her bell or peeked in. I respected her privacy and the web of grief that had spun itself and caught her as ill-fatedly and fatally as a hapless insect in spring flight.

She's the only one of my closest neighbors I haven't spied on, and the only one I never will, on principle.

As for everyone else? I despise their hermetic normalcy too much not to violate it, and for no better reason than the sheer pleasure of hearing it pop. They don't deserve their happiness if that's even what it is. To me it's fake happiness. The margarine version of what the philosophers meant. But it seems to do for the majority, and all the quirks and bland neuroses that fill it up yield surprising substance if you look with hateful enough eyes, hear with spiteful enough ears. If you take a resentful interest, you can make it more than what it is. If you want to destroy it from the minutiae out, you will see the diabolical in the detail, and savor it. A voyeur's incriminating pointillism. Connect the dots and make the damning picture.

But then, maybe this is simply what bored people do.

Pry.

And bored destroyed people pry with vengeance, then justify it by recourse to their pain.

Or maybe it's technology that has made us all so prurient, craving more of the real in our reality TV.

I think the truest reason I do it is to find out all I can about what is find-able, even if it's mostly mundane, because there's so much I can't find out about what matters. I'll never know why my parents died, or any of the de-tails. I'll never get my mind around it. I'll never be whole or unharmed or kind again. But I can know everything about my neighbors' lives, and in so doing, I can ease what is unsatisfied in me.

The spying started years back, with Dave. It wasn't long after my parents' funeral, and just about two years after Dave's father's death. Dave was doing his ineffectual best to help me through the worst, having fashioned himself the local expert on filial grief.

He was on a mission day and night, depositing himself on the couch like some stubborn adjunct caseworker who's decided that his salvation lies in your own, and that stoned silence and snacking are the strongest forms of sympathy.

The fucking toad didn't leave my house for weeks, not even to restock the fridge and cabinets with the purported comfort foods he, and he alone, was consuming with such gusto. He got Mama Kitty to do that. He'd literally call in an order and make it sound like it was for me.

"Yeah, I know, I know, but the only things I can get him to eat are Cherry Garcia and DiGiorno. I'm tellin' ya, the guy's gone. Really bad news. You remember what I was like. It's a miracle he's eating at all. Just get a bunch of stuff—the stuff I eat. If I'm eating regular, sooner or later he's bound to join me. Oh, and bring me some more weed, too, will you? That wheelchair weed you get that's s'posed to make vegans crave corn dogs even when they're on chemo. And trust me, that's how he's starting to look."

There'd be a pause here, with Kitty no doubt duped and mewling on the other end of the line.

Then Dave would jump in, his greedy instincts getting the better of him, turning his tone desperate but still managing to make his grocery list sound like a call to arms rather than a fat boy's food panic at full throttle.

"Please, Ma, just do what I tell you. And hurry."

I have to admit, it did help for a while in some hazy diabetic, opium den sort of way. I hardly ate, but I smoked like a five alarm, and when I did eat, the toxic array of carbohydrates we had in stock were so refined and saturated with chemicals that they were a drug in and of themselves, bringing on the kind of insulin shock once dispensed to mental patients. In combination with booze and gargantuan quantities of THC, you could get a jolt almost strong enough to reboot your brain.

I suppose I should have been grateful for Dave's intervention, but it just made me hate him more, mostly because he'd managed to make his Samaritan opportunism look like his own personal Via Dolorosa, even though he'd done nothing more strenuous than operate the microwave and nothing more self-sacrificial than crap in the upstairs bathroom. And he only conceded that last bit of unholy ground because I threatened to gouge his eyes out with a potato peeler if he ever again subjected me to the miasma of his outsized ass.

Living with this prize primate for more than a month, and seeing all the filthy high jinks he was happy to get up to right out in the open in front of another person (albeit a person who had smoked enough ganja to have gone a shade of gangrene around the gills), made me wonder what he did when he thought no one was looking.

The guy was double-jointed in the knees and would cut and clean his toenails with his teeth, like a baboon. No joke. Totally unconsciously, too, just watching the TV, gnawing away, savoring the Stilton that had been curing there for God only knew how long.

When he was really bored, he'd sit with my old BB gun in my mom's reading chair by the window in the living room and try to pick off squirrels and blue jays in the front yard. He rarely hit any. The accuracy on those things is for shit, and he was always too shaky or bleary to aim anyway. But he sent a lot of unsuspecting creatures flapping and scampering for cover while he cackled with delight.

The day I evicted him, I found him in the kitchen with one of those gallon-size red rubber enema bags they sell in medical supply stores. He'd hung it from one of my mom's old plant hooks on the low ceiling over the sink, and he was kowtowing beneath it naked on the linoleum floor, poring over one of my old porno magazines. He had the white hose of the enema bag planted in his upturned ass and a plastic bucket next to his hip.

When I asked him what the fuck he was doing, all he said was:

"Coffee enema, dude. Great buzz."

It might have been a surfeit of weed or it might have been the lack of it—I don't remember—but this newly blithe and blatant insult threw me into a spiral of shame and disbelief that surprised even me. This could not be happening. Was my grief not enough? Did I deserve this demonic visitation as well?

Exasperated, I spoke at last.

"I have cups, you swine. Why didn't you just drink it?"

Dave grinned wickedly.

"Totally different high when you shoot it. Mellowlike. Awesome. Plus it cleans you out like a meat grinder."

He said this fitfully, gasping and straining as you do when you're exerting yourself in ways that other people shouldn't see.

Stay calm, said a good voice in my head. Focus. The desired goal is to get him to stop.

"Great. Thanks for that detail," I said. "Why are you doing it in here? Did we not discuss this?"

I pointed upstairs.

He sighed impatiently.

"The light's better."

"The light's better? Jesus, God!"

I was losing my tenuous cool and starting to sound uncannily like my father berating my teenage self.

"What does *that* have to do with anything?" I raged.

"The pictures, moron. I gotta be able to see the tits. Plus there's instructions."

Something in me went slack and fell. This was my mother's kitchen, full of clean memories and pleasant smells. A hallowed place. I wasn't going to run and put my head under a pillow while Dave repainted it.

But what to do? Rubber gloves and possibly a dust mask were under the sink. Hugely inadequate, but it was a start, and it was all I had.

I mean, who foresees this kind of invasion? In the kitchen.

Who allows it?

I was just working up the gumption to make a move when Dave said: "Excretasex."

He looked up at me, nodding conclusively, as if this newly minted term of art would make the purpose of this shitshow abundantly clear.

I froze anew, stunned. Staring, but seeing nothing.

Dave mistook this torpor for rapt attention, and added, "Don't you know? It's right here in the mag. I thought you'd read this."

He paused to catch his breath, then pecked with his nose at the annotated centerfold in front of him.

"'The male's ultimate release.' It's all about prostate stimulation or some shit." He giggled. "No pun, dude. Anyway, blowing both valves at once, fire hydrant style. Siamese connection. Fuckin' rocks."

And sure enough—I hadn't noticed this before, coming, as I had, upon this truly sadistic scene from behind—he was wanking like a sport fisherman. Our parlay hadn't even put him off his stroke. It seemed only to have encouraged him. He was breathing harder and faster, rocking on his knees and grunting.

He had turned his now grimacing face half away from me again and was eyeballing the magazine sidelong at close range, snorting feverishly as if it were a scratch 'n' sniff.

That's when I snapped, and some mortally, maternally offended part of me reared and took over. I dove for the cabinet under the sink and flung it open. Still on my belly, hunkering well clear of Dave's weapon, I yanked on the rubber gloves and the dust mask and army-crawled to the stove. Thus armed, I stood in a fury and lunged for the nearest cupboard, which contained, ironically enough, an assortment of the unused coffee mugs as well as a pewter pepper grinder and salt cellar, a china gravy boat, and—*bingo!*—a ceramic mortar and pestle, shaped to look like a concave bowling ball and pin.

Instrument in hand, I turned to face the nightmare on the floor. I stomped my foot on Dave's coccyx and ground his slick face into the magazine until its glossy leaves tore and crunched. Then, in one swift motion, I extracted the hose from Dave's rectum and replaced it with the fat end of the pestle, shoving in the makeshift butt plug all the way to its whimsically indented neck. I threw the hose end into the bucket, grabbed Dave by the hair, heaved him to his feet, and frog-marched him to the backyard, where I tossed him, still naked and frontally engorged, into the hawthorn bushes.

I locked him out then and there. Later that night, I gathered all his things—including his clothes, his wallet, and his asthma inhalers—and burned them in a wheelbarrow out back, well after I knew he had gone. Or, I should say, well after he'd ceased trying to wheedle his way back into the house, pawing with one bloodied palm on the sliding glass patio door and cupping his scratched and shrunken tackle with the other.

That was when I resolved to really humiliate the guy with science. Tape him doing something beyond bestial in the privacy of his own garage and post it on the Internet viewable for a fee.

My hatred boiled over. I was a man possessed, obsessed with the technological opportunities for my revenge, heady with the seeming godliness that secret eyes and ears would bestow on me and the divine justice it could afford. I got a huge thrill imagining it. How I would surveil people's property, note their comings and goings, learn their schedules, then sneak into their houses while they were out doing the weekly shopping or playing the Wednesday game of bridge and install my micro cameras and audio equipment at will. Cleverly conceal them in lamps or VCRs or, better yet, make presents with these things preinstalled.

"Hey, Dave. As a thank-you for all you did for me, I got you this top-of-the-line DVD player. Now you can watch pornos in your bedroom undisturbed."

And I can tape all your whacked-out sexcapades for public consumption and make a tidy profit on the side.

You fuck.

There was life again in that expletive. A plan worth living for. I was in.

4

Dave was my first time out, my trial run, so I went with the preinstall rather than the B and E plant. It was safer, easier, and, I convinced myself, not a crime—or not one they were likely to catch me for. Besides, in Dave's case, it gave me much more pleasure to make a gift of my treachery, even if, or maybe especially if, there was a chance he'd find me out and prosecute. I was able to actually buy the hardware—complete with hypersensitive mini mics for good-quality audio—already rigged at a specialty spy store I found in the Yellow Pages.

This was years before Dave got his home theater and just at the time when DVDs were newly available, so I gave him his first DVD player, which he duly oohed and aahed over and promptly rigged to the TV in his bedroom.

I also gave him what I told him was a state-of-the-art ionizer for his bathroom, which, I explained, could neutralize even the most virulent odors in minutes.

His family would thank me.

"According to the literature," I said, "veterinarians use them in their examination rooms when expressing the anal glands of large breed dogs."

I went on to add that even a few of the more well-endowed urban zoos had installed them in their enclosed walk-through exhibits so as to minimize public discomfort in the monkey ramble and the reptile pavilion.

And that was that. I had my eyes and ears in place. My starter kit of remote violation was up and running.

But it didn't quite go the way I'd planned.

The equipment was fine. Perfect, in fact. I could pan around most of the bedroom, except for a couple blind spots behind the DVD player or in the corners, but none of the action was happening there anyway. In the bathroom

I had full views of the toilet and sinks, as well as the double-wide mirror over the sinks.

I'd had to angle the bathroom shot myself, repositioning the ionizer on a social visit to the house. Dave had put it on the counter between the sinks, which meant that the mirror was out of bounds, and that was just too good to pass up. So I moved the Sanizephyr (as I believe it was called) to a shelf against the opposing wall and told Dave that it wouldn't work properly if it wasn't at least five feet off the floor.

"Methane rises, right?" I explained. "Think of cow burps and the ozone. Same principle."

So far, so good.

Clap goes the clapper board—aaaand action . . .

But Dave's contribution was less than what I'd hoped for. Well, less and more, actually.

Dave surprised the hell out of me in this, I have to say, because what he did when he was alone—aside, of course, from the doleful daily wank under the bedclothes—wasn't sexual. And, trust me, given past experience, I'm using "sexual" here in the broadest possible sense.

But nothin' doin'. Nada. Not a hint of his erstwhile perversity.

I really couldn't believe it. He'd been more than happy to blow out his Siamese connection on my kitchen floor in the good light, but in the darkness of his own private-man hovel he did nothing of the kind.

Turned out he was an exhibitionist, a true performance artist, and they're a real snore when they're at home. No shock, no show, apparently.

Actually, that's not entirely true. They're a snore to the general public. From a sales perspective, they're not, as they say in the trade, money-shot material, but they do have an art house audience, and, as I think we've all learned in the past fifteen years, mostly to our chagrin and peril, the Internet is chock-full of ferrety, owl-eyed freakazoids on the prowl for their own viral brand of strange.

Dave was that for sure. Strange, strange, strange.

And juvenile as hell. Not that that's a shocker. But I don't mean juvenile in the blowing raspberries or making fart noises in your armpit sense. I mean it in the savage imagination unleashed, pulling the wings off Tinkerbell sense.

People say kids are cruel. But kids are actually just wild. Wild as hyenas, except endowed with a hell of a lot more license and imagination. Biologically endowed, not just with cleverness but with tool-wielding capabilities and no moral or empathic sense. They live in a suspended state of mind where anything's possible, or seems so, and the pain of other creatures doesn't register.

When you believe you have that kind of freedom, your first, middle, and last instinct is always to say, "I wonder what will happen if I do this?"

And then all kinds of crazy, convoluted shit unfolds that's impossible to unwind and make sense of after the fact. Even if you watch it happening, as I did, you can't really work out how you, or the artist formerly known as Dave, got there, or what methodic madness made one step follow from the next.

Watching Dave act out in front of my cameras was like having a peephole into someone else's subconscious with said subconscious in the driver's seat on a joyride in the real world, tearing it up as if the whole creation were its own virtual demolition derby. I say virtual because it was as if this creature that had popped out of Dave's pituitary gland and taken the wheel, this sur-real ruler of dreams and nightmares, still thought it was in Dave's head, where cause and effect are rubbery and whim is without consequence. This thing was pure id, as ignorant of the rules of human conduct as any socio-path, but more eccentric.

If you could have spoken to it, its only response to anything would have been, "Huh?"

It was all impulse, and its only mode was melee, like entropy's minion on a tight schedule. Busy, busy, busy, and as random as Russian roulette. With-out conscience or self-awareness or intelligence of any kind. The terrorist's apprentice, bumbling around in the bomb silo.

Be careful what you wish for, I said to myself aloud, as I watched, slack-jawed, while Dave, real and uncut, slowly revealed himself to me. You wanted to see, Nick? Well, see. See well. And weep.

At the time, Dave was living (and still is) about a mile down the road from me in the famously nouveau riche development called Twin Pines. All sub-urbs of major Midwestern cities have their Twin Pines. You've probably driven through a half dozen of them in as many states, either out of sheer desperation for something to do when you were trapped in town for the company convention or because you wanted to see for yourself if the Amer-ican dream really is as tawdry as it looks on TV.

The Twin Pines of the intracoastal hinterlands all look the same, of course. Steroidal lawns, topiary and flower beds landscaped to a fare-thee-well, circular driveways dwarfed by Sheetrock mansions that all look like spacecraft or wedding cakes, or some appalling combination of the two. Here is every status seeker's emerald isle, picked out and placed high on the hills above the more modest, middle-class dwellings on the far side of the wrought-iron fencing. Ever tidy, ever tasteless, coruscating asphalt and concrete, these are the havens of mindless American prosperity where all the local anesthesiologists and mandarins of industry, stranded pro athletes, local-hailing pop stars, and anyone else deeply invested in the symbolic value of lawn statuary has a house. A great, hulking, gauche house to outdo the Joneses.

This, naturally, is also where Dave, the vending machine king, sister Sylvia, and the lovely widowette Mama Kitty make their home. Or did. A few years ago, in an unprecedented show of normalcy, the newly wedded Sylvia moved in with her husband. Next door.

But at the time, the house next door was occupied by a real Gatsby type, though, sadly, not one of the old school. The guy threw a lot of big blowout parties, that's all, with ill-gotten gains of unknown origin and seemingly endless supply. But that's where the comparison ends.

Jack Gordon, né Joshua Goldstein, was reliving his bar mitzvah almost every night of the week for the rest of his life, except he was doing it this time the way he as the Dennis Hopper or Peter Fonda of his boyhood hero fetish would have done it. It was like Jews Gone Wild over there, spilling out over his woefully inadequate two-acre property. It was all leather, denim, and the ravages of cheap libation visited like a plague on the holdout Episcopalian neighbors, one of whom described spectacles like Jack Gordon's as "the lamentable effect of godless shtetl sprawl on what had once been respectable horse country."

Not cool. But you could hardly blame the old buzzard for complaining.

It was a bad scene over at Gordon's place, and it was never self-contained. I spent enough nights at Dave's to know. From six p.m. on you got everything from Bob Seger and the Silver Bullet Band to Guns N' Roses and Poison blasting at criminal decibels and rasping over your skull like iron-filing sandpaper.

After the cops showed up, always too little too late, and just as you might finally be dropping off to sleep at four in the morning, thinking you were indeed living through the decline of an empire, you'd get the adenoidal whinny of a white-trash trophy wife slicing into your temple like an ice pick.

"Jack, honey, is that my diaphragm floating in the pool?"

Vocals just that heinous, I'm telling you. Deadly. Like the very ice pick to the head that killed fucking Leon Trotsky.

Which, incidentally, is why Dave and I still refer to any chick whose voice gives you that ice pick in the head as a Trotsky, and why we especially enjoy banging the shit out of them from behind in parking lots and public toilets, with one hand clamped over their squealing maws and the other steering them like breed mares by their ponytails.

It's standard code at the Swan. We'll say, "Trotsky at three o'clock," and this means that one of us has the job of running interference with the target's friends while the other bumps the sozzled damsel into the nookery of choice and sets about the business of wenching her.

Poor girls?

Yeah, well, no one siphoned the ten shots of Apple Pucker down their throats, now, did they? "Willing participant" is, I believe, the phrase. Or is it "informed consent"? Whichever. Same denominator. As for the rough treatment they received from yours truly and Pig Boy, they can all thank Jack Gordon for that. A nasty bit of deferred revenge ongoing against the screechier sex, and all because some errant schlemiel had a taste for tacky broads and had one too many all-night keggers that shattered the pretentious evening peace of Twin Pines.

But, as I learned via video, Dave took his own revenge much earlier than I did, and more directly.

And this, as I said, is where things got super strange in a hurry and made me almost regret my choice of quasi-criminal pastimes.

Not that I couldn't in part sympathize. I mean, understandably. I knew. Gordon's deafening escapades could have made a madman of anyone, especially his nearest neighbor. Loud music is, after all, a form of torture employed by the U.S. military.

And why? Because it works.

I've been there. I should know. My fraternity at school used it to haze the new pledges, and I was among the supplicants the first year they tried it. They locked ten of us in a room the size of most bathrooms for twenty-four hours straight and played the theme song from *Cheers* on a loop at top volume. We nearly tore each other's hair and teeth out. After twenty-three hours of that, I would have sucked cock for pocket change at a Shriners convention and given the proceeds to al-Qaeda, just to get my hands on the stereo.

So I see why Dave went awry. I do.

It wasn't that he did what he did. It was the *way* he did it that really curdled whatever faith I had left.

I've never seen the guy so focused. He was like one of those serial killers in the movies who makes his own hollow-point bullets or curare-dipped darts or whatever the fuck it is that's supposed to make your home-fabricated ammo most potent. Except, of course, Dave doing this was the *Romper Room* edition, like what you'd see if a bunch of third graders lost their shit on a cooking show.

He'd clearly planned the whole thing, made a shopping list, went to what had to have been at least four different stores to get what was on the list, and prepped his lab—that lab being the bathroom, natch.

One afternoon at about four o'clock, he came into full view of the Sani-zephyr with a tote bag full of supplies, and he laid all the contents of the bag on the counter one by one. His materials included the following: one Kitchen-Aid mixer with beater blade and five-quart stainless-steel bowl, one small Tupperware bowl with lid (closed and full to capacity with a substance that, by color and viscosity, I subsequently deduced to be semen), one Pro-Shot 50cc syringe with pistol grip, one 1-ounce bottle of tincture of iodine, two dozen extralarge eggs (white), one 250-milliliter bottle of Norwegian Promise cod-liver oil, one Hot Melt pneumatic industrial glue gun, one stick of traditional crimson sealing wax, one Bic butane cigarette lighter, one Testors model paintbrush, one tabletop 250-watt infrared heat lamp, and one white porcelain mini ramekin of fresh, semisoft cat shit.

The last offering came courtesy of Trajan, Dave's then sixteen-year-old obese Maine coon who weighed in at a whopping twenty-nine pounds and whose proportionally sizable intestines had been in an uproar since kitten-hood. They were a biohazardous war zone of such offensive and potentially lethal proportions that, after years of prescribing horse doses of metronida-zole to absolutely no avail, several vets had refused to go on treating the beast, and his chronic colitis had flourished unchecked ever since. When Trajan took a dump, the stench was strong enough to wake you out of a stupor from three rooms down the hall, as it once did me, and send you scrambling for the pooper-scooper and the matches as though your soul's salvation depended on it. It was on Trajan's account, actually, that I lobbied most successfully for the Sanizephyr. Suffice it to say, that bloat-bowelled, bomb-dropping sewer-bag never delivered a firm stool in all his miserable life. Ever.

I guess you can see already why we lost the multiplex audience for our amateur Warhol picture, eh? Even the master of Pittsburgh himself, or John Waters, for that matter, and his cack-eating star Divine, would have blanched at the inclusion of Trajan's turds.

Cruel and fucking unusual is what that is. Really.

But that's the id for you when it's unsupervised.

Speaking of which, did I mention that through all this organizational preamble and surgical prep Dave was naked? Yeah. There was that, too. Not such a surprise, considering. There were way too many sartorially unfriendly ingredients going into the devil's roux he was concocting. Purposely so, as it turned out.

Wisest just to work commando and shower afterward, which he (sensibly?) did.

Anyway, first things first. Down to work.

Dave lifted the head on the KitchenAid mixer, revealing its distinctive spade-shaped beater blade. He removed the five-quart bowl, held it to his groin like a bedpan, and pissed into it. A lot. He must have been drinking Mountain Dew all day or taking Kitty's hypertension medication, or both, because he let forth a flood that went on for what seemed like a full minute or more.

He then reached in turn for the containers of fish oil, iodine, and semen and emptied the contents of each into the bowl of piss. He placed the bowl back in position under the mixer head, bent in the beater blade, adjusted the machine's controls to the slowest setting, and left the slop to mix on low while he busied himself with phase two.

He opened the two cartons of eggs, took each egg, and, one at a time, very carefully inserted the syringe into its rounder end. Gently, he guided the syringe in and out of the hole he'd made, puncturing the membrane. He then reversed the plunger setting on the pistol grip and extracted the burst yolk and albumen in a single neat draw. He squirted this glop into the toilet each time, replaced the intact eggshell in the carton, and proceeded to the next egg, until all twenty-four of them were empty and neatly aligned in rows.

This task completed, he reached over and turned off the mixer, removed the bowl from its fixture, peered into it, and sniffed its contents with gagging satisfaction. He then laughed maniacally, holding the bowl aloft in triumph and dancing what I can only describe as some sort of demented Highland fling, until he had to sit on the edge of the bathtub to catch his breath.

When he'd recovered, he stood, a bit unsteadily, brought the bowl back to the cluttered countertop, and proceeded as carefully and meticulously as before with phase three.

Twenty-four separate times—count 'em, twenty-four—Dave filled the syringe with the fetid sepia slop from the mixing bowl and, through the same hole he'd already made, injected it into each empty egg. He then sealed the hole with the glue gun.

Now, I don't know about you, but I'm thinking that right about here is when any moderately disturbed person, let alone a neighbor driven mad by tinnitus, would have stopped. Am I right? I mean, enough is enough. Dave had more than covered the bases set out in whatever vandal's handbook of down and dirty practical jokes he was working from.

Seriously. If, in the mind of the prepubescent vigilante, stink, slime, and stain are the gold standard of noisome projectiles, Dave had done his worst and then some. Any normal revenge-bent eleven-year-old would have just thrown the eggs as is and left it at that, or gone with the tried-and-true water balloon and considered himself well served.

Not Dave.

He is now standing back, looking at his rows of perfect rejiggered eggs. Sealed. Shut tight. For all intents and purposes done. And I'm guessing he's feeling proud of his work, elated by his inventiveness, and his mind, in celebration, is free-associating, maybe ringing off with Stevie Wonder—"Signed, Sealed, Delivered, I'm Yours"—and he's thinking, "Yes, yes, of course, I have done something masterful, sealed what is to be delivered. Only one thing remains. I must sign my work."

Yeah, that must have been it.

I mean, Christ. Your guess is as good as mine.

Fuck if I know what the beasty homunculus wreaking havoc in Dave's right brain was thinking. The deeper wherefores are beyond me. Hell, I defy any alienist to explain it.

One thing's sure. He'd planned his last flourishes from the start. He'd bought the wax and the paintbrush. He had the cat shit warming under the heat lamp. So whatever possessed him had possessed him at the Home Depot and beyond, and now he was just carrying out its orders to the last.

Phase four.

He took the paintbrush, one of the narrow-tipped sort that's meant for gilding or painting model airplanes, dipped it in the magma of cat shit, and proceeded to paint what, given the incarnadine quality of Trajan's stool, looked like a battle-muddied St. George's Cross around the girth and height of each egg. One horizontal band of bloody poo, one vertical. Going all the way around. Cruciform on two sides.

Eat your heart out, Andres Serrano.

That completed, he took the Bic lighter, held it beneath the stick of sealing wax, dribbled a dime-size dollop onto the top of each egg, and imprinted it with the signet ring he wore on his right middle finger.

The last abstracted fuck-you, perhaps?

Or do I give him too much credit?

I didn't know at the time what was engraved on the ring. I'd never noticed it before and I've never seen it on his finger since, but if it was his initials, I guess you have to give the guy some credit for chutzpah, or just dumb belligerence, because it was like putting his fingerprint on the weapon and saying, "Come get me. I'll be in the bunker out back with my canned goods and my RPGs."

Fucking lunatic.

And they could have traced him that way, too, if Dave hadn't hidden or dispensed with the ring and, more to the point, if the partygoers at Jack Gordon's that night hadn't been too drunk and generally disreputable to be credible, even as they stood there rankly splattered with the evidence.

The authorities who investigated the scene—the scene being, of course, Jack's two rowdy acres, pool deck, and aghast guests—might well have classified Dave's salvo as a hate crime, if we had had that legislation in this state at the time.

The St. George's Cross, which was found and identified (or interpreted) as such on some of the less fractured eggshells on Jack's lawn, was seen as a clear indication that the perpetrator was affiliated with the British National Front, or some loosely grafted arm thereof, operating in the disgruntled WASP diaspora, and had carried out his act of vandalism in a spirit of virulent, if shockingly puerile, anti-Semitism.

The letters DOA, which were found imprinted on one of the uncracked wax seals, were seen as an especially sinister touch, but were never conclusively linked with our hero Dave Alders, because his birth and other official records had his middle name as Daniel. Besides, even if what had been interpreted as an O, and assigned such a chilling import, had actually been a

D, for Daniel, a true monogram would have read DAD, not DDA, so the case (weak, at best) against the blubbered bandit was dropped.

Dave must have dispensed with the evidence before he stepped out that night with his bag full of bombs, because none of the goodies—the glue gun, the wax, the syringe, the ring, etc.—were ever found. Trajan himself disappeared that night, too, thereby thwarting any link the county crime lab might have made by means of distinctive intestinal flora. I doubt the notion of a fecal smear ever occurred to those cruller-munching Keystones down at the precinct, but Dave wasn't taking any chances.

Of course, I had the whole thing on tape, but that was mine to do with as I liked and when I chose.

And choose I would. Make no mistake about it.

Meanwhile, every last mucky detail of the episode found its way into our town annals, mostly because the local press went wild over it for weeks, coining all the predictable ringers, e.g., "Fabergé Fiend Fouls Ferragamos." (As if anyone at a Jack Gordon party, except possibly Jack himself, was wearing anything fancier than Frye motorcycle boots. But whatever.)

To this day, that "spiteful prank of partygoer pelting," as one tabloid described it, is known across the predominately Jewish southeastern portion of our state as Eggnacht.

And there, my friends, you have it.

All set down.

Thus, alas, was my crass and terrible introduction to the bizarre bazaar of clandestine photography. I sat goggle-eyed in my basement control room, glued to the monitor, double- and triple-checking the red record light every few minutes, just to be absolutely sure that it was still illuminated and that I was indeed getting all of this.

Truth be told, this abject entertainment was just the right over-the-top shock-and-awe antidote to all the psychic pain, terror, and confusion I was in because of my parents' deaths. I required hyperstimulation and distraction every bit that strong to shut out all the poltergeists of speculation and memory that came crashing in on me full tilt if given the slightest chance.

And that's, I guess, what got me hooked on spying, and what kept it going so elaborately for so long. The need to abscond from myself, to throw off the hounds of my own conscience.

I watched that monitor—or later, my many monitors—for hours and hours on end, and drank until I lost consciousness, finding in that blackness a remote-channeled respite from the horror of the too immediately real.

Forgive me, Father, for I have sinned. It's been thirteen years since your last confession.

This is mine.

I make it in the hope of meted penance.

5

I am so afraid.

Can I say that to you? Or to me? Myself. Nick Walsh. Whoever you are/I am. Can I admit that? Can I stand it?

It's true. The truest thing I can express.

I'm afraid.

Afraid that I am my father.

God. How awful. How truly, terrifyingly awful.

And yet I so want to be him. I really do. I have always wanted that. And I know that that probably doesn't make any sense.

But I want it to make sense. I want it to make sense in the telling. Because my father was not a bad man. He really wasn't. That can be true, even while all the rest is true as well.

It can.

It is. It was.

I remember. I remember so much when I let myself. If I can stand the sear of it, like a hot iron on my tongue, the hiss of contact, the rebellion of every sense against the information.

I remember the trips to the Christmas tree farm when I was a boy, the dry, dry cold and the cerulean sky, the blinding sun splash on the powdered snow, feet deep in places, like sifted flour on the untracked ground, and on the boughs of every tree.

I can hear our boots squeaking on the trail, where other trekkers have trampled the snow into trenches deep and narrow. I can feel the tiny hairs in my nostrils tightening, and I can see Dad's yellow leather work-gloved hand toting the rusted handsaw.

I can feel his competence in that hand, his control, and I can relax into the day and be an animal under the sun and in the air, purely alive and without agenda, following behind.

He will decide which tree is best, because he will know, having judged its lean and its symmetry. He will make a show of consulting me and he will note my objections, if I have any and if they are sensibly put forth.

These are the terms of the discourse. You must make an argument, a case, for the thing you want to express. This is what lawyers do, and so it is what the children of lawyers must do also. This much I know, even at eight, or seven, or six. As far back as that, surely. Emotion will get no response, except occasionally more emotion, and the only emotion Dad shows is anger, often channeled to disdain.

Choosing is a matter of dry judgment, even here, where we are looking at the shape and height of trees and wondering if they will look right in the corner of the room when the lights and ornaments are strung on them.

My father has no aesthetic sense. No receptors for that. For him, beauty registers in straight lines, as order, a pleasing logic in the eye that can, for a moment, relax the grip of his mind on the absolute.

To communicate, I must borrow his language, haul it up, copied and memorized for times like these, when the adjustment is so abrupt. I must narrow my eyes against the light, against the bliss of ambience and appetite, sharpen the focus and speak. Say something astute.

He nods.

"Hold it here, son," he indicates, grasping the midpoint of the trunk where I can reach it, then kneeling to saw at the base.

I watch him do this the way I watch him do everything, like a hospital machine with a pen attached, counting every beat and twitter and recording it. For what? For mimicry. For fascination. I note every dart of his eyes to his fingers, the eyes small and incongruously soft, date brown, the fingers huge, long and thick. Manipulative. Yes. Exactly that. The pull of hands to a task.

My deepest love for him is in that space of intention where he exerts his will on the object and I can see his mind at work, uncluttered by fear or doubt. This is a man. This is a man I want to be. Knowing. Acting. Clear.

I am bursting with silent admiration, bleeding it internally, my chest filled. I am helping to carry the tree, on its side, dragging in the snow on my end, the tip where the angel will go. I am feeling my arms heavy and my shoulders ache. I am watching my boots, which seem big to me, until I look forward at Dad's—huge, punching graves in the snow. I step where he steps and my feet disappear in shadow.

At this age, he is impatient with me, with the things I ask or the things I like and want to do, things he deems frivolous, unintelligent, like taking a ride in the horse-drawn cart filled with hay and other laughing children.

Or this is often how it sounds to me when he replies, a curled lip under his answers. But there is also a firm pedagogy that expects me one day to catch up, say something interesting all on my own.

So many of my memories of him are like this. Snippets. Bits of film clipped out and dominated by imagery and inference, my interpretations of what's happened endlessly branching, like fingers scrabbling for a hold. My experience is dominated by this, my obsession with what was going on in his head, as if it could be read in waves on the air and shield me from his disapproval.

What are you thinking? What do I need to know or presume to get safely through the next five minutes? The next hour? What angers you? I will avoid it. What annoys you? I will slide past. How do I make you proud? What do *you* think is important? I will be that, building the platform of myself out of all the things you admire in other people. Give me the example, and I will make it into something that you can love. More so, something that you can like, or that you can claim as your own without disappointment.

But this business of pleasing is a delicate balance. Dodge and strive. A boy guided not, as he should be, by joy and private inclination, but by what he thinks will get a prize, or some credit from the man above. With fathers, it is every bit this simple, hackneyed, primitive, and stupid. Boys are like savages worshipping stones. "This is God," they say, "this idol of a man. I will sacrifice anything to please him."

My need makes him sound mean, but he wasn't. He was solid and blunt and armed with his education. That's all. Honest to a fault. A man who had made his own way on his own terms, working as a waiter at country clubs to pay his way through college and law school, the first member of his family to educate himself past high school.

As a young man just out of the army, he served veal scallops and single-malt scotch to the businessmen in their tailor-made double-breasted suits, and he swore that someday he would be one of them, a professional, a man of taste and reasonable wealth.

He was much older than most fathers of kids my age, and nine years older than my mother. He was forty-one when I was born.

Maybe that was part of the problem. The gap between us was just too big. The world he had known was nothing like my own. James Nicholas Walsh was a child of the Great Depression, and Nicky boy was coming of age with the Internet.

Dad groomed his hair every morning with the five-inch black plastic comb that he carried behind his wallet in the left-hand breast pocket of his suits. He carried a clean handkerchief in the other breast pocket, and he put his change in the pocket within the pocket at his right hip. All of these things could be reliably found in their accustomed places, the change especially, which he did not remove each evening and which I pilfered once a week from his closet, feeling for the hanging weight in each jacket and sliding my fingers in neatly to filch the coins.

The man was his image: a suit, carefully displayed. Hanging on a hanger or on his shoulders, it was much the same either way.

I was the opposite.

I grew my hair long like every rebellious twelve-year-old boy and took pride in my dishevelment. My looks were so foreign to men of my father's world that one of them, when he met me at a party for the first time, said:

"Your daughter would be quite pretty if she didn't have such big feet."

Another family joke I never lived down.

But who cared? I was an exercise in contrast by design.

Well through my teens, I wore ripped jeans and cutoff T-shirts, especially in summer when I came home from boarding school for three months, randy with the cooped-up flak of the semester and determined to make the most of my freedoms.

I met my friends out back of a neighbor's vacated house most evenings to smoke pot and drink beer and make out with girls in the grass. The cops busted us there one night, having received a report of a possible burglary, and hauled us down to the station for questioning. We'd all been savvy enough to toss our drugs before being tackled by the overzealous third-string SWAT team they sent in, so they couldn't keep us in custody for more than a few hours.

But they did call Dad to have him pick me up at the station, and that was worse than a night in jail. We drove home in a silence that was like a death happening.

When we finally had it out in the kitchen, Dad worked himself into such a fury that he tore the ratty T-shirt off my back. Right off, like wrapping paper. Lifted me clear out of my chair by it, and it gave at the shoulders and pits where I'd trimmed it to show off my pecs.

It was the maddest I'd ever seen him, and the whole time he was ripping into me—chair scraping, cotton shredding—he still managed to sound like an old English barrister taking the wrongdoer down a peg by terms of a gentleman's code.

That was his most effective punishment. Banishment from his good graces. Being thought unworthy, found wanting at the far end of his withering rebuke. He crushed me with slurs I didn't even understand.

Standing there half clothed and sweating out the booze, I was hardly in a position to refute his parting shot.

"You look, you smell like exactly what you are. Uncouth."

I slouched around him like Caliban for weeks after that—*this thing of darkness I acknowledge mine*—doing chores and strewing around copies of Rousseau and Gibbon and even my Signet Classic of *The Tempest* from school, all as a kind of wearying jest, but really just a dash to redeem myself in his eyes, if only by the badge of summer reading.

Dad was such an intellectual climber (and through him, so was, so *am* I) that this Great Books ploy often worked to set things right again between us, or at least give us something to talk about.

He had the autodidact's tic of deep-set insecurity incurable. He was always a sucker for the Western canon, or what a man of good breeding would supposedly just have lying around on his bedside table or on the back of the toilet.

Fuck me, but I loved the old bastard for his love of learning, even if it was put on. How else? I learned quick enough (or is it quickly?) that learning is putting on, or taking on and then keeping for the times when you find yourself alone in your haunted prison, reciting poetry for comfort.

He gave me that, the valuation of knowledge for its own sake. I stole a line for every mood to shore me up against the philistine inside me who wanted nothing more than just to *be* in his own gruff body, hanging from tree limbs and raking his toes in the dirt, running wild all day long on a cocktail of breakfast and testosterone.

That was natural me, and that me took some breaking in the earliest years. But acclimatize the bear to the circus, and he will dance, eventually.

At first I hated to read, when I was a young boy and Dad and Mom made me do it for an hour each day. Hated it. But then, over time, I came to really love it—slowly, in and after college, when I first learned to savor the pleasure of an idea, rolling it around in my brain, feeling for the first time that you could actually get high, really pleasurably high on thinking.

But by then, of course, it was too late. The best of me, done for him and courtesy of him, was all dressed up with no place to go. No place to go but a funeral. Oh, well. At least he saw me graduate. At least I made it partway to what he wanted for me.

That was Dad's greatest gift. He had worked his way into an education. Earned it for himself. But it was given to me as my birthright from day one, not just in the schooling he paid for but in extras as well. By mandate, he gave me the leisure time and space to learn if I wanted to, and I took it. I came home from school every summer, and Dad said, "Study or get a job."

And so, while my friends made cinnamon rolls all day at the mall or mowed lawns for spending money, I chose to study. I took summer school courses, or read on my own from a list that Mom, Dad, or a teacher had given me. I sat by the pool, the pretend gentleman amateur, working on my tan and turning the pages of *The Myth of Sisyphus*, getting maybe every tenth word but feeling really deep all the same for even trying to roll my boulder of a brain up that hill, and then watching it roll back down again.

Mom assigned me most of the literature, Dad the history, philosophy, and poli sci. True to form, he was big on dates and facts and memorization, she on nuance. All the art genes came from her. She could teach you to feel a sonnet down to the roots of your teeth by way of your broken heart, whereas Dad went at your grammar, hammer and tongs.

"Today, you lay the book on the table and you lie on the couch. Yesterday, you laid the book on the table and you lay on the couch."

Right. Got it. First and last lesson learned. A book on the table and a body on the couch. Right here. In this room. Did I say that before? It—the crime—happened here, in Dad's study, which is now mine.

Study.

Study well, boy, and learn.

And with that, the memories snap shut. The pictures cease.

I am in the present again, circled back and caught blank.

Today, which is still so much of yesterday, I lie on the couch beside Monica and I lay what I can of my past out in front of her, telling her all of these things about my parents, my father especially, because she listens, and because lately she asks. It is her asking that helps me to remember, and her listening that helps me to withstand the memory.

Just barely.

"Tell me about your Dad," she says, whispering, close. And she does it in such a smooth, unassuming way that I am able somehow to answer, even though the same question from anyone else would be grounds for dismissal on the spot.

She gets away with it, as with so much else, and I let her, because she is my executioner, chosen especially for this. Standing on the scaffold—for what crime? the crime of omission, I think—I give her the token ring or piece of gold or silver. I put it in her palm and say, "I forgive you," and then she chops off my head.

Except that my head is still like that boulder I read about. Rolling down. I've always got to pick it up again.

"Tell me about your Dad," she says, and smiles gently.

"I hated him and I wanted to be him," I say. "Pretty tired stuff."

"Maybe, but tell me anyway."

"What do you want to know that I haven't told you already?"

"I don't know. Something surprising. Something that no one else knows." She is sitting up now on her elbow looking down at me intently.

"You're no different than anyone else, you know," I say a little angrily. "Everyone wants to know why he did it."

"But I don't mean that. I mean the opposite."

"The opposite of what?"

"Of the devil."

"He wasn't the devil. That's my whole point."

"I know, but you haven't said that."

"That's *all* I've been trying to say."

"Yes, but you keep circling back to the same place."

"What do you mean? What place?"

"I don't know. Hardness, I guess. His demands. His expectations. Your differences."

"Well, that's the way I remember it."

"That's the way you let yourself remember it. But there's more."

"Oh, really? And what makes you so sure about that?"

"Because if there weren't, you'd stop trying. Case closed. But you keep going back because there's something else still there and you need it?"

"So now you're a shrink. Is that it?"

"Don't make this about me."

"Don't make it about *me*, you poser."

"Poser? I've never said I was anything other than what I am. You're the one who's posing. You can't even be honest with yourself. You don't know how."

She flops down on her back and sighs loudly.

We lie in silence like this for a while, both staring up at the ceiling, both hurt, but both working inside ourselves, waiting for the conflict to ease. We can't part this way and we know it. We're both too desperate and, despite whatever I say, we are both way too much in need of the therapy we came for.

After a long time, she says:

"I'm sorry."

She waits longer, then tries again for a way back in.

"He had soft eyes, you said."

To this I manage a strangled:

"Yes."

We are in the most fragile place we ever go to now. One false word and the quiet will flail beyond salvaging.

"There," she says. Carefully, leadingly, placing her finger above the wound, but not touching it.

Still more silence. Then, finally, I say:

"Raspberries."

I almost want to laugh at this, and if I weren't so fucking maimed and terrified, I probably would.

But she gives no sign of anything. She just waits.

Clever girl.

"He loved raspberries."

She nods very, very slowly, but says nothing.

So I go on.

"I remember being very young. We were sitting on the couch side by side watching TV one night after dinner, and we were eating bowls of raspberries with grenadine."

I stop again. I'm going to make her sit for this. See if she can improv and get it right. Squeeze out the confession.

But she's better at this than I am. Not even challenged.

She's so still. Electrically still, like a sound that's too low or too high for me to hear but that registers anyway, somewhere, on my skin or on hers, or between, and she knows she can linger, balanced palpably this way, encouraging, for as long as it will take.

And that's the right word.

Encourage, to make brave.

Why is this little, little thing so hard to say? So hard to remember?

We were eating raspberries. So what?

She'll be disappointed when I finish. There's nothing there. But it's all I can think of.

It's what she wants, so I'll give it to her.

"We were eating and watching the TV, and then I happened to look down at what was on my spoon, and I saw a small white worm curled inside one of the berries, wriggling."

I hang on this, still hoping she'll trip, say the wrong thing or interrupt, and then I won't have to go on with the rest. But she doesn't. She waits.

"I hated insects then," I say, feeling it now, coming strong, the picture running on its own. "I still do. I couldn't believe that there was one in my food, and alive, too. I felt sick at the thought that I'd already eaten one."

Monica smiles uncomfortably, her face squirming with the ick of it.

"I thought, how many worms had I already eaten in all the time I'd been eating fruit? It was horrible. I was probably six or something at the time, the age when discoveries like that are catastrophic."

Monica nods vigorously.

"Around that same age, I once found a spider on my pillow, and for years after that—really, years—I wore socks and a tracksuit to bed every night, my logic being that how could you ever know what was crawling over you while you slept? I'd lie there all night sweating my balls off, but I couldn't bear to sleep uncovered. That's how bad it was."

I'm rolling it out now, blabbing, as if we'd never argued, and there's no stopping me.

"Anyway, I looked up at Dad, probably with those saucer eyes that kids get after they've just bumped their head on the coffee table but before the pain has gotten through—you know, like they're looking at the parent to see if they should freak out—and I said, 'Dad, there's a worm in one of my berries.'"

We both laugh at this and shake our heads. Kids.

"I was full-on ready to pop," I say, "just rigid with it. And I figured he was going to say something harsh, like, 'Don't be a baby, Nick.' You know, shame me into eating it, like it was at the bottom of a bottle of tequila or something."

I pause here, the laugh having fallen out of the story. My voice goes serious and deep.

"But he didn't."

Monica's face falls, too, listening.

"Instead, he said the most soothing thing he ever said to me. And, believe me, I know, it's going to sound really lame and pathetic—like, *Jesus, Nick, if that's the best you ever got, no wonder*—but, well, I don't know, it just worked, and I guess I've never forgotten it."

I hang on this again, wondering, should I make this part up? Lie to her because the truth is so embarrassing? But I'm not quick enough for that, and she is really listening. Her knee is digging into my thigh painfully. She doesn't realize.

"He said," I say, leaning away and shifting her, "'They think the berries are good, too.'"

I smile at this and Monica does, too.

"And then he smiled at me, and he looked right into my bulging, horrified eyes with those soft eyes of his, and—"

I choke here and cough to cover the catch in my voice.

"Like I said, I know it sounds like nothing. But it wasn't. Because it wasn't just *what* he said. It was *the way* he said it. It was bigger than just the words. It was his tone, so sure and so calm."

Monica's eyes are darting across my face, from mouth to eyes and back again, guiding me to finish.

"That was really it, I guess. He was telling me that there was nothing to be afraid of. And the way he did it, with this combination of knowing and helping me to understand, it made everything okay instantly."

I say this again to the wall—"Everything. Instantly."—and Monica puts one fingertip on the forked vein of my forearm, where a drop has fallen. There is nothing on my face.

"I believed him," I say, "because he was who he was. Because he was my dad."

Her eyes are pulling me, and I let them. Her hand has burrowed into mine.

"He took this huge fear and disgust and worry and he just made it disappear. And no one has ever done that again. No one ever could."

It is very late,
And you are sleeping.
I watch over you in the dark,
So that nothing,
Nothing can harm you.
Precious girl.
Perfect girl.
Can you know how much I love you?
Will you?
When we meet at last, as lovers,
Will you know me?
In the shadowed light,
Will you see me in my eyes,
And yourself there, too?
Will you take me as your savior?
Your protector?
Your father, man of dreams and
Eye of God?
Will you?
And for now?
For now,
Will you believe in
What you have not yet seen?
Yes.
I think you will.
With faith and my words,
Set down for you,
What is between us will grow
And live.
Our secret.
In mind.

Sleep well,
My dearest love.
And I will come again,
Tomorrow or the next day.
Soon.
One day I will wake you with kisses,
And you will spend the day in my arms.

6

Another note from Pinko today.

It's been a while since the first one. So long, actually, that until today I'd written that one off as a fluke, or a prank that Dave had lost interest in. I wouldn't at all put it past him to have gotten a sample of my handwriting and found a way to Photoshop it to the purpose.

The pink paper (a pointed choice, I think) has Dave's sophomoric sense of humor written all over it. He's always thought that a guy who wears anything but earth tones is a flamer, and ever since my college rose period, he's never ceased giving me shit about my wardrobe. Not that I've stopped wearing the finer shades now and again, mind you. I wouldn't let the jibes of the behemoth who shopeth at Big and Tall dampen my palette any.

But, having given it more thought, I've pretty much scratched the prankster Dave theory, mostly because Dave couldn't write a poem—not even a serial killer's paean to suburbia as slaughterhouse—if his useless lifestyle depended on it.

He could have cribbed the lines from somewhere, true, but I don't think he'd even know where to look. Plagiarism does take some finesse with a search engine, which cuts Dave out of the running as surely as a rock-solid alibi. I mean, we're talking about the guy who honestly believed for most of his adult life that the winged goddess of victory got her name from the sporting goods company, and not the other way around.

I found the latest poem in the mailbox, again on pink paper, mixed in with all the other junk mail: the Valpak of supermarket coupons, a preapproved offer for a credit card from Sinkhole Bank, a J.Crew catalog (surprise, surprise), and a solicitation from *Taurus* magazine, telling me I'm only ten weeks (and five human growth hormone injections) away from my dream torso.

This latest installment of the lost verses was hidden among all that pulp, and I might have missed it and tossed it, had it not been wrapped around the one and only envelope I search for every week.

Yes, indeed. That would be the thin one with the perforated tabs and the parent company logo that looks more like a parking ticket than a paycheck, and practically shouts: "Cash me, ya broke fuck, and for the love of God, buy some toilet paper!"

There it was. A measly four hundred and seventy-five bucks, and this— God, what can you call it?—this sick-making, pedophiliac's scrawl. This is really not funny anymore. I don't know what to think, unless this is some- body's payback for my spying. Maybe one of the nabes found a camera and somehow traced it back to me. But who? Who would do this? Who could?

There's always Jonathan Katz, I suppose, but that's a long shot. He and his wife, Dorris, were living across the street next to the Blooms, but they split up about two years ago, and now it's just Dorris and the brats in situ, Miriam, ten, and Isaac, twelve. I've had cameras in there for a while now, predivorce and after, but even if Dorris finally noticed one of them and made the con- nection (highly unlikely), I still don't see either of the Katzes as the type to plot or pull off Pinko's style.

Dorris is far too stupid, for starters, a prime specimen of what they used to call the Jewish American Princess, or what the JAPs themselves called a Kugel, as in pudding, as in tasty dish, but brain like a warm dessert.

Jonathan, meanwhile, a pediatric neurosurgeon, poor bastard, is so bitter about the size of his alimony and child support payments (think GNP of Burundi and you're probably in the ballpark) that I bet he'd love the idea of someone posting "Keyhole Exploits of a Divorcée" on XTube. (When I do share my footage, by the way, which isn't that often, as a legal precaution I blur out the faces and any singular household items. But still. You never know who might recognize that cluster of three moles just below Dorris's left armpit.)

Even so, as the TV detectives say, I don't like Dr. Katz for this one. He just doesn't have the motivation. Besides, how many neurosurgeons do you know who have the time, much less the chops, to toss off the likes of "Childe Bride: Bluebeard's Last Seduction"—or whatever you wanna call this "material" I'm getting?

Okay, sure, it's possible, remotely, that Katz is the William Carlos Williams of the criminally insane, but I'm gonna take the under on that. Call it a hunch.

He's since moved to greener stomping grounds, anyway—Twin Pines, wouldn't ya know—and now resides not far from Dave. I'm sure he's rolling in his newfound bachelorhood, happy as happy gets.

And yet, boy, does that man have a pair of lungs. Whoa. And a tongue to match. I'll say that for him. And her, too. I had my cameras in that house for the whole last year plus of their trip down the nuptial toilet—one in the family room, one in the bedroom, and one in the en suite bath—and, Jesus, talk about scenes from a fucking marriage. Holy crap.

You get a couple of Sephardic Jews going at it with all the wrath of the old religion behind them and the pitchfork of the gender wars out front, and it gets nasty in ways that the less ethnic peoples among us just can't wrap our vanilla minds around. Let's just say that, when it comes to spousal abuse, the silent treatment never made it past the Alps, and a good old-fashioned Mediterranean beat down is for the birds when you've got the right vocabulary.

Sticks and stones would have been a relief and, I'm here to tell you, names can definitely hurt you. Not a word went unshouted between these two. Shrieked, actually, at a pitch that isn't even human anymore. My ears are still ringing with it.

I can't believe it lasted as long as it did. I was exhausted just watching. He'd be standing there in nothing but his golf shoes and a jock strap and she, completely starkers (as usual), would be sitting at her dressing table screaming the laundry list of his failings in high C and gesticulating so wildly with a hairbrush that it made me clench my jaw and the cheeks of my ass until they cramped.

Scary, scary shit.

That ended, finally, with him fishtailing so furiously out of the driveway in the white Caddy at three a.m. that there were skid marks halfway down the block. They left the rest to the lawyers, I'm assuming, or the good folks at AT&T, because I never saw the Escalade with the MD plates in the driveway again, though I was privy to a few choice hang-ups on the bedroom extension.

Yeah. I was well wired for them when that action went down, and as with Dave, I came to mostly regret my intrusion. But I stuck to it nonetheless because, like I said before, even all those years after Mom and Dad's deaths, it was still the only thing on offer that was louder than the voices in my head, and I needed it.

I rigged the Katzes the way I rigged everyone after Dave and, ironically enough, under the fiscal auspices of Dave as well. He paid for most of my equipment, unknowingly, of course, but uninquisitively, too, so I can't really feel that bad about fleecing him.

Turns out that liquidity and the good sense (or density, I can't decide which) not to ask questions are possibly Tubbo's only two virtues, and I made efficient use of both. He's the silent partner behind my network.

But he doesn't ever miss a few thou here and there, so who's stealing? Hell, he forks it over willingly, practically foists it on me, because he feels soooo sorry for me, the inert, emotional pygmy of his childhood acquaintance who's, yep, broke again.

He says he's come to love me like a brother. Brothers in death till death, he calls us.

Fucking 'tard.

The technology has evolved a lot since I placed my first Trojan horses at Dave's, so the cameras I have at Dorris's place are the size of ballpoint pens, and the mics are even smaller.

For the install I hired an underworld techie I met through my drug contact Jazmin. You remember her? The dumb cunt who can't even spell her own pseudonym but who gets me the pills that can tame me? Yeah, her.

Anyway, this guy Damian does stash-house surveillance for Jazmin's kingpin connection, and he'll do spy cam plants for anyone else who can afford it. His day job is doing service calls for the local cable and satellite TV company, so he can get access to pretty much anyone's house without arousing suspicion, and he's willing to rig whatever you want while he's there.

That's how I've done all my rig-ups in the past seven years, and that's why I say it'd be pretty damn unlikely that anyone would locate my equipment. This guy's a pro. Precision stealth motherfucker. He could just about slip a camera into your molar while he was Frenching you, and you'd be none the wiser. He's that good.

I doubt *I* could even find my own equipment.

Dorris the porous hasn't got a chance.

The woman really is the bimbo to beat all bimbos.

She's good-looking, I'll grant, in an Anne Bancroft in *The Graduate* kind of way, but she's not blessed with the sultry voice. She's a Trotsky, no mistaking, and a trophy wife of a certain tarnished class raised up by a subspecialist's income to sit in the catbird seat. She was maybe one step above someone you'd have found at Jack Gordon's with her thong in a tree, except she married well.

And she does have a body, true enough, albeit one with a sell-by date that's coming up fast. She's forty-two or -threeish by now if she's a day, and not taking the best care of her skin.

She slathers herself with baby oil and cooks herself into a prune on her back patio every afternoon between Easter and Halloween, or any other time it's even vaguely warm enough to bare her nipples to the elements.

Like I said, the lady isn't a big fan of clothing when she's at home.

And *that* no one needs cameras to see. Every horny kid in the neighborhood has peeked through her hedges on a dare and lathered himself blind at the sight of those dugs.

And why not, I guess.

As Dorris herself likes to say, "If you got it, show it."

And she means it in more ways than one, because much the same could be said for her temper.

Those poor kids are like pound puppies, cowering and practically piddling themselves whenever they spill a glass of milk or grind a corn chip between the sofa cushions or commit whatever other victimless crime kids are prone to. The slightest misstep and Mommy Dearest blows her top like a tone-deaf Wagnerian having her fingernails extracted. Your average shrew is a lap cat by comparison.

Fucking hell, what a noise.

Now that Jonathan is gone, I guess she's got no one else to vent her jilted harpy's spleen on, so the kids take the brunt of it and tiptoe around her as best they can, taking refuge at the worst of times in a makeshift hedge fort they've built at the end of the yard.

If Dorris is in glass-shattering high dudgeon over something—say, a piece of expressionist artwork splattered on the coffee table with a paintball gun—those kids will hide outside even when the weather's fucking Siberian.

I've seen them there on single-digit days crouched and bundled, bouncing on their haunches and blowing on their hands like a couple of street urchins.

I feel sorry for the little varmints. I mean, it'd be downright Dickensian if this weren't Shangri-La La Land and they weren't wearing Dolce down jackets and Bollé ski goggles while playing miniature billiards or whatever other obscenely overpriced novelty game they've managed to cadge out of Jonathan because he left them.

Honestly, can they really take you seriously at Child Protective Services if you make the call from your iPhone while riding around your front yard in your motorized miniature MG?

Still, I'm half tempted to intercept them on their walks home from school and shove them each a pair of earplugs and some Vicodin.

"Here," I'd say, "these are for you. Crush up the pills with the back of a spoon and slip 'em in her Slim-Fast every morning. Put the squishy things in your ears and wait. That should turn down the volume considerably."

But they're surprisingly resilient, as kids so often are. They seem to bounce back and laugh and go on bumbling around, doing the same boneheaded things that threw Dorris over the edge in the first place.

And the parental guilt? Wow. Presents keep rolling in, one upon the next, as if the ongoing storm of the divorce could be drowned out by a bribe.

Which, I guess, to a point, it can.

Except nobody's greasing Dorris. Or not as far as she's concerned anyway. Sure, she buys herself some goodies for the odd night on the town, when she can get a babysitter and when she can wind herself up enough for another turn as a would-be mantrap. But the rest goes to the upkeep of the house and the kids, both of whom are in private school. That's near on thirty grand a pop right there, per annum.

But even if Dorris did have a slush fund for purses and jewelry, I don't think she's really in party mode anyway. She's looking at a pretty leathery, lonely old age if she doesn't turn things around soon, and that's not the kind of pressure that puts you at your best on the singles scene.

I've seen her at the Swan with all the other desperate cougars trying to snag another benefactor for the long, slow slide into retirement. Otherwise, in a few more years, when the alimony payments expire and her face has gone the way of all pumpkins, she'll be working as a hostess at the Capital Grille just to make ends meet.

Time's a-wastin'.

She tried the hard sell on me one night by the bar when she was so drunk that English had become a second language and I was so drunk that I actually leaned in to take her up on her offer. Thank God I pulled back at the last second, having caught an unmistakable, gorge-rising whiff of Eau de Early Old Lady. It was just the barest hint, but, man, I couldn't do it. It was like some primitive species-propagating voice in my head was saying, "Dead ovaries. Dead ovaries. Plow elsewhere."

But I feel sorry for Dorris, too. I really do. I can't help it. Because when she's not yelling at the kids or tying herself to the bed frame so she won't raid the fridge in her Ambiened sleep, she's sitting at that vanity naked doing soliloquies that would tear the heart out of a cyclops.

It's really sad.

Before she married she'd been an aspiring actress. She'd made a few toothpaste commercials, or maybe voiced-over one of those animated ads for feminine hygiene products, but she'd never done anything more serious than community theater. Still, the love of it hasn't died in her, and she's doing her best work, even if it is just to a plate of glass.

Glass, that is, with a camera in it. Or near it.

I think Damian somehow put it in the frame and tilted its angle of sight, because it's a straight-on shot on my monitor. It's now the second camera I have in there. Originally, I just had a wide angle for the whole bedroom, but when I saw her start the mirror monologues a while after the divorce, I had Damian make a courtesy call and rig me a better setup. Now it's like a Bergman movie in there for real.

But look, putting aside all the bile in me, I mean this.

Dorris Katz is in pain. Real pain. And who am I to say that it's any less legitimate than mine, or less debilitating just because it springs from a less newsworthy source? I'm not a big believer in the calculus of suffering. I don't think there's a scale with genocide survivors at the top and washed-up celebrities at the bottom. Not that I don't think you can legitimately say to a person, "Get over yourself, honey, it's a hangnail," or whatever, but I do think that suffering is suffering and is, by definition, subjective, no matter what the cause.

What's more—and maybe this is the Catholic in me, though I'm pretty sure the Buddha would back me up on this—I believe that suffering unites us. The one thing I did get from catechism, the one message that made its way through and stuck, was the idea that Christ was not to be revered because he suffered for our sins or because he suffered more than most—he didn't—but because he suffered *as we do.*

His suffering isn't what made him special. It's what made him just like everybody else. It made him understand what it was to live on the earth as one of us and, so the argument goes, that's why he could not forgo it. It wasn't the final exam, the last push before apotheosis. It was the whole show. The point. This is life, my friend, and welcome to it. He was just lucky it didn't last longer than it did.

He got a taste of this shithole at its worst, and *subjectively* he suffered, just like—exactly like—Dorris Katz. And the likeness goes both ways. Sitting in front of that mirror sobbing her heart out and shouting up to the angels—*Is anybody there?*—or to God—*Why have you abandoned me?*—Dorris—okay, I'm going out on a less than orthodox limb here, but I think I'm right—Dorris reenacts the Crucifixion. She is Christ. Again. And so is every other sorry sad sack sitting in his room suffering immeasurably in his mind.

In her monologues, as I've heard them, Dorris herself is making these same links, links to other people's suffering, though like most of the rest of us she tends to compare pains relatively and berate herself for dealing less well than, say, Mrs. Bloom, or me, with what she believed was a far less tragic fate.

Dorris, like everybody in the neighborhood, whether they've just moved in or were around for the actual events, knows about my parents and the Blooms, about Karen's death and Robin's disappearance. It is part of the lore of our subdivision, something the real estate agents still avoid discussing but which has found its way nonetheless into the ears of every person who has bought property or lived in the vicinity since 1997.

Dorris looks at Isaac, who is now the same age as Robin was when she disappeared, and at Miriam, who is younger and just as vulnerable a little girl, and she asks herself why she can't love them more, or love them better, when she knows that they, too, could be lost on the streets somewhere or in captivity being repeatedly raped and impregnated by some jackal of a man. She knows they could be dead, and that to some tortured parents thinking your kid is probably dead is a relief given the alternatives. She knows all these things all too well, and has made them part of her punishment, further evidence of failure at the one and only thing she feels she was groomed to be: a mother.

She looks searchingly into her own tearful eyes and she asks herself why she could not have made her marriage work, if only for the sake of the children, and to spare them seeing her deflate like this, like the Wicked Witch of the West, cursing and hissing the whole way down into a heap.

So, you see, I do her a grave injustice to say that she's a bimbo or a fleshpot or anything else wholly pejorative, because there is more to her. A lot more.

But who would ever know it? People are only themselves when they're alone, when there's no one there to see it. And sometimes, as with Dave, that's a good thing, because it's the only thing keeping them out of prison or the psych ward.

But with a lot of people, it's just beautiful. Breathtaking. So delicate and subtle and original that you think it might just redeem the whole species. And it's all hidden or reserved, kept in the speeches we make to ourselves in the middle of the night or the excruciatingly long empty afternoons in lonely houses when the pain is so bad that we're on the verge of killing ourselves, but can't. That's the good stuff. The best stuff. The truth. And the only way I've been able to see it is through a lie. A deception. An unconscionable intrusion into someone else's private hell.

Monica's the only person I know or have ever known who's like this all the time. Real, I mean. And she pays, has paid, a high price for it, no doubt. But even she isn't without some pretense. She can't be.

When we're in the presence of another person, there's always a mask, even if that mask is our face. There's no escaping it. And so the vast majority of what we say to each other, whether it's to our spouses, our family, our confessor, or perfect strangers, amounts to cocktail party chitchat all the same, or, at best, a crack audition for that juiciest of all parts we're literally dying to play: ourselves.

But alone.

Fuckin'-A.

Alone, we're genius.

Onstage doing *Our Town* with the other avocational thespians, or in the studio hocking fluoride whiteners and panty liners, Dorris is as Dorris does: a Trotsky Kugel no-talent *who-uh*, as they say in Brooklyn, whose best asset was always and ever her cooz.

But damn.

Alone, Dorris Katz is Antigone. Actually, Medea is probably the more appropriate choice, because, let's face it, she's thought about killing her kids, or being rid of them at least. Who hasn't? And she's thought a million times about how to save them, too, about what motherhood is, in all its triangulated affections, running between father and child and back again. She's thought, too—aloud—about what motherhood is but shouldn't be: the only love you never get over.

She knows a lot, Dorris, and she's wrestling.

She's in there fighting the hardest, timeless human fights that any pretentious patron of the arts ever goes to Euripides or Sophocles to purge himself of in the abstract.

Those tragedies are paper cutouts compared to the source.

Try sobbing until you vomit and going on with the monologue anyway, or cutting your thighs with a dull paring knife because it's the only way to leech out the poison in your underrated soul.

Dorris.

She and Dave inhabit the same world. The same five square miles, give or take. Can you believe that? They've even had a go at it in the sack, which is like something the laws of metaphysics should prohibit, or the voice of an overheated droid should warn you about.

Danger, Mrs. Robinson.

They met through me, of course. At the Swan. And the D-man, being the turkey vulture he is, took up the roadkill I declined.

I can't even talk about what they've done together or how bad she's felt about it afterward, or the fact that she's repeated the encounter anyway. It's enough to give you posttraumatic stress disorder. It has me. Thinking about it is like an abuse flashback. Makes me go clammy all over and want to shower.

I know, I know. You're saying: He's *your* friend, bro. Your best friend if, and I quote, "time wasted together is any indication."

7

Yeah, motherhood.

There's something for you.

It's something for me for sure.

Big.

That's why watching Dorris exercise her sensibilities in front of the mirror made me weep until the front of my shirt looked like a bib, and why watching Dave tup Dorris as if her boudoir were a barn was just too much for me.

Here's one for the books out loud. Take it down.

My mother was murdered.

Full stop.

That in itself is quite enough for anyone, without the coda of Dad as murderer tacked on.

All in the same crime.

All in the family.

I just cannot understand.

And my ignorance is killing me.

I have no information but my own past—the one I had with them, which was so partial anyway. After the age of fourteen I was away at school so much of the time.

I have summers and holidays to go by. And before that, I have the warped view of a child looking up at his progenitors in awe and wonder and, sometimes, impotent rage, as if at the colossi of Easter Island.

Maybe that's right. Maybe our relationships were always mediated by distance and therefore mystery, and that made them both easier and harder, but artificial all the same. And maybe that's why I have so much trouble remembering, because so much of it happened in small bursts, punctuated by long separations.

How much easier it was in this context to build up a theology around my parents. To love them so much and so falsely.

This I know is true, and I know it now for certain in a way that I never did then: it is impossible for me to love a person, or even know a person in any meaningful sense, because I do not believe that there is any such thing as a person.

To me, people have no substance but flesh. Bodies. The rest is purely ideas, a performance on one side, met by projection, and inference on the other. Minds meeting other minds, where minds themselves are just ideas, and the conference between them, illusory. Not a meeting at all. Just a ricochet of mistakes.

I have only an idea of a person, even the person that I call myself. That's all. And when I love another person, or think I do, it is only the idea of that person that I love, and it is only the idea of me that is doing the loving.

And why not love ideas when ideas are so easy to love? So perfect, and ordered, and beautiful, and narcotic. Even chaos has become a theory.

That is the whole history of man, to me. Human events boiling down to this: living, breeding, killing, and dying for ideas, and loving them unrequitedly.

We are no more capable of loving people than we are of loving dirt. We love the ideas that we attach to carcasses, the meanings we ascribe to them, and the image we form of them in our minds, minds that are no more substantial than anyone else's.

Show me where love is, where it exists, and I will show you a cerebral circuit board of signals and crossed wires. Saying you are in love with a person is like saying you are in love with a radio, or a TV, the box itself, not the broadcast coming from it, which is always hopelessly muddled anyway with the broadcast that is coming from yourself.

We are talking past and over each other all the while, and we take the resulting cacophony for music.

So, I suppose, my memories, patchy though they may be, are as legitimate, or as chimerical, as anything else.

I see the picture of my mother in my memory's eye.

It's a lie, but I will speak in the language we all understand, just as I have been doing all along, even to myself.

I will say that I loved my mother, and you will know what I mean. Sort of. We will agree to the common misconception and bask in it.

I will tell you that I smelled my mother's ghost again this afternoon when waking, and you will understand what I mean when I say I trust the hallucinations of my nose to conjure feelings that are not true but that I want to indulge anyway.

I learned this bitter lesson of love from my mother, over time and with repeated frustration. Much and desperately as I loved her and thought I communed with her, or was an intimate part of her and she of me, the fact remains: there was no one there.

My mother was a mirage. I made her up.

And, of course, she helped me along, because she was especially good at faking it. I don't mean that she faked loving me. She bought into that business as much as the rest of us. No, I mean she was good at faking being a person— which is, again, what we all do—but she *knew* she was doing it. She knew she had to do it, and she knew it much sooner than the rest of us ever do or can.

She knew probably by the time she was a young teenager that she was empty, that this person whom everyone called Diana and looked to for responses, opinions, signs of recognition, for substance of any kind—she knew that this person did not exist.

And I'm sure, especially coming as it did at such a young age, that this insight was disconcerting to say the very least. Horrifying, I bet. She probably thought that there was something terribly wrong with her. Who wouldn't? In fact, I'm sure she did, because she spent the rest of her life, and the immensity of her intelligence, first carefully figuring out what was required of her on any given occasion, and then expertly constructing, honing, and perfecting the required delivery.

Psychiatry will tell you that such a person is a narcissist or, more precisely, suffers from a narcissistic personality disorder. But that's reductive and, to my mind, just more proof (if any was needed) that many of the things we call disorders are just unpleasant truths about the so-called human condition that we don't want to face.

My mother was a genius at being a person from scratch, and she sustained that illusion till the day she died, which must have taken more energy than anyone could possibly imagine.

It's boggling, really.

Think of holding up the constant trick of your existence, knowingly, effortfully, and all for the sake of the people around you who haven't got a clue.

That's the part that really gets me.

What can it mean to murder such a person? How do you kill someone who isn't there? And how can they come back to haunt you? I ask myself that all the time. And then I think—maybe that's exactly why she's still here in some form, as much or as little as she ever was (and he, too, come to that), a broadcast still bouncing around in the ether.

I smelled her when I woke today. I smelled her in the form of clay. The grotto, wilted lily smell of a woman's compact, and the residue it leaves on her face; the feather catch of powder and blush, just in the back of your throat, and the candy sweet of lipstick. The humid confines of her favorite cavernous leather purse and all its contents came down on me like a blinding bag, as it did when I was a boy when I would plunge my entire head in there, breathe, and look out through the seams at a world too bright for hiding in.

It was all there again in the scent. The leaky ballpoint pen, the used tissues, crumpled and frayed, her wide lady's wallet with the change pocket that clipped, its belly full of grimy dollar bills that smelled of pencil lead, and crisp new twenties that didn't. There were pennies, nickels, and dimes fallen loose in the bag's cotton lining, mixed with a handful of aspirin and rolls of sugar-free mints. There were pieces of torn notepaper, a paperback book, a hairbrush full of hair. Oh, and yeah—who could forget?—there were always those three or four tiny bottles of Jack Daniel's, clanking.

When you ask the question how she did it, how she pretended so hard for so long, there is the answer. She drank. She drank a lot. And she pretended about that, too, hiding just how drunk she was or how often.

I guess now you know where I get that from.

I wonder, actually, if she puked as much as I do, or if she drank like a woman, a sip here, a sip there, just enough to top you up but not enough to throw your stomach into your throat.

She must have been hungover in the mornings, though, because after I was about ten years old she stopped getting up to make me breakfast on weekday mornings, and I had to fend for myself with peanut butter.

When I was just about ready to leave the house, I had to wake her to drive me to school, and that was like raising Lazarus, I can tell you. It was as if the woman slept in a bog with one arm protruding, and you had to pull her out by that appendage. Dead weight like nobody's business, and a spindly kid on the other end huffing and whining, "Come on, Mom. I'm gonna be late. Again."

I'm amazed she didn't belt me in the face. If some chipper fucker tried to wake me before I was human, I'd smack him clear across the room without even coming to consciousness.

But somehow, she always managed not to take the morning woozies out on me. It helped a lot that before I went to the bedroom to wake her, I'd brew her a cup of coffee that was as thick as the sludge she was sleeping in. I practically had to pour it down her throat from a kneeling position while plugging her nose, like some kind of EMT trainee.

That was enough to get her into her ratty robe and slippers, which is what she always wore in the car. We got into a fender bender once in the school's drop-off zone, and when she got out to give the other mother our number, her hair all wild and matted, her face still greasy with night cream, she looked like she'd escaped from the state asylum.

But what did she (or I) care what the housewives of Pelsher County thought of her? As far as she was concerned, they were a bunch of bubbleheaded cookie-bakers whose only purpose in life was to fatten up the next generation for the slaughter or the factory floor, or whatever else she thought the children of morons were meant for.

Actually, I know what she thought they were meant for, because now and again, at the right hour and after the right vintage, she'd say things like:

"This is a nation of idiots breeding more idiots, a rabble whose only useful function is to fight our foreign wars and donate organs."

Still, I'm thinking she must have been pretty well three sheets to the wind when she said those things, which wasn't that often, because midday, most of the time, when she was probably just mildly buzzed and playful, she rarely had a rude word to say about anybody. She was basically a good person, if a bit caustic on the delivery when you touched a sore spot. And before the drinking got really out of hand, she was a good mom, too.

A mom who even made breakfast.

Weird breakfast. But breakfast nonetheless.

Other kids got Cheerios and Count Chocula on weekday mornings, or at the very least oatmeal with milk and honey. I got frozen fish sticks and canned lentil soup.

I wasn't allowed to eat sugar during the week. Not even after school or after dinner. Only on the weekends and on vacation. So brekkie in the Walsh house was always a savory affair, and the only desserts I ever got, as Mom was so fond of saying, were just ones.

If I'd known at the time that in a few more years I'd be getting no break-fast at all, except what I could forage out of the pantry, I probably would have appreciated the hot meals a lot more, even if they were any kid's nightmare menu for supper, let alone breakfast.

But it's hard to have that kind of perspective when you spend the occa-sional sleepover at various pals' houses and in the morning you get Mrs. Sappy Sunshine serving you hand-squeezed orange juice and blueberry waf-fles shaped like stars and crescent moons.

The comparison was not favorable.

Except on rare Saturdays or holidays, when we all slept late and with Dad's help Mom managed to fork over something resembling pancakes, the clos-est Mom came to traditional breakfast was eggs, invariably scrambled into dry gray balls. Other times I got bean with bacon or cream of tomato soup, which was miles better than lentil, but still.

Breakfast trauma aside, I never really resented Mom's refusal to play home-maker. She was a highly educated woman who didn't take tips from women's magazines. She didn't need the guidance of other women, or the culture, which, as she pointed out, was just a bunch of C-students with dicks sitting around a conference table trying to sell you crap you didn't need, or trying to make you feel inferior if you balked.

Mom was impervious to criticism in this regard. Most regards, actually, but this one in particular. You couldn't make her feel inadequate as a woman or a mother. It was impossible, because her logic was airtight.

To the woman charge she'd say:

"Last time I checked, I had a vagina. QED."

And to the mother charge she'd say something equally cunty but hilari-ous, like:

"Motherhood? What is this 'hood' business? I whelped the bugger. Trust me on this one. I was there."

Where it counted emotionally, she was there, too, or, as I've said, she put on one hell of a performance of being there. And when you're a kid and you're in the presence of the Sarah Bernhardt of the fucking doll's house, you don't know the difference.

Trust me on this one. I was there.

Or don't trust me, and tell me that you would have known better, when even victims of cult abuse love their captors as moms and dads. And why?

Because this "hood" business is actually powerful brainwashing, and damned near impossible to resist.

It sounds confusing because it is. Nobody's love for a parent is simple, and usually it's made up of numerous, opposing points of view, none of which on its own gives a true picture, but which together are more than the sum of their shards.

Contrary things can be true of a person at the same time, and usually are. This was no less true of my mom than my dad. That's just how personality works. It's fickle and abstruse and kaleidoscopic, and trying to order it predictably into something called character is just an exercise in futility and gross oversimplification.

Like mistaking a movie for the real thing, or—hey, now here's a useful simile—like taking a ghost for a real person.

All this—my mother, my father, our family—doesn't need to make sense. It can't. I've learned that much after thirteen years of chewing on it. When I see my parents, especially through the warped lens of memory, and describe what I see, I'm just gilding an illusion. That's all. And that's okay now.

That much is okay.

Though okay in this sense only: this is the familiar pain of the disease that I know is killing me, and I take comfort in the fact that someday it will end.

Meanwhile, the memories are coming faster, though still piecemeal and incomplete. They roll in with the odors like storm clouds from the sea.

Now I am smelling frankincense, and the decomposing pages of old hymnals, and the dank of the old cathedrals we visited together in France. And then there is the carpet again in the upstairs hall of this very house when it was new, and the wallpaper when it was new, too, and I am thinking of Mom teaching me to pray.

I am probably seven or eight, right around the time of my First Communion, and we are both on our knees in the widest part of the hall, where it bends the corner between my room and the guest bath. A crucifix is on the wall above us, a simple dark walnut cross with a yellowed ivory Christ carved in fine detail. It once belonged to my grandmother, who gave it as a blessing for the house when my parents bought it.

Time seems still there in the hallway, with the overhead light falling down on us and through the opened doorways of the darkened rooms, and the two of us are almost touching, head to head, like twins in the womb, bowed, kneeling close, our hands folded in front of us. And now I can hear Mom speaking, softly, instructing.

"The most important thing to understand about prayer, Nick, is that it is not a wish list. The purpose is not to speak but to listen, and if you ask for anything, ask only for the courage to face with compassion, fortitude, humility, and patience everything that God asks of you."

"But what if I can't?" I ask, weakly.

"Then you must do the best you can. That is all that anyone can ask."

"Even God?"

"Yes, even God can ask only that much."

"But what if I fail?"

"You can never fail to do your best. You can only stop trying."

"And what happens if you stop trying?"

"You must never do that."

"Why?"

"Because it is the gravest of sins."

"Why?"

"Because it is at the root of all the others."

"Worse than anything?"

"Yes."

"Worse than murder?"

"It is murder. It is the murder of your own soul."

I told you she talked a good game. She, who I'm pretty certain didn't believe in the soul or, let's say, had serious doubts about it, because she knew she didn't have an identity.

There she was, dressing it up nicely, the whistling void herself, whistling "Dixie." Or was it "Nearer, My God, to Thee"?

What's the difference, when she had whiskey on her breath?

Wait.

Did she?

Conveniently enough, I don't remember.

What happens if you stop trying?

She never said.

But she knew, just as I know. She knew because she was in it, or on the verge of it even then.

It being what?

Well, so many things, really.

First, despair.

There is her gravest of sins. The one at the root of all the others.

Then drinking.

For what?

To assuage the despair? Indulge it? Make it feel good?

Sounds right.

Then, of course, drinking to excess.

And why? Why ever?

Because you can't help it anymore, or because your will is a flaccid rag by then.

No question there.

And finally?

Drinking to death.

Yes. The familiar thing.

Except not quite the way it usually happens.

Not the way it happened to my aunt, for example, Mom's sister, who died before I was born. Drowned in her own vomit.

Or the way it happened to my grandmother. Mom's mom. Classic thing. Her liver tuned to gristle, she turned the color of a golden raisin, and expired. Game over.

But Mom?

She did it her own finagled way, maybe.

You've heard of suicide by cop.

Was this suicide by husband?

Her blood alcohol content was absurd, and so was his. That much the coroner could say. Plus, of course, the wounds to the head. Two each. Point-blank range. Hers between the eyes and out the back. His under the chin and out the top.

Oh, and her liver looked like—well, he was too discreet to say what it looked like. I believe the word he used was "necrotic."

Whereas Dad's was nothing of the kind. Just the usual wear and tear for a social drinker of his age. Being drunk was rare for him. Very rare. Even I knew that.

But being *that* drunk. Never.

So what gives, Daddy-O? Mamacita?

Do tell.

8

I'm awake.
   Again.
   Fuck.
   Very old people must think that every morning. Or the terminally ill.
   Wake up, and the first thought they have is one of two things.
   Either it's, "I'm awake. Again. Yep. Still alive. *Sigh*. Fuck."
   Or it's, "Ahh. Life. Yet another day. Thank you."

Thank you?
   What is that bullshit, anyway?
   The guy on *Dateline* who's got five tubes in his face, is in excruciating pain every waking moment, and can only move the pinky on his left foot, but with that pinky he's dictated his memoir, *Ordeal Is Just a Friend You Haven't Met Yet*, a work of "trenchant beauty and majestic courage that gives a whole new meaning and dignity to the word 'survivor.'"
   Jesus. Give me Jack Kevorkian any day of the week.
   Give me a little genuine grief.
   And you can stick a stake through the heart of the human spirit.
   Mixed metaphor notwithstanding.

Strangely, Monica is here. Still asleep. Right here with me on the couch.
   She's never done that before.
   She's never wanted to, but even if she had, I wouldn't have let her.
   Now, somehow, we've both let it happen, and I can't decide whether it's a good or a bad sign.
   God, she is so beautiful in her sleep. Like an infant, the way she breathes.

She's fully clothed. Even her shoes. So I'm thinking she was on her way out and changed her mind, and I was too drunk to notice.

I remember very little of last night.

I know that Dave and I started at the Swan. The last thing I remember clearly is Dorris Katz sidling up to Dave, all familiar like, the way you kinda presume you can when someone's had his feet in your sheets and his balls in your mouth not twenty-four hours before. But Dave, cretinous scumbag that he is, tried for my benefit to pretend that the two of them weren't on bumping terms and never had been. I knew otherwise, of course, but neither Dave nor Dorris knew that.

Still, it would have been obvious to anyone what was between them. Inexplicably, Dave seemed to think I viewed him as a man of discriminating taste, or an expert dissembler, whereas Dorris must have thought that one more humiliation among so many wasn't worth a fight.

We stood there awkwardly, the three of us, with pained smiles on our faces, playing our assigned roles badly: I oblivious (read: annoyed), Dave haughty (plainly guilty), and Dorris beaten (gulping to forget).

Following Dorris's lead, I finished my three fingers of Jameson and ordered another.

And therewith memory scarpered.

Good dog.

And with it went the vision of Dorris and Dave, as well as whatever meet-up I had with Monica.

She must have driven us home in my car—she doesn't have one—or she's even braver than I thought. Not that I haven't driven blotto many, many times and made it home, and not that Monica isn't suicidal. It's just that she isn't passively suicidal. If she does off herself someday, she won't do it riding shotgun with a blind drunk. She'll take pills, put her head in the oven, *and* kiss a pistol, just to be good and goddamned sure. There'll be no risks or ifs about it, and certainly not those of a bumper car with a sot at the wheel.

I wriggled my way out from beside Monica without waking her, another miracle—she must have partaken last night as well. This, too, is something she never does. She likes her pain straight up and clear. It's what she runs on, which, I guess, is why she's such a wastoid this morning. But hey, good for her. Let her rest. She's earned it. And I like being able to watch her without her knowing it.

I've been doing all the usual online trolling for distraction. CNN, ESPN, weather, Facebook.

I hardly ever post anything on Facebook, but my virtual friends do, most of whom are regulars at the Swan, so it's a way for me to find out what I did the night before and, in some cases, what I need to undo the afternoon after.

None of these people, except Dave, is an actual friend. I don't have any of those. They're just people I habitually molest or abuse while bored and drunk, and who are stunted or desperate enough to take that for real contact, as if now I'd catsit for them or be a groomsman at their wedding.

I ignore most of their postings, unless there's potentially inconvenient damage to be undone—a quick pokey poke in the restroom, say, that was taken for more than it meant—or marginally meaningful records to be set straight—e.g., "No, I emphatically did not flush the contents of your wallet down the toilet while making a point about Obama's tax policies."

Usually around this time of day, while I'm having my Irish coffee (hair of the dog doing double duty), I'll head down to the basement and check my monitors. They're in a small dead-bolted room in the back that could easily pass for a storage area if anyone asked, but no one has. Neither Dave nor Monica, the only two people who are ever here, has ever had any reason to go into the basement, and when one of them is here, as Monica is now, I don't go down there, either.

Lately I've been going days without the urge to do even a quick check on Dorris or Dave or especially the Grubers, who are a relatively new and often wildly diverting addition to the network.

The Grubers live next door to me, to my right if I'm standing in my front door. No one is on my left, because I'm on a corner. The Grubenschwein are my nearest neighbors, and practically spiable without equipment, which is why I haven't had actual cameras in there for so long. The lots here are small relative to the size of the houses that are on them. Side window to side window is only a matter of forty feet.

The property line bisects an apple tree, which we both ignore, I by letting the fruit rot brown and stanky on the ground, he by letting his two Rottweilers shit in my yard—no doubt a retaliation of sorts for the compost.

And by "he" I mean, of course, Edward Gruber the paterfamilias Gargantua, a man of such size and authority and stentorian voice that when he calls his three teenage sons in for dinner on a summer evening he sounds like a subwoofer.

His voice and physique suit his personality exactly. Underneath the paunch and distributed plumpness of middle age, Herr Gruber has the musculature of a Clydesdale and the temperament of a wild boar. With his devil dogs, his dinner plate pecs, and his permanent scowl, he's a bit of a cartoon, to be sure, but he can back up the display, and often has, at the slightest provocation.

This is another reason why I haven't needed hidden cameras to know all that needs knowing about the Grubers. They, especially Edward, do it all out in the open, or a lot of it, such that you get the plot pretty well from a distance.

I once saw him chase his youngest son, Eric, out the front door of their house, both of them at a full sprint, and tackle the kid on the lawn. In Gruber's grip, the boy—he was probably eleven by then, and not small for his age—was like a rodeo calf, his back to the ground and all four appendages held together at a point above him by a white-knuckled clamp of pissed-off muscle and bone.

From a standing position, Gruber lifted Eric thus, a good two feet off the ground, and bellowed his reprimand at a pitch that was so low it was practically infrasonic, like a speech that you'd feel in your chest and you'd have to lip-read to get the meaning of.

When Gruber finished venting, he dropped Eric on his spine and kicked him in the gut, just—and this part you could hear—"to give you something to think about."

Eric vomited himself dry, then lay there on the grass for a good forty minutes before limping into the garage.

From what I could tell, Gruber's personal philosophy seemed to center around the idea that pain is the best mnemonic, and that a traumatized charge, whether human or canine, is an obedient one.

He treated everyone the same way—badly: his dogs, his sons, his wife, even the UPS man, whom he once reduced to a whimpering heap with his thumb and index finger alone because, due to a computer glitch, the guy asked him to sign off twice on a delivery.

Abuse outside the family didn't happen often, but only because it didn't need to. Gruber's reputation spread and stuck. The few people who might have filed charges against him were wise enough not to because they knew what Gruber was capable of, so they chose instead to steer clear of him.

It's just not worth it. Which is the third and most important reason why

I haven't had cameras in that house until this past year. Rumor was, Gruber had crucified someone's daughter's pet rabbit after a scuffle in a bar. Total bullshit, but people believed it and a lot more besides. And given what I'd seen him do without cameras, I wasn't slow to fall in line with the superstition.

My takeaway was neat: you do not want to fuck with this man.

So I let him let his dogs decorate my lawn, and I never make eye contact. Ever.

But cameras?

Well, in the last year my self-care has taken a nosedive, and I guess I'm courting disaster more freely than ever, because despite knowing all that I know about the dangers, I got Damian to rig me up at the Grubers' just about exactly twelve months ago.

Considering how long the Grubers and I have been neighbors, this is ludicrously late in the game to start filming, but clearly my subconscious had grown restless with all this morose waiting-to-die nonsense and thought it was finally time to see if old Gruber was capable of murder.

I can almost hear a gleeful voice in my mind hissing, "Find the cameras, Gruber. Find the cameras. Give this prick his comeuppance already."

The Grubers have been living next door since before my parents died. Their oldest son, J.R., is around eighteen now; the family moved in when he was a toddler. Their middle son, Jeff, is sixteen and the only one of the three who might escape the fate of the chronically abused. He does well in school, is a star athlete (track, swimming, tennis), and keeps his nose clean socially.

In the Gruber family, this means he's never been arrested for petty theft, destruction of property, or possession of a controlled substance. Even Eric, who's only thirteen now, has been nabbed for two of the three. I don't think drugs are quite yet on the radar, or not in sufficient quantities to bring him to public notice. He doesn't drive yet, either, so there's only so much damage he can do.

J.R., meanwhile, carrying the unlucky burden of all oldest sons and the antisocial legacy of a violent tyrant, is joining the marines as soon as he graduates from high school so that he can kill and destroy property and get paid for it, and, much more important, so that he can get as far away from his father as possible while still potentially making him proud.

Ellie, Gruber's long-suffering wife, is as mousy and cowering as you'd expect, the kind of person who's perfected the technique of disappearing even while she's standing right in front of you. Survival skill, for sure. Typical of a brutally battered wife. Quick camouflage. Become the backdrop. Don't run—at the mouth or otherwise.

She'd seen what happened when you did that. We all had.

It was mostly because Ellie was so retiring that Damian was able to work unhindered in their house. While he was there—his purported reason for being there, in fact—he gave them what he called a routine free upgrade on their cable box, including DVR and high def. This would placate Gruber if he asked any questions when he got home from work, though it was doubtful he would since, as we would soon learn, technology apparently wasn't his thing.

Damian took his time. Scoped out and planted in what he thought were the best spots. He decided first on Gruber's den, where there was no computer or modern instrument of any kind—only an ancient electric pencil sharpener, which, judging by the coating of dust on and around it and the few shavings inside it, was rarely used and never moved. Damian put the camera inside it, in the shavings drawer, an ideal spot on the desk, where it faced a brass-studded oxblood leather chair that bore the telltale marks—sunken seat, worn arms—of Gruber's frequent use.

Damian put another camera in the basement rec room, where, from the look of the place—full-size pool and Ping-Pong tables, separate cable and video game setups, and large-screen TV—he presumed the boys spent the bulk of their time. He put the camera in the upgraded cable box, just as he did in the living room. Easy enough.

Three cameras all told. A good spread, I thought, especially since Ellie favored the TV in the living room and almost always had it to herself. I wondered, naturally, if she would prove to be as absent when she was alone as she was the rest of the time. If past reconnaissance was any indication, I figured she'd probably be doing stripteases or stand-up comedy for the benefit of the four walls she was usually so chummy with.

But no, she was just a zombie flicking through the channels for her favorite shows, sipping her Shasta diet cola, eyes aglaze with cheap contentment.

It was Gruber himself who had the most to show.

Damian had done well. Gruber did spend a lot of time in his study, sitting in that oxblood leather chair, working on pet projects mostly, building and painting model cars and airplanes and tanks. He had a pistol collection, too, which he kept scrupulously clean. He often took the guns down from their places in the display cabinet, dismantled them on the desk, wiped, oiled, and reassembled them, then put them back in their places and sat back and stared at them, sometimes for an hour or more.

I was watching him do this one night, trying to get a line on his mind— well, actually, the mind of any person who can sit and stare rapt at a gun for an hour—when the silence was broken by a shrill cry.

Countless silken ties of love and thought.

When I heard it that first time, I thought it was the TV booming in from the next room. It sounded like a female voice, a girl's voice, and I knew it couldn't be Gruber. He just wasn't physically capable of such a high-pitched sound. Besides, a string of words like that would never come out of Gruber's mouth, even under duress or in a mad bout of playacting with himself.

The second time I heard it, just minutes later—the same words in the same order—I was sure it was a recording and that Gruber must have had some electronics in his study after all, maybe an old tape player.

But again, a book on tape just wasn't Gruber's thing.

Was it?

And poetry on tape?

That was just beyond the realm of possibility.

But it was a poem. I became sure when, a few minutes later, I heard the next line floating across the darkness of Gruber's study out of nowhere.

To everything on earth the compass round.

Yep. Sure enough. A poem. Google that and get? Robert Frost. Wait. What? Robert Frost?

And then I remembered.

Yes, yes.

Of course.

Iris.

It was Iris.

Mom had told me all about Iris. How could I forget? Iris, the African gray parrot, had been taught to recite poems.

Gruber had made his money from a chain of fancy pet stores that catered largely to impulse buyers, spoiled twenty- and thirtysomething Twin Pines type chicks mostly, who could be counted on to drop a grand or more on a puppy on a random Saturday afternoon because it was just too cute. That, or they'd get their hormonally befuddled boyfriends to do it for them. Always another whipped guy whipping out his credit card for Missy, thinking it a relatively small price to pay for a regular BJ and some peace of mind of a Monday Night Football. Before the poor suckers had left the store, they'd have been whined not just into the squirming purchase itself, but into spending another three hunge on a bed for the little pissmonster, too, and more still on the required paraphernalia: leash, toys, food, prophylactics.

For Gruber, it was a fine living. A very fine living, especially when you factored in the monthly groomings, which were the bread and butter of the business. Gruber had good relationships with local breeders, which is where he'd gotten his own dogs, and he could guarantee the health of his pets in a way that most other pet stores couldn't.

He always had a half dozen puppies at any one time, as well as a range of reptiles (boas, iguanas, turtles, lizards) and their live fare (mice, rats, crickets). He also had an impressive range of birds, which always included one or two African grays or a macaw among the usual cockatiels, lovebirds, and parakeets.

Gruber had read all about the famous African gray, Alex, who was owned and trained for thirty years by an animal psychologist. Alex, among other African grays who'd participated in longitudinal studies, disproved the notion that parrots could only parrot what they'd heard from their human owners or imitate ambient sounds. Over the course of his life, Alex had learned to identify objects by color and shape and to use his extensive vocabulary to construct original phrases.

Gruber liked the idea of having smart birds in his store, and charging appropriately for them, too. They usually went for six or seven hundred each—easy.

It's hard to know whether Gruber's special interest in African grays had been spontaneous, because, according to my mom's telling of the story, which is the only reason I knew about any of this, Gruber was actually turned on to the birds by Robin Bloom, who at her preposterously young age was not only reading Dante, but Iris Murdoch, too. She'd apparently come across an African gray in a Murdoch novel and had developed a fascination with the birds. Mom told me about the novel—she knew it, of course, and had actually been the one to recommend Murdoch to Robin in the first place. Apparently, the descriptions of the bird and its interaction with its owner were so captivating, so human, that Robin wanted to know if African grays were like that in real life.

She showed up at Gruber's pet store one day, where he did have one African gray in stock, and spent three hours introducing herself to the bird. Every day after that for months she'd show up, head back to the gray's cage, and play with it. She started training it to say hello and good-bye, and to give kisses. She even named it Iris, after Iris Murdoch.

I guess Gruber was really taken with this, and with Robin in general, as everyone in the neighborhood was. So on her tenth birthday, he presented her with Iris as a gift. Robin was over the moon, and after that she was almost never seen without the bird. Mom said that the Blooms bought Robin a hard-sided mesh backpack with a perch in it so she could walk the bird around the neighborhood. Robin was almost never without that backpack, either strapped to her back or propped next to her on the grass as she read.

After I left for boarding school, I think my mom had a rough time adjusting to the empty nest, and so she took on Robin as a kind of pupil adoptee. The Blooms didn't really know what to make of Robin's bookishness, or how to feed it, but they saw that my mom did. So they encouraged the friendship, allowing Robin to head to our place most days for an hour or so after school. Robin was at our house just about any time the Blooms needed a babysitter. Sometimes she even spent the night.

During our weekly phone calls, Mom mentioned Robin all the time. Robin and I are reading this—"It's cute, she's really inquisitive about the characters' motivations"—or Robin and I got an ice cream, or Robin stayed the night and we watched old movies until eleven and fell asleep in front of the TV. I came to think of Robin as my little sister, even though I had hardly anything to do with her.

Mom gave Robin reading lists, just as she had done with me, and fed the kid's addiction to poetry. They did an odd range, mostly stuff my mom liked and had rustled out of the canon: Auden and Elizabeth Bishop, bits of Frost (most of it she said she found too farmhouse macho to bear), Merrill, Milton, the Bard's sonnets to death, of course, and a host of new unestablished poets they'd found in *The New Yorker* and *The Paris Review*.

They laughed at Plath and Sexton, reciting "Daddy" while swooning in a nightgown.

"I mean, honestly, rhyming 'shoe' with 'achoo,'" Mom would howl, "and likening herself to a Jew. Really. It's too much."

Robin was a more willing and dedicated pupil than I had ever been, probably because she was unencumbered by the lusty shackles of male adolescence, which had made seersucker pornographers of more than a few gifted American writers of the twentieth century, so why not their buck devotees as well?

Robin wasn't whacking off to Henry Miller's description of a female orgasm—an accordion collapsing in a bag of milk, I mean, my God—or fantasizing about bending Elizabeth Bennet over her desk and really giving her something to write home about.

Robin had her mind on the material, and her battered old soul locked onto it like a heat-seeking missile. All the pain in those pages, all the thwarted desire, the longing and the channeled ire. She knew it by heart. It was her pain and her loneliness, her alienation that these writers were shouting down the years. Nothing spoke to her more truly, or so Mom said.

"She's such an odd girl. So profoundly sad. So sensitive. So much more seasoned than her age would suggest. It's enough to make you half believe in reincarnation. I keep saying to myself: How does she know this stuff? How does she feel it?"

I'm sure Mom saw herself in Robin, the precocity—both intellectual and spiritual—the knowing more than any kid that age should know about the crushing disappointments of life, and the isolation. It was all there. Mirror image. One silvered surface facing another, and reflecting it back, and back, and back, and back, endlessly until it was almost enough to give substance to nothing. What more could Narcissus himself have asked for?

Robin taught Iris to say lines, and so she did, even after the girl disappeared. Well after. Gorgeous lines and memories echoing through the house, until the Blooms couldn't take it anymore. They asked Gruber to take the bird back. And he did. Gladly, I'm sure. Because he loved Robin, too, and was touched by her, it seemed, as by no one else.

For thirteen years, Iris had been in his study, reciting, keeping the lost girl alive to him. And now to me, as I shuffle around with those lovely, lovely words in my head, going around and around again.

Strictly held by none, is loosely bound
By countless silken ties of love and thought
To everything on earth the compass round.

9

"What are you thinking about when you sit there?" I asked.

Monica was at the window as usual, staring out. I was lying on the couch as usual, staring at her. I'd been on the Net for hours, fully absorbed in articles on *Slate* and *The Huffington Post*, and at first I hadn't noticed her wake and move to the window behind me. But by the time I had, I'd also noticed a strangeness about her, a sense of tension or anticipation, like a mood waiting to break. We'd fallen asleep at dawn as usual, and she'd stayed through the morning and afternoon. She'd slept deeply, and now she was still here, perched on the edge of something, it seemed, but reluctant to step in.

"What to do," she said finally.

"I'm sorry?" I said, momentarily confused.

"I'm thinking about what to do."

I felt my stomach squeeze. No one says that when the thoughts are good. No one had ever said it to me before, not like that, or if they had, I hadn't been attentive enough to care.

"Is it so hard to know?" I asked, trying not to sound afraid.

She turned from the window, placed her feet on the floor, and looked at me with a pitying expression.

"Yes," she said. "Yes, it is."

"Why?" I asked, stupidly.

She laughed lightly.

"If I could tell you the why, I wouldn't need to worry about the what."

Okay. True enough. What was the incentive to talk if she had nothing to gain by it?

"What are the options, then?" I said. "Can you tell me those?"

"The usual," she said.

"Stay or go?" I said.

She nodded. "Pretty much."

"Every time you come here, you're thinking that?" I said, a bit fatigued by the idea.

"More or less."

She gave me the pitying look again.

"You're sorry you asked."

I wanted to slap her.

"Heavy silences scare me," I said.

"I don't get it," she said, screwing up her face. "Do you like to hear bad news?"

The desire to hit her was so strong then that I had to shove my hand between the cushions of the couch and sling my leg over it.

"I'd rather have the storm," I said, "than the threat of it."

She cocked her head quizzically, amused, surprised. The goon had said something *sub-tile*. Almost. Gee.

"It's coming anyway," I blundered. "Either way."

"Sooner or later," she agreed, playfully.

I took my hand out of the couch.

"Right."

She smiled broadly, showing her teeth, her eyes telegraphing the thought: Dummy doesn't mind teasing. Could be fun.

She liked this game, so I would play. It would chafe. But fine.

"Do you dislike me?" I asked. "Or is it that I'm lousy in bed?"

She chuckled.

"You're okay in bed, and I like you. That's the problem."

"Feeling guilty?"

"A little, maybe, because I'm nice." She frowned jokingly. "But not really, because you're so awful."

"Not everything people say about me is true."

She clapped her hands victoriously. I had fallen into the trap.

"It's not what people say about you. It's that you know what people say about you, and you wear it like a badge."

"But it's not me," I said.

"You wear it—"

It was as if I hadn't spoken.

"Like a badge," she finished. "Just so that you can say, 'It's not me.'"

"But it isn't," I said.

"I know," she said glaringly. "So why not be yourself in the first place and stop trying so hard?"

She was serious by the end without quite intending to be, her tone curling sharply around the question.

"Because I don't know how," I said, somberly. "I really don't know how."

This sounded cheap and unfair, the way it quashed the fun we were having at my expense, the kind of thing a weak person says to avoid the truth, except that it was the truth and I was weak.

"You're really not that awful, you know?" she said. "Even awful you isn't that awful, which is why it's so funny. Awful you is like sweet you's idea of awful, and it's kind of transparent and annoying."

"And that's why you want to go?" I complained. "Because I'm not very good at being a jerk?"

She threw up her hands.

"Have you heard a thing I've said?"

"Yes, yes, all right. Look, I told you. I don't know how else to be. I'm trying."

"Trying what exactly?"

"Trying to relax, be myself, figure out what that is. I've never had to do this before with anyone. I didn't even think it was possible."

She turned back toward the window, leaning into the embrasure wall and drumming her head softly against it. She looked bored, disappointed. I was confirming the worst.

"Your mind is a hard place to live, isn't it?" I said, lunging further into the mistake.

"Why do you say that?" she said, raising her head.

"You're just very intense, that's all."

She snickered softly and settled back.

"Ah, right. Intense," she said, closing her eyes. "Yeah, I get that a lot. I guess it's the only word in most people's range that comes anywhere close to reaching me." Her eyes flashed open and darted toward me, then away. "Except that it doesn't."

"Most people have limited vocabularies," I said apologetically.

"Yes," she said. "But you don't."

"So, therefore, I should do better."

It wasn't a question.

"Yes, you should, but it doesn't matter. You're just being lazy, talking the way everyone around you talks, picking up bad habits, covering your difference. We all do it."

"That's gracious of you."

If she heard this, I couldn't tell. She had tilted her head to the side dreamily and was watching the slow progress of something on the street outside—a passing car, maybe, or someone picking up the mail.

"You want to know why I'm looking out the window? Why I'm always looking out the window?" she said with taut exasperation.

She turned toward me, narrowing her eyes cruelly.

"Because this is the quality of your conversation."

She had been watching the garbage truck outside. It was close now. I could hear the whine of its compressor and the jolting release of the brake. The back man called something to the driver—"Up" or "Yep"—and they lurched the twenty yards to the next drive.

"How do you want to talk about this?" I asked. "I'm just trying to find a way in."

"Suddenly now you want to know?" she said. "Or is it just to relieve the discomfort of the silence?"

"Is there a difference?"

"Yes, there's a difference. A big one. Either you want to know me or you're scratching an itch—which is it?"

"I'm trying to minimize the damage," I shouted suddenly. "I'm sitting here looking at you sitting there, way off somewhere in your head the whole time as if you didn't want to be here. But you always come back. And so I ask myself, why? Why does she keep coming back if she doesn't like it or need it or something? What's the reason? Except that I don't really want to know the reason, because I have this terrible sneaking suspicion that it's going to make me feel like shit."

"How could it possibly do that? You do this all the time."

"I don't. I've done it with dozens of people who have nothing going on in their heads. People I picked because they were drunk and willing."

"So you're like everybody else. So what? I told you that already."

"And you're not. You said that, too."

"Yeah, I did, which means you don't have the depth for this kind of conversation. Get it?"

That pierced. I was shouting again. "You don't have any idea what I'm capable of? You've known me all of what? A few months? And that only in snatches between fucks. And suddenly now you're sure of everything about me. Forget it. I'm sorry I asked. You're the one who's incapable of this conversation, clearly, but you'll make it look like it's my shortcoming and, worse still, I'll believe you."

"*That* is definitely not my fault."

"No, you're right. It isn't. And I guess now I've answered my own question. You're here because you enjoy making people feel inferior and stupid, and I put up with it because I think I deserve it."

"Oh, don't be such a victim. God, you sound like one of those weepy fat women who's always whining to her girlfriends about getting dumped every few months by the unobtainable man who wipes his boots on her. Your low self-esteem is not a virtue, and I didn't put it there or worsen it. I'm not making you feel anything. You're here to get laid, and you buzz around me before and after because you can't crack me. I'm not one of your Tic Tac lays that you can spit out after the suck-off, and that bugs you. You don't quite know what to do with it. Well, so what? You're intrigued and you're horny, and you think that means you're in love. Sorry, but it's just not very interesting."

"I never said I was in love."

"I didn't say that, either. I said you think you are."

"What if I am?"

"You're not."

"So you know that, too, huh?"

"Yeah, I know that, too, and not because I know you so well, but because it's so commonplace."

"That doesn't make it any less legitimate. I'm confused and I'm a little scared, to be honest. I wish I could brush this off and you off, too, but the thing is, I want to know you. I want to talk to you. I'm lonely, and not just that, I'm lonely for someone like you who feels things deeply and has been through a lot."

"You don't know what I've been through."

"I know I don't. But I know damage when I see it, and I know you're the only person I've met who can talk to me about my parents, and I think you could only do that in the way you have if you'd been through something terrible yourself. I just want to share with you. I want to know something more about you. Please don't be angry at me for that."

This seemed to calm her. She sighed loudly and put her feet on the floor once more. She stood and came and sat beside me on the couch. She placed her hand lightly on my thigh.

We sat that way for some time.

"I'm sorry," she said, finally. "I'm used to people who don't care or can't understand, and I guess I've blocked myself off from everyone. I've forgotten how to talk."

I put my hand over hers.

"I know it's a lot to ask, but would you tell me something about yourself? Anything?"

She smirked.

"You mean like your raspberries?"

I squeezed her hand lightly.

"C'mon. Don't do that. I'm not a threat."

"Disclosure is always a threat."

"Okay. I get it. But maybe you could think about trusting me just a little. I'm not saying now. It doesn't have to be now. But just think about it. Just think about telling me one thing. Even if it's hard. Will you do that?"

"I'll think about it."

"You'll think about thinking about it?" I said, smiling.

She laughed. "Yeah."

"Okay," I said, putting my arm around her and pulling her to me. "Fair enough."

She made a move to lie down and I squirmed in behind her lengthwise, sorting the cushions beneath us. She folded down into me, wrapping her legs around mine and putting her face into the open collar of my shirt. The tip of her nose was cool, the breath moist and sweet.

I lay back, propping my head gently against the hard arm of the couch, and looked down the length of our bodies, letting my eyes roam aimlessly over our twined limbs and then up the walls and over the ceiling, coming to rest on a shifting pale trapezoid of shadow above the door.

The light was going. The room was blue-gray. The air had turned still with the onset of the evening, and every sound was amplified and dampened, like the felted thump of the pedal on a bass drum. I could hear the huff and squeech of Gruber closing his back door, and the whisper hiss of a passing car, and I could see the single bulb in Mrs. Bloom's upstairs window going on for the night. I thought I could even make out the head of the sleeping giant in the trees over the Blooms' house, and I smiled at myself for being such a baby, still.

Darling,
You must keep our secret.
You must hide it as you hide your heart and mine
In the place where we whisper and smile.
If you tell, if you betray our silence
Life as both of us know it will end forever.
Do you understand?
I will defend this to the last.
You cannot imagine what I would do.

10

The doorbell woke me at noon.

Way, way too early for Dave.

I was lying naked on the couch, entwined in a rope of blanket. Monica had slipped out without rousing me. She'd left a note on the arm of the couch that said, "Thank you." Below that, in tiny letters, she'd written, "IOU one difficult disclosure." Next to that she'd left the print of her lips, barely discernable, in ChapStick. Mint ChapStick.

My girl.

The doorbell went again. Just once. Politely.

Definitely not Dave.

I went over to the bay window and peeked around toward the front door.

Couldn't see the face. Just the body and dark brown hair. Long down the back. Neatly combed, thick and shining.

And then a pair of cutoff shorts, scrawny legs, and sneakers.

A kid.

Some Barbie, no doubt, selling candy for her synchronized swim team or collecting for UNICEF.

No thanks.

Ogre in residence. Move on.

She rang again. Once.

Bing.

Damn it, girlie. Nobody's home. Skip off already.

I waved my hand in a shooing motion.

Come on, come on.

She retreated from the step, looked up at the second floor, then right toward the living room, then left, straight at me in the window. Caught me full on.

Jaybird.

I ducked.

Fuck.

It was Dorris's kid Miriam.

I covered myself with my hands and peeked up.

She waved.

I slid to the floor.

I just flashed you, you little perv, now run. Didn't Mommy warn you about this?

Bing.

Jesus. Was I going to have to look her in the face?

Bing. Bing.

Just great.

I grabbed my jeans and T-shirt off the floor and pulled them on roughly, staggering toward the door.

I yanked it open, still falling.

"Whaattt?"

Yep. Miriam. Unfazed.

"Hi, Nick?" she chirped.

"Miriam," I gasped. "Couldn't you see that no one was home?"

She narrowed her mouth into a line.

"But you are home."

"Technically, yes. But haven't you ever heard of not being at home even when you're home?"

She looked at me quizzically.

"No."

"Haven't you seen any old movies?"

She paused to think.

"You mean like *The Matrix*?"

"Uh, no. I mean like *The Magnificent Ambersons* or *Miracle on 34th Street*. Black and white."

"Oh, yeah, yeah," she said, as if I'd tripped over the painfully obvious. "I saw *Amistad* in school."

"No. No, I mean black-and-white film. *It's a Wonderful Life*. Surely, you've seen that?"

She sighed impatiently. "Only every December."

"Okay. So you like it."

"I hate it."

"School again?"

"Yep." She rolled her eyes. "Boring."

"Do you ever read?"

"Nope."

"Can you read?"

"Duhhhh."

"Right." I leaned toward her and narrowed the door. "Well, I guess I'm going to have to get one of those signs that says, DO NOT DISTURB."

"Nah," she said. "Isaac has one of those on his door. I don't even see it anymore."

I was peeking through a three-inch crack.

"Does your brother beat you?"

"What?"

"Never mind."

I started to close the door.

"Oh, you mean like at tennis. Yeah, but he still sucks anyway. I just suck more."

"Nice."

I opened the crack again to three inches.

"Look. Can you go away?" I said. "I'm tired."

Her voice turned suddenly plaintive.

"But you said I could come by whenever I wanted."

"I most certainly did not!"

"Did so."

"Oh, yeah? When?"

"When you were over a few weeks ago with Dave and everybody was acting like they didn't know each other."

That had the ring of truth to it. Give her that.

Play dumb, Nicky. Play dumb.

"So your mom and Dave know each other, huh?"

"He's over now. He stayed the night again and he won't leave. I hate him."

"Hate? Really? That's strong. More or less than *It's a Wonderful Life*?"

"More. Much more."

"That's bad, then, huh?" I smiled.

She didn't.

"Yeah. It's bad all right."

"Why?"

She crossed her arms.

"'Cuz they're always loud and shouting and locked in Mommy's bedroom."

"Bummer," I said.

She moved closer to the cracked door.

"Can I please come in?"

She put on her best sad eyes.

"Please?"

I had to admit, she looked pretty genuinely upset, unless she was a better actress than her mother. But why would she want to wheedle her way into my house of all places, when most kids, like the Gruber boys, had grown up thinking it was haunted or cursed or both?

"I think he's hurting her," she said, her voice catching in a sob. "Honest."

Terrific. This was all I needed. A child in crisis on my doorstep. She knew what I knew. Clearly. Or as much of it as she'd overheard. Poor thing. Christ, a young kid privy to Dave the satyromaniac goating it up with Mommy.

No wonder the full sight of me hadn't flipped her. She was fleeing Caligula.

I had the visual on Dave and Dorris in the act, and it was bad enough, but what would it sound like coming through the walls? And to ten-year-old ears that don't have the first idea how to make sense of the noise? To kids, if they have the misfortune to overhear it, sexual pleasure always sounds like pain, doesn't it? It did to me. And the idea of my parents getting it on, whatever that was, was way too scary to contemplate.

"All right, all right." I caved. "Come in."

I swung the door wide. She walked under my arm and crossed into the foyer, wiping her eyes. She was crying in earnest now, snuffling and gasping as she went. I led her into the living room and sat her in Mom's old reading chair. She looked like a doll there, sunk in a suede manger, dwarfed by the high back and the wide, padded arms.

"Do you want a glass of juice?" I said. "I have apple, I think."

She wiped her nose on her wrist and struggled into a more upright position.

"No, thanks."

"What about milk? I have that."

"I'm fine."

She wiped her wrist on the side of her shorts. In an effort to recover her dignity, she adjusted the front of her shirt.

"Sure?" I asked.

"Yeah, I'm sure. Thanks."

"Listen," I said, sitting down on the footstool. I leaned toward her, resting my forearms on my thighs. "Your mom and Dave are just having fun. They're only playing. It's just playing the way adults play."

Her eyes were on the floor.

"Well, it doesn't sound fun."

"I know, I know. I thought that, too, when I was your age. But when you're older, you'll understand. Really. Don't worry."

She looked up, skeptical.

"But she has bruises."

Christ. Fucking Dave. Perfect. Just perfect.

He was in for a beating on this one. Later.

Definitely later.

But now.

What now?

Think fast. She's waiting. Tell her something. Anything.

"Don't you get bruises sometimes on the playground?" I asked.

Her eyes locked on my face pleadingly, wanting to believe, to believe whatever I would say if it would make the bad feeling go away. She tilted her head to the side, wondering.

"Sometimes, I guess," she ventured.

"Okay. Well, it's like that. Just a scrape here and there that you get in the course of having fun. Nothing a little time and TLC won't fix."

"But I don't want more time. I want him to go away."

She began to cry again, her chest heaving and shuddering.

"Can you make him go away, Nick? Please?"

I knit my fingers and pressed them hard against my mouth so that she wouldn't see me sneer.

Bastard.

I looked away, out the window toward the street, and pressed harder until my teeth dug into my lower lip.

"Where is your brother?" I asked.

"It's his day with Daddy. They're having pizza and playing miniature golf."

"And you don't go?"

"I go separate. On another day."

I was desperate to change the subject.

"Separate-*ly*," I corrected. "You go separate-*ly*."

"That's what I said. Why are you repeating?"

Not that way, Nicky. Not that way. She's normal. Remember?

"Never mind," I said.

Was she? Normal? Was this normal? Who knew? Just move. Move on. Move the conversation on. Distract her. Help her. But how? I don't know. I don't know. What the fuck do you say to little girls?

"What do you do on your day?" I said, lamely.

But she was having none of it.

"Stuff."

"Like what stuff?"

She chewed the nail on her thumb. Looked at it, dissatisfied.

"Just stuff."

She dropped the hand limply into her lap. I was losing her.

"Miriam, does your Daddy know about Dave?"

Her face darkened.

"No. He said never to tell."

"Dave said?"

"Yeah. Dave said."

"Tell what exactly?" I asked. "That he and your mother are seeing each other?"

She shifted uncomfortably in the chair.

"Nothing. Forget it. Sorry."

I took her by her forearms, too roughly.

"Miriam, look at me. Don't be sorry for telling someone if you think something is wrong."

She squirmed away from my grasp and fixed her eyes once more on the floor.

"I'm not telling someone."

She looked at me reproachfully.

"I'm telling you."

"Okay." I sighed, sitting back on the footstool. I felt like some predatory shoe salesman. Don't touch.

"But why me?" I said, finally. "Why did you choose me?"

She started to answer, then stopped herself. Then started again.

"I don't know," she mumbled at last.

She toyed with the cutoff fringe on her shorts, tugging at it where the loose threads were longest and winding it around her finger.

"I . . ."

She closed her eyes tightly and grimaced, as if that would make the mistake disappear.

"You what?"

She hesitated again, censoring.

"You said— You . . . Oh . . . it doesn't matter."

"It does. What?"

"You chose me. You did," she blurted. "Why don't you remember?"

She fell back heavily against the chair.

I felt my scalp prickle and go cold.

"What are you talking about, Miriam? What do you mean I chose you? How? When?"

She shook her head violently.

She would say no more.

I looked away again out the window just in time to see a very pissed-off Dorris making her way up the drive. She was wearing a loud silk flower-print bathrobe and leopard mules with black feather tufts on the toes. She was striding angrily, as fast as she could in that attire. She turned sharply onto the walk, cutting the corner of the lawn. She stumbled and swore.

I turned back to Miriam. She was still shaking her head, more slowly now.

The doorbell went.

Miriam started.

"Oh, God. It's him?"

"No, no." I touched her hand. "It's your mother."

She pulled away and curled into a ball, pressing herself desperately into the deepest cup of the chair.

"I'm not here. Okay? I'm not here," she cried.

"Miriam, I can't lie to your mother about where you are. She'll worry."

"She won't. She'll just be mad. She'll yell. You don't know."

"It's the same. She'll be mad because she's worried. That's all. C'mon. I'll calm her down, okay?"

"She'll take me back there with *him*. Nick, I don't want to go. I want to stay here with you. Let me stay here with you. I'll be good."

What the hell did that mean? *I'll be good*?

"You haven't been bad, sweetheart," I said. "Don't worry. Everything's fine."

The doorbell went again. Three quick times.

Bing-buh-bing-bing.

She's hopping mad, I thought. This is going to blow. Hard.

I turned to make my way toward the door.

"Please, Nick," Miriam bawled from behind me.

"It's cool, kid," I shot back over my shoulder. "I'll deal with it. Relax."

I opened the door slowly, stern-faced but calm and vaguely condescending. That seemed the right tone for Dorris, who was dressed like a bayou whore but had the glare of a prison camp commandant.

"Is Miriam in there?" she barked.

No hello. No sorry. No beg your pardon.

The gall of the woman. Honestly.

"She's your kid," I spat. "You tell me. Is she?"

"I'm betting on it," she snapped.

She shifted her weight and adjusted the belt on her robe, cinching it tighter and pulling the flap closed over her cleavage.

"Oh, really? And why's that?" I said, genuinely surprised.

"Oh, I don't know, because she seems to be under the impression that you're God or something. Where do you think she got that idea?"

"What?" Had she really just said what I'd thought she'd said?

"I have no idea. What are you talking about?"

"Look, you freak, if she's in there, you've got exactly three seconds to turn her over before I yell rape."

Without thinking, or thinking to stop myself, I said, "As if anyone would believe you."

"I'm not talking about me, fuckface," she crowed. "I'm talking about her, and you can bet my word'll be more believable than yours."

Whoa. Where was all this shit coming from? What had I said the other night? What had I done?

Nothing. Fucking nothing.

The woman had turned her children's home into a bordello, and she was going to claim the moral high ground with me?

Nuh-unh.

"I wouldn't try to play the outraged mother if I were you, Dorris. Have you checked a mirror lately? You look like the cook in a meth lab."

"Right," she hissed, turning on her kitten heel. "You are so fucked, you pathetic, twisted, infantile prick."

She was halfway down the walk before she spun around again.

"I'll be back with the cops in five. Then we'll see who believes."

"Oh, cool it, Dorris," I blurted. "She's here. Unharmed. All in one piece, no thanks to you and Dave. Come in and see for yourself."

She shot me a look about the Dave comment, but decided not to contest.

"You scared the hell out of her," I hissed, "you fucking slag. Can't you at least put her in day care while you ply your trade?"

Miriam had appeared behind me, grasping at the belt loops of my jeans.

Dorris stepped close enough for me to smell the vodka and the sex on her breath. Her face had runnels of sweat on the brow and upper lip and along the trace of sideburns by her ears. She'd dyed them an alarming shade of copper, which only made them stand out more noticeably against the deep-lined mahogany of her cheeks.

She leaned in closer still, close enough to kiss me, and hissed:

"F-U, Nick Walsh. This is not over."

She flushed and pushed me aside, pawing for Miriam as if she were a fork that had fallen down the sink and lodged itself in the disposal.

"Come on, missy. That's quite enough excitement for one day. We're going home."

"Nooooo," Miriam wailed. "I won't go. I won't."

She pressed herself against my legs and wrapped herself around, arms and legs crossed and locked.

"Oh, yes, you will, little lady," grunted Dorris through gritted teeth.

She peeled savagely at Miriam's fingers one by one, then tried for the twined ankles instead, but to no avail. The kid was latched like a poultice.

Dorris bellowed and huffed with frustration, her halitosis souring thickly around us. I turned my head away in disgust, leaving myself open for the strike, which came as swiftly and surreptitiously as the low blow always does.

Bam!

She hiked her knee into my balls.

I felt my throat close and my breathing stop, the familiar jolt, like pulling the panic brake on a train, the lock before the long, hideous screeching of wheels.

As I buckled and face-planted to the stoop, she pulled Miriam, shrieking, by her hair, and force-somersaulted her over my back and down the steps before I could even inhale.

I watched them go, pushing and tearing at each other, my eyes bulged and glazed, frozen as everything else.

Wait it out. Wait it out.

The waves of nausea came and came again, then the trembling, the adrenal haul through the bloodstream, juddering the limbs.

Everything was sideways, but I could see that they were in their driveway now. Dorris had a firm hold on Miriam, an upright full nelson with Miriam's arms pinned back butterfly, Dorris's hands locked at the back of Miriam's neck, and Miriam's feet limp atop Dorris's own, marching forward by force.

The front door opened and Dave appeared briefly in a pair of candy apple red briefs that, even from that distance, I could see were too shiny to be cotton. He stepped out of the way to let Dorris and her cargo pass, and the light caught the bulge of his codpiece.

Yep. Vinyl for sure.

Big as you please in the doorway with a ten-year-old in tow.

He glanced in my direction and laughed, then slammed the door behind them. The glass storm door rattled in its frame.

No mercy, my friend. Just wait. He could laugh at that when the time came. I was gonna hurt him till you couldn't even recognize his face.

Meanwhile, motor control was coming back. Slowly.

I was flexing my hands, then my arms, then my legs—still on my side— then on my back, flat against the stoop, staring up at the narrow panels of the aluminum siding, row after row under the eaves.

If I had a cent I'd have that redone, I thought. It's been—what?—fifteen years? More?

Seventeen. Yeah. Seventeen for sure.

I remembered Mom telling me about it. I was in my senior year at prep, I think, and we were having one of our Sunday phone calls. How's it going? How's school? How was your week? They were having the siding done, she was telling me, and it was going well. Normally I wouldn't have remembered a detail like that, but it was around the time when Mom was getting really friendly with Robin Bloom. Every week I heard a story. The parrot story or a sleepover story or something to do with that kid.

She was everywhere, like a gravitational force that everyone bowed to and bended toward, often without even realizing it. And it wasn't just the neighbors, Gruber, and my mom. It was everyone.

I guess that's why I remembered this particular story so well, because I remember thinking at the time that it was just weird, the power that kid had over people. Even total strangers.

People like the guys putting up the aluminum siding. Gruff tradesmen, you'd think. Thermos and lunch pail kinda guys who'd have spent their breaks smoking and swearing and ogling the likes of Dorris Katz, if she'd been here then, or someone's teenage daughter walking the dog.

But fuck me if Robin didn't charm the pants off one of them. He practically fell in love with her, from the sound of it. Mom said this guy took a scrap piece of aluminum, cut it to size, and made a bracelet out of it. Worked on it every chance he got for a week. Spray painted it with moons and stars and shades of the night sky, and presented it to Robin, ceremoniously on bended knee, like a troubadour.

Crazy.

But that was Robin all over, I guess. This precious, beautiful, sweet fairytale girl that men and women fetishized and fell for. Flop. Flop. Flop. All the way down the line, like daisies under her feet.

And there I was, too, lying under the overhang, all Gumby on my back, my crotch in a knot, thinking of Robin Bloom seventeen years after the fact and wondering: Whatever happened to that bracelet?

Did Mrs. Bloom still have it enshrined somewhere in a Lucite case along with all the other heirlooms of Robin's loss? Or the ones she could bear to keep?

Maybe one of these days I'd ask her. Just go over, ring the bell, and say, "Hey, I've been thinking . . ."

Thinking what?

About what a jewel your granddaughter must have been? Oh, and sorry for your loss?

Is there a decency interval on condolence? Is this unseemly after so long? I beg your pardon, if so.

Finally, I sat up. I'd stopped shaking and the nausea was gone.

Not a sign from across the street. You'd have thought the house was empty for all you could hear or tell of what was going on in there.

A terrible silence.

It made me think of those stories on the news now and again, the kind of thing you can't forget and that gives you the willies when you're just walking down a quiet suburban street. Like the story about that Austrian guy who had kept his daughter prisoner in the family basement for more than twenty years, raping her all that time, and had had seven kids by her, three of whom had never seen the light of day. Never. Meanwhile, the guy's wife was living with him upstairs purporting not to know a thing.

That ruined a restless early morning stroll for me every time. I'd be out walking off the booze before bed just as the sun was coming up, and instead of thinking what I might have once thought (once when?), or let's say what a normal person would think—something like, "Oh, isn't it lovely to walk through a quiet place where people probably leave their doors unlocked and let their kids play unsupervised"—I'd be wondering instead if there was some girl who'd been missing for twenty years holed up in a basement being gored daily and bearing a brood of inbreds to a monster.

And then I'd wonder, how many horrible things are going on right now in any one of these houses? How many quiet crimes are being committed? And not by marauding bands of escaped cons or cat-burgling sex offenders registered on a website, but by family members, who, as the statistics are always reminding us, are far more likely to bring about your demise than a stranger, and are in a far better position to do so without arousing suspicion. Without arousing any kind of response whatsoever. Without making a sound.

Who was ever going to know?

Who would ever even conceive?

Well, I would, for one.

And maybe I was the only one.

But I *could* know what was going on, and what's more, I could do something about it.

Hell, I could be the self-styled superhero of the behind-closed-doors, the savior of the stay-at-home, the supreme violator of privacy who violates for the private good, for the individual good, because he knows that privacy itself is a violation, or could be.

Maybe I could help Miriam after all. I didn't have to guess at what was going on in that house. I could head down to the basement and see for myself, right there on the monitors. Live.

Was this a cause I heard calling? Was this a mission for the unholy? A turnaround for the—what had Dorris called me?—the twisted?

Why, yes, I believe it was.

Whoa.

Hang on.

Wait. Wait. Wait.

Pull back for just one second here, and think.

Help Miriam?

Well, now let's consider that a bit more closely, shall we?

Before you get too overzealous and prosecutorial there, Nicky boy, and start installing a hotline for the police commissioner, hadn't you better remember what Dorris said? What Miriam herself said?

Oh, you're confused. Not getting it, I see. Okay, then. Well, let's review. Dorris said what? That Miriam thought you were God or something. Was that it? Interesting choice of words, considering. Don't you think? And Miriam had said something about choosing. You chose her. She definitely said that. Remember now?

Right.

So?

So, do the math. What does that add up to, smart guy? Still not getting it? Okay. Let's put it this way: What if, purely for the sake of argument, we allowed that you did somehow miraculously turn your atrocious peeping hobby into a superpower that could redeem your rotten soul and, in the process, save the American people from the scourge of their right to privacy? Let's say we granted that particular if for just a moment here. And let's call a spade what it is while we're at it, shall we? It's a pretty fucking enormous and lethargic if to begin with. But let's just say you did it. You became tinker tailor savior spy. Then what?

Well, in keeping with our theme here, I'd say you ought to be a tad worried about what you'll find when you finish all that snooping, wouldn't you?

I mean, what if the perp, the real badass behind it all, the guy on tape for all to see and slam the gavel on—*guilty!*—the really death-penalty-deserving scum of plain-Jane Middle America is, in fact, you?

What if you're the one sticking your schlong in Miriam's sticky bits and telling her not to tell? What if you *chose* her, just like she said? What then, wonder boy? What then? Will you turn the tapes on yourself? I'm just asking, 'cuz before you rush out and buy that cape and tights, you'd better know what you intend.

No recordings of that, huh?

Can't tape the doings when you're in the picture, right? But what if someone else could? What if someone else is watching the red record light while they're watching you?

Hoist, anyone?

Petard, perhaps?

Now there's one of Daddy's quotables for you. Or was it Mom's?

Pretty damn right on the money, no?

Yeah.

I thought so.

Thinkin' twice now a little? Maybe?

Damn right.

Idiot.

11

'Tis the sport to have the engineer
  Hoist with his own petard.
That's the line Hamlet says.
About his college buddies Rosencrantz and Guildenstern.
He knows they're going to fuck him over—and he figures, *Ahh, let 'em try.*
They're bunglers anyway, and they'll just blow themselves up with their own bomb.
'Course, that was before suicide bombers.
Time was, you could bank on the fact that the guy planting the bomb wanted to get out before it went off, and that was a kind of defense against it.
Sometimes.
But now. Blowing yourself up is the point. And how do you defend against that?
And do I even want to? Or is it the point? Was it the point all along?
To catch myself, kill myself, punish myself. That way. Hoist with my own petard. Caught by my own mischief. The subconscious works in circuitous ways.

Yeah, *Hamlet.*
Jesus. Mom made me learn that whole fucking play practically by heart in the sixth grade. She'd have me go through every speech and put it in my own words so that I'd really understand what it meant.
We did it with most of Shakespeare.
So, for example, when Macbeth says the bit about sound and fury signifying nothing, my version was: "Yeah, life. A lot of shouting and shoving that doesn't mean jack shit in the end."
"Exactly. That's it," she'd hoot. "Very good. This is fabulous. Go on."

So I would. I did.

Making Shakespeare into slang for my own edification, and for the ancillary amusement of my mother.

Or was my edification the ancillary bit?

Unsure.

I made her laugh, though. God, I made her laugh.

She was probably smashed anyway, but who cares? Making her laugh was like winning the trophy or getting laid or falling in love. It was a swooning feeling all through me and an inherent sense of value, like I meant something, was worth having all on my own, just for being and being funny.

I didn't have that feeling very often, and even then it was conditional.

Make me laugh and I'll love you. Don't just be. Be a clown.

Or:

"As Ovid said," said Mom, "'If you would be loved, be lovable.'"

Ouch.

Yep.

There was no being in the Walsh household. Not in the ontological sense. "Being" as a noun. As in, a thing or a state. As in, I, Nick Walsh, am a being. A lump. An entity. A boy with certain qualities and not others. A child that simply is. That exists. Period. And so is loved.

There was none of that.

Being was a verb.

To be. To act. To perform.

Then came love.

Maybe.

If you did it right.

It's all there in the Yeats line.

The other one, along with the Ovid, that Mom said all the time, just for the pleasure of the saying and usually half to herself, but loud enough to hear. The one that hurt like a motherfucker when it got inside you and wormed its mellifluous way around.

Hearts are not had as a gift but hearts are earned.

By those that are not entirely beautiful

Boom.

Suck on that and see where your esteem goes.

I wonder if she taught that to Robin Bloom? Or if Robin taught it to Iris? And if so, did Robin interpret it the way I did? As the needle of all insults?

Or was that only something a biological child would do, convolute his own inadequacy in the mouth of his mother? Whereas a mere student would simply take it how it was meant, as a world-weary sigh made into song.

You know, poetry.

Oh, blow me, how it was meant.

Who the fuck knows how it was meant. It's how it was interpreted that counts, and the damage it did as a result. And anyway, it was meant the way I thought it was meant. You can believe that. It had just that whisper-thin edge on it that was Mom to a T. A paper cut that hurt more than a bruise and could never be sewn up or scarred over, but just gaped and ached for the rest of your life.

Yeah, yeah. I know. I get it. Boo hoo. Your poor hothouse flower of a broken heart bleeds nectar. Your crisis is not compelling.

And you're right. Sort of.

But I ask you this anyway, just as a matter of interest.

Why does a little learning always make people cruel?

And pardon me, Mr. Yeats—it is a beautiful line, and I know you were describing the world as it is—but isn't the whole mythic point and gobsmacking punch of love that it doesn't have to be earned? That it's given over, legs in the air, on your back as a fucking gratuity, just 'cuz?

Otherwise, why not call it lunch, and come right out and say that it ain't free?

Or don't say anything at all, if you're so clever. Leastways not to your kid, who's hanging on your every word and etching it all in memory.

Keep your corrosive asides to yourself.

Whaddaya say, Ma?

Mum's the word?

No?

Nice try, but not a chance.

The sport is hoisting with petards.

So, bombs away.

The sport.

It really pisses me off that he called it that.

Like it was fun. A game, and loss of life was just part of the scrum.

Fucking Hamlet.

What a dick.

I mean, what an absolute arrogant, self-absorbed, grandiose douchebag.

And lest we forget, a murderer, too.

Big-time.

By the end, he's responsible, whether directly or indirectly, for the deaths of at least seven people, including his girlfriend, his mom, and three of his very close friends, but he's remembered as the hypersensitive, suicidal flake who couldn't make up his mind.

How stupid is that?

The expectancy and rose of the fair state, my ass.

The guy was just a killer with diplomatic immunity and a big mouth.

But everybody loves the smarty-pants in pain, right?

I was no different. Any spoiled kid who has a vaguely philosophical bent, serious daddy issues, and a bleak outlook on life has thought of himself as Hamlet and thought himself mighty profound and soulful for doing so.

But if you're a guy who went to boarding school and college in the Northeast with a bunch of tribal nimrods, you probably figured out pretty quickly that the only preppy outlets for homicidal teen angst are pisswater beer and team sports, preferably violent team sports.

You weren't going around reciting "To be, or not to be" and musing on the cause of Hamlet's inability to act.

You played lacrosse, or football.

Or rugby, if you were in it purely for the hurt.

Except if you were me, the idea of rubbing groins and grubby shoulders with your frat brothers while doing them grievous bodily harm just didn't have the right zing to it. Concussive sports are for sadists who like it quick and hard, the kind of people who'd go to a public execution and bring snacks. My frat brothers. Masochists like me, on the other hand, went it solo and called it endurance, because it sounded better than calling it what it was: slow torture on the inside where only you could hear you scream.

Worked for me.

Sport, usually endurance sport on my own, is where I put my pain. And where I found it. That's right. My amateur, low-level, not-a-tragedy pain.

I put it in the gym, on the court, in the pool, on the track. Running so long and hard until I got that burn in my lungs for hours after, lifting weights until my limbs gave out, swimming laps for miles, nose in the blue, eyes rolling, brain afloat, going over a poem or learning the map of Africa by heart just so I wouldn't obsess about my failures or my ignorance and cringe.

I practiced my jump shot until I could hit—swish—off the feed pass from every spot on the three-point line, even though I never tried out for the team. On scorching summer days, I stood on the blazing painted hard courts at the country club perfecting my serve at a slow roast until I looked like I'd been in the pool, and the downy felt on every ball in the practice basket had turned matted and gray.

I still play.

Tennis that is. With Gruber's middle son, Jeff, actually, who's a good player already at sixteen. He plays the second spot on the varsity and he's only a sophomore. We hit once a week under the lights down at the high school courts or, when the weather's bad, at the club that his team uses for winter workouts.

It's like going back in time.

When we get a long rally going and all you can hear is the squeak of your shoes and the thwack of the ball, I can almost lose myself in the rhythm of my arms swinging and the loophole of the sweet spot, until it feels as if I'm not exerting any effort at all, or thinking—just fitting, with an audible click, into a preestablished pattern that exists in nature independent of me and is going on all the time.

For that twenty minutes or hour or however long it lasts, I could swear I'm a teenager again. I have the same feeling I had then, that I've joined some cycle, or tide, or silent music and become a passive part of it, like a body being brought in by a wave, catching a ride on an unseen force.

I forget everything.

Even—especially—myself.

It was always that way in sport. The times when it happened, when my heart rate would settle at 150 and my breathing would steady itself faster and I would leave my body, or seem to, and float on the high of physical exertion—those were the times, the few times, when being really was a state of grace, separate from parental expectation and the onus of not knowing who I was.

But it didn't happen that often.

I chased it, pawed for it and the relief it brought me. But it came only when it wanted to, either because I'd eaten the right combination of things at the right time or because I was well rested and in a good mood—or, fuck knows, because the moon was full and Mercury was retrograde.

There wasn't any formula.

It just floated in and blessed me for a while and made me numb to the knife in my mother's laugh and the stab in her tutelage.

That was Mom.

A little learning made her cruel, sure, and the drink made her lethal, but until she and Dad did their last, I had it easy.

When I think about what I've seen in the last thirteen years—Miriam, Dorris, Dave, the Grubers—I'd even go so far as to say I had a free pass on the home front.

If I've learned anything from spying on my neighbors, it's that (to mangle Tolstoy) every family is extravagantly fucked up in its own way, and cruelty has a thousand faces.

A little learning is only one of them, and a minor one at that.

Take Gruber. Now there's a brand of cruel that's almost subhuman, except that he did the kind of appalling calculated shit that animals are incapable of.

Eric took the brunt of it.

Because he was the youngest, because he was the weakest, and because he was a bed wetter, among other verboten things.

Big deal, you'd think, right?

Rubber sheets. Extra laundry. No sweat.

But not to Gruber.

What did Gruber do in response to this comparatively minor domestic disturbance that afflicts millions of "normal" boys and families at one time or another and passes of its own accord without the use of corporal punishment?

He reacted like it was a trial sent from God, inflicted maliciously on him alone, the master of dogs and men, for whom when and where you cleared your tubes practically took on the significance of a religious rite.

Seriously, Eric probably would have been better off if he'd been gay.

One good whipping and it would have been over.

After all, cock is something you could swear off.

But the soiling?

That was beyond Eric's control, and thus beyond Gruber's, so it just brought out the brownshirt in the old bastard.

He broke the boy like a dog, or tried to, mostly because he persisted in believing that this involuntary nocturnal emission was a bad habit or a defiant act for which, as with so many other things, iron discipline was the indisputable cure.

It must have been going on for years by the time I got my cameras in there, because Eric was already twelve by then and onset for this sort of thing is usually a lot earlier than that. Besides, as much of a dirtbag as I knew Gruber to be, I don't think even he would have resorted right off the bat to the extreme measures he was using by the time I got online.

At night, all night, he made Eric sleep in an extralarge dog crate down in the basement. He had it set up by the sectional couch down there with the overhead light on for Eric's added discomfort. The cage was within range of the cameras that Damian had put in the gaming system, so I got to see the whole gulag rigged up in detail—not that there was much to it. It had a padlock on the outside—to which, of course, only Gruber himself had the key—and no blankets or bedding of any kind on the inside. Just Eric, naked and white as new, curled on the removable plastic floor pan.

Gruber had clearly once used the crate to train his Rotties, though now, apparently, having become masters of their own micturition, they enjoyed the privilege of sleeping on luxury plush Fatboys upstairs.

But Eric, he was looking through crossed bars at the couch that was within groping distance. The comfy, sprawling, cloudlike couch that he knew the swaddling potential of because he sat or lay or sprawled on it playing Xbox for hours most afternoons.

Ah, afternoons, and evenings and mornings, too. How sweet they must have seemed. The waking times of day when his bladder was not a liability.

That poor kid. Tortured by his bodily functions. Imprisoned by something he couldn't help or stop.

Now that *is* malicious punishment from God.

Occasionally, for a good portion of the night, if I wasn't with Monica or Dave, I'd sit in front of the monitors and watch Eric sleep. I'd zoom the camera in as far as I could so that the cage and Eric in it took up the whole screen, and I could see every move he made. Sometimes, depending on his position, I could even see the expression on his face.

There was something strangely mesmerizing and calming about it, like watching a fire lick and crackle in a grate.

Often, he had bad dreams, or fitful ones, where he cried out and moaned unintelligible words or nonsensical combinations of real words. Sometimes he woke many times a night, usually with a jerk and a panicked search beneath and around him, as if he thought that rousing himself prematurely would forestall the dreaded leak.

He didn't wet himself every night. Not at all. In fact, he'd go weeks without an incident and come tantalizingly close to release—a month clean was the marker—but then, heartbreakingly, he'd lose it, and the cycle would start all over again.

I got so invested, I'd count the clean nights with him. He said the tally aloud to himself every night before he went to sleep.

"Fifteen days, Eric. Fifteen days. C'mon. You can do it. Stay tight."

The longest he went was twenty-five days, and on that night, the twenty-fifth night, he woke at three a.m. to a puddle. He wept bitterly for an hour or more, interspersing curses with prayers.

"Please, God. Help me . . . fucking goddamn shitty bastard asshole fuck. PLEEEEEEAAASE."

He slapped at his crotch and his face and banged his head against the cage, pleading and swearing all the while like some medieval monk stuck squarely in the dark night of the soul and madly flagellating his way out.

By the time four forty-five rolled around—Gruber always woke his whole family at five and made the boys go with him for a six-mile run—Eric was so desperate to hide the evidence that he tried to lick it up. Of course, he disgorged it almost immediately, and then the puddle was bigger and more obvious.

Gruber came in at five as usual, pounding two pans together like a drill sergeant.

He stopped short as soon as he looked down into the cage.

Given the teasing evidence before him, newly yucked and flaunting right there in the plastic pan, he didn't even have to do his customary white-gloved swipe to know what was what. He realized immediately, and he flew into a rage far worse than the usual tirade he delivered when Eric messed.

He unlocked the crate hurriedly, panting with rage, and pulled Eric out by his hair.

"You conniving little bastard. How dare you try to deceive me."

Eric hung from his father's fists, limp and gangly. There was barely life in him, and no resistance.

I cried like a little girl watching this, raking at my face in disgust, terror, and futile sympathy. Is there any other kind? As he hung there letting himself be hit, I swear I felt I could hear Eric's thoughts in my own.

Just let it happen and it will all be over sooner.

But when? When would it be over? How long had this been going on? How many years of confinement and pain and humiliation?

Here was a boy wanting nothing more than to wrench out his own plumbing or gum it up for good. Here he was hating his poor penis at the very time when most boys were rapturous with the pleasure it gave them, convulsed with self-imposed ecstasy every chance they got.

Not Eric. Never Eric. It'd be a miracle if he didn't lop the thing off before he passed puberty. He'd never be free with it. He'd never love it. Probably never even enjoy it. That, too, would be denied him along with so much else in the wake of this nightmare. Discharges of whatever kind would happen, as they did now, against his will.

Man, I wanted to punish Gruber for this. Waterboard him with piss. An army corps's worth of communal piss. Buckets of it, thick and amber like dark beer, right down his gullet. Choke and revive, slow and drawn out, for years, until he died, not by drowning but of fucking gout.

Wouldn't superhero me do that?

Wouldn't St. Nick take Gruber down?

Yeah, he and what army?

It was no good. I wasn't that man. But I wasn't *that* man, either. Was I? The abuser? That was Gruber on the screen, not me. I was not the culprit. Not yet. So far as I knew. But was being the culprit really so much worse than being the witness? The witness who didn't do anything? Didn't even say anything, who silently complied knowing everything? Gruber was a savage, but I was a coward. Not capable. A gawking fantasist hanging around with the knowledge and the evidence and a wholly Catholic hard-on for justice, but no grit.

No grit.

Eric did his five a.m. run that morning with his dad and brothers on a stomach that was emptier than usual.

And he put his pain into sport. I have no doubt.

Later he would put it into drink. Of that I have no doubt, either. It was in his genes as much as his upbringing, same as me.

That morning the Gruber men came home to Ellie serving up the usual rancher's feast. Eggs, bacon, pancakes. The works. I couldn't see this with my cameras, since I didn't have any eyes in their kitchen, but I could hear the sounds of clinking cutlery and muted conversation from the mic in the family room. I heard the rest from Jeff, who filled in the gaps when I questioned him after our tennis games—what they ate, what they talked about, and what they didn't.

He wouldn't say much.

They didn't talk about much, certainly not about the horror that was going on all around them. Most of what was said was said by Gruber, orders given and yes-sirred, new chores assigned and past ones accounted for as done. Ellie, as always, said nothing. She served and cleared the plates unnoticed, as if sustenance and cleanliness were things that just appeared of their own accord, like dawns and dusks.

Then the house would empty for the day. Gruber off to the shop, the boys off to school, and Ellie to the rest of her housework, or to the family room couch, where she sat reading or watching the tube, vapid as a hole in the fabric of space-time.

Last of all, when all else was finally still and silent, I'd often hear Iris, alone in the dark of Gruber's study, cawing fitfully the words that a girl had taught her so long before. She talked and talked, beautifully, as if she were reminding the darkness itself, as much as the people in it, or near it, of something they could no more remedy than comprehend.

Its pinnacle to heavenward . . .

Its pinnacle to heavenward . . .

And signifies the sureness of the soul.

12

I got a Facebook message from Dave today. All it said was, "We should talk."

No shit, jackass.

We should talk.

Ya think?

We'll do more than talk, I can promise you that.

Such a prick. He knows where I live. He's over here unannounced all the time, but now he's suddenly Mr. Diplomat because I saw him in his red vinyl underpants presiding like Sid Vicious at the Chelsea Hotel.

"Bring it," I said.

Pull your fist out of the hostess and stagger across the street. I'll be waiting.

And he did.

Not fifteen minutes after I sent my reply he was abusing the bell as usual.

I've got to rip that thing out of the wall one of these days and replace it with one of those novelty shockers that clowns hide in their palms, except I need a high-voltage model that's meant for steers or something, so it'll really hurt.

I opened the door and the fat simp was standing there hunched into a navy sport coat two sizes too small, a white dress shirt so soiled it was the color of a smoker's teeth, and a kelly green patterned tie so thick and pilled and awful it looked as if it had been made out of cast-off upholstery from the local Hampton Inn. The Windsor knot in it was the size of a human heart, and the tail barely reached his navel. If I hadn't known him all my life I would have sworn he was an obese sixth grader escaped from a school trip with the debate team.

"What is this," I laughed, "the model UN?"

"A gesture," he said, stone-faced.

"Really?" I scratched my head. "Huh. What kind of gesture would that be, then?"

"Respect."

"Respect," I mimicked, laughing again. "I see."

"I'm trying, Nick," he said, still dead serious, "Don't make this harder."

I clapped him on the shoulder.

"Oh, Dave, my friend, I'm only just getting started. You don't know from hard."

He pulled away and shoved his hands in his trouser pockets. Those at least were his own, an inoffensive gray flannel, inseam, say, 32, waist circa 48. He was the guy that body mass index charts and nutrition fact postings were made for, and he was also the guy on whom they never had the slightest deterrent effect. He went right on shoveling saturated fats and refined sugars as if snacks made by petroleum companies were featured at the base of the food pyramid.

He was a bit thrown by my comment, unsure how to proceed. I'd never spoken to him this way before. He backed away from me on the stoop and swiveled his head toward the Katzes' house, then back again to me. Over his shoulder I could see that Dorris was standing behind her storm door in a lilac terry cloth robe, watching.

"Oh, I get it," I said. "So this was her idea. No wonder you look like you had that outfit foisted on you by a maître d'. You had it picked off a thrift rack by a skank."

He gave me a pained expression.

"Are you gonna let me in or what?"

This was definitely Dorris's mission. Why not get it over with?

"Yeah, yeah, all right, you whipped little errand boy. Come in."

I stepped aside and let him pass, then stepped back into the doorway and gave Dorris two sarcastic thumbs up. She gave me the finger and closed her door.

By the time I'd closed my own door and made my way into the study, Dave was perched on the edge of the couch wringing his hands like a salesman raring to pitch.

This should be good, I thought. Dave the dummkopf talking it out. He was going to be like one of those chimps that primatologists taught sign language, hoping at long last to tap the depths of the simian brain, except all he was going to say was, "More bananas."

"So what's on your mind, big man?" I said, as seriously as I could manage.

He had picked up the TV remote from the coffee table and was fiddling with it, tracing lines and squares between the buttons. When I spoke, he threw it down carelessly and it tumbled onto the floor.

"Sorry," he said, lunging for it.

He was too fat to bend far enough to reach it. He squirmed there pathetically, groping blindly, his tie drooping, the buttons on his shirtfront straining until I thought they'd pop off and pelt me in the face. He wasn't wearing an undershirt.

The oxford cloth pouched to accommodate his bulge, revealing pasty crescents of tufted flesh, each engorged around a single menacing white eye, a line of them down his chest, unmasked, like the dread face of a Hindu god.

"Leave it," I said, shuddering.

He sat back, out of breath, and smoothed his tie back into place.

Krishna the destroyer disappeared.

"Look," he faltered. "Uh . . . you know . . . now that you know about me and Dorris . . ."

He paused.

"Yes?" I prompted.

"Well, there's some stuff we need to clear up."

"Clear up?" He was such a weasel. "What's to clear up? So you're banging Dorris. Big deal. I'm sure by now even the PTA knows that."

A panicked look streaked across his face.

"You think so?"

I crossed my arms and leaned my ass against the desk, shaking my head in disbelief.

"You're a fucking idiot, you know that? Really, it's quite amazing that you can breathe on your own. How do you manage it?"

He looked hurt, then confused, searching my face for cues. Was I joking? Was I being cruel?

"How did you know?" he said.

"Because it was obvious, you moron. The way she moved on you at the Swan the other night, for one. Even someone with brain damage would have known that you two were together. And by the way, you were a complete A-hole to her. You treated her like she was something you'd tracked in on your shoe."

He smiled at this proudly, like he was the campus pussy-bandit being lauded for his prowess by his unlaid friends.

"It's not funny," I said. "I'm not giving you a compliment."

The smile vanished, and he swallowed hard with a grimace, as if he'd just sampled a carton of soured milk.

"And the other night at Dorris's when you two went—ostensibly—to make us drinks. Did you think that would just pass unnoticed? I could hear you canoodling in the kitchen."

He jumped on the mention of the fateful night, relieved. I had brought us around to the subject.

"That's actually why I'm here, Nick."

"Why? To tell me that you make a lousy Rob Roy and that you sound like one of Jerry's Kids when you're turned on?"

"Screw you, dickhead," he shouted, suddenly very angry. "At least I pick on people my own age."

"Not quite," I said, "but whatever."

He kicked one of the near legs of the coffee table.

"I'm not the one who's done anything wrong here. You're the one who has shit to answer for."

He was getting worked up, and very quickly. The asthma was already choking him. You could hear the rasping edge in his breath.

"Answer to whom?" I said, haughtily. "You? That's rich."

"No, not to me . . ."

He broke off, coughing.

He ransacked his pockets for his inhaler, found it, and took a long, deep pull.

I didn't wait for him to finish.

"Monica's a grown woman," I said. "Not that it's any of your business. She's more mature than any of us by a long way. But then, how would you know that? She's never said a word to you. She tagged you as a reptile from the start."

He exhaled loudly and coughed again.

"That little slice has nothing on me," he said, still coughing in sharp, thick bursts. "She can suck my balls."

He slapped his chest a few times, brought up a gob of phlegm, and spit it onto the floor. He cleared his throat. "Anyway, I'm not talking about Monica."

This was intolerable.

"Look, you lowlife piece of shit," I shouted, "the only reason you're sitting here is because I plan to kick the living slime out of you, precisely for the crime of corrupting a minor, so don't even think about lecturing me about the age of consent."

Now I was the one out of breath.

"What the fucking hell did you think you were doing waltzing around Dorris's place in front of Miriam wearing those mail-order ball-hangers you had on the other day? Do you realize she fled over here to escape you, and begged me to get rid of you? She thinks you're hurting Dorris. It's bad enough that she's actually heard you two barking the night away—that will scar her for life, you can be sure—but she's had to see the marks of it, too, all over her mother's body. And to make matters worse, she's had to see the hairy perpetrator himself swanning around at breakfast in his fuck duds as if this were his own private circle of hell. I could kill you."

"Whoa, whoa. Hold on just a second," he wailed, making a halting gesture with his palm. "I've never done a thing to that girl. It's not my fault if Dorris can't afford a sitter."

"Can't afford? You mean won't bother. Besides, Dorris doesn't need a sitter. She needs a parole officer. And you? Are you completely incapable of controlling yourself? Ever?"

He stood up.

"I came here to ask you the same thing, you fucking pervert."

He was unsteady on his feet and sat down again.

He glared across at me, vexed by his immobility, his torso formless and bulked around him like a beanbag.

"Did you think no one would notice your little private lesson with Miriam?" he sneered. "That's why she was over here, you know? You whispered some voodoo spell into her ear the other night and now she thinks you're Jesus in blue jeans."

That was Dorris's phrase for sure. Verbatim. So stupid. And stupider still coming out of Dave's mouth.

"They say that's how pedophiles do it, though, right?" he added. "It's like hypnosis or something. They turn the kids into zombies and get 'em to come to *them*."

"Save Dorris's criminal profiling claptrap for someone who cares, Dave," I said. "I do not want to hear it. I really, really don't."

"Fine." He sighed. "That's fine."

He managed a deep breath. The medicine was starting to work.

"The truth is, I don't care what you do with that kid," he said, "so long as you leave me out of it, and so long as Dorris doesn't find out about it. But don't tell me about how to behave around a kid. I do what I want, and so can you. Just don't get in my way."

I exploded. Pushing myself up from the desk, I stood and took a step toward him.

"I can't believe I'm actually going to defend myself here, but on principle, and to get some peace, I'm going to clear this up once and for all, because, apparently, you and Dorris think the rest of the world is as disgusting as you are, and you feel quite free to accuse from the top of your own reeking dung heap."

"Defend yourself?" he balked. "Who are you kidding? You can't even remember three-quarters of what you do on any given night. Have you looked at your own Facebook page lately?"

"Facebook. Oh, well, now there's some reliable testimony for you. Those people don't have a single brain between them, and certainly not a functioning short-term memory."

"Neither do you, dude. That's my point."

"Oh, is that your point?"

I picked up the fallen remote and dashed it against the wall behind and just above Dave's head. The plastic cracked and the batteries scattered.

"The only point you have is in your pants, you retarded fucking rhino, so why don't you just head back to Twin Pines like a good little pachyderm and yank yourself numb in your bedroom. And if that doesn't satisfy you, well, you can always go back to hate-criming your neighbors. That's usually good for a laugh. Oh, wait, I forgot, your sister's your neighbor now. Well, I'm sure with some help from a search engine and a pair of night vision goggles you could find out where Jack Gordon is living and where all the unguarded entrances are."

He was definitely not expecting that. His face went fuchsia.

He gasped. "You know I never did shit to that Hebrew."

"No, actually, Dave, I know that you did in fact do a great deal to that Hebrew, as you so delicately put it, and I have the evidence to prove it."

He froze.

"What?"

"You heard me."

He couldn't even pretend to be outraged. He was like a kid in a playground batting back taunts. Each protest was an admission of guilt.

"There is no evidence. Even the cops said that."

"No evidence that anyone found."

He had broken into a sweat so sudden and so profuse that the collar of his shirt was darkening.

"You twit," I said, relishing his panic. "You'd be hopeless in an interrogation room. You'd cave like a sand castle in two minutes tops."

He yanked open his tie and unbuttoned the top two buttons of his shirt. His breathing was getting labored again. He reached for his inhaler once more and took another long draw, then dropped it in his lap and fell back against the couch.

Looking at him there, I actually managed to feel sorry for him, the lump of shit. Beating him to a pulp would have been like clubbing a seal. He was down already, and I hadn't even touched him. He was gasping again miserably.

But I had a vice around my own lungs, too, and a thickening in my throat. I was stuck on what he'd said about Miriam.

He was right. I didn't remember. Not much anyway. Not enough.

Not nearly enough to defend myself. He could have made up anything and made me vulnerable to it, and he knew it. He knew the depths of my blackouts better than anyone, including Monica.

What did I remember?

Think.

I remembered Dave snorting and grunting with Dorris in the kitchen, vaguely, and I remembered sitting in Dorris's living room, marveling that I was seeing her house for the first time not through a lens. I remembered my head spinning and my vision blurring and I remembered wondering if I should get up and go to the bathroom to puke. With effort, I even remembered Miriam, or an apparition of her, appearing at my side in her nightgown. But I had no memory of what, if anything, we said or—God forbid—did. None.

There I was lording it over Dave for giving over guilty at the drop of a hint, but I was just as bad, if not worse. I was so self-incriminating it was ridiculous. You could have convinced me of anything, so long as it tarred me as bad.

And then there were the notes. They were in my handwriting, weren't they? It didn't matter whether I'd actually written them or not. Anyone would believe that I had. I was prepared to believe as much myself, and with no help from anyone else.

It was my turn to panic.

"What did Miriam say?"

"That's just it," Dave snarked, relieved to be back on the offensive. "She wouldn't say anything. But she didn't have to. When we came in from the kitchen, she was sitting in your lap. When we asked her about it later, all she would say was that it was your secret and you wouldn't want her to tell."

"That's funny, Dave, because that's exactly what she said about you."

His face went slack then, and colorless, like a waxen mask.

"What would she have to tell about me?"

"What would she have to tell about you? Are you out of your mind? You've practically made her mother into your concubine and Miriam herself an accessory. It's like an amateur porn set over there."

Yeah, Nicky boy, except who is the one doing the filming?

And who is the one making notes?

Quit while you're ahead, why don't you.

And back the fuck off.

"Look," I said, appeasingly. "Just stop debauching those kids, and we'll call it a truce, all right?"

He considered this for a moment, and whether or not to press me on Gordon, but he was too rattled to dig deeper. He knew me well enough to know I didn't make empty threats, and he also knew he wasn't smart enough to outwrangle me. What I had, I had. I'd had it for a long time. He knew that, too. If I'd planned to use it, I would have done it years ago. Hell, the statute of limitations on egging your neighbors with what may or may not have been artwork in questionable taste had most likely run out anyway. What was I really going to do?

Besides, I clearly had something of my own to hide, even if it was hidden from me, too.

"Fine," he said at last. "But only so long as you promise never to set foot in or near Dorris's house again."

"Deal," I said, too abruptly. I extended my hand.

He didn't shake it.

"What's done is done," he mumbled, and something else I couldn't hear. He shuffled into the hallway and took the front doorknob in his hand. As he pulled it, he turned to look at me one more time.

His eyes were full and his lower lip was trembling.

"Hasn't enough happened?" he said.

Dave was gone before I could answer, but what would I have answered anyway?

Enough.

That was not a word I could understand. Never had. The concept just didn't have a value or a quantity attached to it, nothing that would blow the fuse or trip the switch and stop overload.

Overload was the gig. It always had been.

I could hear my father's voice flaring out of the past.

"Must you do everything to excess?"

I never had an answer for that, either, because it was so patently true. Yes, I must do everything to excess. Yes, I must go overboard, beyond the pale, all out.

It's the way I am.

It's one of the many reasons why you don't love me.

I had never said those words to him, but I had thought them. I had thought about them a lot since his death.

It was all just more illusion, the deeply held belief that parents love their children, as if it's a law of nature or something.

Not just how it's supposed to be, but how it is.

No matter what.

That's really how people see it. Children are sacrosanct. They can and often do hate their parents, maybe even all their lives, and that's acceptable. Run of the mill. Their parents fucked them up. Their parents hurt them, neglected them, exercised inordinate influence. Psychotherapy is built on this principle.

But what about the reverse? No one likes to talk about the reverse. No one can bear to think of it. Not as something normal anyway. Parents hating their children. Parents genuinely regretting their children, and maybe even with good reason.

We're always blown away by parents who kill their children, or rape and imprison them. They're monsters, we say with a collective gasp. And maybe they are, but only in so much as all serial murderers and kidnapping rapists are monsters. The motives are no more or less common than any other. Greed, jealousy, rage, fear, psychosis. And the victims are just people.

But it's the child part we can't accept. And why? Because the bond between a parent and child, the one that goes *from* parent *to* child and, in our minds, links the two beings as surely and undeniably as their shared DNA, that bond is brick and mortar to us. It's one of those collective social lies like the solvency of banks that makes the world stand up and function. It's a load-bearing wall. We can't do without it. Relinquish that, and you've lost more than God and country. You've lost a bedrock organizing principle, and from there the rest is chaos.

Parents passionately love, cherish, and instinctively prize their children. As a matter of course.

They must.

Right?

Wrong.

It came as a shock to me when I realized it. Not the part about my father not loving me. I pretty much knew that. There were signs. The shocking part was the second bit, my eventual response to this information, or I should say the more objective-minded part of me's response to this information, the part of me that sympathized with him and thought—lightbulb going on—*Yeah, he doesn't love me.* But why should he? Why inherently should he?

And this part of my mind nodded sagely and went on with the argument.

Okay, so I'm not the person my father would have chosen as his child. Not the blue-ribbon winner. Not his type. So what? Does that make him a bad man? A bad father? Or—and here's the kicker—even a particularly unusual one?

Well, that hardly seems fair.

I mean, you have a kid and you raise him. You provide for him. You do your best. When he finds a worm in his raspberries, you try to assure him that the world's not such a bad place. But beyond that, maybe you just don't dig him. You don't think he's a gem. And maybe he isn't. How is that your fault?

He's a person like anyone else. Average. Joe Dimwit on the street. But he's your kid, so the love—the passionate, all-encompassing, I-would-die-for-you love—is supposed to follow. Must follow. Except in your case, and maybe in a whole lot of cases that nobody dares to talk about, it doesn't follow. It just doesn't.

It can't. Because love is spontaneous. It either is or it isn't. You can't build it out of good intentions or yeoman service. You can build solid fathership out of those things, and even a kind of love, love as in *caritas* or maybe even *agape*, something distant and noble and really hard to pull off in anything but name. But you can't build the love that everyone is looking for, love as in *eros*, as in apple of my eye, blood of my blood and body given up for you.

You just can't.

So don't sweat it, because, like Gruber's youngest son and his renegade bladder, you just can't help it. And what's more, you're not alone. You're not the only one.

Far from it.

It's everywhere.

Gruber's sons were just people. People who were lesser than he wanted them to be, and the way he saw it, that lesserness reflected poorly on him. It didn't, of course, but he was sure it did, because the narcissism of parenthood is impenetrable.

As impenetrable as the solipsism of childhood. Children grow up trapped in their heads, thinking that the rest of the world disappears when they shutter their eyes. Parents, meanwhile, raise their children thinking that the kids are just extensions of themselves, prototypes, or prize pigs to be judged at the county fair.

All Gruber could see in Eric was a bad grade, a lower score in the competition than his vanity had conditioned him to expect. It had nothing to do with love or lack of it, except love of self, preening of self, the unbridled arrogance of spreading seed.

Dorris, on the other hand, was miserable and rejected and clobbered by conscience, and she was in over her head with Dave Alders. She didn't have an ounce of extra left. Not even for herself.

Is it a wonder her kids went begging?

And I knew myself that Miriam was no specimen. She wasn't a prodigy or a beauty, or even particularly polite. She was just a ten-year-old kid in cutoff shorts and sneakers. She just was. A fact. The middling yield of a failed marriage, and probably not a pleasant reminder thereof.

It—all of it—was painful and sad and it was hard to watch, but it was nobody's fault.

Not really.

Even Dave himself.

A face—a man—that not even a mother could love.

If you would be loved, be lovable.

The poor frump walked out my door blubbering over the overbearing past and the persistence of wrong in the present despite all that had gone before.

"Hasn't enough happened?" he'd said.

Well, now that I have found my voice, I say:

What is enough?

You have set a promise on my brow.
You are mine.
I have chosen.
You have chosen.
The occasion is auspicious.
Today is the day of your namesake.
Did you know?
We are bonded in the word
In the day, the single day,
And in the hour.
The last hour of that day
Is ours.

13

Mrs. Bloom's kitchen was green. All soft and garden-dwelling shades of green: sage, pea, olive, lettuce, and moss. Going into it was like coming into a peaceful forest glade after a long journey, as you might in a dream or a children's story, and finding there a cottage and a kind old woman who makes you tea and tells you all is right with the world.

I don't know why I went there, except, I guess, in the desperate hope of finding exactly what I found.

How rarely that happens.

So rarely, that you think it could not have been an accident, that you must have been guided by something or someone, or drawn in by a presence of which you were unaware but that worked on you like a beacon, both beckoning and pointing the way.

But I don't really believe in any of that.

The truth goes more like this.

I keep waking to the same day over and over again. Always waking to an intrusion or an unexpected row. Usually both.

Today, I wanted that to change.

When I woke, I wanted something about the hours that lay ahead to be substantively, purposefully different from all the hours that had gone before. I wanted refuge from the grinding ring of time, and the exhausting, formulaic way that exposure to my fellow vulgar beings made me feel matted and wrung, like a piece of dirty laundry torturously washed but never made clean.

I hadn't spoken to Mrs. Bloom in years. Since before her husband died three years ago. Or was it four by now? Even five?

Fuck's sake, Nick, look it up.

The synagogue would have a record. He was memorialized at Temple Israel, you may recall.

You were there. Sort of. Hanging at the back and around the edges, too vagrant to approach.

Man, the sources of shame are so many. So very, very many. And ongoing.

Ah, so what?

Go ahead.

Ring the childless widow's doorbell, why don't you?

And then run away, you worthless fink, just like the neighborhood hoodlums on Devil's Night.

Why not toilet paper one of her trees while you're at it? That at least would be congruous. A petty deed follows a callow act.

But don't stand there with the audacity of your need hanging out like a hemorrhoid.

Make one right choice.

For once.

Please?

'Course, I didn't.

I couldn't.

And I can't say why.

Unless you count my problem with enough. Or more specifically my problem with the placement of that all-important "is" between the angry repetitions of that word.

Enough is enough.

A tautology that is not.

To other people it's a phrase that means *stop*. Clear as day. To me it's just some asshole repeating himself, like Gertrude fucking Stein spooling Shakespeare.

Enough is enough is a rose by any other name is Tourette's.

So shut the fuck up.

Against my own better judgment, weak and sarcastic as it was, I went. I went to Mrs. Bloom's and rang the bell—*buong*—and stood there nervously on the step waiting, maybe half hoping she wouldn't answer, but really just so thankfully relieved when she did.

She looked years older. Many years older than the three, four, five years it had actually been. Yet in some eerie way she looked younger, too, a bit the way a yogi looks young after years of meditating in a cave, as if she'd shed the worldly burdens that make wrinkles groove themselves in a face and signal pain.

Whatever pain there had been had washed through her and left a beautiful plainness behind. She was free. You could see that. Not afraid, and wholly ready for death when it would come—though not, as I had thought, waiting for it, resigned or in defeat, but with a fullness of mind and self-possession that was nothing short of astonishing.

I saw her and I couldn't say a word.

"My goodness!" she cried, her faded denim blue eyes alight with surprise. "Nick Walsh. Lord, how wonderful to see you."

She stood there like some ecstatic maestro, with her white wispy bush of hair all standing on end, beaming with such unexpected warmth that I honestly didn't know what to do. I had rehearsed this first exchange so thoroughly, or thought I had, but now when it came to it, the preparation was useless. It had nothing whatsoever to do with what was there in front of me or how I felt in the full glare of her generosity. To me—so down and low and derelict as I had become—her welcome was like a slice of sky as seen from the bottom of a well.

I could not respond to it. Nothing in me would move or speak or make a sound.

She saw this and did not flinch. Or even change her tack. She wouldn't be thrown by my awkwardness. She reached through the door frame and took my hand.

"Come in," she said.

And I let myself be led.

Her foyer was similar to mine. Wide and open, it poured you into the house. Linoleum tile, also green, shaker sideboard, simple dendrite chandelier, four forty-watt teardrop bulbs.

The living room was to the right, same as mine. No wall. Then a den or study or office to the left with wall. And then the kitchen, through a central funneling hall, back and to the right. All the houses on the block had been built at the same time by the same developer. The plans were uninventive. The Bloom house was pretty much the Walsh house, flipped on the other side of the street.

We went straight back to the green kitchen, which was full of subtle shafts and shadows at that time of day, the sun hazed and gray-cast through the trees out back, and the windows not as clean as they could be.

"Sit," she said.

And I did as I was told.

She had that sort of command in her voice, but no animus.

If I believed in any of that shamanist shite, I'd have said that Mrs. Bloom was a power animal, but maybe one that was off the beaten path—like, say, a giraffe, daunting but somehow disarming at the same time, an herbivore (so no worries there), and secure. Really solid. As if its size had given it authority, but perspective, too, and so had made it calm enough to be kind.

"Coffee?" she said.

I shook my head.

"I'm having some," she added, her back to me.

She was pouring water into the machine.

"Won't you join me?"

"Okay," I said, blankly.

She smiled, half turning toward me.

"Good."

She put the paper filter in the basket and measured out six scoops. Her hand shook slightly and she spilled a few grains. With her free hand she brushed them casually onto the floor.

I wondered if she was a tidy person but not a compulsive one, the kind who would sweep that up later. Or would she, like me, forget or not care until the bits became palpable underfoot and she had to shuffle the bottoms of her feet together before getting into bed? Was that the line of her cleanliness? Or was the whole house littered with small remains, crumbs, bits of paper, and mouse turds all fallen onto the carpet and ground slowly into the pile?

Her place didn't smell bad. Just stale, as if the windows were rarely opened and the sun was not allowed to penetrate.

She brought milk and cream to the table with two mugs, an earthenware bowl of white sugar, a matching spoon, and two metal teaspoons. She slid one mug and spoon in front of me.

"Do you like demerara?" she asked. "I think I have a bit if you do."

"No," I said, too brusquely. "This is fine."

I smiled to myself. I hadn't encountered that term for years. Demerara. I don't think I'd ever heard it spoken aloud. She really was like someone out of a storybook.

And here I was encroaching like a leech. I'm just here to suck your blood; don't mind me. I mean, God, lady, slap me or something. I opened my mouth to say as much, but all that came out was, "I'm sorry."

The words hung there like a silent fart that you're waiting for the other person to smell, hoping like mad that it will dissipate before they do.

"I know you are," she said at last, which I hadn't at all expected. "But don't say it."

Don't say it.

Don't say it ever, or don't say it again?

I was confused.

"Because it's inadequate?" I asked.

"Because it doesn't belong," she answered, consolingly but with an undertone of sternness.

"You mean it's rude," I said tartly.

She leaned forward to catch my eyes, which were safely back on the sugar bowl.

I was thinking of Eliot's line about coffee spoons, and the way Mom had once said it to me when I was in elementary school after she'd come back from a conference with my teachers.

"Oh, Nicky, my love, I need a martini. And quickly. Those people. God. What a *parade* of Prufrocks."

And then she waved her arms, laughing and saying the line, cueing me to join.

I have measured out my life with coffee spoons.

I looked up very slowly to meet Mrs. Bloom's eyes. She took my chin in one hand.

"No, Nick," she said. "I don't mean that it's rude."

She sighed, dropping her hand to my arm and patting firmly.

"I mean that it's polite."

She stood up and crossed to retrieve the coffee. The machine was burbling and belching out its last steam.

"I don't want polite," she said, grasping the decanter, "and neither do you. I've had far too much of polite from everyone. I don't think I could take it from you, too."

"But I owe you an apology," I countered. "I've insulted you by coming here. I have no right. No place."

"You've insulted me by saying you're sorry. And for that"—she smiled self-mockingly—"I generously forgive you. But your coming here—" She paused thoughtfully. "Well, you have no idea."

She poured the coffee and placed the decanter on a trivet in the center of the table.

"Nick." She sighed, easing herself back into her seat. "Seeing you is like a holiday from seeing the rest of the world. The polite world where polite doesn't give a damn."

She replaced her hand on my arm, then the other, and shook my wrist for emphasis.

"But you do give a damn. That's why you're here. I know that. And that's also why it wouldn't have mattered when you came so long as you didn't tiptoe in with flowers or send a prompt card. I consider it a compliment that it took you this long."

"A good deed of omission," I ventured. "How convenient."

She laughed.

"Oh, bosh. Don't be so hard on yourself. It wouldn't kill you to take a little credit for something, you know."

"If only it would. I'd be giving myself A's across the board."

She frowned disapprovingly.

"Don't ever wish for death."

She put a half teaspoon of sugar into her mug and stirred it for a long time, slowly, the metal spoon tinkling a lazy tidal rhythm, like a ship's bell in a deserted harbor at night.

"You must have more discipline than that," she said.

I thought of letting this go. It seemed, at first, so out of place, the misfire of an old woman's mind. But I felt a blush of anger in my ears, automatic, marshaling to the defense, and I knew that the remark was quite well placed after all.

"Discipline?" I spat, more derisively than I'd meant to. "What's that got to do with it?"

Her voice grew suddenly sharp.

"Everything. It has everything to do with it."

Well, well, I thought. A fierce heart beats in Old Mother Hubbard.

But the flash of temper didn't last. She seemed to regret it immediately.

"Effort," she murmured, pursing her lips empathically, "is all that is required."

And slip slip. As fast as that, the past was there again—again—and I was on my knees with Mom in the upstairs hall praying in front of the crucifix.

What happens if you stop trying?

You must never do that.

Why?

Because it is the gravest of sins.

Why?

Because it is at the root of all the others.

"You sound just like my mother," I said.

"Well, then she understood a great deal and you should have listened to her."

"I did listen to her. All I did was listen to her and repeat. I can still hear her voice. Every single day, at every turn. All that fucking—sorry—all that poetry she spouted coming back to haunt me. I was thinking of her just now, in fact, looking at your sugar bowl, hearing one of those damn lines."

She looked immensely pleased, then sad, her features seeming to fall into her thought.

"Yes. I know just how you feel. I had to give away that bird, God help me. Oh, that bird. Do you know she sounded just like Robin, the intonation of her voice, the pitch. Just perfect. Like a recording. It was incredible."

She paused, putting her fingers to her mouth to stifle a sob.

"Horrible," she whispered.

It was then that I knew my real reason for going there. To feel worse. To watch this resilient woman cry, and to provoke it.

Nice work.

Keep at it and you'll unravel years of her famous effort by nightfall.

Key word: *her*.

Her effort.

The labor that has given her rest.

Another casualty of your ego.

And these thoughts, too, just more arrogance.

"Don't flatter yourself," she said, seeming to read the self-censure in my face. "It would take a great deal more than your guilt to unsettle me."

Couldn't have said it better myself.

"You've really done your homework, haven't you?" I said instead.

She cocked her head and nodded, raising her brows to the obvious, as if I were a lazy pupil slow to catch on.

"Discipline," she said decisively. "I told you. Know where you stand and stand there. Once you know yourself well enough to do that, you'd be surprised how easily you can read other people."

"But that's just it," I said. "I don't want to stand here."

She blew a raspberry of dissent.

"You most certainly do. I've never seen a person so in love with his grief."

"Oh, and you're not?" I blurted.

"In love with my grief?" she said. "No. Lord, no. That's never been my problem. I have others. Plenty of others."

"Like what?"

Her eyes narrowed and darkened, but there was fondness in them still. We were having her conversation now, and she liked it that way.

"Like terror," she said, flatly. "I have a great deal of trouble with terror."

"Pardon me, Mrs. Bloom," I countered, as usual too rough in tone, "but bullshit. You look like you're about ready to invite the reaper himself in for a drink."

"One for the road," she joked, lifting her mug to the toast.

"C'mon. Seriously, you can't pretend that fear is your big problem."

"I don't have to pretend. If there's one thing in this world there's no pretense in, it's terror. Terror is not polite."

"Terror doesn't send cards and flowers?" I jibed.

She smiled wryly.

"He most certainly does not. But then, you know that well enough yourself. He comes in like a wrecking ball cut loose. *Kerplunk.*"

Yes, I know terror well enough, I thought. You are right there. But it does not come through the wall and lodge, as graceless as an unexploded bomb. It comes like a virus in stocking feet. A creeping malaise. Just the barest scratch in the throat, a dry swallow. The prodrome of terror is just this small, a bad dream, a waking too early, an unease when the light is coming up, unease at the very fact of the light coming up.

How is that? you say, when you are still capable of wonder. What is so wrong with the dawn? Or the night? Or these things that I see every day, and have always seen every day, but which now are so—so terrible.

How to explain exactly what *is* so terrible. You cannot.

"Kerplunk" is not the word I would choose.

But I do not have a better one.

Even memory fails here.

No parrot's line to fill the gap.

Uppp . . . wait.

Wait.

Here's one.

Just in the nick.

Clear your throat and enunciate.

Whereof one cannot speak, thereof one must remain silent.

Teach that to a parrot.

Yeah.

We are never at a loss for words, are we?

Even for a loss of words.

Time passed in Mrs. Bloom's kitchen the way it passes when I'm writing this.

Hours lost.

Total absorption.

Talking with her was like being on a really great first date, a chaste date, but a great one nonetheless: the kind where you look up to order another bottle of wine and the restaurant is empty and the waiters are closing out the till.

We just talked and talked and talked, and then she heated some leftovers and we ate, and we had more coffee afterward. And it was just as she said it would be. A relief from every other strained conversation.

For me, that even included the ones I had with Monica, because there, in that kitchen, with the reclusive, the surprising, the godsent Mrs. Bloom, there was nothing at stake. No ground to take or concede. No sexual taint. No teetering desire. No threat of any kind. And no booze, pills, powders, or weeds of any kind, either. Nothing. I was flat-out clean in the presence of another human being for the first time since my parents had died.

And whaddaya know? I remember everything we said.

Everything.

She told me a lot about my mother, especially my mother and Robin. Things I didn't know, but which rang so achingly true that I knew they must be.

"Your mother had an obsession with words," she said.

"Yes, well, she was an academic at heart," I replied. "I guess you know she had a PhD."

Mrs. Bloom rolled her eyes.

"God, who didn't?" She threw up her hands. "She wore it as a badge of her superiority, and with it she made it very, very clear early on that my husband and I were not on her level . . . that no one in the neighborhood was on her level, except, with the right coaching, Robin. But that was much later. At first it was a hard transition for them. Very hard, I think."

She paused, remembering.

"You know, I'll never forget it. She and your father had us over for dinner once when they first moved into the neighborhood. You were just a baby. They were like any young professional couple coming out of the teeming think pot of New York and finding themselves in the—what did she call it?—the great cultural wastelands of the company town, I think it was. Whatever that meant.

"Anyway, they were desperate for company. Your mom especially. She seemed so shocked by motherhood and the whole of her new life. She always seemed to be looking around in disbelief, as if saying to herself: God, what have I done?"

Mrs. Bloom frowned.

"Our evening together was a total failure, of course. We had very little in common and not much to say to each other. And, well, as you know, your mother was no cook, so we couldn't even take refuge in the food."

She pulled a sour face, her mouth forming a moue of distaste, her nose crinkling in rebuff.

"Well, you see—" She sighed conclusively. "Your mother was bored, I think. Just terribly bored, and she remained that way for the rest of her life, except when she was with you or Robin. You were the bright spots in her terrible mistake. But the rest of the time I think she was dying of boredom. She was certainly dying of boredom that night with us.

"So . . . I guess she did what bored people do. She got drunk. My, did she get drunk. And she said sharp, insulting things, most of which my husband and I couldn't make head or tail of. Only her tone gave her away. Thinking back on it now, I suppose it can be a great blessing not to know enough to know when you're being put down. Ignorance can be bliss. Or protection, anyway, when you're having dinner with the likes of Diana Walsh. Then the real digs can't hurt you. You just coast under them none the wiser, and it just seems as if you're watching a scene in a play and wondering why the hostess is so awfully upset."

She looked at me sympathetically, as if she knew that this had happened to me, and I nodded knowingly.

"That's how it was that night, anyway," she went on. "I remember that so well. I didn't feel hurt by the things your mother said, because I didn't understand most of them, or I didn't value the things she was chiding us for lacking enough to care. She cared about the lack much more than we did. Maybe because it meant that she could find no company with us. No like mind, as she might have said. And that was clearly very painful to her. Very painful. And that's what I saw in her that night. A woman lashing out in pain and missing her targets entirely—which, of course, only infuriated her all the more."

She laughed regretfully.

"Oh, it was dreadful. I felt so terribly sorry for her. I wanted just to reach across the table and take her hand and tell her that it was going to be all right. And I would have, if I hadn't thought that she would slap me away. But that was your mother for you, crying for help in the same shrill voice that was bound to turn help away."

"Bound to?" I said angrily. "You mean *designed* to. She was so perverse. So incredibly perverse. I mean, you don't say 'Mayday, Mayday' and 'Die, peasant, die' in the same breath. But that was standard issue for her. You're lucky you didn't understand her. I did, and it damaged me for life. It was made very clear to me many times over, and in just the way you describe, that I was only just intelligent enough to know how stupid I was. I was not a bright spot in her mistake. I *was* her mistake."

"Oh, Nick," she cried. "Don't say such a thing. You must know how smart and sensitive and wonderful you are. You must know that."

"On my best days, I know, a little," I said. "And the rest of the time all I can see is the shortfall. What I lack. What I'm not. And now that my parents are gone, that's all I'm left with."

"But that isn't true," she insisted. "That simply isn't true. The person who came to my door knows his value, and wants to live and be happy. And he even knows his mother loved him very dearly."

"I don't know. Maybe. But I also know that my mother was a pompous bitch. She should have worn a sign around her neck that said, BEWARE OF THE DOG."

Mrs. Bloom's expression hardened with determination, but her voice was oddly pleading.

"Yes. Okay, so your mother was a pompous bitch. So what? She was also a wonderfully complex and brilliant woman who gave my granddaughter the best of herself—the absolute best of herself—and for nothing more than the pleasure of the giving. Do you have any idea how much your mother meant to Robin? Do you?"

"Some idea," I said. "But not all."

"Well, you should know all. She meant the world. She saved Robin from the doldrums of being such a strange and lonely child. That poor girl was a wretched orphan who had lost her mother and her whole sense of self, and she didn't have a soul in the world that could understand her.

"Lord knows I tried. But I was never bookish in that way. I didn't have the equipment. I gave her all the love anyone could give. I cooked for her—all her favorite foods. I played with her and tried to make her laugh. I nursed her when she was sick. I gave her hugs and pats and constant encouragement, and I think it helped a little. But I couldn't do the main thing. I couldn't open her mind. I couldn't free her capabilities.

"Your mother did. She took Robin, who was so isolated and folded in on herself, unfurled her like a flag, and set her flying proudly at full mast. And for that I will be forever grateful to her memory."

She looked away out the back window and sighed long and loud.

"Her own mother could never have done as much, I'll tell you that. Karen was just a freewheeling sprite lost in a haze of drugs. She abandoned Robin on our doorstep and went off to destroy herself.

"But your mother picked Robin up again, and I think she even managed to take away the pain of that first abandonment. She filled that hollowed-out child's mind with beautiful words, and those words were like magic spells for all the hurts of the past. They shielded her, and I think they healed her."

She reached out and grasped my shoulder as if to transfer the passion of her thanks.

"Did you know that your mother even bought books and maps and study aids for Robin? All the time. She even gave her one of those miniature tape recorders to carry around with her, so that she could recite poems into it."

Her contagious gesture had worked. I was paying very close attention, staring at her face.

Her blue eyes were swollen and plump, like two berries popping from the reddened whites of her eyes, shining through the meniscus of tears.

"Oh, what was it your mother said all the time?" she said. She put her forefinger to her lip pensively.

"Emphasize the spoken word? Was that it?"

She mulled this. Shook her head.

"No, it was something fancier than that."

"The oral tradition," I said. "Cherish the oral tradition."

"Yes." She clapped her hands lightly. "The oral tradition. That was it."

"She thought that language was meant to be heard," I explained. "And you're right—she always gassed on and on about that."

I spoke in my mother's exaggerated voice:

"'Nick, there is a direct line from Homer to Beckett through Shakespeare. The Bard wrote plays for a reason . . . And why? . . . So that his words would be heard. *Aloud* . . . Remember, the muse sings. She does not scratch like a chicken in the dirt. It is the lowly so-called artist who does that, and he can make no claim to any title higher than scrivener.'"

Mrs. Bloom doubled over, slapping her thighs. I struck the table and threw back my head. It must have been a minute straight we were like that, tears rolling down both our faces, our breaths coming in gasps and great heaves of silent laughter.

"You do perfect imitation," she hooted finally.

"Yeah, well, I ought to. I had to listen to it all day. Jesus. You know, she gave me one of those recorders at one point, too, but I just used it to play pranks on my teachers and friends, and then I lost interest and threw it in a drawer and forgot about it. I probably still have it somewhere."

"Not Robin," said Mrs. Bloom, the evenness coming back into her voice. "Heavens, she carried that thing everywhere, I can tell you. Recording everything—dinner conversations, her own thoughts, the cat purring. Everything. It drove me crazy after a while. I had to take it away from her for a day or two just to get her to run around outside and get some exercise."

She chuckled wistfully, her eyes clouding with memory.

"But, oh, Nick, it really was her salvation. Her absolute salvation."

And so she was mine. Mrs. Anita Olga Ivanova Bloom. Was my salvation. Or do I overstate? Was she instead my goad? My gadfly? My lost soul's mate for an evening? Whatever.

I was there, it must have been, until midnight. Finally we said good night.

"You are welcome here, Nick," she said as we parted. "Anytime."

She paused deliberately, then added:

"But only if you want to. Only then."

And I was so grateful to her for that last bit, which she emphasized and meant. In other words, don't add me to your guilt trip. Come if you want, I'll be glad to see you, but don't bother if a dragging case of the shoulds comes into it.

"I don't want anything to do with shoulds," she'd said. "I've damn well had enough of those."

As I was turning up the lawn, she shouted, "Oh, and Nick— If you're ever polite to me again, I'll slap you. Got it?"

"Got it," I said, heels together, saluting.

You were the bright spot in her mistake.

Well, well.

People say the darnedest things.

Could she have known what that would mean to me? Or did it just come out that way because Mrs. Bloom had a folksy way with words and always believed the best about people?

No matter.

It was a pretty thought, and I held on to it.

I sucked it like a placebo. Like some blameless vital sugar pill placed blindly on my tongue.

And it worked for a while just the same, because I believed so damned hard that it would.

14

I told Monica about my visit with Mrs. Bloom.

She kept saying, "I can't believe you went over there."

"I know," I said. "I know. But I'm so glad I did."

I hadn't seen Monica in a while, longer than usual. I'd been preoccupied, what with Miriam, then Dorris, then Dave, and finally Mrs. B. I hadn't been watching my monitors as much, either, with the exception of the nightly check-in with Eric. But even that had been whittled down to a few peeks at lockdown. Just enough to get the count, how many days clean, and to get the gist of his disgrace.

What had Monica been doing all this time? When she called, especially after a hiatus like this, I always wondered what made her call. How did she decide it was time? Did she consider it at all? Or was it just cycles of the moon, or her hormones, or the need to feed?

Her life beyond these walls was unknown to me, and I suppose I had kept it that way, not wanting to know, not wanting to complicate or debase the delights of fucking a stranger.

But my desire to know was getting stronger, and had only increased since our last encounter, our fight, which had not really been a fight between Monica and me, but rather a fight between me and myself about whether I did or did not want to know this woman and whether the growing sense that I was falling in love with her was being fed or stifled by how little I knew.

For me, love had always been built on ignorance, on what I did not know and could at first only dimly perceive. This was true of people as well as places and things. Sometimes all three at once. The act of love itself was an act of the imagination, a brightening and furnishing and peopling of sets that were dark. Love was the lights coming on. But they were my lights. They were my scenes and my lines and my voices, too. My show, all made up and directed, my arm grinding at the back of the toy box, manically and musically and beguilingly to its own tune.

Until what?

Until weariness set in.

And then the disillusion, the inevitable heartbreak of recalling, of seeing as if for the first time, that it was always just you there playing by yourself in the dark.

But that was the sustaining hope, wasn't it? The fantasy of creation? The great leap. Athena from the head of Zeus. Galatea from Pygmalion's hands. Wanting your thoughts, your characters, your representations to come alive, to live, grow, and think for themselves. To talk back and, eventually—the best prize of all—to turn and love you in return.

I had reached that point.

I wanted Monica to come alive for me, to exist independently. And then I wanted her to come to me and relinquish her independence willingly out of love.

Okay. So start with existence. The what, the where, the who, the how, and so on. What did she do with herself? Did she have a job? How did she get money? Where did she sleep? Who the fuck was she?

I'd never even known where she lived. She'd claimed not to *live* anywhere, but what did that mean? Was she off in the woods in a cardboard box? Was she squatting in some kid's tree house? Or was she fucking the night watchman at an office park and sleeping on the chairman's couch?

"I stay," was the most she'd ever said. "And then I leave. I'm a gypsy. I don't believe in property."

"You don't *believe* in property?" I said. "What? As in, you're a communist?"

"No—" She laughed. "It's not that I'm against ownership across the board. I mean that I don't trust it personally, that I can't tie myself to things."

"I don't understand," I said.

"It's a lifestyle choice, not a political conviction."

"But what does that even mean?"

"It means that I've only got one foot on the earth. To own, you have to be on all fours. You're a beast of burden, which is fine for some people, fine for most people, but not for me. I can't do it. I won't. And renting is almost as bad. I can't do that, either."

"Really? That's a little extreme, don't you think?"

"Maybe, but it's how I am."

"But it doesn't make sense. I get the ownership thing, sort of, but what's so wrong with renting?"

"It involves a contract, and contracts are chains."

"Chains? Now you really do sound like Karl Marx."

She laughed, shaking her head. "No."

"Contracts are obligations," I said. "Nothing more. Just tethers, and tethers are good things. They give us something to hold on to."

"No," she said firmly. "They give us something that can hold on to *us*, and I can't have that. Every time you sign your name you tie a knot, and before you know it you're in a net."

"Yes, a safety net."

"No. A trap."

I sighed, frustrated.

"Trap or not, you can't get along in today's world without ever signing your name. It's impossible."

"No, it's not. Just unconventional. Maybe a little impractical, but I get along. Actually, I don't even *have* a signature."

"Bullshit."

"I don't. I don't need one. I don't want one."

"So what? You do everything in cash and you've got a piggy bank? Or is it a wad under the mattress?"

"A coffee can, a ziplock. Whatever's handy."

"You're serious."

"Dead serious."

"You have no address, no ID. No driver's license, no social security number? Nothing?"

"Nothing. As far as the official world's concerned, I don't exist."

"Jesus," I said, only half joking. "Are you wanted or something? Am I harboring a fugitive?"

"Well, yes, I suppose you are. 'Fugitive' is a good word for what I am, but not the kind you mean. Anyway, you only entertain me for a few hours at a time, and you've done so without realizing, so I don't think it really counts as harboring."

"Oh, I entertain you, do I?"

"Yes, of course you do, in many senses of the word, some of which are offensive to me, or would be if I cared to object. But this is all for your own amusement as much as mine, and"—she coughed fakely—"edification, too."

"Mortification is more like it."

"Anyway, you shouldn't worry. I'm untraceable."

"Well, that's a relief. Such a nice quality in a girlfriend."

"Oops. Careful, sly. You're slipping." She smiled coyly. "You said girlfriend."

"So?"

"So am I your girlfriend now?"

"Theoretically."

"Ah. Well. That's all right then. You had me worried there for a second. Girlfriend has the stink of ownership about it. But theoretical? That's not bad. I don't mind theoretical at all."

"Good. I'm glad to hear it," I said, though I wasn't glad in the least. "You're every guy's dream girl. All the benefits, none of the strings."

"Tethers, Nick. Tethers. Keep it straight."

"Right, right. My mistake."

I laughed hollowly.

Theoretically. Mistake.

Not exactly words to get your dick hard, but what was I going to do? I wasn't wild about untraceable, either. Illegal is what it really meant. You couldn't be untraceable without breaking the law, even if you were independently wealthy, and Monica wasn't—I didn't think. Anyway, she'd exist on paper somewhere if that were the case, and there'd still be the snag of tax evasion. Monica wasn't the type. Not acquisitive—she'd just said as much. If there'd been an inheritance, she'd have ditched it. Besides, if she was keeping her money in a coffee can, she couldn't have that much of it, unless she was banking for herself, like some minor drug lord with pallets of bundled cash piled high in mini storage.

Not likely.

Money was coming from somewhere, some way. Trickling in. And I wanted to know how.

"So how do you support yourself?" I asked forcefully. "I doubt you're waiting tables under the table."

"Cute," she said.

"I'm serious. How do you make enough money to float, or whatever it is you do? You have to have pocket change."

"True," she said cryptically.

"So?"

"So it's none of your business."

"Maybe it isn't, but tell me anyway. I want to know."

"No."

"Oh, come on. You owe me one difficult disclosure, remember? Sealed with a kiss."

"This isn't difficult. It's private."

"Yeah, well, in your mind that's the same thing. So spill it."

"Look, it's really not very interesting, and by telling you I'd be compromising my—" She broke off, searching for the word. "My coworkers."

"Coworkers? Wow. Now there's a euphemism if I've ever heard one. Don't you mean pimp or partners in crime or something?"

"Fine. My partners, if you like, except that that implies a formality that doesn't exist between us. We're not bound and we're not equals."

"What are you then?"

"Traders, I guess you'd say. We trade."

"Trade, huh? Interesting. Well, we know you're not in banking, so I guess that leaves—what?—call girl taking . . . or giving it out in trade? Or are you on the barter system? Will flex for food."

She clucked her tongue.

"You really are such an ass. Fine. Here it is. I steal. Okay? I steal. Satisfied?"

"You steal?" I said, patronizingly. "I see. Well, I almost guessed. Just a bit too far right on the left wing. Not communist. Anarchist."

"Oh, please. There is no *ist*. I told you. It's not political."

"Exactly. No rule, no rules."

"No, no. It's exactly the opposite—I need the rules in order to break them. Without a system, there'd be nothing to cheat. And that's what I do, okay? I cheat the system."

"That's intelligent of you. Most anarchists miss that fatal flaw in their platform. If everybody did it, there'd be no game. Not everyone can be a parasite, after all. There has to be a host."

"I'm not a parasite."

"Uh, yes you are."

"The host is bloated and rotting anyway, so who's to complain?"

"Not me, certainly. But I am curious how you're able to do it."

"What do you mean, able?"

"How do you do it? How do you steal exactly?"

"Very simply. I go into a store. I take. I leave."

"You shoplift?"

"Yes."

"But not just for yourself."

"Well, sometimes, if I need something special, but usually I pay for the small things. Not worth the risk to steal those. It's the bigger things, the more valuable things I go for."

"Like?"

"Like clothing, CDs, the higher-end stuff at vitamin shops and drugstores."

"Please tell me you're not stealing Sudafed?"

"You can't anymore. It's behind the counter. But no, I'm not."

"Did you ever?"

"No."

"Well, that's something, anyway. So what do you do with this stuff once you have it?"

"I told you. I trade."

"Dare I ask with whom?"

"Dare I ask? Please, Nick. Drop the daddy act, okay? You're not so clean. In fact, as it happens, I believe you know the guy."

This caught me off guard.

"I know your fence?"

"My fence? Are you for real? You watch way too much TV, Nick. No, I believe you know my partner."

"All right, your partner. Who is this guy you trade with?"

She paused to let me sift through the possibles. Dave? Not Dave again, surely. Please not Dave. What about J.R.? No, Gruber would kill him. Some numbskull at the Swan then? Some faceless Facebook friend? No clue.

"Does the name Damian sound familiar?" she said at last.

Fuck.

Fuck.

Fuck.

And fuck.

I thought.

And said nothing.

"I take it from your face," she said, "that you know him. But then, I knew that already, so let's drop the inquisition, shall we?"

"He told you about me?"

"No. Of course he didn't."

"Then how?"

"You called once when Damian and I were meeting."

"But he never says my name. Especially not on the phone."

"Yes, I know that. I work with him, too, remember? He sounded strange on the phone that time, different, more formal, so I sneaked a look at his cell later and saw you on the recent calls."

"Later? So you're 'entertaining' him, too, then, I take it?"

"Jesus, Nick. Get a grip, will you? No, I am not."

"Why don't I believe you?"

"Oh, I don't know, because you're paranoid and massively insecure."

"And you're a career criminal," I blurted. "Or are you going to maintain that you're actually the one proverbial honest thief out there?"

"I'm not going to maintain anything. I don't have to."

She glared at me.

That much was true. She didn't have to maintain anything, least of all me, or us, and the prospect of that sundering, I realized, had come all the way around in the course of only a few months from being the expected and unremarkable collateral damage of fuck-buddying to being a crippling loss that scared the fight and the sass right out of me. She was alive all right, and talking back, my gimcrack creation, but would she stand or run?

That would depend on what she knew.

"So he never told you about me?" I asked, my voice scarred with fear.

"No. I told you, no. He never told me anything."

"And you never asked?"

"No. Why would I? He doesn't know that you and I know each other, and he sure as hell doesn't know that I snooped around in his phone."

"So why didn't you ask me about him?" I asked.

"Because I respect your privacy. What you do on your own time is your own affair."

"You mean like you respected Damian's privacy?"

"That's different. He's different. I have to protect myself. I've had to learn that the hard way. I had a weird feeling. I had to know."

"So what do you know?"

"Just that you know Damian. That's all."

"Really? You had to know, and that's all you know? I don't believe you."

"Fine. Take it or leave it, Nick. That's all I know, and it's all I want to know."
She stood up.

"Never mind. It doesn't matter. This conversation is over."

She shied past me at the door and I didn't move to stop her. It was the only time she'd ever left without touching me, without that tacit promise of return, and all I could think of was that word 'untraceable,' a word that sounds exotic and fantastic and desirable until you need, and then it sounds tinny and sharp, like the pin being pulled from a grenade.

"Am I capable of harm?"

It was the last thing I asked Mrs. Bloom that night.

"Do you think I'm capable of harm?"

And she answered in that same gnomic way she'd answered everything else.

"We're all capable of harm."

Yes, yes, but *me*, I'd thought, scratching at the palm of my hand. What about me? Me, Nick Walsh, individually, not me, son of the tribe that was thrown out of paradise?

But she didn't have an answer for that. How could she? What experience did she have of harm, except as its transitive recipient? Needle to daughter to mom. The gut punch of grief. Then something or someone to Robin to surrogate mom again. A sideswiping act of God. And last, the common thing, heart attack to husband to wife. Widow.

She knew the butt end of harm. That she did. But not the fist of it. Not the kind of mind that writes megalomaniacal love notes to little girls, or abducts them, or gives birth to them and leaves them on doorsteps. Even what Karen had done was unfathomable to her.

As for the rest, she couldn't bear to look.

And yet she had looked at me, really looked at me sitting there across from her, the sugar bowl and the coffee mugs and the welcome rudeness between us. But she had looked at me unknowingly, just as I had harbored Monica unknowingly, so it didn't count.

You didn't know what you were looking at most of the time.

You just didn't, even when you thought you did, even when you believed you actually were all of those flattering things you told yourself you were.

Shrewd and circumspect and discerning. Intelligent. You still didn't know. Even Albert Speer said that. Right, Dad?

Tra-la!

And herewith—cymbal crash—a rare line from Pop for the occasion.

One seldom recognizes the devil when he has his hand on your shoulder.

So true, old man, so true. You had your hand on my shoulder all the way. Through the test scores and the study habits, the final exams and the colleges of choice. You favored the small schools, where the faculty-student ratio was low and you felt the experience was more hands-on, more conducive to the transfer of knowledge, or the feisty pursuit thereof.

"You'll get lost at a big university," you'd said. "You won't get the individual attention. You'll get survey courses taught by graduate students and shooting-star professors who are too preoccupied with their book tours and speaking fees to give you the time of day."

You said not to apply to Columbia, because Harlem was a hole. You said that NYU was mediocre, and, anyway, too full of Jews. You let me try Harvard as a long shot, because you couldn't resist the cachet, but we both knew I didn't have the numbers, and we both turned out to be right.

So I loaded up with the small schools, the ones with tasteful surnames and remote locales, and the forgiving admissions policies for dreamers who didn't test well.

I had the test scores of a space monkey, but I wrote an essay about God and how I'd spent my last winter vacation on a retreat at a monastery in Spain. Your idea, of course. The monastery and the essay. But it worked. I got in to all those buttoned-down middlebrow schools that you'd be proud to wear on your sweatshirt. And then I chose one of them and went there, because you, Daddy, thought it was the best.

Yes. You had your heavy ham hand on my shoulder saying, "Good boy" or "Work hard," and when I turned to look at you, it's true, I did not see the devil. I do not see him still, except in the traces of a bad deed that happened so quickly, so passionately, it might have been any one of us on the wrong day with the wrong confrontation.

A lapse and eternal damnation.

Yes, surely, you are among the damned, if there is such a company, wandering, groveling, stewing somewhere, in some time or supernumerary dimension, but you are not a cliché of the damned, any more than you were a cliché of the devil. You do not smell of sulfur. You smell of slow determination and your golf bag, and the Brylcreem in your hair.

So how was I to know? How am I to know? Does the devil play golf? And where were the horns under your hairline? Was Satan so impeccably groomed? Or just Lucifer, who must have lost his luster on the descent?

I don't know, Dad. I don't know.

I do not recognize the signs.

Even in myself. I do not.

Because I do not know the answer to the question: Am I capable of harm? Deep harm. Fatal harm. Diabolical harm. And under what conditions? Perhaps that is the only relevant question. Not if, but when?

"We are all capable of harm," she said.

And that is what she meant.

No if. Just when.

But to that I would add the real question, and that is the question I did not ask, because it is the question to which she could not possibly have or wish to know the answer.

The first question is routine.

Am I capable of harm?

Why, yes. Of course. Obviously.

That is only a matter of placement and provocation and incalculables so numerous that you had better not think about them, or you'd never get out of bed in the morning.

But the second question: How much?

How much harm am I capable of?

Ah. Well, that is something else entirely.

And that is not a question you ask an old woman sitting at her kitchen table of a companionable evening, even if you think she's the goddamned oracle of Apollo. And why? Because you do not really want to know the answer.

You know it already, which is why you asked the question in the first place, or half asked it, and then skulked away, soothed and appeased by a platitude.

The truth is, one seldom recognizes the devil, even when the hand on your shoulder is your own.

15

You see, this is why I hate Facebook.

Actually, there are a lot of reasons why I hate Facebook, prime among them being the fact that, despite hating Facebook, hating the very idea of it—its saccharine amity, its overweening groupiness, its inane, interminable blah, blah, blah—I've joined the nodding herd and posted a profile on it anyway, just like every-fucking-body else.

Yes, I've spent the time—way, way too much time—on my profile, deciding—no, it's worse than that—painstakingly culling what's cool and not cool to say about myself, what sounds right but is marginally true as well, or fibable if pressed.

I've taken the five hundred warped webcam snapshots of myself, been duly horrified by the results—am I really that rubber-faced? slab-nosed? droop-eyed? edemic?—and tried all the ameliorating effects—sepia, pencil sketch, black and white—but to no avail.

I've selected, from the measly offered list, what's safe or advantageous for the world to know about me, which amounts to very little—name, home-town, relationship status ("Other"?). And in the end, I've clicked that oh-so-apposite submit button and posted my self's thumbnail to the ether, like the love letter or the last orders hastily dispatched, going elsewhere, nowhere, and everywhere all at the same time.

Ridiculous.

But I submit.

To the religion of social networking.

And then what happens?

Well, exactly what you'd expect to happen. You get repeated, rapid-fire friend requests from all the fuckups, lamebrains, asswipes, and outcasts that you never kept in touch with all these years for a reason, and you find out they've become exactly what you'd expect them to have become: married, kidded accountants, salesmen, software designers, and schoolteachers, all posting this year's crop of family photos from the mid-March getaway on the Mexican Riviera or the Oktoberfest booze-up/corn maze with the kids.

And then, of course, there's the thimbleful of people you actually want to find who, apparently, don't want you to find them, and for all the same reasons stated above. You're their good-riddance classmate, cabinmate, teammate, regretted hand job, rim job, spit swap of whichever sad and shady stage of life and venue where the floor was tacky underfoot and the goings-on were best (and, thus, ruthlessly) repressed.

Friend request ignored.

Sure, you make a few connections on Facebook. Emphasis: *few*.

But you spend the rest of the time marveling at why it is that Jimmy or Joanie or whichever other generic and superfluous Your Name Here that you, in a moment of weakness, accepted as your friend thinks you give a rat's ass that they are, at this very moment, having a glass of conscientious Pellegrino in the tub and reading *Eat, Pray, Love* for the fourth time aloud to imminent progeny number three—it's a girl!—in utero.

I mean, fuck.

And yet, as I found out today when I logged on to my account, if it could—and, yes, I'm here to tell you that indeed it can—it gets worse. Because not only is Facebook home to the mind-numbingly logorrheic stay-at-home mom and the quietly desperate actuary languishing in his six-by-six-foot cubicle. It's also home to that holed-up cyber-psycho who has a special message just for you.

Or for me, as it happens.

And no, thank you, the rank ironies are not lost on me here. It couldn't have happened to a ruder pest. The peeker is being poked. The spier has been spied. I get it.

Nicky boy has a friend request from a stalker who is calling himself Iris Gray.

Iris Gray.

Can you beat that?

No photo, natch. Instead, per Facebook's template, just the blank outline of a male. Silhouette. White on blue. A male.

Okay, whatever.

But it's the message attached that's the real eye-burner.

It says simply: "What about those pink notes?"

A strong opening move, wouldn't you say?

King's pawn to D4, or something.

Not that I play.

But this player definitely has my attention.

And then some.

I'd even go so far as to say I'm scared. Truly. I mean, it was one thing to keep finding these notes, convinced, as I had pretty well become, that it was all my own work—and the excessive drinking that was making me forget. But now it's official. Someone else knows. Someone else is in possession.

Of the paperwork, or its implications, at least. And maybe more.

It's Gruber, of course.

Who else could it be?

Unless it's one of Gruber's boys, but I can't see that. What's the possible motivation or means? Mental means, I mean.

Eric's in a crate half his life, and when he's not, having been rendered semiretarded by this treatment, either he's at special school still trying to grasp the rock-bottom rudiments of the three R's or he's in front of the tube playing ultraviolent futuristic war games on Xbox.

Jeff and I are pals and see each other often. No grudge there, or I'd know about it.

J.R. is so steeped in anabolic steroids and militia camps I doubt he's even on the grid. At the breakfast table not long ago, he announced that the U.S. Armed Forces were too PC for him to bother with—"too concerned about civilian casualties to get the job done in the sandbox."

I'm sure by now he's been so indoctrinated by the weekend warrior set that he thinks computers are Orwell's telescreens, part of the vast government panopticon watching *us*. If he knew about the cameras, he wouldn't be in the least surprised, and he sure as shit wouldn't write to me on Facebook. He'd kick in the back door, throw a hood over my head, and spirit me upstate to one of his deer hunters' goon forts where I'd wake up in a circle of inbred Dave types feasting on muskrat and questioning my loyalty to the secessionist U.S. of A.

Mrs. B. is the only other person who knows about that bird, or knows that it's alive and well, and she would never use its name as a pseudonym. Just thinking of Iris made her cry. Besides, she'd never use a pseudonym, much less designate herself as male. She'd never use the Internet. She doesn't even have a computer.

But then again, neither does Gruber.

Does he?

Not in his study anyway.

Yeah, but between them, his boys must have more hardware than they can keep track of. Judging by the look of the basement, that house must be a graveyard of motherboards. Besides, there are always Internet cafés and Internet courses for idiots free at the public library.

It's Gruber.

That Nazoid.

He's found the cameras.

Either that or Dave and Dorris have hired him as their bodyguard for Miriam.

That's possible.

Absurd, but possible.

Gruber would know Dave as the perpetrator of Eggnacht, if nothing else, and given Gruber's flaunted heritage and general comportment toward anyone whom he even suspects of being sub-Caucasian, I'd be surprised if he didn't send St. George's oaf a commendation on behalf of the Aryan Brotherhood when he saw Jack Gordon with egg on his face splashed across all the local papers for weeks.

Either way, alone or in Dave and Miriam's employ, it's Gruber.

Gotta be.

Gruber, who thinks he's being all stealth calling himself Iris Gray because he doesn't know that I know that he still has that bird jailed in his study piping the sonnets of Robert Frost in a perfect imitation of Robin Bloom.

Or does he know it?

No. That's paranoid.

Even if he did find the camera in his pencil sharpener, how in hell would he trace it to me? And wouldn't he be just as likely to do what J.R. would do in the same circumstance? Walk across our adjoining patch of grass and put me in a wheelchair?

I dunno. Maybe he's learned a thing or two about restraint in the hopes of spending his retirement as a free man.

How likely is that, though, really?

A lifetime of brute force without even so much as a Filofax, and suddenly he's the cunning hint dropper of the photon dot? The friend finder of Facebook? And more unlikely still, the stealth pink planter of black valentines?

Nick, man, your nerves have gotten the better of you. Take a breath. Have a piece of Nicorette and use your head. Chew on this for five and get a grip.

Right. Okay.

Question: So who's left?

Answer: Jeff.

Question: No, come on?

Answer: Yeeees. Think it through.

Have I been too quick to dismiss my singles partner?

Really? Jeff? Clean Jeff?

He is the only one in that house who's brainy and tame enough to do it. There is that. But why? I can't figure it.

He'd probably be thankful for the cameras—fodder for his day in court if he ever got one. Besides, I've never filmed him doing anything in the least incriminating, or even embarrassing. The guy's a machine of schoolwork, workouts, and sleep. He's like a prisoner of conscience in his own home. Model inmate.

But what do I know?

What did I know about Monica?

True.

Maybe that's why he's so withdrawn and impersonal, never much for talking over beers after a game. I always thought it was life in H-block that had rendered him near mute, but maybe it's me. Maybe all this time he's been playing not tennis but chess.

Oh, Christ. Who cares? I don't have the energy to speculate anymore. At this point it hardly matters. The game is on and I'm ready.

Do your worst, Iris Gray, my man, whoever you are.

Let's see what you got.

Friendship, is it, you're requesting?

Or a duel?

Fine.

Click.

I accept.

Meanwhile, today I finally had the stomach to go downstairs and check out what might be going on at Dorris's place. I haven't dared to look since Dorris as Mother Brown gave me tonsillitis of the scrotal sack on my own front stoop. What's more, I haven't cared to look since Dave pulled his whole *Law & Order: Special Victims Unit* routine a few days later.

I actually yanked out the wires on the monitors, Katzes' numbers 1, 2, and 3, and they stayed yanked until this evening when close scrutiny of the Grubers yielded nothing more than the usual lobotomized Ellie lambent before the light-emitting diode in the living room, Gruber himself in his study lovingly fellating the snub nose of his Walther PPK, and Iris, inspired as ever, interjecting spots of Hopkins, I think it was, at intervals.

My heart in hiding stirred for a bird.

There was no sign of the boys.

I had to change the channel.

On KatzBO, the only news I got of the hostage Miriam was through Dave and Dorris's conversations about her, which of course took place postcoitus with the two of them flopped like a couple of leopard seals after a meal, seeping sebum and electrolytes onto the black sateen sheets. Word was, Miriam was conducting a strike of sorts in her room, door locked, lights out, and Justin Bieber on repeat crooning at his bluest and mooniest.

Bless her, she maintained my innocence of all but sympathy and kindness, or so said Dave, who had been assigned the wearisome task of prying the truth out of her, or whichever distortion of the truth would best suit Dave and Dorris's need for a scoundrel to blame their damage on.

She held firm, Miriam did, even in the face of bribes to do otherwise, or so claimed the exasperated Dave, pounding the teak headboard with his fist.

"She won't give," he shouted. "She won't fucking give."

"Shhh, baby," cooed Dorris. "Shhh."

Baby?

There is no hell where Dave is anyone's baby.

"Listen," Baby said, hefting his wet bulk onto an elbow, "can't we just take her to a doctor?"

"Are you crazy?" Dorris wailed.

"No. No, listen. I mean, can't we just take her in and say, 'Hey, Doc, can you take a look and tell us if anyone's been messing with her?'"

"If anyone's been *messing* with her? I can't believe what I'm hearing. What do you want him to do, a pap smear? She's ten, Dave."

"No, I know, but I mean, can't the guy just get out his headlamp and find out if her Heimlich is still intact?"

"Hymen, you idiot. It's hymen. Even I know that. And no, he can't. No geriatric pediatrician is going to go spelunking around in my daughter, especially not without Jonathan finding out about it."

"What do you mean?"

"He's in the field, genius. Pediatrics. They all know each other. Trust me, he'd find out."

"Well, can't we go out of state and find some hole-in-the-wall, low-budgie guy who'd give us what we want?"

"Low-budgie? This isn't a snuff film, you complete shithead. This is my daughter. My God. What am I doing? What *am* I doing?"

She leapt out of bed, enraged.

"Get out," she screamed, pointing savagely at the door. "Get out of my house."

"What, baby? What?" said Baby.

She tore the covers off the bed.

"Get the fuck out. NOW!"

Dave slid to a sitting position, legs akimbo, all flaps and folds and mounds of flesh.

"All right, all right. Don't lose your shit. I'm going." He groaned, throwing his feet to the floor.

"Damn right you're going." Dorris sneered.

After that, the usual screeching and cursing that Dorris had done with Jonathan went on for a while between the two of them as Dave dressed. Dorris did all the screeching, while Dave merely grunted a series of nasty, half-inaudible asides as he searched for his clothes and other accumulated belongings under and around the furniture. He threw everything into a couple of pillowcases and walked out without a parting shot or even a glance in Dorris's direction, as if he'd just had the sudden urge to do some spring cleaning and had forgotten that Dorris was even there.

Dorris collapsed in a heap on the floor in the pile of covers she'd ripped from the bed, wailing herself senseless until, exhausted, she fell into a juddering trance and finally a leaden sleep. At some point later in the evening,

I checked the monitor again and saw that Miriam had joined her, spooned in on the near side.

As expected, the reply from Iris Gray was prompt. Friend request acceptance accepted. Then an invitation to chat on the IM. The lower right-hand corner of the screen popped up.

"Hello."

I obliged.

"Hello."

"Thank you for accepting my request. I know the subject is touchy, but I needed to get your attention."

"So you have it. Now what?"

There was a long pause on the other end, so I opened a file in Word to keep a transcript. Here's how it went.

Iris: "Now we get acquainted."

"I'm not in the mood to dance," I replied.

"So don't dance."

Long pause. I could think of nothing to say to this. Then Iris again.

"Talk to me."

"I am."

Pause again. Then me again.

"I don't like being manipulated."

"I'm not manipulating you. There was no other way."

"Why no other way?"

"Because you had to see for yourself."

"What did I have to see?"

"The notes. The evidence. The handwriting."

"And why did I have to see it?"

"Because you wouldn't have believed me."

"You don't know that. And now I don't know what to believe."

"Maybe not, but trust me, this was the kindest way."

"What do you mean, the kindest way?"

"The kindest way to tell you. To show you."

"Yeah, well, trust me, it's not kind."

"None of this will be easy. You've been through a lot. I know that."

"Then why not leave me alone?"

"Because you want to know."

"Know what?"

"What I have to tell you."

"Then just tell me. I told you I didn't want to dance."

"I will tell you. But slowly. There's a lot to know, and it will take time."

"I'd rather just have it out and over with."

"It will be, eventually. But not all at once."

"Who are you to decide what I should know when?"

"I'm trying to help you."

"Or fuck with me. How do I know you know anything worth knowing?"

"It's not a question of worth."

"So you don't want money?"

"God, no! Whatever gave you that idea?"

"Money to destroy the evidence. Seems pretty straightforward to me."

"The evidence belongs to me. I will never destroy it."

"Then what's the fucking point?"

"I told you. You needed to know. You deserve to know."

"Or maybe there's nothing to know, and you're just having fun at my expense."

"Calm down."

"Fuck you. You plant crazy notes trying to frame me for something horrible, and you expect me to be calm."

"No one's framing anyone. Relax."

"I say again. Fuck you."

"I think you may be confused."

"Uh. Negative, asshole. Not confused. Just really, really pissed off."

"Don't be. Look, Nick. The notes can't harm you. But you have to go slowly."

"How about I rip out your liver slowly?"

"In the end, if that's what you want, then be my guest. Maybe I deserve it. But just hear me out."

"Then fucking talk."

"I am. I will. But you're going to have to trust me."

"I will never trust you."

"That wasn't a request."

And that's where Iris blipped out. I sent three or four more stabs, but no answer. Just the slow blinking of the cursor. Black on white.

About an hour later I got a message in my inbox. It said: "I'll be in touch. Trust me."

Goddamned manipulative son of a bitch.

I have no choice.

Since he'd started seeing Dorris, Dave hadn't been at his place much, but now, after the Heimlich maneuver and its aftermath, he was back to his old ways. Homebody nothin' doin', holed up in his home theater smoking dope and watching movies so bad they'd gone straight to video unrated, and so loud and grossly special-effected they made the house beams shake.

I knew him in this mode. Had been there, asphyxiated by my own brown breath, sealed tight in his subbasement, and buffeted borderline retarded by the sound track of *Demoniad III: The Pains of Hell* booming at me through five channels. That entertainment center was like something out of *A Clockwork Orange*, and Dave in it was like something out of Kafka, or a cheeky commercial for pest control: a giant roach smoking a roach.

I knew what he was doing even if I couldn't always see it—the cameras were still upstairs in the Sanizephyr and the antiquated DVD, which Dave now used exclusively for nightcap porn. But I knew what Dave was doing because I knew Dave. He wasn't complicated. He was lying back and letting Mama Kitty lick his wounds for him, because tongue therapy with Mommy was all bonking Dorris had ever been about. Mama Kitty was the first whore. There would never be another. He'd lie in her smothering embrace for a while longer, and then he'd be back out in the scene, looking for her next epigone.

I was making bets on how long it was going to take for my doorbell to start ringing again. Either that or I'd see him at the Swan with his nose in a pint of pale ale and his dick in a sling, blubbering to himself like an old hobo about the great injustices of the world and the cold treachery of womankind.

Most of us drink to make the rest of the world palatable to us, but Dave drank to make himself palatable to others. He figured, rightly as it turned out, that his cerebrum was only sophisticated enough to chew gum or walk down the street, not the idiomatic two at once. Thus, if he was drunk—language center compromised, motor function deranged—all his remaining brainpower would be given over to trivia—standing, leaning, bringing glass to lips—and he'd be constitutionally incapable of insulting anyone or, in fact, of doing anything more injurious (to himself or others) than braying at passersby in the parking lot. And that, only if he wasn't simultaneously taking a piss.

That was the mistake he'd made with Dorris. He'd let slip a clearheaded lacuna between bouts of effortful dishevelment and—*whomp!*—out had flopped Little Lord Schnastypants with his parasitic twin Ignoramus attached, and the honeymoon was over. The workings of Dave's mind were revealed, and the horror of recognition dumped in Dorris's lap like a placenta.

There Dorris, having lapsed carelessly into sobriety herself, beheld all at once the full and terrible form of the hydra-headed shegetz in her bed and, what's more, the clear and present danger he posed to her ten-year-old female child, whom, she then realized, he regarded as little more than a junior hole.

She'd known, of course, about Jack Gordon et al's treatment at Dave's hands all those years ago, and the insidious ramifications thereof—never forget!—but she'd convinced herself that the skinhead had grown out his hair, had hung his Bova boots in the garage, had expunged the offending hieroglyph from the epidermis of his left deltoid, what have you. He'd changed. She herself had changed him by the very fact of their congress.

Besides, as she told herself in the mirror when the weak-signaled distress calls of her conscience could sometimes be heard above the brainstorm of alcohol and drugs, assuaging her lust with one of the unbrissed was really no worse than succumbing to the occasional BLT.

Is it any wonder then that the dawning of sense came down so hard and heavy on them both? Or so quickly? It saw its chance and it took it. Two sots sober at the same time and so much—shall we say *cultural*?—volatility between them. It was like a critical imbalance of nature rectifying itself with a bang. The ill-fated strike of lightning undone the second time around.

"Phew!" said God and all the angels when it was done. "That was a close fucking call."

And it was, too.

Better to have Dave back at the Swan or in his basement debilitating himself—in either case, for the public good.

Alternatively, his keeping would be back on me.

A reluctant brother.

But, *ach*, I tell myself.

Don't fight it.

This is all part of the punishment.

But Miriam. I felt responsible for her. And something else, too. Drawn, I suppose. Curious in a way that made me squirm and still suspect that there was some truth to what Dorris and Dave had accused me of, even if Miriam herself had denied it. Maybe it wasn't the truth of having violated or coveted her, or even of having attempted however ineptly to seduce her that drunken night while Dave and Dorris were safely out of eye and earshot in the kitchen.

But there has been more contact since then.

I confess.

Although I do not know how to feel about it.

My clearest time of day—I've said—is late afternoon when I am writing this and prodding myself to life with all the iridescent gels and syrups of the convenience store and the galloping black bile of the barista.

As cruel coincidence would have it—this is also just about the time of day when those straggling dribs and drabs of public schoolers are taking their ill-advised and too entitled shortcuts home across the backyards of iffy neighbors like me. School must be out by now for summer, or very close, and remedial courses begun. Most kids are playing video games all day at this time, or watching movies, or heading off to camp.

But not Miriam.

She bows beneath the burden of her book bag, eyes on her feet. She knows the way so well. She cuts down the property line between Gruber and me, having crossed the main road behind my house and crept into the subdivision the back way through a door of loose planks in my fencing.

I've gotten so I can time this, three forty-five or thereabouts, sitting at the table in the kitchen, sipping, eyes over the brim, scanning for the sneakered foot, skinny leg, half-girl to slide through the slit of pine picket and out, full body, into view.

She lingers under the apple tree sampling the new-sprung fruit. Finding it sour, she stomps the rottens on the ground instead, if there are any so early in the year. She likes the way they splat and flatten into cakes that she can pick up and fling.

She finds a clear spot and sits. She has a family of dolls in her bag, which she removes and assembles in the grass, tilting them on their stiff legs to make them speak: whole listing, jerking conversations, back and forth, right hand to left hand and left to right, her face giving wild expression to their dance.

She looks up at the house occasionally, but sees nothing. Or I think she sees nothing, because her expression does not change. The mouth is a weak bow of longing and the eyes are like caves in her face. She stares, she scans the sun-blazed windows of the house for movement, as if they, too, are un-fathomable eyes, and then, downcast, she goes back to what she is doing.

The dolls tussle and shout, throwing stiff-limbed punches and kicks, hurling insults in Miriam's voice. Then, abruptly, they stop, and Miriam sits breathing, holding the figures apart. Slowly, slowly they come together, and there is the relief of an embrace, the rigid heads unmeeting, the cartwheeled arms and legs turning on the dry axis of the chests grinding like the foci of five-pointed stars.

And then there are tears coming down her face, washes of them in sheets. Her cheeks and chin glisten. Her lungs sputter and protest like flustered wings in the cage of her chest, and a rain of sputum comes down in front of her.

It must tell you everything about me that I do not go to her then. That I do not open the door and go out and take her in my arms and cradle her to calm. Not as many times as I have seen it. I have not gone.

Instead I sit in fascination, the live picture framed in the window, so perfectly real, this interior life outside, for me, and voluntary. A prayer, a sacrifice, a ritual. It is the doing and the loneliness that count, and would make no sense if someone answered.

She leaves me offerings, or arts. A fallen starling, so softly dead, rung round with wreaths of berries and branches and sprigs of greens and dandelion. A trail of pebble cairns leads to a small trench, furrowed by dirty fingers, and in it there are figures she has fashioned out of sticks and bundled grass. They are gathered over plates and cups made of wrappers, bottle caps, and broken glass.

As I watch her there on the ground, crouched small, assiduous, answering the urge, so female, to make her plastic figurines enact relationships and eat and drink from tea sets made of trash, I wonder what it is to be a girl, vulnerable for life, who will never grow into a form that can protect her from the prying eyes and minds of men like me. She is what she will always be in this world, an animator by craft, a greenhorn yearning in a dry world to wring emotion from dead things.

And I am what I have always been, a vacuum of personality sucking its only substance through the holes in its skull. What I have seen, what I have heard, I am. The pastiche of stolen words and pictures that belong to other people and places has become the hodgepodge of me. Things observed, overheard, remembered wrong. Things that I do not even understand are there in me, sewn in, waving in the wind of an inspection, saying: This guy has absolutely no idea who he is. He's made it all up, and I'm the proof of it.

You cannot expect such a person to go saving people, fantasies of same notwithstanding, even when the drowning man in question is a little girl crying her pipes out in his backyard and leaving handicrafted signals of distress in every bush and cranny. He simply cannot help. He cannot act, because that is information going in the wrong direction—out—when he is only ever taking in, absorbing, copying—and that, poorly.

It's no good.

I'm not going to *do* anything.

And yet I watch. I wait for her and I watch, and I think she knows I'm watching. Yes, she knows. Of course she knows. We are communicating, if only in the deferred language of objects.

I put a crow's feather upright in the ground at the head of her starling, and a canopy of bright leaves over her tea party. I put the print of my hand in a clearing of soil at the base of the apple tree, and beside it she puts the print of her own.

Back at Facebook, I've been waiting on Iris. Waiting for his information, if he has any.

Over and over, I've kept thinking about what he said.

"You needed to know. You deserve to know."

Deserve?

"Deserve" was not a word I would have expected from an extortionist, or even a whistle-blower for that matter, unless it was followed by the words "to die" or "to be gang-raped in prison like the rest of your chicken-hawking kind."

I mean, it's weird. This guy thinks he's got me on child rape, right? So why is he taking care of me, or seeming to? Why take the "kindest way"? And if I'm the author of these notes, then what could he tell me that I don't already know? He doesn't know I'm blocked on the memory. Yet he said, "I think you may be confused." Confused how? Confused as in, you, wretched pedophile, caught in the grip of your monstrous perversion, aren't thinking straight. You don't know that little girls are not for the taking. You can't see the right way. So now I, equalizer/vigilante therapist, am here to set you straight. Was that it? Or was he using "confused" euphemistically, like some hit man in a gangster movie as the prelude to a really ugly move? As in, let me help you get clear here, pal. The ground rules are these. *Snap.*

And yet he said I could torture *him* in the end if that's what I wanted. So how does that make any sense?

There's nothing to do but wait.

And trust.

I can see the appeal of letting myself fall into someone else's hands, advisedly or not. It doesn't matter. The slipping feeling, the ease of it is intoxicating in a new way. To be led blindly and not to resist. To exercise no choice but this one. To follow. And after that, all the following is done without thinking. It simply proceeds, like water flowing through channels, finding the weak points and carving new ones very slowly, unnoticeably, without pain, until there is a gash of its passage through rock.

I recognize in this the appeal of my sexual past as expressed in my body through sport. There is, of course, the surge of victory, of domination, which we are all supposed to be in it for. The win. But there is something incredibly erotic in a loss, especially a loss that is delivered on the other end, as in tennis, with balletic ease. The volleyer praised for his touch and his soft hands places the ball in the corners, an elegant slice, a curt punch, and the running man on the baseline, all feet, scampering, desperate, outpaced by a sliding, taunting, floating untouchable shot.

Put that way, I accept. Fully now, without caveat, I accept.

I will be led and—laughing now at this next bit—pummeled softly.

How dime-store is that?

16

It's not that I care that Monica's a thief. I don't.

Good for her. She's making a living outside the system, as she would say, but within it. She's solved the modern problem of life. People work to earn to live, but either they work so much that they have no life and no leisure time to spend and enjoy what they earn, or they earn too little to afford anything good in the free time they have.

If they have kids, they have no free time either way, and all monies go toward maintaining the untenable working parent lifestyle. Modern man and woman are enslaved, whether at home or in the office or both. Their entire lives are spent trying to bring about something that never materializes—a gulp of air, a moment of rest—and they die having achieved and enjoyed nothing.

That is, unless they cheat, or are very, very lucky. It used to be said of the underclass that they preferred welfare, because why work at a shit job eight or ten hours a day for bare sustenance? At least on the dole or selling drugs you have a life—or can have one, can spend time alone, can even spend quality time with your kids. Imagine that? But nowadays the same can be and is said of the middle and upper middle classes as well. Everyone is living on the red line of sustenance, and sustenance of what? A crowded, work-suffused, sleep-deprived, leisure-free nonlife in which all desires and personal satisfactions are firmly sublimated until they pop out like hernia, in the form of extramarital affairs and tax evasion, teenage kids in dog crates, fat men in fetish wear, little girls in the crosshairs, and guys watching the whole thing on video.

No, I couldn't judge Monica. I admired her. She had said no to the social contract right up front. She hadn't shaken meekly on the terms and gone about shuffling her feet like the rest of us, just waiting for that secret moment to transgress. Her whole life was a transgression.

Perfectly consistent.

A house of lies.

And yet within that antimatter, something of its opposite managed to exist. There was substance in the core of the illusion, substance created by and dependent on the illusion, but not itself of it.

In this, I could see my mother again so clearly. Exactly this quality, this technique. Substance from absence. A complexity of personality so fine, so delicate, so elusive, eliciting a collector's fascination. Disbelief. How is it made? Reaching in—there is something there, I see it—and grasping nothing.

But Monica was different in one key respect. She was living in the world on her own terms, whereas my mother had capitulated to tradition. To her, the word "wife" was an execration, and "MOM" was exactly what it looked like on the page in caps: a yawning maw between spread legs or, as she so bitterly put it, "the opposite of WOW."

Diana Walsh did what was expected of her. She followed the rules, and then she cheated with booze. And in so doing, I ask you: Did she do more or less damage than Monica?

Stupid question.

I mean, who is the real anarchist here? The petty thief siphoning a pittance off the system? Or the wife and mother knocking the knees out from under the next generation?

Monica wasn't belittling a toddler somewhere, or beating or raping or stabbing one of her own at home with the very hands that were supposed to be caring for it. She wasn't warping minds irreparably with the unmatched omnipotence of a mommy or a daddy in those first five years of life. She was nothing. Not even a threat.

You want to destroy a civilization? You don't do it by taking to the streets and banging down doors, or by living outside the system and making balaclavaed forays in.

You do it in the living room and at the kitchen table. You do it in all those irretrievable moments when a person is made, when all manner of freaks are coached into their freaky being by people who are doing only what is expected of them.

Nothing is as radical as normal. I'm telling you. Fucking nothing.

Which, I guess, is why Monica made me feel safe, and why her association with Damian or any other underworld characters wasn't much cause for concern. It was just one more thing we had in common, and maybe one more thing that would make it easier for Monica to accept me once she knew everything. When she found out about the spying and this journal, if she hadn't already, she would have to see it as my cheat, and so, presumably, she would understand it.

Maybe she would take or was already taking refuge in my transgressions, just as I was taking a paradoxical kind of refuge in hers. She was a floating tent to me, and so maybe to her I was a cozy cesspool. I would have put that description on Facebook if I'd had the balls. It was the truest thing you could say about me, but it would take a person as untethered as Monica to accept it.

Would she ask me to change? Would I ask her? Wasn't that always the mistake?

Stop thinking, Nick, and it will fall into place.

No. That's wrong.

Something else.

The program is all upside down and backward.

So let it be.

Let her know everything.

And then what?

Then see.

Just sit back and see what happens.

At our tennis game Jeff was his usual self. Reticent but pliable if you cared to work at it. And this time I did. I felt like kicking him in the head, not so much because of what I thought he was probably doing to me, but because I wanted to see him surprised by pain.

He was far too controlled and prepared. I wanted to get something spontaneous.

With most people, this would have worked. Problem was, pain was too much a regular part of Jeff's life in his father's house. A random boot to the bean wouldn't have surprised him at all. He had a mask for that, too.

But this was a changed world for me. The world of everything upside down and backward. I was thinking in a whole new way.

We were sitting side by side in the lounge at the club, sprawled across a couple of those shapeless low-slung armchairs off in a corner away from the

TV. I'd brought some beer and coaxed Jeff into having a couple. In this, he was unusually amenable, seeming not to mind or much resist, for once, my insistence that he join me.

"How's life at home?" I asked.

"The same," he murmured.

"Meaning what?" I prodded. I wasn't going to let him retreat into monosyllables again. "Your older brother's still a psycho, your younger brother's still on death row, and you're doing your best to make yourself invisible, just like your mom?"

He looked at me, surprised, then returned to peeling the label off his bottle of beer.

"Pretty much," he said.

"Yeah, well, guess what?" I continued. "Life's about to change."

"How do you mean?"

"I mean you and I are going to talk for once, maybe even act if we really get crazy."

"Act how?"

"I don't know. You tell me. How do you act?"

"Like this," he said, throwing up his hands. "You know. I don't."

"No, I'm not sure I do know. I know that you mope around and you look moody like every teenage guy who can get his dick sucked, but beyond that you're a blank, and that's starting to worry me, frankly. Nobody's *that* blank, and it's always the quiet ones who're the worst. They're always the ones who turn out to be conducting experiments on small animals and homeless people in abandoned warehouses. You know what I mean?"

"Yeah, I know what you mean," he replied, too knowingly.

"So?"

"So?"

"So what's your sideline? Are you doing dental work on house cats, or dropping burning bags of shit into the pretty royal blue mail collection box outside Kroger's?"

"Someone did that?" he said.

"Yeah, a few weeks back," I lied. "It was in the papers. Didn't you hear?"

"No."

"Some kids, they think, on a dare. Lit all the mail on fire, blew open the swinging door with all the gas buildup, and blew the shit with it. Talk about a dirty bomb."

I laughed.

Jeff didn't.

"Come on," I said. "You've never done anything like that?"

"Hell, no. You know what my dad's like."

"Yeah, I do. And the apple doesn't fall far from the tree."

"What does that mean?"

"It means your dad is unhinged, and your oldest brother is, too. Your little brother's well on his way to certifiable. Christ, it's like pattern baldness with you people, except it comes through the dad. Fucking congenital. And then, well, life in the compound just makes it a sure thing, doesn't it? Nature-nurture one-two punch?"

Jeff took a long swig of beer, but said nothing.

I took a long swig, too, for lubrication of the mood. I could feel the flow of meanness rising in my throat and the splash in the back of my brain.

"Or are you gonna tell me that you're the anomaly? You'll break the mold?"

"I will never be like my father," he said, "if that's what you mean. Never."

"Why's that? Because you study hard and you're athlete of the year? You think you can work your way out of your genes?"

I knew as soon as I said it that this was the wrong thing to say. I doubt he even knew what I meant. His mind was like a maze, full of walls and dead ends. He would simply stop if the stimulus was off, if he was too frightened, or bored, or confused. I was going to have to thread my way through blind, by feel.

The heat in my thoughts had fallen, too, the rush of cruelty having slackened with the miss.

That would be my guide. Could I feel myself hurting him, feel my progress inside his head, hand over hand? I would know by my own measure the correlation, proportionally direct, of my pleasure to his weakness: one to one.

We sat in silence for a while and I knew I was losing him, but I couldn't see where to strike. Where was the way in? How would I get him to show me what he was hiding, if anything? Or was he really that blank after all? I was watching him closely, staring in a hostile, predatory way, but he was too shy to look up, too accustomed to shutting down, and too blunted by brute force to notice the subtlety of another person's need to violate in thought.

The idea of scanning for a person's emotional vulnerability—seeking it out in the armature of their defenses, finding it, and sticking it, just there, like a beetle on a board, and watching with almost sexual pleasure as the legs curled and squirmed around the insult—that would probably never occur to someone like Jeff. Unless? Unless he was that rarest of breeds, the seamless sociopath, a machine of damage, all brushed stainless steel on the outside and all ripping rapier blades on the inside, dicing livers, hearts, and souls without spilling a drop.

A chilling thought, but a useful one. I was thinking about surfaces. Perfect surfaces. And I was looking at Jeff's face.

And that's when I saw it. Right there. So obvious. So bare. Of course. The thing they all had in common, all three boys, the thing that was so blindingly apparent in them and, for that reason, almost always overlooked. You had to be a stranger to see it. If you'd known them all their lives, you took it as much for granted as they did. But if you knew them the way I knew them, if you knew Gruber, you knew that it was the only untried point of attack, the blindside all out in the open where even the old man had never thought to hit.

It was the one blow that Jeff—that any Gruber—wouldn't see coming. He'd fold into it like dough around a baker's fist, because he wouldn't know that it was violence until it was too late.

I was looking at Jeff's head. His blunt, bent, blond head, straight nose, full lips, cut jaw, loose curls, like something on a Roman coin, the coloration gold and rose and cameo—absurd—and the russet framing stubble around the mouth and chin. Ridiculous. You gorgeous motherfucker, I thought. Right there. Right fucking there.

And it was true. I haven't even said it here. In all this time, I haven't even thought to mention it, but they were all like that. All three of them. Gorgeous motherfuckers. Blond, blue-eyed, bold-featured, lean, and strong: a goddamned gift basket of dick. Just the gang of choirboys you'd pay to pull a train on you. They were that unreal. You'd see them running up the street beside Gruber at six in the morning like flanking cherubim with the sun coming up in their hair and their long, limber legs striding, and you'd think that the apocalypse was upon you, and hallelujah, it was hung like a horse.

You thought it, and you didn't. And then they were just those kids across the street again, taking their arresting beauty in stride.

The Grubers had a black housekeeper for a while, who had a less reverent way of putting it. She called them Snap, Crackle, and Pop. If Mom could have seen them like this, all grown up and shining, she'd have had a snide one for it, too, like: "Ah, twice blessed, it's the three graces in drag."

Yes, you're beautiful, I thought, and that's it. That's exactly it.

Had I said it out loud?

I must have, because Jeff put down his beer and made a move to get up.

"Where you going, big guy?" I said, grabbing hold of his knee.

"Somewhere else," he said. "This is the wrong place for this conversation."

His tone was stern but strangely intimate as well. The flattery had penetrated. The target pinged.

Hang on, I thought. You have him.

Hang on. Just a little longer.

Carefully, gently, I put my hand on his shoulder.

"Jeff," I said. "Jeff, don't go."

A pause.

"Talk to me," I pleaded.

Would he recognize the phrase?

Talk to me.

So girlish.

You fucking little bitch.

He coughed, embarrassed, and covered his mouth with his hand. I felt him tense and then release beneath my fingers.

Move now, I thought. Quickly.

I slid my hand to the back of his neck, my thumb pressing around the side, over the rope of muscle, and past to the soft, pulsing groove of skin and vein where the life would let out if you sliced it.

Just there where the blood is thickest between the heart and the brain.

He closed his eyes and pushed a loud, heavy trumpeter's breath through his lips, his cheeks inflated then collapsed.

And I felt the answering sting in my intention.

With my free hand I seized my beer and finished it. I reached across and finished the remainder of his. I pulled a fresh one from my bag and handed it to him.

"Here," I said. "It helps."

He grasped it, twisted off the cap, and took a long, nervous series of gulps. Wiping his lips with the sleeve of his sweatshirt, he said, "Thanks."

His hands were trembling.

There, I said again to myself. There is your permission. Steady now. Breathe.

A surgeon's touch. Is cold and clean.

Shhhh. Breathe.

I slid out of my chair to the floor. On my knees.

Careful. Careful.

Under.

Just under the trip wire.

And clear.

Clear on the other side.

I crept closer.

My knees against his foot, my chest against his knee, patella to solar plexus, prie-dieu.

My hand, my right hand, was still there on the nape of his neck, cupping, supple, yet firm, contracting, the soft spot where the will would relinquish.

"I'm sorry, man. I'm sorry," I whispered.

Squeeze.

He dropped his head. Chin to chest.

Low over his lap. The lips slack.

I leaned in, my thumb still pressing beneath the ear, my fingers curling on the other side. Just tight. The heel of my hand full contact, the base of the skull. Soft cell where the spine goes in.

Wait.

Just there.

And now?

And yet.

Another pause.

What?

Is this the smooth transgression I intend? The scarring of a face with teeth?

I opened my mouth to do it.

I leaned in.

And I *was* going to bite him.

I really was.

But the art comes through on its own.

No warning.

It does not obey intention.

The world is upside down and backward, Judas, said the voice in my head. So kiss.

Soft sell.

Soft shell.

Cracking.

King's pawn to king's pawn
Is pawn to pawn.
Sliding felt over lacquer.
And clack.
The pieces fall.
Sliding tongue over teeth.
Then clack.
Teeth to teeth.
The pieces.
Fall.
They fall, as master and disciple, as killer and wife, with a kiss.
And so a conjugation.
I kissed. He kissed. We kissed.
I kissed thee ere I killed thee.
But no matter.
I left no trace.
These acts are only ever in the mind, whatever the mess on the floor.
Am I right, Mother?

How much time passes in a kiss?

How much information?

Who has any way of knowing from the inside, where time and information are both the same and both immeasurable? When an act is an act in the mind, the motion hardly matters and the means of calculation are all awry.

Jeff tasted like acne. Suppurating acne and its corrective cream, like caulking and the pith of a black banana. He did. And he tasted of malt and the hops and the sugar in the beer with a bit of bleeding gums at the back, like the finish on a tannin-steeped wine or the harsh in a macerated cherry.

They were not flavors I knew intimately.

He was not one of my ghosts.

Jeff stood abruptly and reached for his bag.

I stood, too.

"Face-to-face not your style?" I grunted, tripping slightly on the chair.

"What?" He stopped. "No. What are you talking about?"

"I'm talking about Facebook, asshole," I shouted.

A doubles posse of old men in sweat suits sitting by the TV turned briefly and looked in our direction, shrugged, and looked away.

"Facebook?" Jeff said. He looked frightened.

"Yeah, Facebook. You use it, don't you?"

"Everybody uses it. So what? God's sake! What are you talking about?"

Committed now, I thought. Just pull.

"I know that you've still got that bird in your house, Jeff," I hissed.

A cramp of puzzlement made its way across his face, then the slackness of dumb fear.

"How—?" He broke off, shouldered his bag abruptly, and pushed past me into the lounge. Striding fast, he kicked open the double glass doors to the parking lot and walked out of the club.

I left my bag and followed, running.

I caught up with him at his car. I grabbed him by the collar of his track jacket and tried to pull him down, but he was surprisingly strong. He took hold of my wrists and squeezed until I lost my grip, shoving me back against the adjacent car and leaning into me with all his weight. He butted his forehead against mine and held us together, bone on bone, his mouth tearing into the rictus of a silent scream, his eyes squeezing shut.

He held us there, sobbing openmouthed, tendrils of drool shuddering between his lips, his hands shaking violently now, seeming to scramble to my shoulders for support, then, at last, falling to his side as he himself fell back against his car, his head canting backward onto the roof.

He took a deep, frightened breath, his eyes searching the sky, his head loose-necked and lolling. Then he reached for the door handle behind him, and in one swift motion rolled himself into the car, slammed and locked the door, pulled out and away.

His bag lay forgotten on the pavement.

When I got in tonight there was a note from Iris in my inbox. "Chat at midnight," it said.

So there I was at midnight waiting with my Word document open, ready to copy and paste.

At twelve oh two a.m., a blip.

Chat box up.

"You there?"

"Yep."

"Good."

A pause.

"I'm going to help you to trust me now."

What the hell do you say to that?

"OK," I typed, then erased it. Too passive.

"Fine," I typed, then erased it. Too bitchy.

Finally, I settled on his word.

"Good."

Another longer pause. Then:

"She is as in a field a silken tent."

"What?"

"At midday when the sunny summer breeze has dried the dew."

Oh, gimme a fucking break with this shit already.

"And all its ropes relent."

"I'm not doing this," I typed.

He went on.

"So that in guys it gently sways at ease."

"I'm signing off if you keep this up."

"And its supporting central cedar pole,

"That is its pinnacle to heavenward."

And then I recognized it.

Of course.

The Frost poem. He was reciting the Frost poem.

Such a dolt.

Furious typing.

"I already know you've got that bird, asshole."

This shut him up for a minute.

Then: "Ah, so that's who you think I am. I see now."

"Right, so can we stop the crap already?"

"Nick, Iris doesn't know the whole poem."

"Maybe not, but Google does."

Another short pause. Then from Iris:

"You had to Google it, huh?"

I said nothing to this. I was done. I was moving my hand to quit Facebook when one more transmission made it through.

"Your mother would have been so disappointed."

17

Trust me.

I'm going to help you to trust me, he'd said.

But what can that really mean?

What helps me or anyone to trust another person?

Knowing their secrets? Knowing who they are? Where they've been? What they're capable of? What they've done in the past and so are likely to do now? Knowing them all your life?

Ha.

We trust people on these bases all the time, but they are false bases. There is nothing to them. And at some level we know this, or, perhaps if we are less lucky, we are at one time or another confronted with the shattering betrayal that forces us to know it.

There is no knowing someone well enough to trust them. Ever.

Because the knowledge involved is of the wrong kind. Inductive knowledge, which is really just belief. Nothing more. I believe that such and such will happen in this particular way in the future, because it has always happened that way in the past. Induction.

That is trust for most of us, trust not just in people, but in the whole way of the world—trust, as the philosophers said, that the sun will rise tomorrow, that the ground will hold us upright, and that the green piece of paper that says ONE DOLLAR has a dollar's worth of gold behind it in the treasury. In God we trust.

In trust we trust.

It's nothing.

You see?

But the person who is Iris Gray knows different.

That person knows that there is only one kind of real trust: the trust based on self-betrayal.

This is my standard, and he shares it. It is his standard as well.

It goes like this.

I know that a person is telling the truth only when it costs him something to tell it, when it goes against his interests, or his pride, or his vanity. Only when all other possible reasons—the self-interested reasons—are exhausted, and there is nothing left but the vulnerability, or the shame, or the risk of a person having disclosed something he should not have—only then can I believe that what I am hearing is the truth. Only then can I trust.

In betrayal I trust.

And so Iris unveils himself to me as an offering of trust, because his ano-nymity is the thing he values most, the thing he relinquishes, strange to say, most self-effacingly.

Iris and I share the same inverted principles, because Iris and I had the same teacher, the teacher, as Iris said, who would have been so very disap-pointed that I did not know the Frost poem off by heart.

Twelve sixteen a.m. The chat box was still open, and my index finger, poised above the Q for so long, had pulled back, retreated with my thumb from the command key, and hunkered, like a startled crab, on the desk.

Okay. The tests of trust. Betray yourself.

Prove that you are who I think you are.

A few easy ones first. The ones I did remember.

I typed.

"Hearts are not had as a gift . . ."

And the reply came quickly.

". . . but hearts are earned. By those that are not entirely beautiful."

Check.

Good.

Now again.

I typed.

"I have known the evenings, mornings, afternoons . . ."

Wait.

And blink.

Blink.

Blink.

Reply:
". . . I have measured out my life with coffee spoons."
Yes!
Check.
Okay.
Now the last one. The only one that only *she* would know.
"Nel mezzo del cammin di nostra vita . . ."
Come on.
Come on.
Be there.
Be her.
Blink. Blink. Blink.
Answer, damn it.
Answer.
Let this be true.
Let it be real.
Come on.
Come on.
Blink.
You know it.
You know it by heart.
Blink.
Don't be afraid.
Blink.
Then scroll.
". . . mi ritrovai per una selva oscura."
My God.
I fell back in the chair.
My God.
It's her. It's really her.
"She's alive."
I said it out loud.
"I don't believe it."
I slapped the desk with both hands.
And again in disbelief I said aloud: "It's really her."
Wait, wait.
One more time to be sure.

I typed.

"And the translator was . . . ?"

A smile emoticon appeared.

Blink.

:)

Then blink again:

"Robert Pinsky."

My fucking God.

Robin Bloom.

It really is Robin Bloom.

Twelve thirty-five a.m.

"Nick? . . . You still there?"

Pause.

"I'm here."

Blink.

"You okay?"

Count of five with the cursor.

Thinking.

One . . . two . . . three . . . four . . . five.

Then typing:

"I can't believe it's really you."

"I know, I know. I told you there was a lot."

I smiled, typing:

"The name and the male template were kinda stupid, though."

"Yeah, well, Facebook is kinda stupid, but it was the best way to reach you."

"You must know where I live."

"I wasn't going to show up at your door."

"Actually, I'm glad you didn't."

"You're welcome."

"But why not just write me as Robin Bloom?"

"Think about it, Nick. That's a stupid question."

"What? I don't see how."

"I don't want to be found. Even digitally."

"I think most people presumed you were dead."

"Right, and that's the way I want to keep it."

"Really?"

"Yes. Really."

"But there must be other Robin Blooms on Facebook. If you used a template, who would know you?"

"There are, but I don't want to be one of them."

"You'd rather be dead?"

"So to speak, yes."

I was stuck again with the full force of meeting her. I couldn't think of what else to say. There were so many things to ask, and all of them were huge and intrusive and not my place, but I wanted to know. I wanted to know everything there was to know about why she had left, where she had been, how she had survived, and why she hadn't come back. And then, of course, there was this whole business with the notes. What the fuck was that about? Why me? Why contact me? And why in this roundabout and—I still thought this—manipulative way?

Still, I was overjoyed. Meeting her again was like meeting myself or my twin. The connection was so strong, the shared past, but so was the estrangement, the divergent paths we had since taken. She was the only other person in the world who knew my mother as well as I did—maybe better—and that idea both thrilled and frightened me. It made me nauseatingly jealous, too, I realized, as if Robin somehow had the power to usurp my identity, my people, the emotional things that were mine.

I felt cruel suddenly, and angry.

"Do you know that your grandmother keeps a light in the window for you?"

No response.

"She lights it every night and puts it out every morning."

Still nothing.

"Don't you think it was bad enough for her to lose Karen? Losing you, too, was like death to her. Don't you think she has a right to know that you're all right?"

"Iris Gray is typing," said the prompt.

I waited.

Then the scroll advanced, a chunk of text appeared.

"Nick, you know nothing. When you know more, when you know the rest, you can give me your informed opinion. Until then, take my word for it, you don't know what you're talking about."

Something in me softened. I knew she was right. But I also felt loyal to the old woman across the street, the woman with whom I had shared probably the most pleasant, healing evening I'd passed since my parents' deaths.

"I saw her recently," I typed. "She actually looks great. She's a strong and wise old lady."

"I'm glad to hear that . . . It sounds like adversity has deepened her."

That's a shitty thing to say, I thought, but I wasn't in a position to say so, or to retaliate on Mrs. B.'s behalf. I'd spent an evening with the woman once in thirteen years, an edited evening, truth be told, in which we had both been on our best behavior despite our claims to being compassionately impolite. I would defer to Robin for now about the woman who had raised her.

"Why deepened her?" I asked. "Was she so shallow before?"

Pause.

"Simple," she replied.

Another pause. Then again:

"She was simple. One of the cookie-bakers, your mother would have said."

I laughed aloud. This was Robin for sure.

"Yeah, that's vintage Diana all right," I typed.

I laughed more and typed again:

"I can just hear her now: 'The Philistines are upon us, Mr. Lloyd.'"

"Laughing," Robin typed. "I loved that book."

"I hated it," I replied. "Total chick book, though, so no surprise."

"No way. *Emma* and *Pride and Prejudice* are chick books. *The Prime of Miss Jean Brodie* is for crones. Crones, through and through."

Now I was roaring. Typing with tears in my eyes.

"True, true. Bitter old crones. And young ones, too, I guess, huh?"

"Absolutely. I was born wizened, inside and out."

"And your grandmother wasn't."

"Nope. Not a bit."

"C'mon, she's a really nice lady," I replied. "Don't be so hard on her."

"Yes. Definitely. She was always that."

"So. Is that so bad?"

"No. I suppose not. Not always."

"But?"

"But nice can cover a multitude of sins."

I thought for a moment, remembering what Mrs. B. had said about the insult of good manners.

"It might surprise you to know that she said something very similar to me the other day."

Nothing.

"Robin?"

Pause.

"Look," I added. "She really does get it, you know. She knows that she never understood you. She knows that she didn't have what it took to nurture your intellect, or to make you really happy. But she tried. Surely not measuring up to you was not a sin?"

"I never said it was."

"So what was it then?"

Silence.

Oh, come on. Make your point if you're so sure of it.

"Robin?"

Still nothing.

Funny how you can feel a sulk through cyberspace, the other person pouting behind her screen, empowered by your having had the last word, rather than herself. You hang there in the white, your last transmission dangling, looking, as words isolated on a page so often do, stranger and stranger and more and more meaningless the longer you stare.

"Robin?"

"Yes. I'm here."

"Help me to understand."

"I'll try."

My turn. Ask again.

"So your grandmother wasn't a woman of the world. She didn't get you. Okay. But why is that a sin?"

Another pause.

I couldn't help it. I could feel the anger resurfacing.

"And don't ridicule simplicity of mind the way my mother would have, because that's just snobbery."

That got her.

"As far as I'm concerned, ridicule has nothing to do with it."

"So what, then?"

"It's just that simplemindedness can be a form of neglect."

"OK," I replied. "Explain."

Iris Gray is typing . . .

Scroll up.

"My grandmother saw what she wanted to see, which was the good and the easy and the nice, and the rest just didn't exist for her."

A pause. Then:

"She lived in denial."

Don't we all, I thought. Big deal. If that's the greatest sin you know about, Robin, then you've had it way too easy in life.

How could she? How could she say this to me? To *me*? My father had killed my mother and then himself in this very house, and had left me to live in the scene of the crime. Robin knew this. Every detail of it. Jesus. Denial—you must be kidding.

But I was the meek one who knew nothing, apparently, the rube confined to questions. I sent a controlled reply.

"But, Robin, what harm did that really do?"

More typing on her end.

"The people who lived in the towns outside the concentration camps lived in denial, Nick. Do you think that denial did any harm?"

I let loose then, growling at the screen in frustration as I typed.

"Oh, come on. I can't believe you just said that. That's absurd. Absolutely absurd."

"That depends on your perspective."

"Yeah, I'd say so, and I'm beginning to think that yours is more than a little warped."

"Of course it's warped. It's mine. But to each of us our pain is everything, especially when we're children."

"You're saying that your childhood was a holocaust?"

"Yes. To me it was."

Unbelievable. The woman was out of her mind.

"Pardon the intrusion of reality here, Robin, but I think that, in order to count, a holocaust has to have destroyed the lives of more than one person, and not just in her own mind."

"As I said, Nick. You know nothing."

Maybe, I thought. And maybe you're a crazy bitch.

"I know quite a lot, as I believe you are aware."

"Not nearly enough."

"Yeah, so you keep saying. We'll see."

"Yes. We will."

A long pause.

I was fuming now. The presumption of the woman.

Still there was the calmer voice in my head.

Take it easy, Nick. Take it easy. Get the information you want.

Typing.

"All right, all right. So you said you were going through something horrible."

"Yes."

"And your grandmother ignored it?"

"No. I said she denied it. She willfully didn't see it."

"So you think she knew and didn't want to know, is that it?"

"Let's just stick with our metaphor—she told herself that the inch of ash on the windowsill was from a fire at the chemical plant down the way, and that the smell of burning flesh was a potato blight."

"So there were indications and she didn't see them. We all do that."

"No. You're not listening. There was evidence and she chose to explain it away."

"What evidence?"

No response.

Too soon for that, I knew.

Redirect.

"So now you think she deserves her suffering?"

"I think that she can handle her suffering and that it's not altogether a bad thing that she does."

I sat back in my chair flummoxed, my head swirling with ignorance, a hundred questions, a hundred angry retorts, raging curiosity—no, much more than that—a highly discomfiting need to know, and then horror, disapproval, indignation—all of it contained, I saw then, in one question.

I typed it very slowly, looked at it there on the screen for a long time, and then tapped a hesitant return.

"Robin, what happened to you?"

The question hung there for what seemed like several minutes or more, tacked to the scroll in the pop-up box, words on a screen, sent and landed.

What happened to you?

And the damned cursor at the end of it, flashing like an exclamation point, or a silent, taunting chime.

Blink. Blink. Blink.

What happened to you?

No response.

And still the words were there.

Too much all at once.

The words to sum up a life, perhaps a family. Her life, her grandmother's life, her grandfather's life, maybe even her long-dead mother's demise. The events that changed everything.

There was such a long, long pause on the answer. Time enough for me to regret the question many times over and to type numerous apologies and take backs and never minds, and then to erase them just as quickly.

I was beginning to think she had gone, when finally there came the leading Robinesque reply, the unsettling kind of answer that I was going to have to get used to.

"What happened to me, Nick?" she repeated.

A short pause.

Scroll up.

"The same thing that happened to you."

18

There was nothing of interest in Jeff's bag. An Ace bandage for his bum ankle, a can of spray for jock itch, a couple of bottles of Vitamin Water, two extra racquets, several packages of Tourna-Grip, three dirty white terry cloth wristbands, two pairs of athletic socks, a towel, and some loose change. Pretty straight up. Nothing of value except a set of his house keys, which I kept. The rest I tossed in a Dumpster behind the Dunkin' Donuts across the parking lot from the racquet club.

Poor guy. I felt bad for him now. Now that I knew he wasn't Iris Gray. He was going to be reliving our special moment over and over for the next few months, maybe the next few decades, either rapturously or torturously, depending on his turn of mind and his tendencies.

If he was gay, he'd never kissed a guy before, that was for sure. Even I knew that, and I'd never kissed a guy before, either. From the feel of it, I'd say he'd never kissed anything more animate than his own forearm while dreaming hot and wet of an at-long-last consummated amour.

Per the monitors, nothing had changed at the Grubers' in recent days. J.R. was still spouting at the breakfast table, quoting snatches of *Mein Kampf* and *The Protocols of the Elders of Zion* and raving about the great socialist conspiracy of the rainbow coalition as embodied, naturally, by President Obama, whom he referred to as B.O. or the Manchurian candidate and denounced as a puppet of North Korea.

Eric was still in his cage, though only one dry night away from freedom. He'd taken to consuming no liquids after noon, and no liquids whatsoever with caffeine or alcohol, or so he'd told Jeff over an especially gory game of *Grand Theft Auto* while reclining on the couch in the basement.

Jeff himself, also reclining and slaughtering virtual hookers willy-nilly with his right thumb, had upgraded from Vitamin Water and was drinking large quantities of the latest rip-roaring fitness drink, which I believe was called Ursa-Fuel Ultra. I'd seen it in the local GNC, had thought about trying it, but had read the label and passed. There was no mistaking it, though. It came in a Day-Glo yellow can with black lightning bolts on it. It was definitely not FDA approved (or even dreamt of), and was probably filled with all kinds of test-tube aminos that no one had even named yet. Its dubious claim to fame and most potent ingredient was alleged to be a derivative of polar bear bile—hence the name—which, when consumed in sufficient quantities, could "fortify" your metabolism (whatever that meant), presumably making you capable of digesting and extracting performance-enhancing nutrients from anything—including rusty nails, plywood, and concrete. Or something like that.

I guess that's what you do when you're a teenage guy in the suburban Midwest, your dad's a storm trooper, and you're afraid you might be gay. Not the reaction I'd expect, but not exactly a curveball, either. Sit back, drink yourself green with overdoses of creatine and B vitamins, and take out your aggressions on a video game.

I was as desperate for distraction as they were. It was four o'clock in the afternoon, I'd been up for only an hour, and I was already well into a fifth of Jameson.

I was obsessed by one thought.

Robin said there was evidence.

Evidence that her grandmother "chose to explain away."

I'm looking at the transcript of our chat, and that's what it says. That's the part she wouldn't answer.

What evidence?

There was only one place I could think of to go looking for it. Only one other person I could ask.

But how could I dare to do it? How could I intrude again on that poor woman's grief, and this time not to commiserate but, essentially, to accuse. Because that's what it would mean. Even just to ask about what might have happened to Robin, to ask about some alleged evidence of harm done to a child—that in itself was to judge, or at the very least dredge up the worst of the past. And yet, if Robin was telling the truth, we were now talking about my past, too.

The same thing that happened to you.

That's what she'd said.

Carefully chosen words.

Make me do the work. Make it matter to me. Take a man whose own past is a mystery to him, and make him believe you hold the key to it, make him believe that your story, true or not, is his story, too, and he will go running all over creation to find the answer, even though all he is really doing is playing out the family drama of a disturbed runaway looking to take revenge on an old woman. What better way to hurt her grandmother, justifiably or not, than by sending me over there to give the old woman the only piece of news that would hurt her more than the news she thinks she's already had?

Oh, yeah, don't mind me, Mrs. B., I'm just here on your doorstep once more, the bearer of bad news—again—here to tell you that—well, um—this may come as a bit of a shock—it being the last straw, camel's back trauma of your life and all—but, uh, well, you know that *thing*, that really awful *thing* that you thought you knew all these years? Yes, yes, that's the one, that dreadful conclusion you'd been forced to reach after going so long without hearing a word, and with which you've finally managed to make something approaching a separate peace—yes, precisely, the death of your granddaughter, thank you—well, as it turns out, you were wrong. We were all wrong. Your beloved granddaughter is, I'm pleased say—fate being what it is and all—your granddaughter is actually alive and, in a manner of speaking, well.

Physically well, I mean, or we think so anyway. We haven't seen her. Just chat room stuff, you know, typing back and forth, but she seems . . . uh . . . coherent, I guess you'd say, if a bit pissed off, and maybe a shade unreasonable, but that's to be expected after so long on the run, and really it's quite a miracle in a case like this to find— What's that? Oh, yes, yes, we're sure it's her. Yes. Absolutely sure. No question about it. We gave her the usual Dalai Lama tests and such, and she picked out all the right items, knew all the right quotations. No, there's no question it's her. Yep. Alive and kicking, as it were.

Anyway, we just thought you'd like to know, so that you can go about contemplating why she hasn't seen fit to contact you in all these years or to alleviate your suffering in any way—oh, and of course, first things first, so that you can stop putting that silly light in the window, eh? No point now, really, is there? Salt in the wound and all that.

Okay then, well, that's that. Message received. Damage done. My work is finished here, I think. Do take care, Mrs. Bloom. Yes, nice seeing you again, too, and on such a happy occasion. *Ta-da.*

Fuck me if I was going to go over there and abuse that woman, holocaust (small *h*) denier or not.

There had to be another way.

There just had to be.

And then I remembered.

Dave's conversation with Dorris about Miriam.

I was looking for evidence of abuse, right? Standard stuff—cuts, bruises, welts, maybe broken bones. Stuff, if it was bad enough, that a teacher might notice or, yes, a doctor might have to treat. A pediatrician. Dorris had said that Jonathan's profession was a small world. They all knew each other. It had been only thirteen years. Robin's doctor might still be around, maybe even still practicing. It was worth a shot.

Jonathan has his practice over on Mission Lake Road, and a tricked-out website to go with it, of course, so it wasn't difficult to get in touch.

"He's in surgery over at the hospital every morning until noon," said the receptionist. So I left a message with her saying it was an urgent private matter and if he could get back to me soon I'd be grateful.

He called back late that afternoon, probably out of curiosity more than anything else. What the hell is my ex-wife's neighbor doing calling me? he must have been thinking. Whatever he was expecting, it certainly wouldn't be about the long-lost Robin Bloom—he'd have known about her only tangentially, the same way Dorris knew about her, through the gossip mill, or maybe through some neighborly tea and sympathy session with Mrs. B. when they'd first moved into the neighborhood. Go and pay a visit to the sad old lady next door and bring a basket of fruit. Just the kind of thing she'd have hated.

He wasn't exactly chatty on the phone, but then, who knew what Dorris had told him about me.

"Nick, Jonathan Katz here. You left a message with my service."

"Yeah, yeah. I did. Thanks for calling me back so quickly. I appreciate it."

He was all business.

"Not a problem. What can I do for you?"

"Look, I know this will seem a little strange and out of the blue, but it's about my neighbor, and your old neighbor, Mrs. Bloom."

"Anita Bloom?"

"Yes."

"The widow?"

"Yeah. The one whose granddaughter disappeared thirteen years ago. Remember hearing about that?"

"Oh, jeez. Yeah, I do remember that. I was sick to death when I heard about it. What a thing. Terrible. They never solved it, right?"

"No. They've never found her. But that's the thing. See, Mrs. Bloom and I have gotten pretty close over the years, you know, with what happened to my parents and all, and she's asked me to look into things for her, keep an eye out, that sort of thing."

"Didn't the cops do all that years ago?"

"Yeah, but you know how that goes. By now it's essentially a closed case. Missing presumed dead. No leads. It's nothing formal between us, but she just asked me to look around, maybe follow a few different angles. She's getting old, and I think she wants to make one last push for closure."

"Why not hire a private detective?"

"Probably a money issue, but I think it's a privacy thing, too. She doesn't want to deal with a stranger. Besides, they did hire one years ago, right after it happened, while Mr. Bloom was still alive. Nothing substantive came up."

"So, I don't get it. Why are you calling me?"

"Well, here's the strange bit. I've come across some information that suggests there may have been some sort of abuse going on—maybe in the home—or maybe outside. Unclear."

"What do you mean by abuse?"

"Well, I'm not sure yet. It might be nothing—my source is a bit unorthodox . . ."

"You mean unreliable."

"Maybe. I don't know. You come across a lot of false leads and strange people in this kind of thing, people claiming to know things they don't."

"Yeah, I'm sure you do."

"But I gotta check it out. Thing is, I don't want to go to Mrs. Bloom with every piece of lint I pick up, especially when it's something really sensitive and possibly hurtful like this. Not until I know more, and not unless I have to."

"Sorry, Nick, but I'm still not getting you. What is it you don't want to go to her with?"

"I need to know the name of Robin Bloom's pediatrician. The one she would have seen thirteen or more years ago if she'd had a broken bone or

some other injuries that might have been a bit off the run, might have indicated she was being abused."

"Whoa, whoa. Wait a minute there, guy. Slow down. That's privileged information. I couldn't tell you even if I knew—which I don't, as it happens."

"But you work in the field. It's a small world, no?"

"It doesn't matter, Nick. Don't you get it? It would be highly unethical for
me to give you that information. Highly unethical."

"I'm just looking for a name. That's all."

"No, that's not all you're looking for, and even if I could get you the person's
name, he'd tell you the same thing I'm telling you. But in his or her case, it
would be illegal, not just unethical, to disclose the details of Robin Bloom's
medical history without her or her legal guardian's prior consent."

"Look, I know all that, and if it comes to that, if there's something in it, I
can probably get Mrs. Bloom's permission, or get someone who can get it—"

"Nick, I don't want to hear any more of this. Do you have any idea how
creepy you sound? I understand you're trying to do some good here, or you
think you are, but it's just wrong to go about it this way. I can't help you. I'm
sorry."

"Jonathan—wait, okay? I hear you. I really do, and I get what you're saying.
But I need to find out the truth here. I need it."

"I can see that, but it doesn't change anything from my perspective, I'm
afraid."

"She was a little girl, Jonathan. Can't you appreciate that? A crime may
have been committed and swept under the rug."

"Then go to the authorities."

"I can't. They wouldn't act on the questionable lead of a neighbor thirteen
years after the fact."

"You're right, so why would you expect me to?"

"Because it's personal."

"You're damn right it's personal. Personal to that poor girl, who is in all
likelihood dead, and personal to what's left of her family, which is one tortured old woman who's got enough to go to her grave with without you pil-
ing it on by the shovelful."

"But what if what I find could give her some peace?"

"That's hardly likely, and you know it. If you find anything at all, it'll be
something you won't want to tell her. You're already afraid to ask her for the

name, because you know that this can bring about no good. I don't even want
to know why you're so obsessed with this, but I can tell you that your story
sounds like a load of shit. I don't think Mrs. Bloom has asked for your help
at all, and I think my wing-nut ex-wife was actually right about something
for once. You're a sick, sad alcoholic, and you think your own suffering has
given you carte blanche to do whatever comes into your head. I'll tell you
this once, Nick. Leave it alone. Leave it be, and I'll forget we ever had this
conversation. And never, ever contact me or my wife again."

He hung up.

I was watching Eric keep vigil for what he hoped would be his last night in
the crate—there was no way he was going to let himself fall asleep—when
Jonathan called back. It was late, just past three. I was at the bottom of the
bottle of Jameson. Feelin' fine. Jonathan sounded sleepless and upset.

"Nick, Jonathan again."

I said nothing.

"I'm going to give you what you want."

"That's gracious of you," I slurred. "Why the sudden change of heart? Ethics flown with the night bird?"

"I've been up all night tossing over this. There's something on my conscience, and as much as I dislike you, I've decided that you may be the only
person reckless enough to do something about it."

"How's that?"

"Look, as it turns out, I've met the man you're looking for. I met him once
golfing at the club just a few weeks after Dorris and I moved into the neighborhood."

"Does he live in the neighborhood?"

"No, no. He just golfs at the same club. A lot of the docs do. You were right
about that—it's a small, tight circle in pediatrics out here. Anyway, I'm going
to make this short, so pay attention. I can tell you're well on your way to
oblivion, so get a pen."

"Hold on," I said, weaving my way upstairs to the study with the extension
in hand.

"Got it?" he said.

"Yep. Go."

"Okay. His name is Simon Cunningham. C-U-N-N-I-N-G-H-A-M. He's retired now, but he's in the book. Lives in Twin Pines, not in my section, but in one of the ones over the hill. Shouldn't be hard to find him. Otherwise you could probably still find him at the club."

"All right."

"Now, listen carefully. I want you to remember this. You may need it if you want him to talk to you."

"I'm listening."

"Good." He sighed, and I could hear him taking a long sip of something with ice in it. "So, as I said, when Dorris and I moved in a few years back, I met Simon at the club through some mutual friends. We played a round with a bunch of guys and had some drinks afterward. Simon and I got to talking and he asked me where I was living. When I told him, he asked me where specifically. Said he knew a lot of the people around there. When I said we were living next to the Blooms, he did what everyone does when that name comes up. He said how sad it was what had happened with their daughter and then their granddaughter. I've known that family for forty-five years, he said. Treated Karen when she was a baby. Treated Robin, too.

"He said this while we were still on the course and still sober, and he didn't say a lot for the rest of the round. He went very quiet and broody, which, again, I attributed to having brought up the Blooms. They're a downer for everyone, and he seemed to know them better than most. But later, in the lounge, after we'd had a few drinks, he said something completely out of nowhere that at the time didn't mean a whole lot to me but which now I can't stop thinking about. I just can't help believing that he was talking about the Blooms."

He took another drink and shifted his position. I could hear fabric rustling very close to the receiver, as if he were lying in bed or reclining on a couch adjusting pillows.

"So we were sitting in the lounge together drinking, and he said, 'Listen, Katz, remember something for me, will you?' He'd only known me for a few hours, mind you, and I'm a good thirty years younger than he is, but his tone of voice and the look on his face were uncomfortably intimate, as though he'd lost track of where he was and thought he was talking to a contemporary he'd known all his life. He paused for a long time, looking right into my eyes in the saddest, guiltiest way, like he wanted to confess something but couldn't bring himself to do it . . . Then he said something really odd."

Katz took another long drink and sighed heavily. His breath shushed loudly across the receiver.

"He said, 'Keep this in mind every day for the rest of the time you practice medicine. Do that for me, will you?' Sure, I said, of course . . . I figured, you know, placate an old man when he's drunk. Just let him say what he needs to say and move on."

"Makes sense," I said, leadingly.

Katz coughed and went on.

"So I said, 'What is it, Dr. Cunningham?' And then he said this thing that I couldn't forget even if I tried. Not even if I tried, and I have tried. He said: 'When you remember the oath you took, when you try to remain true to it in your practice, remember this. Sometimes the greater harm is done by doing nothing.'

"I must have looked very puzzled, because he added, 'What I mean to say is that your worst professional regrets—the ones that haunt you all your life—those are much less likely to revolve around the things you did than the things you failed to do.'

"He said that last bit while looking away, and it trailed off with his voice. He didn't say another word or even look at me for the rest of the evening. And that was it. I've never seen him since, and I've never, until now, quite understood what he meant. But I can't escape the feeling that he was talking about the Blooms, and by keeping silent myself, I can't help feeling that I am perpetuating whatever harm he felt he may have done to them by keeping silent in the first place."

"I see," I said.

"Maybe I'm all wrong on this—and I hope I am— but I just had to tell you. If it's nothing, then Simon will think what I thought—that you're a loose cannon and a lunatic, and he'll tell you to piss off. But if I'm not wrong, well, maybe he'll tell you something worth knowing, and maybe some of the harm can be undone. If that's the case, you might be right—something good can come out of it, if only peace of mind for some of those concerned."

I could hear him breathing and sipping again on the other end.

Finally, I said, "Thank you, Jonathan. I can't tell you how much this means."

"Don't thank me, damn you. This phone call never happened," he growled, and hung up.

I stayed up with Eric until five, when Gruber hauled him out clean and slapped him across the face like a Jewish mother when her daughter gets her period. Welcome to the pains of life, fella. Good job.

I stared at the name on the piece of paper in front of me. Simon Cunningham. Katz was right. It was in the book. So were ten others, but only one MD. Address in Twin Pines East.

Beneath the name was my scrawling shorthand of the convo with Katz. The pen had been a good idea. The details of the exchange came mostly as a surprise to me when I reread them that afternoon.

19

Nothing more from Robin yet. But then, she probably figured there was no need. She probably thought what Katz and everyone else thought about me. Wild-headed freak. He'll do anything. Let him run the rushes and see what he shakes out.

And they were right. But who cares? I thought. I had nothing to lose by pestering an old man about a patient he'd had thirteen years ago. If Katz was telling the truth, Cunningham was probably ripe to confess, privacy be damned. He was retired anyway, and like Katz he could always deny we'd ever spoken, chalk it up to the delusions of a selective amnesiac alkie shut-in who spies on his neighbors for fun.

I showed at Cunningham's address at two in the afternoon. I'd gotten up—actually, more like sobered up, I hadn't slept much—earlier than usual. With the help of some bracing chemicals, I showered, shaved, and made myself generally presentable as the kind of guy you could spill your sins to on your doorstep on a serendipitous Thursday afternoon.

What the hey? I bet you'd be surprised how many people are sitting at home alone day after day just waiting for some white-shirt-wearing do-gooder with a bowl haircut and a face as bland as a boiled egg to show up as if by God and take your past from you like a backpack full of bricks and just walk away with it.

I was going to do that for Dr. Simon Cunningham if he would let me. Present myself, like the great saving Mormon man (without the magazine and the spiel), and make myself the receptacle of his bad conscience.

How could he refuse?

I walked up the concrete walk, over the lawn-serviced lawn, past the oxidized birdbath and the knee-high sculpted Cupid with bow, all wavy hips and baby tits, gone pumiced and gray with the rain. I saw the mold tinge on the north side of the house, and the blanched exposure on the south.

I ran my hand over the modular white stucco wall, and I rang the irregular bell. It sounded like a water bird drowning, or landing, or abortedly taking off. A frantic beating of wings and splashing and a strangled squawk. An outdoorsman's novelty gag, I guessed, like the talking bigmouth bass. Get a chuckle every time.

I was forever ringing bells on doorsteps, or having them rung. The same day over and over again, and I'm on either end. Ring. Answer. Ring. Ignore. Ring, ring, ring. Tell me your troubles, I'll tell you mine. Babble, chatter, make meaningless noise. Punctuate the time, and the awkwardness of the transitions. You and me and everybody else, coming and going, a world of cars and stoops and living rooms and nothing in between.

Is this how they envisioned suburban life when they built here? All of us going from couch to garage to parking lot, to cubicle to parking lot to store, to garage to home theater? None of us ever walking more than a hundred feet, and never dressing for the weather because we aren't out in it long enough to care.

Did they expect us to be fat, agoraphobic cave dwellers who never mingle or play out of doors, never stroll or loiter or happen on each other by chance, except possibly through the intercession of our dogs? When they built these pods and segues of modernity and plastered them with the promise of a dream, did they know how stunted they would make us? How deformed?

Generic, yes. Unoriginal, sure. They planned for that and wanted it. We all did. We do.

And so you know as well as I do how it went, at first, meeting Dr. C.

The details hardly matter.

The man and his home, the furniture and the decor, what he looked like and how we shook hands. It was all exactly as you'd expect. The same. He was a retired pediatrician. Fill in the blanks. Kindly, glasses, cardigan sweater, duck hunter, teetotaler, grandfather of three.

What did I care anyway? What do you?

He could have been a caterpillar smoking a pipe or the witch behind the wardrobe, and I could have been the Grand Inquisitor or a hole in the ground. It didn't fucking matter. He was a mouth that said these words and I was the ears that heard them.

He told me what I needed to know, and he did it because, like me, he didn't give a tinker's anymore what happened to him, and he thought he deserved what was coming.

He led me into his study. The club chairs, the side tables, the desk. The diplomas, the snapshots, the taxidermy. On stands, in frames, and on the walls. And that groggy gray light of a lake-effect afternoon, coming in low through the dirty, too small casement window.

I told him what I was there for. I told him about Katz's tip. I didn't have to say much.

"I should have been stripped of my license," he said when I'd finished.

No intro, no explaining needed. He was ready as guns and bursting with it, and then I knew that it was all coming out. Every bit. And I wouldn't have to do a thing to ease it.

"You see a lot of things as a physician, Nick," he told me. "Even in a small family practice. And most of the time you are bound to be silent. What is said, what passes between a doctor and his patient is as sacred, as protected as what passes between a parishioner and his priest. But a child—a child cannot speak for itself. Not really . . . Their bodies are a complete mystery to them, like something separate, unattached, and they come into your office so frightened and surprised by the things that just show up, that just happen to them, and they don't know why. Injury, trauma, sickness are confusing. They have no causes or consequences associated with them. They are just events, just more time passing, some discomfort, and maybe the introduction of instruments or substances they've never seen, never imagined. But none of it means anything intellectually. Only emotionally, and even then, only dimly in the present, as something like a sore throat or a sick stomach, that they wish would go away . . . And then when it does go away, it's gone. Forgotten in the eternal present."

He smiled tightly.

"Except, of course, that it isn't. It isn't gone. It exists somewhere, stored away. Influencing. Because like every other thing that happens in childhood, no matter how small, it remains. It gets recorded in every detail, and it composes the person who ultimately becomes the adult."

"The child is the father of the man," I said.

"I'm sorry?"

"Oh, it was just something my mother used to say. It's from a poem."

"Ah," he said, nodding. "Well, that's right. That's exactly right. I'll have to remember that."

He seemed then to drift away into his thoughts, as though sifting through them for the right thing to say. He was silent for several minutes, and then abruptly, he said:

"HPV. Do you know what that is, Nick?"

"No, Doctor. I'm afraid I don't."

"Human papillomavirus," he said.

"Okay," I said, still not knowing.

"Robin Bloom presented with the human papillomavirus. HPV."

This is not what I came for, I thought. He's gone. I'm going to get a list of childhood ailments and a watery stare. Yes, yes. Robin Bloom. I remember. Let me see. She had mono and strep, too.

"She presented with HPV at twelve years of age," he said, fixing me with a look that was clearer than my own, and piercing. "Do you understand what that means?"

Twelve years of age. He put the emphasis on "twelve." Why was the age so important? Too young? Too old? No idea. His eyes were waiting for an answer.

I shook my head.

"HPV is a venereal disease, Nick. You must have come across it in college or somewhere along the way. It's practically the common cold of sexually active young people. It generally causes warts and sometimes other growths to appear on the genitals."

"Uh. Look. Wait—" I groaned, putting up my hand. "I don't think I want to hear this."

"I don't care whether you want to hear it or not," he growled. "You're going to hear it. All of it. I have never said this to another human soul since the day I said it to Anita Bloom, and I need to say it. I need you to hear it."

He looked blankly at the floor, and added, in an almost automatic way: "Robin Bloom had—"

He broke off for a moment, overcome, then resumed in a choked whisper: "—warts on her vulva."

He paused again.

"And," he continued, "she had them clustered in and around her anus and rectum as well."

"Oh, Christ. Please, Doctor," I said.

"Listen," he shouted. "All you have to do is listen."

"I'm sorry," I said. "Go on."

He waited.

"Please go on," I said again. "What did you . . . What was the treatment?"

The red faded from his face. He seemed able again to focus on the facts.

"Usually you burn off the growths with liquid nitrogen, but that frightened Robin too much. So I gave her a topical solution instead. Something you'd apply twice a day."

"And this cleared them up?"

"I assume so, yes."

"What do you mean, you assume so? Didn't you follow up?"

"No," he said loudly, curling the word firmly on his tongue. "No," he said again, more quietly. "I did not."

He fell silent again, the back of one hand pressed tightly against his mouth. Then, abruptly, he cast the hand wildly in front of him.

"Don't you see? That's the point. I didn't follow up, not with Anita Bloom, and not with anybody else. I didn't report what I'd found to the authorities, which is what I should—what I was legally bound to have done."

He fixed me again with the piercing stare, then closed his eyes wearily with a nasal huff of self-disgust.

"And that's why you say you should have been stripped of your license?" I said at last.

"Yes. That and more."

"And why didn't you report it?"

"I've tried to answer that question hundreds of times myself—thousands. Why? Why? Why? . . . There are so many answers, and none that justifies what I did. What is it that people say? There's a reason for everything, but not an excuse. I have a lot of reasons, but no excuse."

I felt the familiar pang of self-pity.

"At least you *have* reasons," I said. "I'd give my health, my soul, my house, and everything else I could think of to have those. Knowing why means a hell of a lot more than you might think."

He shifted in his chair, seeming to relent slightly at this.

"You mean about your parents," he said.

"Yes."

He nodded knowingly.

"I guess what I'm telling you, son, is that knowing the reasons doesn't free you from the pain or the guilt or the shame. Not at all. And while I realize that I may seem to be speaking from a position of privilege in the sense that I have more reasons than I know what to do with, and you have none, I can only tell you that it doesn't help. It only gives you something else to chew on and to run through your brain over and over again. It's just more ammunition."

"I can see that," I said. "You're as torn up as I am. But it doesn't matter. Even if what you say is true, I still feel as compelled as ever to know why what happened happened, and I'll do almost anything to find out."

"You'll accept any substitute," he offered.

"Yeah, I guess that's right. If I can know something, solve something about the mystery of Robin Bloom, I can—I don't know—feel some relief. Maybe not in the end, once I know, but now, while I'm searching."

He considered this.

"Yes, searching can be very distracting. But then, one way or another the search comes to an end, and you're left again with the past, still there, just as it was before. Unchanged. I have lived with the past, with this piece of the past for so long."

He sighed heavily.

"Isn't it strange, Nick? Here you are looking for relief, yet perhaps all you can do is give it. I have waited for so long to tell this to someone. I didn't realize that fully until just now. But it's true. I've been waiting for you, or someone in your shape and with your purpose, to hear my confession. And now at last you are here, my merciful ear, and not at all as I expected you."

"Really? What did you expect?"

"You know?" he said. "I really have no idea. Just not you, oddly enough. Not the son of a man I golfed with. I guess you didn't know that, did you? Your father and I golfed occasionally, not that that's so surprising in these parts. All the doctors and lawyers and entrepreneurs golf at the same club. Always have done. They're bound sooner or later to bump into each other's tragedies, whether they know it or not."

He chuckled softly.

"The most innocuous, lackadaisical of sports—hardly a sport at all—and yet the things that have been said on golf courses . . . I suppose they've shaken the world, haven't they? All those presidents and their coconspirators, all the power brokers divvying up the world between them, all tooling around like overgrown babies in their toy cars and chasing a tiny dimpled white ball around in the grass. Puts it all in perspective."

He chuckled again and shook his head at the irony of it. He picked up a small lacquered pillbox lying on the side table by his chair and examined it closely, as if for the last time. I thought he was going to hand it to me and tell me that it held some special significance for him or for me, or maybe for Robin Bloom. But after a few moments he put it back on the table and left it there.

"By the time she brought Robin to see me that day," he said, "I had known Anita Bloom for thirty years. I knew what she had been through with her daughter Karen's death, or I knew what little she would share with me, and what I had observed. I had been invited to a memorial service they'd held for her. Anita was a very devout and private person, an innocent person. When Karen died, she was so bewildered, so thrown back, because she had never had any contact with that world before, the world of drugs and over-dose and runaways and crime. She didn't know how it killed people. She didn't know that a dark shadow lay just on the other side of the white picket fence. She had no idea.

"And somehow, even after Karen's death, she managed to keep an awareness of that dark world at bay. She went on living in a dream, and I think she wanted to keep that dream world alive for Robin. She thought it was the best thing she could give her.

"That day, when I told her what I had to tell her about Robin, about the HPV and what it meant, I knew she'd had nothing to do with it. It wasn't a case of domestic abuse. I knew John Bloom, too, and he was as drawn into and invested in her dream world as she was. He hadn't done this. He hadn't known. I'd have bet money on that. A lot of money.

"No. I looked into Anita's eyes and I saw that she was as horrified as I was—and absolutely ignorant as well. She broke down right there in my office and begged me not to say anything to anyone. Not because she didn't want to help Robin or protect her. She wanted that more than anything. But to acknowledge that Robin had been molested, possibly raped—well, that would have shattered the world she was trying to maintain. It would have shattered *her*. She would have broken into a million pieces under the strain. It was too awful to face.

"And so, I told myself that it was okay to let Anita and John handle it themselves, privately, because I told myself that whoever had done this awful thing was not living in that house. Robin was not in danger in their hands. They could and would protect her. Withdraw. Hide. Whatever it took."

He fixed his eyes on me guiltily.

"Now, you may say that circumstances had already made it clear that they couldn't protect Robin, that they had failed in that already. And you would be right. But I wanted to believe in them and their made-up world— No, that's not quite true."

He paused and thought. Then, seeming to land on the avoided thing, he added:

"I didn't want to hurt them anymore. I couldn't. I simply couldn't. And so, I suppose, without quite knowing it, or wanting to know it, I sacrificed the welfare of that little girl, just as her grandparents had and did, to protect an illusion of safety and the fragile sanity that went with it.

"And I have had to live with that for thirteen years, not a single day of which has passed without a painful reminder of my role in what ultimately happened to that poor child."

He stopped as suddenly as he had begun.

I burst in.

"Listen, Doctor. I've come here, as it turns out, to do more than listen. I hadn't intended to tell you this, but there's something I want you to know, and I think it will help."

He looked up with just the barest glimmer of hope in his eyes. Then he dampened it and his eyes were dull again with the years of ceaseless self-recrimination.

I stopped for a moment and wondered. Is this what Robin would have wanted? As angry as she was? If, in her eyes, her mother was to blame for seeing the evidence and explaining it away, wasn't the doctor even worse? Wasn't he the arch-criminal in her memory? Wouldn't she want him to go on suffering to the end, to be deepened also by his grief, for as long as guilt would last?

Or was I being too hard? Was I being too naive? I was struck suddenly by another passing thought. Had Robin known that I would come here all along? Had she set me on this course purposely, dropping the single word— *evidence*—and then the linking pronoun—*you, the same thing that happened to you*—into the lap of a man who wanted nothing so much as to solve his own mystery? Did she know? Had she forgiven? And did she want this kindness for the doctor, after all?

I couldn't puzzle it out, and I didn't want to. I didn't care. I was going to tell what I knew. It was the right thing to do.

"Doctor," I blurted, "Robin Bloom is alive."

His face didn't change.

"She's alive and well. I've spoken—I've corresponded with her."

Again nothing.

His eyes moved back and forth slowly from one corner of the room to the other, but seemed to see nothing, as though he had hold of a difficult idea and was following it through to its end. At last he said:

"I know."

I thought I had misheard.

"What?"

He fixed his eyes on me.

"I know that Robin Bloom is alive," he repeated sternly.

"But . . . then how—?"

He smiled bitterly.

"I told you. Knowing won't release you."

He paused, waiting for this to sink in.

"Do you know, Nick?" he said curiously. "How very strange. Right now, you look just as Anita looked that day. So startled. So innocent. You really have no idea, do you?"

He ran his palms along his thighs vigorously, as though to warm or wipe the sweat from them.

"Well, why should you?" he said. "I have the missing piece."

The smile faded from his face, replaced by a furrow of sympathy in his brow and a small twist of regret on his lips.

"What was it you said?" he asked. "The child is the father—something?"

"The child is the father of the man," I repeated wearily.

"Yes, that's it. The child is the father of the man. That's very good. Very good."

He half smiled again.

"The Robin Bloom that lay on my examination room table that day thirteen years ago—almost to the day, I would wager—*that* Robin Bloom is the mother of the Robin Bloom you've just met. She knows all her secrets. She remembers *everything*."

"I'm not following you," I said. "I don't see how—"

He looked again at the small lacquered box on the table, picked it up, and held it.

"Why is it," he said, turning it over in his hands, "that we always think life is preferable? . . . You know, I've always argued fiercely with my colleagues over that point. Medicine is polluted—positively wrecked—by this notion of life at all costs. Life almighty. As if it were the opposite of harm. Keep the patient alive."

He lifted his arms above his head.

"*Save!*"

He dropped his arms with a slap.

"But save what?" he said. "We never ask ourselves: Save what? What is the thing, the creature that we are saving? . . . So Robin Bloom is alive. You say that as if it could cure. But the Robin Bloom who is alive—who is that person? *How* is that person? That is the relevant thing. Should I feel exonerated by her life? By the fact that she is living, when she is corrupted so thoroughly by the past? When she is the very miscarriage of her own disease?"

He clutched the lacquered box tightly in his fist, as if he meant to crush it, and winced. Then he replaced it once more on the table. He opened his hand, revealing a whitened palm and the angry red hexagon the box had imprinted there.

"I did not expect it to be you," he said again. "You see, this is so marvelously done, really. I will have my confession but no relief, and you will have your reason and no relief. She has seen to that."

"I don't understand," I said.

"I know you don't, son." He sighed. "Neither did I until just now. But you will understand, and you will wish that you did not."

He stood then and crossed the room to the desk on the far side by the window. He opened a small drawer and took out a piece of paper.

"I received this in my mailbox—no postage, just as it is—three days ago."

He crossed the room again, slowly, and handed the paper to me.

It was yellowed with age, but uncreased, as if it had been kept in a sleeve or between the pages of a book.

The top of the page had the logo of the Twin Pines Country Club, two pine trees flanked by the letters TP on one side and CC on the other, and beneath that, the club's sanguine motto: "Where the grass is always greener."

As my eyes moved down the page, I recognized it as a scorecard for a game of golf. I'd never actually seen one before. As many times as I'd been to Twin Pines Country Club as a child and adolescent, I'd never once been on the golf course. I'd always been on the tennis courts or sitting by the pool.

But it was clear enough. Hole, par, handicap.

On the left-hand side of the card, the players' names were written by hand in pencil.

Simon Cunningham. James Walsh.

It was dated June 16, 1997.

James Walsh.

It was jarring to see my father's name on a piece of paper like that after so long, a piece of paper that he had no doubt touched, that might have once borne—perhaps still bore—the marks of the oil or the salt on his fingertips.

I raised the card to my nose.

Just paper. Old paper. And dust. The dust made largely of the flakes of other people's skin.

"You said you used to play golf with my dad," I said.

"Yes," he replied. "I did."

"So?"

"Yes, so? That's exactly what I thought until you showed up at my door today asking about Robin Bloom. Until *you* showed up. Not just anyone. You. And not just anytime, but now. Unlucky thirteen years after the fact."

"But you said you thought it was almost to the day—the day of her exam. The card is marked the sixteenth. Today is the twenty-ninth."

He laughed.

"I don't remember the exact date, of course. Only the month. It was a beautiful June day. I remember that because I remember looking out at the sunshine glaring off the glass of the parked cars in the lot and thinking that it was going to be a gorgeous night for our party. My wife and I were throwing a party for my colleagues, as we did every June for thirty years. I remember I kept staring out at the sunshine so that I wouldn't have to keep looking into Mrs. Bloom's face, and I remember berating myself for thinking about something so selfish and mundane as our party and the weather while I was telling a mother that her child had probably been sodomized right under her nose. I got very drunk that night. Drunker than I had ever been. Damn near killed myself. I was throwing up for days. Haven't had a drink since . . . Yes, it was a day in June. That much I'm sure of."

He sat down again heavily in his chair.

"The name and a day in June, and then you," he said. "What else could it possibly mean?"

He paused, waiting for this to penetrate.

I waited, too, for the information, so long in coming, to break through.

But why a card? Why this card? This was a clue for me, not for him. So what? What was it I'd missed? I looked again. I looked not just at the date, but at my father's name written next to Dr. Cunningham's, and a few notes, presumably about the course, that were scribbled on the bottom and sides of the card.

James Walsh.

I read it again and again. James Walsh. James Walsh. James Walsh. Like knocking on a door, or calling into the dark without an answer. I stared. I echoed. I heard my father's name repeated. I looked at the nonsensical short-hand at the bottom of the card. And then, finally, I thought I saw. I thought I saw and then I saw. It came into focus slowly, landing on my brain as a thought. Not just the name, but the script itself. My father's name and the notations were written in *his* handwriting. His slightly more sloped—or as I had once thought, more drunken—version of my own handwriting, perhaps scribbled in the dark.

It was his hand for certain.

The same hand, the blemished hand that had written those terrible poems on those faded pink pieces of paper.

"You know it now," the doctor said with conviction. "I can see it in your face."

I nodded, but I hardly knew what I was saying.

"She must have . . ."

I looked at him for confirmation.

"Yes, she must have taken it from his pocket."

"The left-hand breast pocket," I said flatly. "Next to his wallet and his comb."

Dr. Cunningham frowned.

"I'm sorry, Nick. I'm so very sorry."

What happened to you? I thought again.

What happened to you?

And then again I heard the knowing answer.

The same thing that happened to you.

Nick, she'd said, you know nothing.

And then he.

He'd said.

I told you.

Knowing won't release you.

But still, I'd said, I don't understand.

And he again.

I know you don't, son, but you will, and you will wish that you did not.

I'm sorry, he said.

He said he was sorry.

Sorry.

But what did that mean?

To be sorry.

What did it ever mean when you were an accessory to the harm?

"You're sorry?" I shouted suddenly, brandishing the paper. "Then why did you show this to me? Why? You could have kept it from me. You could have kept your ridiculous silence."

"Because, Nick. Don't you see? It was her or me. She contacted you, yes? She led you into the trap. She led me, too. But when I realized it only just a short time ago, I also realized that this was the better way. It's part of my penance. I owe you—I owe *her* that. It's only right that I be the one to tell you. You were going to know one way or the other. I knew that as soon as you said she was alive. I knew that she'd been in touch with you, just as she had been in touch with me, and that it was all playing out, piece by piece, just as she had planned it, as I said, almost to the day. How long do you think she thought it would take you to make your way to me through Jonathan Katz? How quickly can desperation follow a trail? She knew exactly. And honestly, I think she was, in some tortuous way, trying to soften the blow."

"What, by having me listen to every clinical detail of what my fucking father did to her?"

"To have you understand slowly, because there was so much."

"God. You sound just like her."

"Well, then I'm right, aren't I?"

"You're right? Right about what? That I'm the last to know? Yes, I get it, finally. I get it. You're right about that. But you're wrong about one thing."

"I'm sure I'm wrong about a lot of things," he said. "If I knew before you, it was only minutes before, when I realized that it was Robin who'd left me the golf card. Until you showed up, until you said she was alive, I'd had no idea who could have planted that or why."

"It wasn't the date or the name that she wanted me to see," I blustered on angrily. "Or not just that. It was the handwriting."

"The handwriting?"

"Yes. It's my father's handwriting."

"On the card?"

"Yes. On the card. But not just there. I've been getting things in my mail-box, too."

"Ah. Well, there you have it then. We are each only half informed. What things?"

"Things like your card. Things that didn't make any sense until just now."

"What things, Nick?"

He sounded alarmed.

"Notes," I said. "Love notes. Poems. Whatever. Sick shit that he wrote to her then. All this time I thought it was me. I thought the handwriting was mine, and I've been forgetting so much lately, I thought the notes were mine, too. Or I thought somebody was messing with me, playing a prank. I don't know. It doesn't matter now. It's just more of her evidence."

"Evidence?"

"Yes, that's why I'm here. She told me there was evidence. Evidence that her mother saw. Evidence of what was happening to her. I thought she meant physical evidence. Literally. On the body. I thought she was being hit."

"What did she say that made you think that?"

"Nothing. I guess that was just the worst I could imagine."

I laughed.

"Quaint, isn't it?"

"No," he said sadly. "No."

He squinted, as if reading his answers from a prompt that he could barely make out. His voice, his thoughts were slow to catch up.

"Violence is what you know," he murmured. "It's where your mind goes."

He hesitated again, removed his spectacles, wiped them, and replaced them on his face.

"It's where she knew your mind would go," he continued, sure of the line now. "It's the place where you two cross paths in me, ironically."

He nodded.

Yes, he was onto it now.

"I saw that, too, in my practice," he said. "Kids who'd obviously been hit, and hit by their parents, the parents who brought them to see me. I knew that look. The look of the guilty party. That's why I knew that Anita Bloom hadn't known, hadn't even conceived of the possibility of what had happened to Robin. That's also why I knew that look in you, Nick. Just now. That look of not knowing, of not understanding. Do you see? That's why it was better for me to tell you the truth, for you to hear this from me. I was wrong before. You will have some relief, after all, if you let yourself, and perhaps so will I."

He leaned forward in his chair, his fingers long and lean, outstretched, parallel, as if holding something light and fragile for me to take.

"Listen to me, Nick. Listen. I have it now. All that I needed to tell you, all perhaps that Robin, by her own double-edged means, meant for me to tell you. Your father did this. Yes. He did. There is my confession. What I saw. And there is his, in the card and in the pages you have seen. It happened. I can attest to that now just as you can."

He molded his hands around the malleable bulb of air between them.

"But," he added, his voice stronger and firm, "and this is the part you *must* hear. You are not your father. You will never be your father."

He enunciated this next part very slowly and deliberately:

"Nick, you don't have it in you."

I snorted derisively.

"Oh, and you know that for certain, do you?"

"I know it as well as I know anything, yes. You are innocent of this—this crime. You are innocent of all your father's crimes. They are not yours by inheritance, or implication, or anything else. And especially not by temperament. You are your mother through and through, Nick. Her words, her ideas, her love for everything refined that makes people worthy of anything. And you are only as guilty as the rest of us, no more."

"All my father's crimes," I repeated. "Where is the end of them?"

"Here!" he shouted. "Right here!"

I lurched in my own chair, startled.

"You must stop this now," he said more softly. "This—" He searched for the word. "Self-torture."

He collapsed then, exhausted, his hands limp against the arms of the chair, his head fallen back, eyes closed.

He was done. There was nothing more to say, even if he'd had the energy to say it, which, by the look of him, I doubted. His lips had gone pale, the lids of his eyes were parchment thin and spider veined. All the verve of revelation had gone out of him, and he could barely muster the breath to mutter good-bye as I stood to go. He looked at me once more with pity and exhausted sympathy, rolling his wan, hollow-templed head to the side and raising weakly the first two fingers of his right hand in farewell.

I hated Robin then.

I hated her more than I hated my father.

More than I hated myself.

20

I came home from Dr. Cunningham's to find Monica sitting on my front steps in the dark. It had been a week or more since I'd seen her. I'd lost track of time, and given all that had happened, seeing her felt like starting over, like we'd have to reintroduce ourselves on all but the most superficial of terms.

She must have seen the wretchedness written all over me. I couldn't imagine who wouldn't. I felt like a hundred and sixty pounds of rotting meat left out in the sun, like a body thrown from a plane crash and lost to rescue, just barely conscious and dying on the bone.

She didn't say a word. Not: Where have you been? Not: Jesus, you look like death on a stick. Not even: What happened to you? She just walked with me into the house, poured me a tallboy of Jameson straight, set it beside me on the table by the couch in the study, and sat down.

We sat there for a long time in silence before we began to take off our clothes. There was nothing sensual in the act. Nothing intentional at all. Monica fetched a blanket from my bedroom and we lay together full length on the couch beneath it enfolded in each other's arms.

We fell asleep that way, or I did, and when I woke, as usual, she was gone.

For all I know, she was never there at all and I dreamt her. She would have been the only comfort I could have taken and then been left by without apology, hurt, or explanation.

I didn't know how I was going to tell her what I knew, or if I ever could. I knew only that I had to find Robin right away, to speak or write to her now that I knew all that she had wanted me to know.

I got up at noon—we had been to bed early—and went immediately to the computer. I logged on to Facebook and sent a message to Iris Gray: "I need to talk to you. Now. I'll be waiting."

At four p.m., still nothing.

But it didn't matter.

I wasn't going anywhere. I had nowhere to go. Everything had led to this, and I was going to be here for it. Right square in the center. Sober. I wanted to be in this pain, this particular, real, differentiated pain, and remember it vividly.

I could wait.

I walked into the kitchen to make more coffee. Out back, I could see that Miriam was there again, right on time as usual, book bag toppled on the ground disgorging its contents—notepads, pens, dolls, a juice box—all dumped, strewn, displayed under the apple tree.

Over the past week, and with my help, Miriam's starling shrine and tea party have spread and morphed into a village. We work in shifts. Every day she is here at or just before four. She stays until five or six, adding, shaping, building. Then she goes home for dinner. I go out around seven and work until dark.

On Monday afternoon she built a gazebo with a thatched roof made of bark and pine needles, and on Tuesday afternoon she fenced in a cemetery, complete with flat rock headstones inscribed with names and dates in permanent black marker. On Monday evening I dug the outline of a soccer field around a patch of grass, posted netless goals, and trimmed the turf with a pair of scissors. On Tuesday evening I painted in the boxes, lines, and center circle with some Liquid Paper I'd found in my desk. On Wednesday she wound a cobblestone road through the center of town, and that evening I built side streets off of it.

Today, she was working on something new, or planning it, standing over, scrutinizing the site. I smiled and walked back into the study.

I closed the laptop and took it to the basement. Downstairs I opened it again—still logged on to Facebook, still no Iris Gray in chat—set it off to the side on the table in front of the monitors, and sat back to wait.

What was doing these days with the nabes?

I hadn't spent as much time with the cameras since my game of shadow building had started with Miriam. Why would I? Watching the live telescreen of my rear window was far more diverting than closed-circuit situation tragedy on rerun any day of the week. Besides, and more to the point, running down Robin and the inflicted past had made everything in my small-screen life feel one-dimensional by comparison.

There wasn't much to see.

At this hour, Dave was never in his bedroom or bathroom, probably not even in the house. Best guess, either he was golfing—yes, you guessed it—at Twin fucking Pines Country Club, or he was having his triweekly rub 'n' tug at Zora's, the full-service "gentleman's spa" downtown that's staffed by all those platinum, pie-faced heroin whores from Siberia and Ukraine who didn't quite make it on the tennis circuit.

Ellie, meanwhile, was watching *Ellen* or *Oprah* or some other palliative for hausfraus, catatonic as usual on the couch in the living room. Eric and Jeff were gaming, limp and supine in the rec room, and Iris, the original and best, was, for once, at an apparent loss for words, pulling lazy loop-de-loops on her swing and emitting the occasional bored squawk.

But a fight was on at Dorris's, or so it seemed.

She was in the family room railing at someone in the next room.

". . . so much . . . you don't do any of it. Tell me one way—aside from your three hours twice a week with each of them, which, let's be honest, you usually combine to three hours once a week with both of them—tell me one way that your life is different because your children are in it."

Ah. Of course. Jonathan. Who else?

"Tell me one way," Dorris went on. "That you've changed, except for the worse. You're living like a bachelor just out of college, drinking as soon as your coat is off, going out every night, dating women half your age, and you're going to tell me that you love those kids more than I do? I don't think so."

Jonathan came into view from the kitchen carrying a tall glass of liquid with ice.

"Well, I do love them more," he said, sipping and almost laughing. "Just listen to you."

He had the swagger of a free man. Good for him.

"Yes, well—" Dorris sneered. "It's very easy to love people you see once a week at the amusement park. I promise you, it's a little harder when they treat you like the hired help and call you a bitch to your face."

Now he was laughing outright.

"Well, you are a bitch. What do you expect?"

Dorris hurled a throw pillow and missed.

"They've made me one, damn you. You've made me one. It's like I've got three kids and no one to help me."

She burst into tears.

"I help you plenty, honey," snarked Jonathan, still amused. "Just ask my accountant."

Dorris grunted through gritted teeth and beat her fists against her thighs.

"God, it's incredible. You think your money buys you the right to be a complete bastard all the time to everyone."

She stalked to the couch for another throw pillow, seized it, and twisted it violently between her hands.

"I'd give up your fucking money in a heartbeat," she shouted. "In a *heartbeat*—if I could get one crumb of kindness from you, one iota of emotional support . . . if I could get you to do one thing just for me that you weren't already doing for yourself . . . You can't starve a person of human contact and walk away feeling benevolent just because you're paying the bill. It doesn't work that way."

Jonathan took a self-placatory sip of his drink.

"No, actually, that's exactly how it works. Exactly. To the dollar amount."

He jabbed at the air with his index finger.

"And don't tell me you're doing so much for those kids, because you're not. You're about as attentive as a potted plant."

"As if you would know—" she began, but he barreled over her.

"I'm not paying to walk away. I'm footing the bill while my ex-wife has a very public nervous breakdown and leaves my kids to live by their wits or die of shame."

"What the hell are you talking about?"

"How can you possibly pretend otherwise? For God's sake, Dorris, your name and number might as well be written over the urinal at that trough you've been visiting down the road. You didn't think I knew about that, did you? The Swan, is it? Where you go to grovel at the feet of that fascist you've been schtupping . . . I may be out every night, it's true—to dinner, mind you, not at some sleazy hole-in-the-wall—having the healthy, mature social life that I missed while married to you, but you're out there tripping and slurring like a leper with bells on, begging the last of the uninfected to fuck you."

"That's a total lie and you know it."

"Really?"

He yanked an envelope from his breast pocket and threw it on the coffee table. Its glossy contents fanned out.

"Sure looks that way to me."

Dorris picked up the photographs and flipped hurriedly through them, her face clenching and clouding with rage.

"How dare you! How fucking dare you? You've been following me?"

"I'm far too busy for that—" He paused awkwardly. "Let's just say that some things have come to my attention, and I thought it best to stay informed."

"Informed?"

"Yes. Somebody's got to watch out for those kids."

Dorris threw down the pillow she'd been throttling, shifted her weight haughtily, and crossed her arms over her chest.

"Wait, I'm sorry. Am I hearing this right? You've had a private detective following not just me but the kids?"

Jonathan hesitated, sipping repeatedly.

"Miriam, mostly," he murmured at last.

Dorris plunged her hands into her hair, bent forward at the waist, and thrashed her head backward in disbelief.

"Good God!" she shouted. "You've had a private detective following your daughter?"

Jonathan looked away and didn't answer.

"That is really beyond . . ." began Dorris, but lapsed into a groan of disgust.

Jonathan turned on her, hard-eyed.

"It's for her protection," he snapped.

"Protection?" Dorris howled derisively. "From what?"

"Don't play dumb, Dorris. You told me yourself that Nick Walsh made some kind of advance to her in this very house."

"I'm not so sure anymore. Miriam denies it. And there's been nothing since."

"Nothing since?" he replied. "God, you really have been on the moon. There has been a lot since—a hell of a lot—but, of course, why would you know that when you're either out cold or demented and servicing all comers twenty-four hours a day?"

Dorris ignored this last jab, her voice falling to a shocked whine.

"What do you mean, a hell of a lot? When? Where?"

"Every goddamned day, Dorris. Every day. Right across the street at his house."

"What? But I . . . But how?"

"On her way home from school every day for two weeks, she's been creeping into his yard through the back fence and staying for hours. Actually, school has been out for a week already, but why would you know that, either?"

He threw up his hand sarcastically.

"What mother would?"

Dorris was standing there blinking, too stunned to react.

"And I can tell you," Jonathan went on, "she's counting on your ignorance. She must be pretty desperate to be out of this house."

Dorris began to cry again, moaning piteously.

"Oh, relax," said Jonathan, impatiently. "It isn't that bad. She's been safe so far, thank God."

"But what," gurgled Dorris, "has she been doing all day for the past week?"

"Hanging around the school yard alone, playing on the swings. She spends most of the early afternoon at the public library watching old movies and playing around on the computer. God forbid she actually read."

Dorris sighed hugely.

She sat heavily on the arm of the couch, recovering her breath.

After a moment she looked up.

"And your disgusting paid informant has been lurking in the background for all this?" she said, the command coming back to her voice. "Following and watching a little girl?"

She laughed abruptly.

"Let me guess—he's a fat guy in orthopedic shoes who wears short-sleeved button-down shirts."

Jonathan waived his hand at her dismissively.

"I don't think you're in much of a position to denigrate fat guys, Dorris, or their attire. But regardless, *that* fat guy has been doing your mothering for you, and quite possibly averting a disaster, so don't even try to make an issue out of this. In fact, if I were you, I'd be looking to brush this under the rug as quickly as possible. My God—do you know how this would look in front of a judge? I'd get custody in a nanosecond."

Dorris bolted up.

"You don't even want custody, you selfish son of a bitch. You're just looking after your . . . investments . . . That's all we are to you—investments. Them especially. You don't care about those kids! You just don't want anyone putting their fingers in your pie."

Jonathan smirked.

"'Care' is not a word I would emphasize, if I were you. It's not your strong suit. Or fingers in pies, for that matter."

Dorris tried to slap him, but he ducked away.

"Fuck youuuuu!!!!" she screeched, wheeling her arms in front of her, trying to land a blow, and failing.

He dodged her easily. Swilling down the rest of his drink, he slammed his glass on the coffee table, gathered up his photographs, and shoved them back into his breast pocket.

"You know, the beauty of these"—he slapped the pocket—"is that I don't have to listen to this anymore. I've got everything I need to take those kids away from you, and—believe me—I will if you keep this up. You should be feeling pretty bloody grateful that your daughter is in one piece and right here where we can see her, when she might very well have ended up like that poor Bloom girl."

Dorris balked.

"That poor Bloom girl? Where the hell is that coming from? You didn't even know her. All anyone has ever heard of her is gossip, pure and simple. Nothing more."

"Tell that to her mother."

"Her *grand*mother. Her mother was a crack whore who died after dumping the kid on the doorstep."

Jonathan raised his eyebrows and smirked.

"Sound familiar?"

Dorris pushed past him toward the kitchen. "I don't have to justify myself to you, mister."

He ignored this, speaking to the empty room.

"It happens every day, Dorris. Every day some kid goes missing and dies in circumstances you don't even want to think about. And every day a hundred more kids come down with some rare disease and die of it slowly and painfully. I should know—I see them year in and year out, suffering and struggling and dying."

He shook his head angrily.

"How dare we take our own for granted? How dare we let them out of our sight for one minute? You don't deserve what you have, and if I were that woman next door, watching you throw everything away out of sheer laziness and self-pity, I'd want to kill you."

Dorris shouted something long and involved and unintelligible from the kitchen or the hall, but I didn't try to work it out.

I'd heard enough.

This was getting like the old days, and I wasn't game.

I stood up, snapped the laptop shut, took it, and walked out of the room, yanking the door shut tight behind me and locking all the locks.

Ah, so Jonathan had been watching, and for a while now, too. So what? What was there to see? The fact that I was spending more quality time with his daughter than he was?

Well, I was.

No crime in that.

Exoneration, if anything.

Let those two peck each other to death, and let his fat man in orthos send him his reports. I had more important things to do.

21

At eight p.m. the words came on the screen.

Friends in chat: Iris Gray.

Jesus. Finally.

I typed without thinking, "I know."

There was a long pause, then the scroll up from Iris.

"What is it that you think you know?"

"I know that—"

I froze. What did I in fact know? Now that it came to saying it, I couldn't put the words in order. I erased what I had written, then wrote:

"My father—"

My father what?

Raped? Sodomized? Infected?

"My father wrote—" I wrote, then erased.

How sentimental, I thought. How appallingly loyal after all this time. I can't put it down. I can't even put it down.

Coward, I shouted. Say it. Just fucking say it.

But say what? What had he done precisely? No one had said that he had done anything but write notes, and even that was only implied. Wasn't I used to strategy? Didn't I know what it meant to play with someone? So now I was on the other side of it. Think it through, then, why don't you, like someone who is making up the plot, not the mouse in the maze running blindly.

Be skeptical for one second.

To infer something, going backward in time and scraping together means and motive from the guilty conscience of a pediatrician and the gamesmanship of a runaway, that was one thing, but to accuse outright, that was quite another. This wasn't just loyalty to Dad. This was loyalty to the truth, or, barring that, as Dad himself would have said archly in a court of law, loyalty to the other side of the lie.

"My father," I typed again and sent.

No, no, no. Say it.

"What he did to you." I sent again.

"Stop," she wrote.

And again.

"Stop."

Fuck.

You've fucked it up. Right up.

She's right. Just stop.

I stopped.

I waited for more.

But there was no more. Just the word "stop." Twice. A hand in my face for stuttering. You fucking retard, you're stuttering. You're stuttering to the victim.

"OK," I sent. "I'm sorry."

Nothing.

Now what?

But I'm not sorry.

No, I don't know. I am and I'm not.

Why have you put me in this position?

I'd waited so long for this conversation. I'd thought it was all I wanted, and now I couldn't speak. I didn't know what to say.

So don't say, I thought.

Ask something. She wants you to ask.

Try again.

Slowly. Be careful. Be . . . *subservient*. Was that it? Again? Be less. Less knowing, less informed, less worthy. Give her the power, because she deserves it. Your role is to bend down. To regret. To take blame. In his absence, you are the surrogate for blame.

Blame for what, though?

Just ask.

"What did he do to you?" I wrote.

I reread it several times.

It was direct. It was a question.

I was comfortable with that.

Somewhat.

Right.

Send.

I sent.

And this time the answer came quickly.

"I don't know."

I stared. Frozen again.

I had expected a lot of things, but not that.

"You don't know?" I sent.

"No."

How could she not fucking know? All of that had led only to this. All that "evidence," and no testimony? Really?

"I don't understand," I typed.

A pause.

"I don't remember," she replied.

I was shouting again. How can you not remember? How can you presume?

"How is that possible?" I typed.

"I don't know. I don't know," she answered.

Keep her here, I thought. Don't panic. Find out. Dig. Needle in for the sliver and grasp it. There is something there, a motivation at least.

Find it.

I typed.

"But something did happen. I mean, the medical record alone—"

I stopped, erased this, and typed again.

"Where did you get the golf card?"

Again the answer came quickly.

"From him, of course."

"But where?"

"In your bedroom."

My bedroom? What?

"What? When?"

"At night, of course."

Stop with the "of courses" already, you arrogant bitch. If you were here, I'd slap you.

Calm, Nick. Calm, I said aloud to the screen.

"What were you doing in my bedroom at night?" I wrote.

"The sleepovers with your mom."

"So you remember them?"

"Yes, why wouldn't I?"

Yes, why wouldn't you? No reason to forget that. No play on that angle, right? You and my mother lying around in your nightgowns watching old movies, throwing out lines, and throwing back gin. She'd have given you gin, I know that much. Oh, just a splash in some orange juice won't kill you. Live a little. You're young. And you'd have taken it just as I did, because you were in love, and because Auntie Mom was irresistible, was she not?

Gin was like mother's milk to her. [*Laugh.*] And therewith [*bow*] memory scarpered [*flourish*]. Good dog.

Yes, I know the tricks of memory, too, and the things you wake up to after.

A little vomit, a little strange, a little VD in the morning.

That stings.

"So he came into my room at night when you were sleeping," I wrote conclusively.

"Yes."

"How often?"

"A few times."

"And one night you took the golf card?"

"No."

"I don't understand."

"I found it."

"How do you mean?"

Nothing.

"This doesn't make any sense," I typed. "You say you were asleep. You say you don't remember. So how do you know he was there?"

No answer.

"What does a golf card prove?"

"Nothing," she replied. "It wasn't meant to prove anything. Only to show you. I found it on the floor by the bed and kept it. That's all."

"So," I repeated, "how do you know he came into my room at night?"

"Because, Nick. The notes. He wrote those notes in my diary."

A silence here. The silence of getting it slowly, as designed. My brain moves in patterns.

Wide ruled. Pink. Sharp, marginless edge. Jesus Christ. Why hadn't I seen? The notes were cut from her diary.

A young girl's place to keep her thoughts. Write every day, said Mother. She bought it for you, no doubt. Pink pages, yellow cover—was it?—and a pretty locking clasp on the side with a key to it.

Christ, were they both seducing you?

She typed again.

"He left the notes for me to find in the morning."

And what he did or didn't do in the darkness you don't know, I thought. Did he watch you sleep? Did he drug you? Or had Mom done the sedating for him? Did he spoon you nighty night? Did he rub up against you, warts and all, while you slept the sleep of the drunk?

"So you really have parted with the evidence," I wrote. It was all I could think to say.

"Some of it."

"But why? Why not send a copy?"

"I told you, because I needed you to believe."

"But why? Why me at all? Why did I need to know what he did? What possible purpose could it serve?"

"This has never been about what he did, Nick."

"What are you talking about? That's all it's been about. The notes. The card. The diagnosis."

"No."

"What do you mean, no?"

"I told you there was a lot, and that you would have to know it slowly. That you would have to hear it for yourself, find it for yourself, and hold it in your hands."

I didn't answer.

"Nick," she wrote. "This is only the beginning. You had to know this to understand the rest. I'm sorry."

"But you're not sorry. You're wronged, and you want me to suffer and atone somehow for him."

"No, I told you. This is not about what he did."

"Then, please, tell me. What the fuck is it about?"

A pause.

"What I did, Nick. It's about what I did."

This was more of the game and I could see it. I could see myself running to her bait and devouring it, knowingly devouring it and waiting for the next.

But knowing wouldn't stop me. I would run through as led just the same, and at her pace, with her cadence, every turn as she designed it, laid out and bending in careful order to the last.

"Wait," I typed, and waited.

You can't just trip over my father, I thought. He's not just a stone along the way to be kicked. I won't let you defame him offhand as part of *your* story. You will have to give something.

"Tell me that what he did doesn't matter," I wrote.

And she replied immediately.

"I don't know what he did. Or not all of what he did. I have flashes, and then I can only guess. And I might be wrong. I only know for certain what I did after, and that's the part that matters. What's left over is what counts. Your father is one piece, one motivation. There must be so many others that explain it, that explain me, but I can't put them all together because I don't know what they are, either. I only know the result. I have to live with the results."

"So you don't know?" I repeated.

"No, I don't know. I don't know what actually happened. I don't know how or even for certain if he gave me that infection, though I don't know who else could have. But I do know that he wrote in my diary at night and I know that what he wrote wasn't right. And I do know that I turned up at the doctor's office scared to death with something filthy and contagious growing on me, and I know that the doctor and my mother lied about it to me and to themselves and that it ruined all of our lives forever."

You don't know who else could have? Who else could have infected you? But it could have been anyone, anyone else you don't remember. You have flashes. Flashes of what?

"What do you have flashes of?" I wrote.

"Him," she replied.

"Him how?"

"Kissing me. Touching me."

"So you do remember?"

"I see it. Quickly. Like in a film. In pieces. Very small pieces. But not all."

I was hardly listening. I was reading the words but not fully taking them in. Only leaping to the next reply, charging back. Prove it. Somehow. Make it real to me.

But how?

Would she know? If he had been there, she would know. So ask. Yes, ask. A piece of information. A flash. But wait— There is no going back if she answers. If she knows it, then it's true. Truer than anything else. Can you handle that?

You're a beast for even thinking it. So what? So what? She's accusing. So let her accuse. Fuck her. Ask.

I was mad now.

So, Robin. You were there.

"What did he taste like?" I typed and sent.

You bastard.

Yeah, yeah. I'm a bastard. You want to play? Let's play. You were there. So say. If you know so much, what did the old man taste like? What did he smell like? Get that and I'll believe you.

Scroll up.

"Blood," she replied.

Good answer, little girl. Good answer. But maybe just a bit overdone for effect. Back it up.

"Why blood?" I sent.

Typing.

Scroll.

"Because he bit me."

Really? Hmm, creative. Okay. More. Back that up, too.

"Where?"

How long would she pause on that one?

Not at all.

"My mouth."

Stands to reason.

No, that's a movie you saw. Not a flash like in a movie. It *is* a movie. He tasted like your blood? Too easy. I don't believe you.

"Bullshit," I sent.

A pause.

"When we meet I'll show you the scar."

She was laughing at me. How could she be laughing?

Push harder. Ask the last.

Fine. Laugh at this.

"What did he smell like?" I sent.

Be careful now. Don't ruin it. Either you know or you don't.

No pause. Iris typing.

"I'm not doing this."

There. You lying sack of shit. Got you.

"You lie," I sent.

Nothing.

For a long time, nothing.

Then, from Iris: "Funny you should ask."

No. It can't . . .

She can't know. She doesn't know. Don't listen.

I didn't reply.

"Sometimes lately," she wrote, "I could swear I've smelled him. Like he's been in the room."

She couldn't know that without—

Without knowing.

Right? Right?

Still I didn't reply.

Don't give. Don't fold. She's lying.

Scroll up.

She wrote:

"I've been thinking I'm crazy. I've smelled your mom, too."

There. See.

You have your answer.

No lie. You know it's no lie.

"I can't describe it," she sent. "How do you describe how someone smells?"

A pause.

"But it was them. I just knew it was them. By smell. Am I crazy, Nick?"

Yes, you're fucking crazy. We're both fucking crazy.

She knows, I said aloud. She's telling you the truth.

Believe her.

"No," I sent at last. "You're not crazy."

Not crazy.

Then what?

Now what?

I can't.

I can't do this.

You said you're not doing this, and I can't do this. But you are doing it. Fuck. But I can't.

"Fuck," I sent and quit.

Exit chat.
Close out.
Shut down.
Exit. Close. Shut. Fuck. Out.
I put my head on the desk and wept.

22

I smelled bacon. Frying bacon.

Here we go, I thought, opening my eyes. Here we go. Saturday morning, 1984. Again. Except, where's the rest? I smelled bacon, and toast maybe, but not the pancakes or the creamy sweetened coffee, or the snow shovel and the bitter air.

Incomplete.

Strange.

Very strange.

Was this the diminishment of sharing? If Robin was getting the ghosts, too, was she taking some of mine away?

My God. That's right. Robin had said she was getting this, too. That happened. It wasn't a dream. She did say that.

Yes, I'm sure. She did.

The whole of the previous evening came rushing into consciousness at once. Dad. The sleepovers. My room. The diary. Jesus Christ. The diary. And then the smells. She said she was getting the smells. Mom and Dad. Like they'd been in the room, she said. Like they'd been in the room.

But I could hear sounds.

Shuffle, pat, twang, shuffle.

There were definitely sounds. Coming from where? The kitchen? Utensils, pans, cupboards? Back and to the right.

Yes, the kitchen.

Shush, scrape, muffle, twang.

Definitely the kitchen.

I'd never had sounds before. Only smells.

What the . . . ?

I lifted my head from the desk.

Sticky.

The side of my face was sticky, and the desk, too.

Vomit.

Yep.

Sleep in your own sick.

Again.

Lucky.

You're still breathing.

I wiped my face with my T-shirt, also vomitous, shrugged it off and into the trash basket.

The usual receptacle.

Schlop.

Clean it later.

Now, I said, see about the sounds.

Now.

Stand.

Oof.

Bump.

Right yourself.

Steady.

Don't be a pussy.

Go.

Go in there and see your illusion.

Walking around.

I stumbled wall to wall in the hall into the kitchen.

Dizzy, weak, thick-tongued.

I looked.

Shit.

Sure enough.

There was someone.

There was an old woman standing at the stove with her back to me, humming softly.

Was she? Really humming?

No.

Could she?

She was humming that song. What song? I knew it somehow, I knew the lyrics. But from where?

Spring will be a little late this year,
A little late arriving in my lonely world over here.

This is how it happens, I thought. This is how you go mad. It starts with dreams and smells, then escalates to sounds and sights. Songs you know and people you don't. Togetherness in the kitchen.

Am I dreaming or waking?

I don't know. I don't know. I have dreamt this dream before. I remember, this dream of waking, being awake, while all the while I was sleeping.

This has the quality of a dream. Surely. An old woman at the stove humming an old song that Mom sometimes sang around the house. My mind's extrapolation of what my mother would look like now, except that I can't picture it quite, so I can't see her face. Her face is the back of her head even when she turns around. Isn't that how it goes? She can turn her head like an owl, all the way around, and I will only ever see the back of her head.

So interpret the dream then, I said. Yes, interpret, if it's a dream.

But can you interpret a dream when you are in one?

You can if you are dreaming about dreaming.

But am I?

Who cares? Do it anyway.

Okay, okay. Ease off. I'm frightened. I feel sick.

So what? Go on. Tell me. Go on. Now. Tell me.

All right, all right. Fuck.

Umm.

I see . . . [*smell of bacon still, spoon clanking, pot rustling, a figure of a woman*]

I see the back of my mother's head. Why? Because . . . [*still humming—that creepy humming*]

I see the back of my mother's head because my mother never faced me, because my mother didn't have a face.

Is that right?

Maybe.

So?

So what else?

What do you mean, what else? *What* what else?

So can she talk, my old lady?

Find out if she can talk.

I . . .

"Hello?" I said tremulously.

Aloud?

Must have.

She turned abruptly.

"Well, hello there," she said, flashing a reassuring smile. "At last."

A face.

She has a face.

It's not Mom.

It's not Mom at all.

It's Mrs. Bloom?

Mrs. Bloom was in my kitchen.

Did she die in the night over there, in her green kitchen across the street, and now she's in my kitchen over here?

"Mrs. B.?" I croaked.

Definitely aloud.

She turned back to stirring what she had on the stove.

"I came by earlier," she said, turning toward me again, seeming to notice for the first time that I was half caked in my own puke.

She grimaced.

"I rang the bell for a long time, but there was no answer. Then I tried the door and it was open."

She returned to her stirring.

"I hope you don't mind terribly, Nick. I wouldn't normally just walk into somebody's house uninvited, but when I stuck my head in and called your name, I was—" She paused, editing herself. "Well, I was overwhelmed by the smell, to be perfectly honest, and I got worried."

She laughed nervously.

"You know, all this time I've been thinking that I was the one they were going to find rotting in my house someday, no one the wiser, and I guess I panicked. I thought, God, he could be dead in there, or dying, and no one would know."

Her eyes widened with concern. She laughed again, more genuinely this time.

"So, anyhow, I thought I'd check on you. I tried to wake you several times, but it was no good, so I thought I'd clean up a bit and cook you some break-fast while you slept it off. Of course, you had nothing in the fridge, so I went back to my place and brought over this."

She gestured at a carton of eggs, the pack of bacon, some milk, bread, margarine, and orange juice.

"That's very kind, Mrs. B., really," I said, suppressing a gag. "But I'm feeling pretty rotten and—"

"And I thought to myself," she continued, as if I hadn't spoken, "I bet he hasn't had a home-cooked meal in years, and a proper breakfast in longer than that."

She fixed me with that piercing stare of hers, seeming to reprimand and console at the same time.

"Am I right?" she said flatly.

"I'm—" I stammered. "I'm really not a breakfast person. I'm hardly ever up before evening."

Why was she here? Why was she really here? This wasn't just weird because I'd woken in a lake of my own sick and someone other than Dave had found me that way, or because I was standing clueless and horrified in my kitchen feeling as though I'd just slept with my grandmother. It wasn't even weird because I'd thought I'd smelled a ghost and found it rattling my pots and pans. It was just weird. Period.

"Why don't you go and get cleaned up," she said, seeming to sense the need for a better explanation. "I'll have this ready in a minute. Then we can talk."

Why don't you get out of my fucking kitchen, I thought, still staring, still only half believing that she was real.

"Gatorade," I said, afraid to approach.

She looked puzzled.

"There's Gatorade in the fridge," I explained, extending a limp arm.

She nodded, opening the fridge. She crossed the kitchen with the bottle and handed it to me with a worried frown.

"See you in a few minutes?" she asked.

I took the bottle and said nothing.

I spent a long time in the shower, drinking and puking, drinking and puking. Rinse and repeat.

When I shuffled back into the kitchen at least forty minutes later— probably more like over an hour—I was sure Mrs. B. would be gone. But there she was, sitting at the table, drinking a cup of coffee and looking pensively out the back window into the yard.

Please no Miriam yet, I thought, panicked.

I looked. Nope.

Remembering our promise not to be polite and feeling immensely grateful for that now, I checked the impulse to apologize. Instead I said:

"This is what I do."

"Yes," she said resignedly. "I see."

She had put away the breakfast things and either dumped or eaten what she had made, because there was nothing on the table or the counter for me.

"I've been in touch with Robin," I blurted, surprising myself.

She blinked over the rim of her cup, took a sip, and set it down.

"I thought you might," she said calmly.

"Why?"

"Oh, I don't know, because she brings chaos in her wake. Always has done."

I grunted, pulling a face.

"Yeah, well, I do pretty well on the chaos front myself, as you can see."

She smiled weakly and looked away.

"But you only hurt yourself," she said.

"Not true, not true," I objected. "That's where you're wrong. I've left a trail of half-wits in my wake that you wouldn't believe. AA meetings all over town are filled with my rejects."

She chuckled politely but said nothing. She let her eyes rest on the floor, staring blankly.

I was out of excuses and not-so-charming repartee, so I sank heavily into a chair across from her at the table. I thought about getting up to get another Gatorade, but couldn't bring myself to move, so instead I stared at a fixed point on the horizon out back, hoping to quell my nausea the old-fashioned way.

The silence grew heavy and uncomfortable between us.

Whatever she had come for, it was bad. Really bad. Her former equanimity was gone, replaced by an emanating dread. Looking at her full on, I could see why she had waited out my shower. She was spooked. Deep down spooked in that childish, afraid-of-the-dark kind of way that makes you park yourself in the lobbies of public buildings or doctors' offices because you're just that desperate for company, and because you're under the mistaken impression that the bogeyman doesn't do groups. I knew that feeling well. I'd sat for hours in all kinds of places where I didn't have appointments, just so I could loiter unnoticed and soak up the bland solace of the herd.

Mrs. B. was here for that. Because she needed somewhere to be, and someone—anyone—to be with. It didn't matter where or whom.

"How long have you known?" I asked.

She started slightly at the sound of my voice.

"Known? About what?"

"About Robin. That she was alive, I mean."

She looked relieved.

"Alive?" she said knowingly. "Oh, Lord. Since she left, I suppose."

She closed her eyes wearily and pinched the bridge of her nose between her thumb and index finger. She looked up at me, blinking away the fatigue.

"I realize that it's become something of a cliché to say this, but it's true in my case. A mother knows."

She searched my face, as if for confirmation.

I nodded attentively.

"When your child dies, a light goes out," she said, nudging her coffee cup away toward the center of the table.

She kept her eyes on the cup.

"I knew about Karen days before they came to tell us. I knew in the middle of the night. Sat bolt upright from a deep sleep, wide awake, and I knew."

She paused thoughtfully.

"It was like drowning. I couldn't get my breath. I wanted to scream or cry out for help. I didn't know what was happening to me. But I couldn't make a sound. My throat was closing and my tongue was like sodden bread. Suffocating. Heavy. It was horrible."

She draped her opened palm across her throat and stroked it, soothingly.

"And then, just as suddenly as it had come, it passed," she said.

She let her hand fall to her lap.

"Everything relaxed. Everything in me went limp and weightless and—do you know?"

She looked at me intently, seemingly amazed again by the memory.

"I felt more whole and complete than I have ever felt in my entire life before or since. It was the profoundest peace I have ever known, and it was the moment—I'm sure of it—that my only daughter left this earth, the moment she let go of all the pain and struggle of her short, troubled life and just went."

I hesitated to point out that she wasn't talking about her only daughter now. She was talking about her granddaughter. Surely a grandmother didn't just know. But clearly, Mrs. Bloom drew no distinction between the two. Robin was her own as much as Karen had been, telepathy of the womb be damned.

"You know," she said, taking another long, pensive sip of coffee. "When I was a girl, my mother gave me a necklace for my fifteenth birthday. It was in the shape of a heart, a silver heart, and at the center there was a stone set in it. A large square aquamarine. On the back she'd had the jeweler engrave the words 'My heart walking around.' That's what she always called me, you see. She'd say, 'You're my heart walking around.' It wasn't until I became a mother myself that I understood what those words really meant. She meant them quite literally. Having a child is like having one of your vital organs out walking around in the world. *The* vital organ, and when it stops, you stop, too. That's what happened the night Karen died."

She placed her palms flat on the tabletop and looked at her arthritic hands. Her eyes wandered regretfully over each bulbous swelling, each cruel bend of bone.

"With Robin, nothing stopped," she said. "On the contrary, it went on and on and on, and it's still going. Every day, I can feel it here in my chest, like the sound of something very loud but very far away, rolling on. Robin is alive because her pain is alive and it has a presence in the world like a germ or a shock wave, spreading where she sends it."

Her face clouded and she looked out the window again toward the sky. She squinted against the light.

"This morning it was very close to home," she said.

"How do you mean?" I asked.

"Oh, I don't know. It's not just one thing. It's a lot of things. Little things. Things you'd easily miss if you weren't attuned to them. Things that build up and cluster at certain times, or have done over the years. Or maybe I'm just getting old"—she smiled, waving her hand to indicate her unsavory surroundings—"and smelling death everywhere."

I smiled, too, sheepishly. The smell of my own accumulated sick in the morning, overpowering, and I wasn't even aware. That's when you know you've gone morbid—when your stink is completely undetectable to you and yet strong enough to draw the neighbors.

"I saw something in the paper," she continued. "An obituary for an old family friend I haven't thought about in years. I saw the picture. It wasn't a particularly recent picture—he must have been at least five years my senior— so he looked much the way I remembered him. Startlingly so. Like someone who shouldn't have died. Like someone popped out of my memory as big as life, and there he was in a notice telling me he was dead."

She sighed and patted my arm.

"When you get to be my age, Nick, this is what happens. More often than you'd care to acknowledge, you start seeing people you know in the obituaries column."

She shuddered.

"And you feel a cold, sharp thrill go through you."

She turned her gaze back to me and blinked concertedly, as if trying to bring me and this moment back into focus.

"Anyway, there he was, looking out at me, big as—well, big as death, I guess, and . . ."

She trailed off.

And when you thought of death, big as death, you thought of me, I thought. Thanks a lot. I'll just go over and see Nick, big as death over there, still clinging to life but barely. Practically putrid. Jeez, you can smell him from here.

So kind. Really, thanks.

"That's terrible," I said at last, trying to sound sympathetic, and failing. "Is there going to be a service?"

"I expect so, but I couldn't go."

"Why not?"

"It's complicated," she said. "It's been far too long, for one thing. Far, far too long. I should have been in touch ages ago, I suppose."

"I'm sure the family wouldn't hold that against you," I said. "You didn't hold it against me."

"No." She sighed. "You're right. I'm sure they wouldn't."

She looked away again distractedly.

I wondered if she was thinking about Robin. I was surprised by her lack of curiosity on the subject of our recent contact. I had spent so much time thinking about what to tell her and what not to tell her, about protecting her from painful knowledge or false hope, but none of that turned out to be of the slightest importance now. I was all wrong again in my assumptions. She, too, the simplest of women, or so I had assumed, knew more than I did, and might well have laughed at my naïveté or manipulated it.

She wasn't grieving the death or disappearance of a child, after all. That was for storybooks. She was grieving the survival of a child, the separate, rogue survival of a child. Was that it?

Dr. Cunningham had said as much himself. It wasn't the fact of a life. It was the quality of that life, the tenor of it, its reach and ambient effect. Mrs. B. had made Robin sound like a noxious presence in the world, a nuclear accident or a plague, not a sweetheart abducted and mourned. Yet surely she was that, too, the girl the construction worker had made the bracelet for, the girl Gruber, of all people, had doted on so fondly.

I knew from my own experience what Robin had become: bitter, vengeful, self-righteous. I knew how she could bleed into and poison her surroundings.

But—

There was still a but.

An extenuation of memory, an ideal that I held on to.

"Has Robin been in touch with you?" I asked, pretty certain I knew the answer already.

"Oh, yes, yes," she said. "All along."

She waved her hand dismissively.

"Robin made sure I knew where she was, or where she'd been. She knew enough to conceal her whereabouts. She had no intention of being found or of coming home. That was clear. She was teasing. I got postcards from all over. Gag postcards usually, as if she were on vacation and it was all a big joke. It was her way of letting me know how angry she was."

So much for a mother just knows, I thought. So much for that light in the window. Robin had been manipulating this from day one. The punishment, the revenge, had started early. There was no mystery at all, and the only loss was of trust and innocence. Mrs. Bloom's as much as Robin's.

She turned to me abruptly.

"Nick," she said, breathlessly. "I'm frightened."

She covered her mouth with her palms and clenched her eyelids, as if shutting out an ugly sight. A tear rolled out of each eye and pooled on her fingertips.

"I'm so frightened—" She gasped.

I took hold of her wrists, gently guiding her arms to her lap and taking her hands in mine.

"Mrs. B., what is it?" I asked. "What are you so frightened of?"

She raised her eyes to me slowly, puzzled.

"Of her," she whispered. "Don't you see? Of what she'll do."

She was trembling.

"Something must have happened," I said. "Something that made you worry so much now, after all this time. What was it? What's changed?"

"The postcards," she said, as if the revelation had just come to her. "She stopped mailing them."

"And you think that means something has happened to her?" I asked.

"No, no," she cried, frustrated by my lack of understanding. "I've still been getting them, just not through the mail."

"I don't understand," I said, even though of course I did. I wanted to see if she did, too.

"She's been here, Nick," she said. "She's been delivering them herself in the mailbox by hand."

Yes, I thought. She's been making the rounds.

For once, I was the one who sounded informed.

"Yeah, I know," I said. "No postmark."

"So that's how she's reached you?" she said.

"That and online. She found me on Facebook. Do you know about Facebook?"

She frowned searchingly.

"I've heard the term, or I've read it somewhere, but it doesn't mean anything to me."

"It's a way to find long-lost friends." I chuckled bitterly. "Among other things."

"So she sent you some kind of message on this Facebook?"

"Well, that, and she's been leaving me notes in the mailbox, too. Same as you."

She squinted thoughtfully.

"But what would she have to say to you?" she asked.

Catching herself, she added:

"I'm sorry, I didn't mean it like that. But you didn't know her, did you? Not really."

"No. Not really. Mostly through my mom. And yeah, I thought exactly the same thing. Why me? Why now?"

"And?" she said.

"And what?"

"Why you? Why now?"

"I have no idea," I lied. "I thought you were going to tell me."

I pushed my chair back, its legs scraping painfully on the linoleum, and went to the fridge for another Gatorade.

"Hell," I said, yanking one from the shelf in the door and wrenching off the cap, "I didn't even know until now that you knew she was alive. That's how stupid I am. All this time I thought you were grieving for her, hoping, waiting for her to come home, or for someone to find her, and instead the opposite is true. You've known all along and you're terrified of her coming back."

I kicked the refrigerator shut. It sealed with a loud suck.

"It's not the opposite," she said firmly.

She paused, checking my expression, then resumed more gently.

"That's wrong . . . It's both . . . It's all . . . I have grieved *and* I have been afraid. I have worried *and* I have longed for her . . . But I have also wished that she would stay away."

She paused again.

I could feel myself getting angry. I'm so tired, I thought. Tired of this convoluted past and its sick characters that just won't die or conform or stop. I turned toward the sink, my back to her, and took a long, sloppy drink. I wiped my mouth with the back of my hand and belched loudly.

"Victims are not saints," she added sharply, as if in retort.

"Yes," I murmured more tamely. "I'm aware."

This was my territory now. On this I could well instruct.

"The things that have happened to you," I announced sarcastically, "are just the things that have happened to you. They don't make you who you are."

I turned to face her.

"They don't make you special or entitled or excused or fucking good," I spat, furiously.

"Nick," she cried. "I didn't mean—"

"I know, I know," I shouted, turning away again. "You never meant any of it."

I hurled the half-filled Gatorade into the sink. It bounced out of the basin, threw a jet of purple Riptide Rush against the backsplash and the window, skidded across the counter spewing as it went, and spiraled onto the floor, where it came to rest on its side beneath the cupboard overhang.

Mrs. Bloom gasped disapprovingly.

I gripped the sides of the sink, enraged.

"You never meant for harm to come to Robin. You never meant for harm to come to Karen. But it did, didn't it? It did. And now what you did or didn't mean doesn't matter anymore, and the little girl that everybody loved to love and loved to give things to, she's a barking freak coming in for a landing at home sweet home. So deal with it. Finally fucking"—I choked—"deal with it."

I leaned down and vomited into the sink. The heave itself was silent, just an effortless pouring forth, but the viscous gush of syrup and bile that came out of me landed against the flat stainless steel of the basin with a horrible, thick smacking sound and slithered with a half-muffled screech down the drain.

I ran the water for a moment and put my head under. I laid my head on my arm and draped a dish towel over it. I stayed that way for a long time, breathing as deeply as I dared and waiting for the wherewithal to move.

As far as I could tell, Mrs. B. didn't stir. She didn't make a sound. I might as well have been alone except that I could feel her woundedness pulsing behind me like something I'd run over in the road.

When I raised my head at last to look at her, she was sitting with her hands folded loosely in her lap. Her eyes were closed. She opened them hesitantly and let them drift to my face, slowly, exhaustedly, as if she were looking out of obligation at something gruesome or pornographic that she did not wish to see. I suppose she was.

"You see," she said resignedly. "She has ruined this already. And we had only just begun."

She stood to go.

I didn't try to stop her.

She was right and I knew it.

But I would make an effort to minimize the damage.

"Look," I said. "Don't be hurt. That anger is for her, not you. It's just that she isn't here and—"

She cut me off.

"Yes. That's always been it. What she leaves you. You have to work with what she leaves you. And what she leaves you is always broken and sharp and impossible to pick up without cutting yourself. That has always been her gift. She puts an obstacle in your way so that you have to move it. You have to grapple with it, and when you do that you hurt yourself, and then she has what she was after all along."

I pushed myself away from the sink. Bolstering myself with one hand, I made my way around the U of the counter toward where she was standing.

"We don't have to let her win," I said. "Not entirely."

She shrugged meekly and turned away.

"Let me at least walk you home," I insisted.

She walked through the doorway into the hall.

"If you like," she called back, with just the barest hint of a lilt in her voice.

I smiled. She was forgiving me already. By this evening she would have left this behind, sloughed it off with the other detritus of the day and the hours and the years. It just wasn't important.

That, anyway, was how I imagined her mind working: like a drive-through car wash, or one of those newfangled, self-cleaning lavatories, a stainless pod with a door to let experience in and a spray to wash it away again. A remarkable fluidity.

She had come to me for solace, and I had failed her, even confirmed her worst fears. Okay. So she would let it go and move on, slide into the next moment clean, and me with it, waiting for what would happen next and showing up. Nothing more.

Nothing more complicated than that.

I followed her to the front door, opened it for her, and made a show of offering her my arm.

She smiled warmly.

"You," she said, nudging me.

"I know, I know." I laughed. "But here we are."

"Indeed," she mused, taking my arm. "Here we are indeed."

We walked in silence across my neglected front lawn, across the empty street, glazed and sleepy with the afternoon sun, and down the gentle slope of her own lawn, where an undefiled little girl had once sat reading Dante and Frost and Hopkins, and taught it all to a bird.

When we reached Mrs. B.'s doorstep and turned to say good-bye, I said:

"Mrs. B., can I ask you something very personal?"

"Of course you can, Nick." She nodded her assent. "Please."

I hesitated, looking up toward the house, puzzled.

"That light in the upstairs window. The one you light and put out every night and morning. I always thought it was for Robin." I paused, scowling into the sun. "But it's not, is it?"

She scanned my face, surprised and, it seemed, slightly disappointed.

She shook her head.

"Oh, no, dear. No."

I waited, but she said nothing more. She, too, was looking up at the house, at the place where the light would appear this evening.

"So then," I said at last, "who is it for?"

She put her palms together in a prayer position in front of her chest and brought her fingertips to her lips. She raised her eyes to my face.

"Dear boy," she whispered.

She leaned in slowly and deliberately and kissed me very softly on the cheek. As she stepped away, she raised the back of one hand and lightly brushed the place she had kissed.

"Why, it's for you, of course," she said. "It has always been for you."

She smiled sadly, turned quickly, went into the house, and gently closed the door behind her.

I turned and crossed her lawn again, thinking this time not just of Robin's past, but of my own, and of how Robin had said the two overlapped. "The same thing that happened to you," she'd said. What happened to me is the same thing that happened to you.

I stopped on the easement to collect my mail. When I got back inside, I set the mail on my desk and went through it. There was all the usual junk, which I threw directly into the bin on top of my soiled T-shirt. There was a small package, a yellow bubble mailer with my name written on it in black marker, but no address, stamps, or postal marks. I tore it open immediately and a single old Maxell sixty-minute microcassette tape fell out.

Robin had been by.

Among the junk in the bin I could see my copy of that week's *Pelsher County Gazette* partially folded back on itself. I fished it out and flipped to the obits page.

It was the only picture on the page, and she was right. It was old. Soft-focused and forgiving. The face hopeful and bland. Nothing like the man now. Beneath the photo the listing read:

> Dr. Simon T. Cunningham, beloved and venerated
> pediatrician and long-standing pillar of his com-
> munity, died Tuesday at his home in Twin Pines.
> He was seventy-two. The cause of death has not
> yet been officially determined, his daughter Joclyn
> said, though he was found lying comfortably in his
> bed, and by all indications appears to have died
> peacefully in his sleep. Apart from his daughter
> and his three grandchildren, Dr. Cunningham is
> survived by his wife, Lelah, and his sister Rose.

23

At nightfall, the light went on in Mrs. B.'s window. Hours and hours later, I was still sitting at my desk thinking about Doctor Cunningham, wondering if there was a code phrase in obits for suicide, and if so, was it "died in his sleep"? Or, more to the point, "appeared to die in his sleep"?

Life just wasn't that neat. It didn't wait for you to make your confession on the off chance the right confessor would show up, and then check you out that same night, done deal.

I kept thinking of that lacquered box. Now *that* was something he could have waited for, or waited with, grasping it in hand, as he had done (firmly enough to leave a mark), then popping it open for the last. I saw it in his face, his whole body—the resignation, the relief. He was done. As soon as he said those words—"You must stop this now"—he was done. And that box, or what was in it—it could have been anything; he was an MD—was his ticket, his door out.

Good for him. He had had the courage to do what I could not. And despite everything that's said about suicide and cowardice, and everything we boast about our unbelief, at the end, when we are alone with an irrevocable choice, we are all afraid to be so insolent in the face of the unknown. It takes courage.

Robin. There was chaos in her wake all right. A cluster of harm, and now death. It was enough to make you believe in spells. No wonder Mrs. B. was so afraid. I was afraid now, too, and exhilarated in a way that I didn't trust. I didn't want to be alone, either.

I wanted Monica with me. I wanted to hide myself in her presence and stop thinking or feeling anything except the most primitive impulses—hunger, fatigue, desire—and the satisfaction of all three with her. I'd never felt the need so strongly before. I wanted to rush down to the Swan in the hope of finding her there, or of finding someone who knew where she might be.

But she didn't have any friends. She didn't have any acquaintances. Just her so-called partner, Damian, and me.

Damian. He at least had a phone.

I dialed his number and left a message. Have Monica find me. It's important.

I went to the front door and unbolted it, in case I was passed out when she arrived. I left it open most nights for the same reason, which is how Mrs. B. had found it this morning when she'd sauntered in unannounced.

I made my way down to the basement for the first time in I didn't know how long. I'd lost track of time and everything except Robin and her goose chase. I hadn't even thought of Dave or Jeff or Dorris and the rest. My own life had grown up around me, even if still in a virtual world, online, in the past. What did it matter? I was alive again, immersed, and not in someone else's life, but my own. Someone else's life as my own. The same thing.

What did that mean? The same. Robin and I did not have the same past. Did we? And yet I could hardly deny it. Even Mrs. B. seemed to think so. What else was that light in her window but an apology? Or a small cheer from the side of the course that says, "Come on. Almost there." I hated that idea. Mrs. B. cheering. Hurrah for the chin-up cripple, who runs in his special race.

The basement seemed like a foreign place now, though it had been only— what?—a few days? I wasn't sure. All the usual markers had fallen away, and my thoughts had stretched across the emptiness.

I went to open the locks on the monitor room door and stopped. I couldn't do it. I couldn't bring myself to go in there and shame myself again with all that I would see or try to see. For the first time the distraction felt too heavy, too tedious to carry out. The unlocking of the door, the powering up, the scanning for movement, action, argument. It had become like everything else: routine. I was dulled finally to its shock. I had developed a tolerance to this drug, too.

I stood there fiddling with my keys, waiting to know what to do. It was late. Very late, I thought. Maybe close on dawn. Who knew?

I shoved the keys in the front pocket of my jeans and lumbered up the stairs. Just inside the basement door my eyes fell on the flashlight that I keep on the shelf there. I picked it up and switched it on, then off again. Not bright, but bright enough.

I took it, closed the basement door behind me, hustled through the hall and out the front door. It was still pitch outside, but warm. My guess was four o'clock, but it might have been three, or even earlier. It didn't matter. There was time.

Yes, I thought, this night is like any other night in the middle of the night. And it was, surely, but somehow it seemed more replete than all the others I had known. More potent, like something my father would have enjoyed and acted in or on, energized by the passivity of the dark. In the dead of night he had been a different man, a bolder man.

I would be a bolder man, too. I would act. Now. Here. I would stop thinking. I tapped the keys in my pocket. I felt the weight of the flashlight in my hand.

Barefoot, I made my way down my lawn to the side of the house, over to the property line, and across to Gruber's backyard. I stepped in a cold, wet pile and felt it paste thickly across my instep. I knew what it was by the stink of it, but I turned the flashlight on anyway and shined it on my foot. I swore disgustedly and turned out the light. When I got to Gruber's patio, I scraped my foot against the edge of one of the stones, smeared the rest on the grass, and kept on toward the back door of the garage.

I fished my key ring out of my pocket, separated the subset that was Jeff's, and fiddled with each key until I found the one that fit. I eased open the door, slid inside, and closed it behind me.

I put my palm over the flashlight and turned it on. I let the light leak through my fingers as I scanned the space; then I trained the full force of the beam on what I couldn't quite see.

Gruber always parked his cars in the driveway, and now I saw why. He used his garage as a workshop, mostly for carpentry, from the look of it. There was a sawhorse in the middle of the space, with an electric circular saw perched on top of it and a long, wide piece of lumber half cut. There was sawdust and discarded trimmings all over the floor radiating outward from the horse. Beyond that, each on its own island of newspaper, lay various pieces of furniture—bookshelves, side tables, coffee tables—that Gruber had stained and varnished and set aside to dry.

I threaded my way through these obstacles, careful not to upset anything, and stopped at the inside door to the house. I stood for a few moments, listening for any hint of motion inside. Nothing.

I waited a moment longer.

Once you do this, I thought, you'll have to take what comes. There will be no going back and no reprieve. If Gruber catches you, you're dead, right here and now. Suicide by Gruber, I whispered and smiled. He won't miss.

Was that why I was here? Or was this just the most reckless thing I could think of? No, I hadn't thought. I hadn't planned. I had no idea what I was doing here or what I would do once I got inside. I had made a right turn out of my door. I had the keys to this house by accident, and now I was here by accident. What other accident was inside?

And then, strangely, I was hearing my father's words, like an incantation in my head, the words that I had read so many times, for so long thinking they were mine, and then had read and reread many times again in the last forty-eight hours, knowing they were his.

I possess this quiet place and all its houses.

At night, I am the dream of stealth to all my silenced people.

A sort of god, unknown.

It was true. So, so true. As I slipped the key in the lock I felt exactly what he had described. All of it. The potency of the transgression, the terrible possession of people and places that are emptied yet filled by sleep, the power of quiet violation. I felt immensely dulled by it, drugged, so oddly calm in this invasion of someone else's home.

He was right. It was unmistakably sexual, a predatory high that was bound to be addictive to almost anyone who could take that first breaching step over the threshold. But it was something else as well, something cozier, cleaner, like love.

A tongue of silent invitation.

Each dear, dear nesting thing.

And somehow doing this to Gruber, of all people, made the thrill of it that much more intense and immediate, like ramming my buttered fist right up his hard-walled ass.

I opened the door and went in.

I stood in Ellie's country kitchen looking at the flaxen-haired stuffed dolls in overalls perched on the glass-fronted crockery hutch. I looked at the painted wooden sign on the wall that read, GOD BLESS THIS HOME, and the dwarf bonsai in a pot by the sink. I listened to the fridge humming and tinkling, and I stared at the blue-white light of the digital clock on the stove. I watched several minutes pass. I took my pulse. Not bad. Sixty-five.

I wasn't frightened at all. In fact, as I stood there observing the clock, watching the two dots between the numbers tick the seconds off—*bip* . . .

bip . . . bip—feeling the soft drumming of my heart on my fingertips, and listening to the hum of the refrigerator in the kitchen of a house I had just broken into, I realized that I was more relaxed, more at peace—actual peace—than I had been since early childhood. I felt engulfed by an ameliorating sense of fate that seemed to say: What you do or do not do now will make no difference. It will all just unfold.

Believing this, I felt an immense relief. I was not responsible. I was not in control. I was in the picture and the picture was whatever it would be. I thought of what Mrs. Bloom had said about the night Karen died. That release. The worry gone.

I felt the lightness of indifference.

I walked into Gruber's study and turned the flashlight on full beam. The guns were on the wall, the pencil sharpener was on the desk, the red chair was pushed in, and Iris's cage was in the corner, covered with a brightly multicolored beach towel.

"Jesus Christ," I said, clutching my chest. "You scared the living shit out of me. What are you doing here?"

Miriam was standing under the apple tree, picked out, a shadow among shadows.

"What are *you* doing here?" she said smartly.

"It's my house."

"So?"

"So? I live here. You don't."

"I know," she said, dropping her chin. "But still."

She was right. But still. It was the middle of the night and I had come across the back from Gruber's to stand in my own backyard and do what?

I softened my tone.

"Miriam, how many times have you done this?"

She blinked innocently.

"Done what?"

"Been here in the middle of the night?" I said firmly.

She crossed her arms over her belly nervously, clutching her elbows with her hands.

"This is the first time."

"Are you telling the truth?"

"Yes."

"Honest?"

She stamped her foot in protest.

"I swear."

"Okay, okay. So what are you doing here tonight?"

She looked at the ground, frowning, trailing an exploratory toe back and forth across the grass.

"Can't sleep."

It was a better excuse than mine, and I understood it, given what I'd seen transpire between Dorris and Jonathan of late, and what Jonathan had said about his extra pair of eyes and ears tailing Miriam. Did Miriam know or sense she was being followed? Was she still? Or was it just the operatic custody battle resuming at home that had left her unable to sleep? I knew all this, but I said the chiding parent's stock phrase anyway.

"You should be home. It's not safe—really not safe—for a girl your age to be out on her own in the middle of the night. Don't you know that?"

"I know." She dropped her arms to her sides and looked off longingly into the dark. "It's just that . . ."

I know, I thought, and looked out, too, in the same direction, toward the main road behind my house, and the flaw in the fencing that led to it, all quiet, enchanting, the way out and the way home again, and yet the backdrop to so much pain.

Let her tell you about it then, I thought. Just let her say.

"It's just that what?" I said, leadingly.

She shrugged.

"I feel better here." She considered this briefly, then added, "Safe."

"But you're not safe. I've just said that."

She scowled woundedly and said nothing.

"I'm sorry," I said. "I didn't mean . . . Go on . . . What do you mean by safe?"

She took a long time to answer, swallowing hard, determined to hold back a show of emotion that she was too proud to show.

"I don't know," she said, haltingly. "Like I belong. Like all this stuff"—she indicated the village—"is a place for me. And you're here, too, and I don't feel lonely."

It was simple and beautiful and true, what she'd said, more so than she could know or I could tell her. It was more than I'd thought she was capable of, and I didn't know how to answer.

It was how I felt, too. We'd made a secret world—as a man and a girl we had made it—and it wasn't wrong, and in it—I could sense this now myself—the dark held you and hid you from everything that was wrong in the real world, and it was precious for that reason.

Carefully, respectfully, I sat beside her on the ground and took a long look around at our creation, or what I could see of it in the dark. And as I looked, and thought and smiled proudly, I felt myself soften to the idea of her and the intimacy we had shared in this place, an intimacy that was in no way shameful or base or to be defended against, but something, on the contrary, that I could recognize as my own. I had felt this before, in the distant past, as a child myself playing with other children, and until this moment I had forgotten how full and wide open a feeling it was, how freeing and—Miriam was right—safe it seemed, even, or perhaps especially in the middle of the night.

"Me, too," I said thickly, my voice swelling unexpectedly with tears.

"Really?"

I put my arm around her shoulders and squeezed.

"Yeah, really. Building this with you has meant a lot to me. I didn't know it until just now, but it has. A lot. You have no idea."

She smiled up at me, pleased, but not quite understanding.

I slid my arm off and away from her self-consciously and replaced it at my side.

"When you get older," I explained, "you don't do things like this anymore. You forget or you don't have time or nobody brings it out in you, and it just goes away. And you miss it. Only you don't know that you've been missing it until you have it again. Like now. Do you know what I mean?"

She nodded.

"Sort of," she said.

"It's like what you said," I went on. "A feeling that everything's okay and that all the hard things about the real world don't exist. Nothing exists but this. And it's how you want it to be."

She nodded again, more emphatically.

We sat silently for several minutes then, looking at the sky and the dark houses and the empty street, and listening to the soft breathing of the trees. I was on the verge of telling her about the shape of my sleeping giant in the growth of leaves above the Blooms' house, but then I wondered if it would seem too strange to her. I thought better of it and didn't. I plucked a fat spear of grass and wound it around my finger and began tying it in knots. It broke and I threw it aside.

Abruptly, there was the sound of her voice.

"Do you . . . love . . . me?" she said.

She said it so haltingly that, at first, I thought I had misheard.

I waited, watching her face, half pleading for an escape.

Had she said it? Had she meant it? That way?

Please don't have, I thought. Not that. Not now. Not from her. Not that same question the other way around. But she *had* said it, and meant it. She was waiting for an answer.

But what answer?

Don't do this to me, kid.

It was there, as always, so quickly—my father's longed-for voice saying the thing he had said to me once so long ago in response to this same question?

Yes, it was his voice, not mine. And memory's.

Dad?

Silence.

Dad?

Do you love me?

Silence.

Then:

As your mother says, love is not had as a gift . . .

No, no, me. Not her. Please. Not that. Me. Just answer me.

More silence.

Long, grueling silence.

Then, sighing, at last:

Don't do this to me, kid.

Yes, he said it just like that.

I do remember.

And now I know why.

I have known why before, but now I am on the other side of it, and I know it more completely, more painfully, in a way that explains the anger he felt.

Because I feel it, too.

Because the real answer, my answer, is this:

I do not love you, kid. I'm sorry. I'm so very sorry, but I do not love you.

You are too plain. Not mine. Just . . . just not enough, and I'm sorry.

But it is not my fault.

And it is not your fault, either.

And *goddamn it* why am I in this position?

Why?
Because it is the other side and it hurts, too.
You see?
Not to love hurts, too.
To be on the other side of love,
not loving,
hurts, too.
Now you know.
And what's worse,
now you have to lie about it.
Or don't.
Lie to a child about love,
or don't lie and rip her
as you yourself were torn
by the wrong words.
Don't do this to me, kid.
I straightened stiffly and coughed.
"Miriam, listen," I said, too loudly.
She started at the resolve in my voice.
"This is very important," I said, more softly, "and I want you to hear this,
really hear this, okay?"
She made no sign that she had heard, except the sign of not making a sign.
She was hurt already.
"Okay," she murmured, too late and too timidly to sound sure.
I touched her arm.
"I mean it."
"Okay," she said, pulling away. "I said okay."
I pulled up more grass and began to twine it nervously around my fingers.
"Love is a strange and complicated thing," I said, wincing at the tiredness
of that phrase. I was going to flub this and I knew it.
"Just to say the word 'love' isn't enough," I added firmly, wincing again.
I checked her face. It was still closed and wounded.
"A lot of people will do that, and they won't mean it, and it will hurt
you in the end . . . It will . . . because, you see, love is not just something you
say. It's something you do. Love is easy to say, and very hard to do. Do
you see?"
Again she made no sign of recognition.

"So people say it a lot, and then they don't do it, and that's worse than not saying it at all."

I paused clumsily.

This wasn't going to work. I could see that. The damage had been done, the desired answer not supplied. Nothing else would penetrate. Still, I couldn't stop myself from trying. The guilt was too strong.

"I know none of this makes much sense now, but it will, which is why I want you to remember it."

"I'll remember it," she said flatly, standing fastidiously and brushing off her shorts with hard smacking motions on her rear. "I'll always remember it."

She barreled past me and sprang across the yard to the mock village. When she'd reached it, she turned to shoot a last punishing look in my direction—she had Dorris's flair down pat—then she turned back and with all the willowy force her small body could command she kicked down the gazebo and stomped on it. It made a light whiffing sound like a house of cards collapsing, and then a mild series of cracks as she trampled it. Unsatisfied, she dropped to her knees and tore out the tea party with her hands, flinging dirt and leaves and litter all around her like a panicked bird wrecking a nest. She stood again to destroy the cemetery and the streets, but I caught her in time, grasping her roughly by the shoulders.

"Stop," I shouted, shaking her. "Don't do this, Miriam. Please."

"Let go of me," she screamed, her voice slicing through the night air.

It was a terrifying sound. I dropped my hands at once and stepped back. She lowered her voice, but only slightly, to a half-stifled sob.

"You're a liar and I hate you."

She turned and flew out of the yard, her arms and legs flailing furiously, her body thrashing from side to side like a kite whirled in an angry wind.

I followed her as far as the end of my drive to be sure she wasn't going anywhere but home.

She ran down the property line her accustomed way and across the street to her house. She had left a front window ajar on the ground floor, her way out, presumably. She lifted it higher, pulled herself through to the waist, toppled inside, and shut the pane behind her.

I turned and picked my way back to the house, shaking and wiping the cold moisture from my face.

As predicted, I failed.

I was no better than he was—Dad, the man who was too honest—who couldn't say the words outright—*I love you*—and so had chosen to moan aloud at his condition instead, and my forcing of it.

Don't do this to me, kid.

But what I had said to Miriam was worse.

Some gasbag parry of the question posing as wisdom.

Love is a strange and complicated thing?

What was that?

I'd have walked out, too, in Miriam's place.

But Miriam isn't my child. Surely that counts?

No. It doesn't matter. In the end it doesn't matter. You should have just lied and told her what she wanted to hear. You should have said I love you and worked on the feeling afterward. Maybe it would have come with effort in time.

Now all you have is the mistake.

24

When I came into the house, Monica was there waiting for me. She was sitting at my desk looking at the obituary for Dr. Cunningham with a slack expression on her face.

"Hey," I said.

She looked up, momentarily startled.

"Oh, hey."

She tapped the paper with the back of her hand.

"Did you know him?"

"A little," I said.

"Your doctor?"

"No. A friend's."

"Yeah?" she said. "Which friend is that?"

"No one you know."

She threw the paper on the desk, seeming to accept the dodge, and turned toward me.

"So what's the emergency?"

Her tone was hard and superior, as if she were talking to a hysterical child prone to blowing life's little mishaps all out of proportion. I felt a pang of embarrassment. Embarrassment that I had been so in need, so without emotional resources as to beg someone I hardly knew—via someone else's voice mail no less—to come and rescue me in my own home in the middle of the night.

"It's passed," I said curtly.

She raised her brows skeptically.

"That was quick."

"Emergencies usually are."

This came out reproachfully instead of coolly, the way I had meant it to.

"Yeah, well, that's one of the downsides of being untraceable," she said. "Can't rush to help a fuck buddy in need."

"Since when do you say fuck buddy?" I asked.

She shrugged.

"Since I got a fuck buddy, I guess."

I did not like this mood, whatever it was. Not now especially. She could be of no help to me like this.

"Glad to know I've made a lasting contribution," I said, trying to match her nonchalance and failing.

"I wouldn't say lasting," she scoffed. "Isn't that the beauty of fuck buddies? They come and they go?"

I smirked.

"Usually."

She nodded, pursing her lips dismissively.

"Why are you so hostile?" I said.

"I'm not hostile." She smiled fakely. "I'm just not making an effort to be nice."

"Was it so hard before?"

She thought about this for a second.

"Yes, actually. Often it was."

"So why bother? Why did you show up at all?"

She looked away.

"Look," I said. "I don't judge you about Damian. I just didn't know how else to get in touch with you. I'm sorry if it put you in a bad spot."

"It didn't," she said.

"So what is it then? Are you angry that I called you to ask for help? I know it's been a while and maybe you figure I have no right, which is true, I guess, but I've been . . ."

I couldn't think of how to describe it.

She straightened attentively.

"You've been what?"

"I've been through a hell of a lot."

"Really?"

She still had that condescending barb in her voice.

"Yeah, really," I snapped.

She took this in.

"Where were you tonight?" she asked. "Your car was here. I thought I heard a voice outside."

"I was next door," I said without thinking.

"At four in the morning?"

"Looks that way."

"What the hell for?"

"I had the keys," I said, as if this made sense. I slumped down on the arm of the couch. "I don't know. I really don't know. Just working something out with my dad, I think."

"Through Gruber?"

"Sort of. And through stalking around at night."

She didn't ask me to explain.

"It's an incredible feeling," I said. "Being out in the world when everyone else is asleep. Walking around in people's private spaces. It makes you feel powerful and privileged, like you're looking at what the world would be like if you could peel back the cover and see underneath."

She nodded.

"Yeah, I know what you mean. Being able to access that world in different ways is really the only thing that makes life livable. That's sort of what shoplifting is like for me. That, and living out of a coffee can. The whole soft-criminal life. It keeps it interesting and off center."

She shuddered and turned the corners of her mouth down.

"If I had to live in the waking, working world all the time, doing what I'm supposed to do—I mean, Jesus, there's no place more depressing than a mall or a Wal-Mart—but when you're stealing or casing or you're there in the middle of the night, everything about it changes."

"Exactly," I said. "So then you know what I mean. All that shiny, plastic coating on everything and everyone melts away. And—I don't know—it feels more honest somehow." I paused, thinking about the cameras. "But it isn't, really."

"No," she agreed. "It isn't. But it's how we survive."

I searched her face for disapproval but found none.

"I can't," I said, letting myself fall from the arm into the body of the couch. "I just can't do this anymore."

"Do what?"

"I don't know. Play this game. Be artificial. Be strategic. Be angry. All of it.

I'm tired. I'm so fucking tired and I have no explanations for anything. Just more parties to the suffering."

She came and sat beside me on the couch. She put her arm around me and kissed my temple.

"All these people caught up in an invisible person's pain," I said. "Me most of all, and I don't understand it. I don't know why we're all still talking about it and trading pieces of something that happened so long ago. I mean, how does one person cause that much wreckage?"

"You mean Gruber?"

"No—well, yes, actually. Now that I think of it, I mean everyone on this block. It's the same thing over and over again in every house. But I was talking about the doctor and Mrs. Bloom, and, fuck, even my father."

She sighed heavily.

"I think the causes and the effects are hard to separate. That's all. Everybody is somebody's cause and someone else's effect. Everybody's doing harm and being harmed in big ways and small ways. That's life. Family life. Relationships. Love. Even doctors and priests and accountants get caught up in the tussle. It sounds stupid when people say that we're all connected. But it's true. How could it not be? We're all stuck here together maneuvering in the same small space. Contact is inevitable."

"And that's why you live so cut off from the world?" I said.

She thought about this, rolling her lower lip gently between her thumb and index finger.

"Mostly, sure. The less contact I have with other people, the safer, the cleaner it is for all of us."

She smiled, poking me in the chest. "And you're not exactly a hub yourself, you know. If you didn't need to get laid so often, you'd never leave the house."

"I go to the gym almost every day."

"Only to get laid."

I laughed.

"No, to stay in shape."

She laughed, too, nodding, sewing up the conclusion.

"Right. So that you can get laid."

"Well, okay, maybe partly, but it's mostly emotional. It's mostly because—you're right—otherwise I wouldn't leave the house enough, and because it's the only way I know, other than booze and sex, to manage the pain."

260 | Norah Vincent

She pulled a mock serious face.

"What pain?"

"Don't be an ass. You know what pain."

"Yes, right, I know. How could I forget? How could anyone forget? But I'm curious to hear you say it. Describe it."

"No."

"No, I'm serious. I want to know what it feels like. What it really feels like." I shot her a rebuking look, then looked away.

"If you don't know, I can't tell you."

"Oh, come on. Enlighten me. Here's your chance. Why not?"

"Because it doesn't work that way. I can say, it's pain, it's terror, it's desolation. But what does that mean? Describing it doesn't get you any closer to the experience. It's like trying to describe what it feels like to be high. The closest you can come is . . ."

I didn't want to say this part.

"Oh, forget it," I said, waving my hand dismissively. "You don't want to know anyway."

She leaned forward to get the rest, prompting.

"The closest you can come is?"

Is hurting other people as much and as often as you can, I thought but didn't say. Just so that you can have some company. You know, break hearts occasionally, if you can, even if they're soppy stupid half hearts and easy marks, and even if the very notion of breaking hearts is just too embarrassingly Harlequin to admit.

So, keep that crap to yourself.

And leave the hearts out of it.

So what, then, if not that?

More often insult, appall, or if all else fails, offend, and then you'll have something in common with the other crawlers that you seek out every weekend at the Swan. What else can be done? Reducing them to your condition or thereabouts is all you have to comfort you because on some days—don't all the buzzards know—being broken solo is worse than sitting on a bar stool mean drunk and mindfucking the unsuspecting stranger.

"The closest you can come," I said at last, "is having it done to you."

She took this in, unable to suppress a smirk.

"So you'd have to find my parents and kill them," she said archly, "and then I'd know."

Reluctantly, I smirked, too.

"Or, ideally, have them kill each other. Yeah, then you might know."

"Right. I see," she said. "Well, besides that, what?"

"I don't know," I said, my voice going mean. "What have you got in your grab bag of pain? . . . What's the worst thing that's ever happened to you?"

That took the tease out of her voice quick enough.

She sat up.

"Unh-unh. Nope," she said, shaking her head vigorously. "I'm not going to share something painful on a dare just so that you can shoot it down as lightweight."

"Maybe I won't. Is it lightweight?"

"And what if it wasn't?" she said, suddenly angry. "Wouldn't you feel like the biggest self-pitying prick in the world if I could one-up your pain? Wouldn't you feel pretty foolish if you found out . . . I don't know . . . What would even count as worse to you? . . . Ah, it doesn't matter anyway. I don't think you would feel foolish. I think you just wouldn't know who the hell you are anymore. I mean, who are you if you're not the wounded man under the thundercloud?"

"No one," I said, still partly trying for a joke. "Not a soul."

She wasn't buying.

"Right. So I guess you see why a person might not be so eager to share herself with you. You make it pretty impossible on both ends."

"How's that?"

"Me and you. Either I'd feel dismissed right at the moment I'm most vulnerable, or you'd disappear."

"God," I groaned. "I really am my fucking mother."

She didn't reply.

I wish I could hurt you, I thought, and almost laughed at how cheap that sounded, even just in my head. Still, there it was.

"I don't really have the power to hurt you, though, do I?" I said instead. "I mean, honestly. You don't respect me enough."

This fell between us like something wet and foul-smelling spilled on hard ground. We both recoiled.

"It's not that," she said, trying to deflect.

"What, then?" I insisted.

There was no lightening this now.

"I don't have to explain that. There is no explaining it."

"Can you try? I'd really like to understand."

"This again." She groaned dismissively. "Why?"

"Because I care what you think. A lot. Sorry. Believe me, I wish it wasn't true, but it is, and I know you don't feel the same way, and I know it's irritating, but I just want to know why."

"It's not a question of why. You know that."

"No, it is. It is. People say it's not because they can't be brutally honest, or they don't want to take responsibility for what they really think and feel. But there is always a reason—at least one clear, identifiable reason."

"But even if there were, what difference would it make?"

"It might help me."

"How could it possibly help you?"

"To use the rejection for something productive, I guess."

"Productive? That's got to be one of the most harebrained and self-indulgent things I've ever heard you say. Rejection isn't productive, Nick."

"You're wrong. My whole life has run on that principle. Rejection can be made into fuel. You can live on it, and that's better than letting it kill you."

"But it is killing you, you idiot, and you know it. And besides, you can live perfectly well—much better—on support and acceptance and good will." She laughed sarcastically. "Everybody's doing it."

"Yeah, everybody's doing it. Right. Look around. That's my point exactly. Nobody's fucking doing it. Nobody that I've seen. And I'm no different. I never had acceptance. What I got . . . what I got a lot of was rejection. Over and over again. So I learned to use it. And now acceptance and support wouldn't even work if I had them. I wouldn't know what to do with them."

"Oh, for God's sake . . . so what? What do you want from me?"

"The details."

She burst out.

"Please. Really, this is just—"

"Come on. It can't be that hard."

She was back to rage instantly.

"Hard? What the fuck do you know about hard, you spoiled little brat? God. This is so basic, and you don't have a clue . . . You really don't, do you? . . . Well, here's the truth that would smack you in your arrogant head if you gave it half a chance. It's the luxury of the loved and whole and privileged person to seek out reasons for pain and make them into food. Real, total devastation isn't like that. You don't think about it. You don't examine it. You don't convert it. And you don't get off on it. You get away from it any way you can, if you can, and you stay away. You survive and you thank God that you have, and you look for any hint of happiness or kindness wherever you can find it, and you hold on to it for dear life."

She glared at me.

"And if you want your ridiculous detail, there it is. I don't love you—whatever the hell that means to you—because you're a baby. You're a self-satisfied, lucky baby who thinks he's a tragic hero because he's joined the vast majority of the rest of the human race in finding out that life is hell."

She laughed nastily.

"You wish you had the power to hurt me? My God, do you have even the smallest inkling of how . . . *luxurious* and oblivious to actual suffering that is? Like the richest man in the world looking down on the bloody writhing pile of human misery and wondering why—O great sadness—he can't have his fresh figs today . . . It's unbelievable."

She stopped as abruptly as she had begun, turning her head to the side away from me and staring blankly at the floor.

I was looking around the room absently, watching, out of habit, the glow of the hall light reflected in the windows across from us. The black of the nighttime windows was just barely beginning to fade. The sun would be up soon.

"I guess your story must be pretty damn bad," I said, wearily.

She shrugged.

"No worse than anyone else's."

"When you think about the ragpickers in India," I agreed.

"Oh, fuck off."

"Jeez, Mon. That's got to be four 'fucks' for you tonight alone. And there I was thinking I had the foulest mouth."

She turned up the edges of her lips derisively.

"Foulest mouth. Biggest pain. Deepest soul."

"Okay, okay. Let up a little, will you? Jesus."

"You wanted to know."

"I know, I know . . . So I got it. Honest, I got it. You don't have to elaborate any more."

"I won't."

"Of course."

"Right," she murmured.

264 | Norah Vincent

"For what it's worth," I offered, "everything you said was true. I can't deny that."

She sighed impatiently, but I went on.

"And I'm really sorry for it. Sorry because it's so shameful and exposing and petty—you're right about that—but sorriest because it's cut me off from you. Maybe it's cut me off from everyone . . . No—of course it has. You can't go around hurting and offending everyone as a matter of course and expect anything but solitary confinement. Or a good, hard slap in the face."

"I'm sorry," she said gently. "I lost my temper. I shouldn't have said anything."

"No, no. It's good. I'm glad you did. You told me what I wanted to know. It's what I've always wanted to know, and I feel like I've been asking you to tell me this in a hundred ways since we met. That's what was always behind your moods, and I knew it." I put up an appeasing hand. "Sorry, more self-pity."

"Oh, forget it," she said, batting my hand away. "Just forget it. Who am I to say anything to anyone?"

"Someone who's been through a lot, I think."

She smiled sadly.

"Maybe I just read all that in a book."

"Well, it doesn't matter. It's true and you were right."

"All right. If you think so." She put a heavy hand on my back. "Now maybe we should just leave it at that."

"Yeah, okay," I said, forcing a squelched laugh. "Just give me a sec."

She smiled again, and moved her hand along my spine.

"Sure."

It wasn't very long before I had the impulse to move, or maybe I was just lost in the echo of all that she'd said. Replaying. I was sitting on top of the pit, she'd said, watching it all obscenely.

So I was, I thought, so I was. So come and see.

"Come on," I said, standing awkwardly. "I want to show you something."

I led her to the basement steps.

"You want to see something really criminal?"

I turned and barreled down the stairs without waiting for a reply. Monica followed slowly. By the time she had gotten down the stairs, I had the locks and the door to the control room open and I was powering up the system.

The screens blinked into life, revealing mostly empty or darkened rooms. A light had been left on in Dorris's bathroom, but nobody was there.

I pointed to that monitor.

"This is Dorris Katz's master bath."

I pointed again.

"And this is her bedroom."

Monica squinted and leaned closer.

"And these two," I said, indicating, "are Dave Alders's bedroom and bath. Too dark to see much."

I moved to Gruber's basement, where the light was on as usual, even though Eric wasn't in the crate.

"This is Gruber's basement," I said. "His youngest son's a bed wetter, and every time he has an accident, he has to sleep in that crate for a month straight without incident before he can go back upstairs."

Monica's brow furrowed.

"Man," she said, shaking her head.

I pointed to the next monitor.

"This is Gruber's living room—also dark at the moment, unfortunately— where his wife spends her life watching TV. And this is . . ."

The light was on in the study.

Jeff was sitting in Gruber's chair.

"What is he . . . ?" I blinked and touched the screen. "Uh . . . and this is Gruber's middle son, Jeff."

I tapped the screen gently with the nail of my index finger.

Monica pulled my hand away to get a better look.

"What is he doing?" she said, squinting again.

"Your guess is as good as mine," I replied.

"You were just there, weren't you?"

"Yeah, but he wasn't."

"He wasn't home?"

"He wasn't awa—" I stopped and corrected myself. "I didn't see him."

She turned back to the screen.

"He wasn't awake?" she said.

"Well, he sure as shit wasn't in that chair."

"Do you think he could have seen you?"

"I don't know. Maybe. If he was hiding."

She grasped my shoulder and shook it, turning me toward her.

"Nick, what did you do over there?" Her eyes were wide and piercing. "Tell me."

"Nothing," I said testily, wrenching free of her grasp and turning sharply back toward the screen.

"You went into the house and did nothing?" she said flatly. "*Riiight.*"

I didn't reply.

I was looking at Jeff. He had something lying on the desk in front of him, but the angle of the camera made it impossible for me to tell what it was. It was a blurry mass in the foreground, the focus of his gaze. His face was blank, without expression, as serene as I had ever seen it.

Gruber's voice came booming from behind the camera. He must have been in the doorway.

I jumped.

"What in God's holy name are you doing in my study, boy?" Gruber shouted.

Jeff looked up calmly, but said nothing. His eyes fell again to whatever was on the desk.

Gruber must have looked, too.

"What—?" Gruber said, panicked.

His hands came into view from the top of the picture, reaching across the desk, taking up the thing that was lying there, and raising it closer to his face to get a better look.

"I told you never, ever to go near—"

Jeff's eyes were locked on Gruber's face.

"What?" he cut in, curiously.

"I said," Gruber began, but Jeff interrupted triumphantly.

"I heard what you said." Then, acidly, he added: "It's too late. You're too late."

Gruber said nothing. Jeff was still watching him intently.

"What did you really think was going to happen?" Jeff said. "Something had to. Eventually."

This was already beyond what Gruber could do. This wasn't going to be a conversation. But then, it was clear that Jeff had never intended it to be.

This was bolder than Jeff had ever been, something planned and reckless at the same time, and I wondered if I had pushed him to it. Maybe after all the beatings and humiliations and hard treatment, a kiss had finally ruptured the torpor that had held him in check for so long. He'd chosen his mother's way, fitting oblivion around him like a drug and taking the bruises less brutally as a result. But now he was wide open, and everything inside was coming out.

Monica was standing beside me as shocked as I was and feeling the same mute tension of something terrible impending. But she seemed more thrilled than concerned, hunched and greedy for the reveal, as if this really were just happening on television as entertainment and she was the riveted audience, willing the plot to resolve.

I started to ask if she was all right, but she waved me away impatiently. "Shhhh."

Gruber was still looking at the thing in his hands.

Jeff saw this with satisfaction, then dropped his eyes thoughtfully and began to speak.

"All this time . . ." he said calmly. "All this time I thought so much about how to be your son."

His voice broke slightly, and he paused to gather himself, swallowing and breathing through his nose.

"I tried so hard for so long to figure out how to please you . . . And, you know, all I ever did was fail. Always—fail. And you hated me. You hated us all. Still. The same as ever."

His face took on the puzzled expression of a person saying something aloud for the first time and experiencing his own words as a revelation.

"So then I thought, okay, this is never going to change. This is the sentence. Do the time. Just survive . . . And, you know, I thought that would be enough. I'd make it through, leave, and never come back—start again somewhere else and spend the rest of my life free. There has to be a better life out there, I thought. I'll find it. And this place—you, all of it—will just go away.

"But then somewhere along the way I realized that that wasn't true. The world isn't really a better place at all, and just surviving isn't enough."

He sighed heavily.

"Because you take it all with you. No matter where you go, or who you're with, the world you walk into always has you in it, and you're not just some easy guy who did his time and shook it off and kept on going. You're the kid who grew up in your dad's house."

He looked up accusingly at Gruber, his brow contorting fiercely.

"And you know who that guy is? That guy's a really pissed-off, broken-up son of a bitch who takes after the old man."

He stopped, checking Gruber's face again for recognition, or the progress of an emotion he had sought to provoke.

"And that's why, if you want to know," he said, nodding at what Gruber still had in his hands. "Because I can't have a better life. I can't get out. I'm stuck here with you no matter what I do . . . and while I am . . ."

He was struggling through a sob.

"I'm going to get you back, you rotten scumbag piece of shit, and I'm going to keep on getting until you die of it or you kill me . . . Yeah, that's right—until you kill me, if you even have the balls. I'm not afraid of that anymore. Go ahead."

He gestured at the guns on the wall.

"Take your pick."

Gruber didn't move or say anything.

Jeff swiveled in the chair, raised his right leg, and kicked his foot through the glass display case. He kicked three more times around the edge of the first point of impact, and the whole of the left pane came down in pieces to the floor. He reached in, picked out one of the pistols, and sat back in the chair, holding the gun loosely in his lap. He lifted it limply.

"I thought about using one of these to do it," he said, glaring into Gruber's face. "But I wanted—I wanted to feel it, you know? I wanted to feel the life going out of her . . . I wanted to feel her heart stop beating and her whole body go slack. I wanted to squeeze and see if she would fight or if she would know what was coming. I wanted to look into her eyes and see if she was afraid, or if something there would go blank when her neck snapped."

Gruber roared, "Noooooo."

"Oh, Jesus," I said, moving to flip the switch. "I'm turning this off."

Monica grabbed my wrist. "Don't touch it," she snapped.

Her eyes were hard on the monitor.

Jeff was smiling thinly, his eyes shadowed with satisfaction.

"Does it hurt?" he said. He seemed to be asking Gruber, but then he answered as if to himself.

"I don't think so. Maybe I should have done something that hurt. Slowly. Maybe the vice in the woodshop? Would that have worked?"

Gruber made a lunge forward with one arm, but Jeff pointed the gun toward him.

"Ah, ah. Take it easy, old man. Back off."

Gruber pulled back slowly. Still cradling Iris in his left hand, he brought her body to his cheek, held it there, and closed his eyes.

"Oh . . ." He moaned. "She was inno—"

Jeff reared up out of the chair.

"Innocent?" he screamed. "Is that what you meant to say? Fucking innocent? Well, guess what. So was I. So was Mom. So were all of us, *father* . . . But somehow you couldn't feel for us what you felt for her, could you? You couldn't protect us and pet us and baby talk to us, could you? You couldn't bathe us and feed us by hand? You could hardly bear to be in the same room. Why was that?"

He paused, rhetorically, reading Gruber's face and the truer signal of his hands, which had begun shaking violently.

"You know, I thought about that, too, when I was killing her."

Gruber moaned again, and pressed Iris closer.

"Well, right before, actually. I thought, what is it about her that he loves so much? That he *can* love? So damned much. And I couldn't get an answer. I couldn't figure it out."

"You have no idea what you've done," Gruber said, his voice now shaking, too. "You have no idea."

"I've done what I meant to do," Jeff hissed ecstatically. "And maybe a lot more, which as far as I'm concerned is a bonus."

"You—" Gruber began, but Jeff cut him off, screaming again, his voice breaking hoarsely with the effort.

"No, *you*. It's on *you*. All of this is on you. Every part of it. And me? I know exactly what I've done. And the only thing I regret is having to watch you snivel over a bird. A fucking talking bird."

He still had the gun pointed at Gruber, but he had loosened his grip on the butt. Now he let it slip from his fingers onto the desk. He placed his hand over it.

Monica turned to me, her eyes frightening.

"Which door did you use to get in?"

"What?"

"Over there." She pointed at the monitor. "Which door did you use? Back or front?"

"Back," I said. "Through the garage. Why?"

She turned and bolted out of the room. I could hear her stomping up the stairs and across the foyer. I heard the front door slam open wildly against the coat closet wall. I lurched to follow her, tossing my body up the stairs as fast as it would go. I came out the front door just in time to see Monica disappearing around the back of Gruber's house.

I slowed, as if momentarily confused about which way to go, except that that wasn't the confusion. The dawn was coming up, soft and gray, but yet strangely sharp as well, picking out the edges of things, layering the contours of depth and width and breadth contiguously. The space before me seemed to stretch by halves again as long, and bend into looping pools of light and shadow. I had been staring at the monitors so closely—the flat, square, flickering view—and now I was running in round dimensions.

I was moving as fast as I could, and yet it felt as though I was running in deep sand. I shouted aloud in frustration, growling to push myself on, yet Gruber's house seemed to be receding atop a scrolling belt of grass. There was a loud, dizzy shushing in my ears and a cool weightlessness in the back of my head, as if someone had left open a door to my skull. As I ran, seemingly in place, I heard again those freeing words that I had heard in Gruber's kitchen an hour before, words that now came down on me like a trap: *What you do or do not do now will make no difference.*

I heard the shot as I rounded the side of the house and I fell into the cool wet receiving grass.

25

I never lost consciousness as far as I know. And yet the gap in time between falling down and seeing Mrs. Bloom's face hovering not two feet above my own cannot be accounted for. Was it five minutes? Ten? Or was it only two?

I don't remember thinking anything. I don't remember knowing why I was lying on the lawn, or where I had been going when I fell there. Not at first. I knew only that Mrs. Bloom was kneeling beside me, looking down at me with those serene, pale, pale blue eyes and smiling a paper-thin smile of relief that I wasn't dead.

"You're all right," she said. "You're all right."

The palm of her hand was on my chest, pressing gently.

"How do you know?" I said, teasingly. I don't know why.

She slid her hand across and up and down my torso.

"Well, let's see," she said gamely. "No holes. Do you hurt anywhere?"

I shook my head.

"Nick," she said, very seriously, "I thought I heard a loud bang."

Then I remembered.

"Yes," I said. "I was running."

She looked puzzled.

"I was watching, and then I ran—"

I bolted up. "Monica—"

"Okay, wait," she said, placing one hand on each of my shoulders. "I've called the police."

"Yes, but—" I tried to get up again. "Has there been another shot?"

"No," said Mrs. B. "Nothing."

I looked toward Gruber's house.

"There?" said Mrs. B.

"Yeah," I replied. "One of Gruber's guns."

She nodded worriedly.

"Who is Monica?" she asked.

"A friend. She went into the house. I was coming after her."

"Why, for heaven's sake, would your female friend be going into Edward's house at five in the morning?"

"Because of the gun," I said, without thinking.

Mrs. B. frowned and fell back on her haunches. She dropped her hands to her sides and let them trail helplessly in the grass. She was looking at Gruber's house.

I let my eyes wander to the morning sky behind her head, the horizon going rose, touched with salmon in the west, and tracers of clouds, blue-gray. I was thinking how calm it seemed, the facade of our cake-decorated world, how dreamy drawn in crayon, and simple, like a first grader's rendition of where he lives. The house, the chimney, the sun in its sky, the green grass, the brown tree, the lines of behavior all distinct, yet softly realized in wax. Here is our neighborhood, our neighbor. See? You can touch the child's drawing and feel paper. You can see what he wants you to see. And there will be no more to go on. This is what you get. By way of view and by way of warning.

When I looked back at her, Mrs. B.'s face had transformed. The concern and strange jocularity of our exchange had given way to a much stronger emotion. Her eyes had gone glassy with horror and amazement. She had risen on her knees and her back was rigid with alarm.

I turned to see what she was seeing.

Gruber had emerged from his house through the front door. He was walking very slowly toward us across his front lawn. His bright white undershirt was stained with patches of bright red blood. His face, grooved and sunken above the sharp border of his shirtfront, was like a peach pit, slimed with sweat and tears. He was carrying Monica in his outstretched arms.

I could not look at her.

I looked at Gruber instead.

I watched the banded muscles of his thighs strain beneath the ruined skin, poking as incongruously as his head, from the starched white of his undergarments. The boxer shorts hung loosely beneath the belt of Monica's body, pulling and wrinkling with each step. Gruber's left knee kept banging against Monica's dangling left wrist.

I looked back at Mrs. Bloom. She had raised her hands to her mouth, as I had seen her do when overcome before. Her breath drew in sharply, hissing, the nostrils sucking tight around her outstretched fingers. The fingers themselves were raw and cracked and only partially extended, the swollen, angry joints having wrenched and wrangled the digits into a claw.

I thought again of the power animal. No power at all. A meerkat or a prairie dog, upright, gnawing its nails in fear.

Gruber strode purposefully to where Mrs. Bloom and I were sitting, knelt beside us, and laid Monica on the ground. Her knees, still bent, fell to the side away from us, one on top of the other, slim as fence posts, and the wet white rubber bottoms of her Keds flashed up at us like fish. Her head rolled to the side facing us, and at last I could look. The eyes were open, the mouth closed.

I thought once again of the walnut ivory crucifix in the hall upstairs. The one where Mom had taught me to pray. The position of the knees to the side like this, the head turned the opposite way, so pale against the dark wood. The Christ, she called him. *The* Christ. Like an object: *the*. An object for the eyes to worship, but so powerless, so beaten, the knees to the side, piled, and the head the opposite way. The torso twisted open. Like this.

"My God—" said Gruber. "Anita, I didn't know. I didn't know she was . . ."

Mrs. Bloom's hands strayed across the surface of Monica's jeans from the ankle to the waist, the V of the bent knees, the Braille of the rough, faded seam.

"I know, Edward," she said softly. "I know. It's not your fault."

She moved her hand to Gruber's own and took it, holding it up and tossing it lightly as if to feel the weight.

"She came running in," Gruber said. "I don't know how—I couldn't believe it was— And Jeff had the gun in his hand. She went right for the bird and—he'd fired before he even knew who or what—"

Mrs. Bloom put up her hand to silence him.

"Edward, please. It's over now." She looked for the first time into the dead familiar face. "She's gone. She's finally really gone."

She turned to me.

"Is this your Monica?" she said.

I nodded. *This*, she had said. Not she, but this. Is *this* your Monica? *This thing of darkness I acknowledge mine.* Yes. This was mine. My mistake. My illusion. Yet another. My Monica who was no Monica at all.

"How—?" I began, but she interrupted.

"How could you not have known?" she said.

I nodded again.

"She's changed," she said, brushing the hair back from the forehead. "More than I would have thought."

"How do you mean?" I asked.

Mrs. Bloom let her eyes linger lovingly on the face. She looked up at Gruber.

"Wouldn't you say, Edward?"

Gruber was slow to reply. When he did, his voice was thick with tears.

"I would have known her anywhere." He cocked his head to the side. "That face." He swallowed hard. "That face," he said again.

Mrs. Bloom shook her head.

"So much like Karen." She sighed. "Astonishing."

She clucked disapprovingly and frowned, as though a trick had been played on her in bad taste.

"That is who I see," she said. "I see Karen. That awful, late, late, ravaged Karen, who came home that day to abandon her baby."

She gasped sharply, as if startled, offended again by the memory.

"God, that day," she said. "She was dead already when she came to us. Her skin was the color of old washing. Her face was the face of someone drowned, and I tell you, Edward, I would not have known her anywhere. Had she not been standing on my doorstep calling me Mother, looking out from behind the . . ." She searched for the word. "The accident . . . of herself, I would not have believed that this was my child. I would not have believed that this empty, senseless, bedraggled thing was something I had loved into being."

She reached down and touched the cool cheek, which was not ravaged or drowned at all, but startlingly clean and blameless and young and beautiful.

"Like this," she said. "She looked just like this."

She ran her thumb across the brow several times, above the plane of the dead eye, but she did not close the lid.

"Do you know?" she went on. "That day, she hadn't even named her. A year old and she hadn't named her."

Her thumb came to rest on the bridge of the nose.

"And I just thought that was the most terrible, haunting thing I had ever heard. A baby with no name. It made me sick to think of it."

She let her index finger trail to the lower lip and beneath it, tracing the neat bow shape.

"I wanted to erase that memory," she said, her voice abrupt with sudden anger. Then soft again. "I wanted to give that child the most hopeful, living name I could think of."

Her eyes drifted to mine, gently intense, straining for connection, some catch of understanding.

"Your first robin of spring," she said. "You know it?"

I nodded encouragingly.

She smiled gratefully and looked back at the upturned face beneath us.

"When you see your first robin of spring you know that the dark, cold shutting in of winter is almost over and your heart leaps a little bit every time."

Her eyes checked me again.

I blinked slowly in reply.

"And then you tell someone. You say—I saw my first robin of spring today. And your heart leaps again."

"Yes," I said. "Yes."

She paused.

"Well, I wanted this girl without a name to have that leaping heart, that sign of an end to darkness and cold and shutting in. That's what I wanted. That's really all I ever hoped for."

"And she did have it," I said. "She did."

"And yet—" She shrugged toward the body lying on the ground. "Here she is with another face and another name in the same place, practically on my doorstep. Isn't that something?"

She looked toward her front door and then back again to the spot on the grass where Robin lay.

"Just steps apart," she said. "And so many years between—so much running and struggling and trying to get away, and all only to come back to this same place."

"No," said Edward mournfully, but neither of us acknowledged him.

"People say that time passes," Mrs. Bloom continued. "But it doesn't." She considered this, then added, "It bends."

She made an awkward S shape in the air with her gnarled hand.

"And sometimes, I think, when it bends, things that were far apart pass close together, and you can see the resemblance."

She reached in front of her, as if to touch Edward's hand again, but mimed the action instead.

"And you can almost reach out and touch something that happened twenty-four years ago, or something that will happen twenty-four years from now—and when you do, you realize that they are part of the same event. How strange. Back then, I was looking forward at this"—she emphasized the strange name—"this . . . *Monica's* face, and now I am looking back at Karen's."

"You saw a ghost," I murmured.

"Yes," she agreed. "And I am seeing one now."

"That's exactly how I feel," I said. "She was right there in front of me all the time, and I didn't know it. And now that I do know it, she's gone."

Mrs. Bloom peered at me quizzically.

"That part I still can't understand. Why pull you into this? Why haunt you?"

I shrugged.

"It's complicated."

"Of course it is," she said knowingly. "But that's something I would have expected to say to you. And yet, it was you—"

I didn't wait for her to finish.

"Listen. What I said the other day—"

She cut me off.

"Was confusing," she said. She sat up straighter. "What did you mean when you said I never meant harm to come to her, and yet it did?"

"I was upset. I was embarrassed that you found me that way. I didn't mean anything."

"But you did. You said it meaningfully. You were referring to something in particular."

"Let's not—you said it yourself. It's finally finished."

"No," she said through her teeth. "If you are accusing me of something, then do it directly. I deserve that"—she laughed, remembering our pact—"discourtesy."

"I'm not accusing you."

She leapt on this.

"Then she did."

"Yes," I conceded. "She did. But I think she was wrong."

"That's not for you to decide."

"Maybe not," I said.

Grimacing at the arrogance of that, I added:

"No. You're right. It's not."

There was no way to get out of it now. Why, anyway? All of my secrets had turned out not to be secrets, had turned out not to be mine at all.

Yet I hesitated still. It all seemed too public. Too exposed for this disclosure. Gruber was still kneeling there in the grass across from us, his massive chest and arms defeated, his army-tidy whites now bloodied so starkly, all of him redundant, ridiculous in this disaster. But even he knew, even he had grieved. He was part of this, too, and had been during every one of the last thirteen years, carrying his piece of this alone, unknowing, to place it now on the table in its empty fitting spot. The odd shape snapping into place. He, too, was standing on the other side of an event, and marveling at the proximity.

"Dr. Cunningham didn't die in his sleep," I blurted nervously.

No one spoke. Gruber was scratching his forearm anxiously and working his wrist in tight circles, as if to massage an injury. The wrist cracked loudly and he stopped. Mrs. B. touched his thigh consolingly and moved it away again. She hadn't taken her eyes off my face.

"I saw him the day he died," I told her.

I paused, measuring the words.

"He told me about seeing Robin. What she had wrong with her, and what it meant."

I paused again. Could I drive this home?

"After he told you, he never said anything to anyone. Ever. Until me. That day. And it killed him. It was killing him his whole life and then it finally did kill him. The whole time we were talking, he was holding this box—a pillbox—and it must have been full of whatever he took."

I turned to Mrs. Bloom.

"That was your obit in the paper, the one you saw, and that was why it frightened you so much. You knew what it meant."

Mrs. Bloom lowered her eyes. I raised my voice.

"You knew what he knew and you said nothing."

I let that fall on her, watching her face. Did she know this line of thinking? Was it hers? Was it worn and glazed with living, like someone's name carved in a table? Or did it pinch like new?

I leaned closer.

"Is that what you're worried about?" I asked. "Is that the accusation you expect? Well, sorry, but it's not the news. It's not the reason."

She looked up at me surprised, almost hopeful, as if the accustomed burden might actually fall away this easily.

I leaned back from her, sighing loudly.

"You're just like everybody else in this. You know that? And, God, are there
a lot of everybody elses. You weren't kidding. Robin spread. She fucking me-
tastasized. She had us all writhing and dying over our private crimes and
our dreamed-up hidden loves for her, and all the time it was just the edge of
it. We were all peripheral."

I laughed nastily.

Gruber sneered in my direction, his eyes bulging with fury.

"How do you like that?" I slapped my thigh inanely for emphasis. "Surprise!
You are not important."

Mrs. Bloom flinched, but made no move to pull away.

"You wanna know why she was after me?" I croaked. "You really wanna
know?" I leaned in again for the blow. "Because my father was fucking her."

A large globule of my spit landed on Mrs. Bloom's chin, and a smaller one
on her cheek. Immediately, her hands went up to her mouth, as I knew they
would, but they could not stop the sound. Mrs. Bloom screamed into her
hands, low and throaty, and the cry was strangely alien and menacing, like
the cheers of a stadium full of people heard from half a mile away, or the
clamor of an insect colony amplified on the sound track of a film.

"He was the one," I shouted. "He's the one who gave her that disease you
didn't want to know about. He's what you would have found if you'd bothered
to look. He's what she was running away from—what she had to run away
from—because nobody wanted to know enough to make her safe."

There. I'd done it. I'd pounded in the last stake, Robin's coolie still, doing
the small work delegated, and right on time. This is how it is in the hell of
other people, I remember thinking. You have at each other, and then you eat.
Tear each other to pieces with pettiness, and dull teeth.

Gruber barked and swung at me, landing an awkward openhanded thump
on the far side of my head. Mrs. Bloom threw herself on his arm screaming
"*No!*" as he supported her weight over the body. She pushed away from him
with both hands and let herself fall onto Robin's chest, her face fitting neatly
in the sleek exposed arc of the neck.

She stayed there, howling. Gruber sneered at me over the pile of them,
threatening what would come. Even through his mindless rage and his pulp-
faced stupidity, I could see that he was horrified and shocked by what I had

said about my father. I could see all of his thwarted animal affection for that once lost little girl who was now lying dead at his feet—all that affection thrashing into the fundamental baseness of his nature, violent as water. But for the bodies between us—the particular bodies that they were, each with a call on him, one cold and one begging—he would have come at me like nothing tame.

I wish he had.

The history of places, Anita had said, and futures, passed as close as trains. Which is moving and which still? Which now and which then? Which real and which illusion? We were looking across time both ways now. There could be no more separation.

Over Gruber's shoulder, just barely cresting the gentle rise of our street, I could see two police cruisers rolling into the subdivision, dreamily silent and slow, their blue and red beacons swirling weakly in the thin morning light.

Mrs. Bloom had quieted. She was whispering into Robin's ear a long string of words that I could not hear. It sounded like pages rustling. Gruber had placed his opened hand on Mrs. Bloom's back, his massive palm and barreled fingers spanning her withered form.

And that is how I left them. I stood slowly, mechanically, turned and walked across the lawns that had separated two gunshots by thirteen years. The stage of our tragedy, as usual, overdone.

Does everyone have to die?

I always wondered that as a kid when Mom took me to the theater to see the plays we'd been reading together at home. *Hamlet* especially, but the Greeks, too. Everybody fucking dies. It's relentless. And when I said this to her afterward, when we were all shuffling out of the theater like people who'd been beaten about the head and shoulders with a work of art, I'd say, "Isn't it a bit unrealistic?" or "Why do you want to feel this way on a Saturday night?," she'd always laugh at me a little meanly, and I knew she was thinking: What child of mine is this?

But I meant it. And I still do. It's too much. Why do we need it? Why do we seek it out even when life itself doesn't supply it? Can't we just enjoy simplicity? Kick back and do nothing extreme? Can't we just have parents who die in their sleep, and doctors, too? Can't we just have little girls who grow up smiling in their sundresses and throwing their arms around their fathers' necks? Can't we just have one major tragedy per acre in a generation? And otherwise, is it impossible to say, let's just have a boring mothers knitting, children doing homework, dads coming home sober from a hard day's work and eating dinner with the family kind of place. You know, a neighborhood?

They exist, don't they?

In theory.

Just not here.

Yeah. Just not here.

Gruber and Mrs. B. could deal with the cops, I figured. Send them over to me when they were done. They'd want to know why Robin had gone running into the house, and I'd tell them I didn't know. That's just how she was, I'd say, and shrug. Who knew why she did anything. Only she knew the real story, and she was dead. And Gruber and Mrs. B. were too tangled in their own dramas to wonder about mine. It was over. The details didn't matter anymore, if they ever had to anyone but Robin and me. What could I tell them anyway? I was just Monica's fuck buddy with a bunch of TVs that nobody knew about?

Ah, right. The TVs. Didn't want to be caught with those.

They were foremost in my mind suddenly, or I made them be, because, as usual, it was better than thinking about and sorting through the endgame on the other side of the street. Just click into self-preservation practical mode and get rid of the evidence. No, not the evidence. It wasn't evidence. It was garbage. I needed to take out the garbage.

On my way down to the basement I stopped again at the shelf at the top of the stairs. There was a black rubber mallet lying there. It was Dad's. It was one of his favorite tools. Came in handy for all kinds of things: pounding in dowels without leaving a mark, mercy killing chipmunks that got stuck in the glue traps in the garage meant for rats and mice, and, now, whirlwinding a tantrum over closed-circuit TVs. Perfect.

Now that's the kind of catharsis I can get behind.

No *Oresteia* in the world can beat the sound of solid-state smashing.

26

"... couldn't possibly matter less, darling, really."

It was my mother's voice for sure. The sound quality was wretched, crackling and hissing through the dusty plastic pores of the speaker in my old handheld tape recorder. But I was absolutely sure. That was my mother's voice. Her arrogant, alto, elocutionary voice alive again in my ears.

After I pounded the entertainment center good and hard—there wasn't a salvageable circuit left—I did what Robin expected me to do. All the pieces in place. I went right upstairs to my bedroom, to the drawer in the far bedside table, the disused one, where all the other artifacts of boyhood lay untouched in a grave of junk. There it still was, under the reporter's notebook with the miniature pen shoved straight through the spiral binding, under the pile of medals with their threadbare ribbons still attached: gold, silver, bronze; tennis, hockey, track and field. There, just where I had left it so many years before, was the Sony microcassette recorder that Robin knew I would still have, a pair of ancient AA Rayovacs still wedged into it.

I went to the fridge for new batteries. For courage, I went to the case of Jameson in the garage. I inserted the tape, side A, and pressed play. For the first time in thirteen years, I heard my mother's voice.

Six words.

Pop.

That's all it took.

And I was shaking all over.

I stopped the tape.

I took a long drink, and then another.

I leaned down, fished my earbuds out of my gym bag, and plugged them into the receptacle on the side of the recorder. I rewound the tape to the beginning, lowered the volume, and pressed play again.

". . . couldn't possibly matter less, darling, really."

Another voice then, high and thin. A child's voice, startlingly sure and precise. Peevish, too.

Robin. It had to be.

"It matters to me."

Mom, again, exasperated:

"Why on earth would he possibly matter to you? I don't see—"

A loud sigh.

". . . Oh, honestly, I refuse to argue about something so immaterial, especially with you."

Robin, shouting:

"Are you deaf? I just said it matters."

A long pause.

Mom, beseechingly:

"Darling, would you?"

She must have been raising her glass.

"You've had enough. It's barely seven."

"Don't chide," she said exasperatedly.

"All right," said Robin, more calmly. "But then you'll listen?"

"Yes, then I'll listen."

With an abrupt click the recording stopped; then with another click and the shushing, scraping sound of the recorder being moved, perhaps into a pocket or under a book, it began again.

My mother, again, midspeech:

". . . us, darling. Join us. Your paramour and I have just been going over your leavings."

There were the distant sounds of someone—my father, presumably—coming into the house, and the sound of rustling paper closer to the mic. There was a long pause full of more rustling and shuffling, then my father's voice in the room. He sounded rigid, as usual, precise and distant, but underneath there was a strain of something else. Fear? Surprise? Brewing rage? I couldn't say.

"My leavings?" he said.

Mom, knowing she has the upper hand and enjoying it immensely.

"Yes, yes. Your compositions, dear." More paper rustling. "Here."

Nothing from Dad.

"You really are a dark one, Jimmy. I had no idea you were a poet"—

snorting—"an execrable one, but—who knows—you might have given Lord Alfred Douglas a run for his money. Your very own love that dare not speak its name, and all that."

A long silence. Excruciatingly long.

Finally, Dad, sighing hugely: "Oh, Christ . . . Christ."

Mom: "I should say so."

Another long silence.

Mom, enthusiastically, clapping her hands: "Let's begin at the beginning, shall we?"

Dad, woundedly, almost under his breath: "Why? . . . Why?"

Robin sobbing.

Mom: "You leave her out of this. She's said all she needs to. You do this with *me* now. *Me.* Your wife. Your equal. She does not have to defend herself any—more."

Pause.

Dad, meekly: "I can't."

"You will. If it takes all night. If it takes the rest of our lives, by God, you will."

"Please, Diana. I beg you. Do not pursue this."

"Pursue this? What? Are you completely out of your mind?"

"It's a mistake."

"Oh"—laughing bitterly—"it's a lot more than a mistake, little man. Believe me."

"No—this. This conversation is a mistake. Can't you ever just know when you're out—"

He faltered.

Mom, in disbelief: "Out what, precisely? I hardly know. Is there a word, a phrase for it? Outdegraded? Outshocked? Out of my pathological depth? Tell me. I'd really like to know. Which 'out' am I?"

Dad, shouting: "Just out. Out, damn you. There is nothing to say. There is nothing clever you can say."

"Do you think I'm trying to be clever? Do you really think that this is some kind of—of contest?"

Silence.

"My God. You do."

Dad, almost whining: "You see? Already you have misunderstood everything."

"I don't think so."

"No, of course you don't. You never have. You never do."

There was the banging, crashing sound of something being overturned, and the splintering of wood. The coffee table? A chair?

"Oh, fuck, Jimmy. For once in our dreary, clawing, petty life together this is not about who is more intelligent."

Pause.

Faintly, a bottle being unscrewed, poured. Dad's first drink? The coroner's one of many? Or just a few very large ones? More shuffling of the tape recorder being moved again. Out of his line of sight? Or hers?

Dad, determined: "Listen, Di. Just listen to me. You do not want . . . you do not want to do this."

Mom, reenergized: "Oh, but that's where you're wrong, dearest. After all this time, don't you know me any better than that? Why, I'm just now engaged." Laughing. "This is my sweet spot. This is where I live."

A huge sigh from Dad, the *humph* of him sitting down. Then, resignedly: "Yes. This *is* where you live, isn't it?"

A pause. Dad resuming angrily: "Don't I know you well enough? Yes. I know. I know . . . The tidy life was never enough for you. No, not you . . . The four walls and the square meals and the ease of never having to worry about anything practical . . . because *I* was doing it . . . none of that was good enough for you. You wanted this. You wanted to see the guts on the table and everyone ruined."

"Oh, come, come, Jimmy. You can do better than that. A transgression of this magnitude requires a more forceful deflection."

"You little bitch."

"Yes, that . . . and?"

Dad, in disbelief: "And? What are you saying, 'and'?"

"The rest, love. The rest. We know what I am. We have that. But you? Where are you in this demonology? Surely you rate now. Perhaps not before, I agree—straight man, company man—but now, now that you are . . . sharing yourself. Well, you've graduated to a whole new circle of hell, wouldn't you say? Or is that unclear? If it's unclear I could—"

Dad, sobbing: "Oh, God, Diana . . . please."

Mom, resuming, acidly: "Oh, all right then. Since you can't bring yourself to articulate. Let's see. How shall I put this for you? The tried-and-true ways of tearing up a marriage—is that it? . . . Yes, the usual thing, making a housemaid and whipping post out of your wife, cheating, whoring, lying, stealing—that—all that—just wasn't nearly the right kind of kinky for you. Not enough for me, you say? Ha! I'll give you not enough. You couldn't just be the husband who's absent and emotionally obtuse and fucking his secretary or the babysitter. You had to be the husband who's fucking the baby . . . I suppose I should count myself lucky that it wasn't *ours*."

"Don't you even think of bringing Nick into this."

Mom, hugely: "Oh, I wouldn't dream of it. Our son? I can barely remember who he is. You've managed that beautifully. I see him twice a year at holidays if I'm lucky, and in the summers he's practically a stranger—sullen, evasive, hostile to everything I've tried to teach him, banging around with that Alders creature, systematically erasing everything that's original and worthy in him. Yes, you've made a model man out of him. He'll be as bland as bread when you're through with him."

"When *I'm* through with him? It's you who's done the number on him. Sending him away to school might just barely have saved him—might. *If* he survives you, and that is by no means a given, it will be a miracle if he can ever look a woman in the face, let alone take one to bed."

A barking laugh from Mom, then:

"You really are something. By all means, blame me. Blame me for filling the void, when it was always, always you he wanted and adored. God help him, he thinks *you're* God. To this day. He really does."

Dad, ignoring her: "Do you have any idea the effect you have on men? Do you? Because it's not what you think."

Mom, appalled: "This—none of this—has anything to do with me. Do not—"

"No, really. Do you? It's quite—how did your father put it on our wedding day?—withering? Yes. 'She can be a bit withering,' he said, 'but you'll be all right, I expect.' Priceless . . . You'll be all right, I expect . . . Jesus, he knew."

"Oh, my dear, is that our euphemism now? Withering? Is that the story line? The all-conquering member withers before the *terrible breasts of Boadicea*?"

Dad, bewildered: "What are you babbling about? Who are you playing for?"

"Oh, myself, as always. Myself. Someone has to do something to raise this beyond— God, I am standing in front of a man, for all intents and purposes, a man of resources and breeding and middle-class pretension, and we are talking about the faulty mechanics of his penis. Again. Why he can't get it up unless the victim is bald below the belt. Is there anything else? Is there ever anything else? Is there any stage of evolution beyond which a man's virility, and his harridan wife's fanged deflation of same, is not the great exoneration for all his troglodyte crimes? Forgive me if I had hoped to give this a loftier gloss, but the cliché is *kill*ing me."

"Listen to yourself, Di. This is why— Oh, Jesus, are you incapable of responding to anything directly—as yourself—to me, as myself? We are not one of your poems. We don't scan. You can't cite your way out of this. This is real, people to people, life as it is. It doesn't shine."

"Well, well, the night bard instructs." A gurgling scream. "You make me sick. You think because your prick is hard and you can put pen to paper and scribble, that you can make this . . . this violation stand up and declare itself legitimate. No, you are right enough in that. It doesn't shine. It shames. Reading this, tasting it, sour and stinking as it comes up in my throat, I am ashamed of every word in the English language. You have accomplished that. How can you have? . . . Oh, that's why you did it, of course—to destroy the thing that you could never touch, the love and living drive in me that you could not approach because you are so incapable, so artless, so utterly without sensibility. You can't . . . Oh, it's so much worse than ignorance. You don't even stand under the same sky."

"You arrogant—"

"You have deliberately, methodically—how else for you?—defiled what is beyond—no, more than that—what is *beyond* beyond you—what is so far outside your box-trap subsistence as to be only dimly available as some kind of *sore* on your procedure. The flannel man cannot feel awe in the presence of the sublime, and so he howls at his inadequacy."

"Shut up. My God, shut up, you pompous bitch. Do you really still think that anyone cares about all that useless academic slush that's splashing around in your head? You're nobody. You have always been nobody. Same as me. A big, towering second-rate mind in a paddock full of idiots. If we'd stayed in New York you would have found that out very quickly, *dar*ling. You'd have been laughed out at the door. But here you could stew in all your thwarted ambition, talking down to all the animals. Well, that's over. No one's listening anymore, if they ever were. Well, no one, that is, except your ripe acolyte over here."

Mom, showing her first signs of weariness: "And we're back to your excuses. The siren nymphet, too plump to resist. How original."

"Yes, I know. My defense isn't worthy of you. My reasons are the same as everybody else's."

"Every sick—"

"No, not sick. That *is* unworthy of you. You, of all people, should be able to grasp this, should be able to talk about it in a more sophisticated way. Do you think your feminist outrage is any less imaginative than my transgression?"

"Feminist? We're talking about the seduction of a child, Jimmy. What could it possibly matter the sex? Hers or mine, or yours, for that matter? She and I are not allies because we are women, and you are not the enemy—nor are you to be excused your . . . indiscriminate humping—because you are a man."

"It was not indiscriminate, any more than your taking on the role of her tutor was indiscriminate. What did you see in her? . . . Hmm? . . . What? . . . Do you even know? . . . I'll tell you what. You saw sensitivity, intelligence, beauty, promise, safe harbor, the possibility of love without judgment. Isn't that right? Well, that is what I saw, too. That is what I hoped for. Maybe I sexualized it, yes, because I am a man—that is what we do—and maybe I tried to ennoble it with borrowed language because I was ashamed of my inability to express the enormity of what I felt, but how could anyone not see and adore, not want to touch and possess this marvelous, pure—"

He broke off again, unable to find the word.

Mom, softly: "Image."

Dad: "What?"

Mom, repeating pensively: "This image. She is an image, Jimmy. That's all. The image of what we have lost. You cannot possess it."

Silence.

Dad, crying now—or I think it's crying—awkwardly, jaggedly, coughing almost. He does not know how.

"Oh, Di. Help me. I am so afraid."

Mom, sternly again, but with a strain of softness left: "I can't help you. I can't help any of it. It's done. It's all done."

Dad, strangled: "Is it? Is it really?"

"Yes."

"Done?"

"Yes."

More crying.

"Please, Di. Don't give up on me. Not now. I need you."

"You have never needed me, except as cover."

Dad, begging: "That's not true. You know that's not true."

Nothing from Mom. Just the sound of Dad whimpering.

Then, at last, Mom, resolute: "You've ruined her."

Pause.

Dad, incredulous: "What?"

Nothing.

Dad again: "What did you say?"

Mom, nastily: "I said you've ruined her."

"What do you mean, ruined her? How can you say ruin? What a terrible word. Can you possibly mean that the way it sounds?"

"I don't know, Jimmy. How does it sound?"

"Like she's a soufflé or a pair of suede shoes. My God, Di."

Again, nothing from Mom.

"Like used up, trashed. No longer pristine."

Still nothing from Mom.

"Jesus, you're not even going to contradict me."

Mom, finally, feigning control: "Jimmy, stop. Really. You're making a fool of yourself."

Dad, on the offensive at last: "No, no. That's it, isn't it?"

A pause with Dad puffing and laughing mirthlessly.

"You know what I find incredible? Unimaginable? After all this, yes, I've just now realized it. You're not angry. You're not even shocked. You're—what is that expression on your face? Jealousy? No. That would be human . . . My God, you're disappointed."

A loud guffaw.

"Don't be absurd, Jimmy."

Dad, almost whining with disbelief: "'Ripe' is not the wrong word. Or it wasn't until— Jesus, your private delicacy has been spoiled, hasn't it? And now you don't want it anymore."

"I couldn't expect you to—"

"Yes, that's it. Your all-consuming vanity has been pricked. The prize stolen right out from underneath you. Good God. You really are a monster.

Well, my withering wife and partner competitor, standing so proudly under your own sky, I've had her. I've had your little dumpling protégé. And now you don't want her."

Dad, laughing hideously: "I've had her. How do you like that? Over and over and over and—"

Robin, screaming: "Stop it!" Sobbing. "Please stop it."

Mom: "You absolute bastard."

Loud shushing and scraping again. The tape recorder being moved. The sound of running footsteps and the rhythmic brush of fabric on the mic, a slamming door, sobbing, fumbling. *Click.*

There wasn't much left on that side of the tape. It was all blank—I checked. I turned it to side B, saw that it was fully rewound, and pressed play, hoping and dreading that there was more.

Click.

Door opening. She must have been in the downstairs bathroom. Nothing else is that close except the front door, and she was obviously still in the house. The brush of fabric again. The recorder is in her jacket pocket, maybe, a loose linen thing with room. Must be. The fabric brushes slowly as she moves. Back and forth with her hips. Standing, walking, sliding past.

Robin: "Let's go."

Mom: "We don't have to do this. Not ever."

Robin: "I'm fine."

"Are you sure?"

"Yes."

"Darling, I'm so sorry you've had to hear—you must disregard—people say things—this is about us. This is a very old argument."

"And this is my life. I won't ever forget any of this. Ever."

Nothing from Mom.

More shushing.

Robin: "I'm going back in."

Mom: "But what for?"

"To try to understand."

"But you can't. I can't."

"I have to try."

Shushing and rustling, in the background my mother's low block heels on the floor crossing the foyer, echoing flatly.

Shushing. A gasp.

Dad, stage-whispering sharply: "Forgive me."

Footfalls stopping.

Mom, booming: "Jesus, Jimmy. What are you doing? Have you utterly lost your mind?"

Nothing from Dad.

Robin, her composure lost, crying again.

Mom, tremblingly: "Jimmy. Let's just—"

Dad, firmly: "No. You were right. It's done. There is no going back."

Mom: "Not this way. Not with the chil—"

"Yes. This way. With. We always said this, Di. With. This was always the choice. The choice, not the resignation, remember?"

"Not like this, Jimmy. Not like this. The child. Think of the child."

"Yes. We knew it would come. We knew it would come when we didn't want it, and we always said we would choose it then, when it was hardest. That was how we would know, you said—when it was hardest—and we would make no excuses, because there would always be excuses to be made, always last appeals that would seem so sweet in the terror of finishing. But resist, you said. And I agreed. Resist the temptation to run when the temptation is strongest."

"I was wrong."

"The gun within reach, you said. Live life to the fullest with a loaded gun within reach. Do you remember how often we said that? How many times we clinked glasses over those words and laughed and shouted that our life was recklessly complete because the way out was right there, lying on the table, and we chose not to take it. Until we did. Well, we are there now, my wife. We are at the point of picking up the weapon that has always been in full view. We put this here for that."

"We were kids, Jimmy. Stupid, arrogant kids full of high ideas we didn't understand. We were drunk. We were alone in the world."

"We weren't kids when we put this here."

"*We* didn't put it there. How long have you had that?"

"Oh, Di. Don't back away now. You have always been my courage."

"Jimmy, stop this. Now. Stop it."

"I will stop it. It will all . . . just . . . stop."

"Jimmy, listen to me. Listen, will you? Just take a few minutes and let me tell you—"

"Tell me what? What can you possibly tell me now? That's an escape. We have to take what we have chosen."

"We will. All right? We will. But let me tell you—"

"What?"

"About—"

Dad screaming: "About what?"

Mom, chillingly calm: "About Robin."

Long pause. She has hit the mark.

Mom, slowly: "I want to tell you about Robin. And I want you to tell me about her, too. And I will listen. And she will listen. Here. Right here. Between us there is everything to say."

The pause then was so long I could hardly bear it. I thought several times of turning off the tape. Turning it off and burning it so I would never be tempted to listen to this again. What you hear once now, said the voice in my head, you will hear for the rest of your life. And I knew that it was true. Pieces of this would be with me forever, thrown language splattering the walls of my mind indelibly. But I could not stop. I would not. I had heard too much already. And too little.

Finally, Robin's tiny frightened voice broke the silence, and when I heard what it said and remembered that I had seen those same words on a computer screen just days before, it was like the last heavy bolt of a combination lock sliding out of grasp and the strongbox opening.

"Talk to me," she said.

And then more softly, "Please?"

All we want is an explanation. Some way to understand. Still and always that. After we have pulled the trigger, somehow, or let it be pulled for us, maybe a little on our behalf, after we have witnessed something unspeakable, we want to understand what we have seen and known, because seeing and knowing are never enough when the shock is so strong. It cannot penetrate, and it cannot dissipate, either. It does not even seem real. It is only pain—illiterate, dumb pain that we are desperate to disintegrate with words.

Mom, terrified, trying to be strong: "Robin, sweetheart. Look at me."

A pause.

"Please, darling. Look at me."

A longer pause and the slightest break in my mother's voice as she begins: "You have been my precious gift. Always . . . Talking with you has been like talking to a better vision of myself . . . like seeing and walking beside and sharing perfect language with someone I would have hoped to be . . . I have never been your teacher. You have been mine—my example, and my admired friend. Yours is the most expansive and supple, quick and capacious mind I have ever known. Feed it. Promise me, darling. Feed it every day and cherish it. It belongs to you, and nothing—not I . . . not Jimmy, nothing bad that has ever happened or will happen to you—can ever take that away. It is all just more experience . . . *Nothing is either bad or good.* Remember?"

Robin, mechanically: "*But thinking makes it so.*"

Mom: "Yes, darling. Yes. That's it. Keep that. Keep it close always and it will comfort you and free you from all of this. I promise."

Robin, crying: "But I don't want you to go."

"I know, darling. I know. But this is your freedom."

Robin, crying harder: "I don't understand."

"I know. But you will. You will. And you will thrive in the only possession you will ever need. Your home is in your mind, your gorgeous mind. You will need nothing else. Anything else would be a hindrance. We—we are in your way, just as everyone else will be in your way . . . Every weak loser clawing for a piece of you . . . every adoring lover and friend and teacher and pupil . . . all of your inferiors . . . You must shut out all of them—shut it all out with sentimentality. It has no place in you."

Dad, gruffly: "That's enough, Di. You've said enough."

Mom: "Then let her go, Jimmy."

Dad: "I will. I am."

Mom: "No. Let her go now, and you and I will finish this alone. That is how we said it would be."

A long pause.

Dad, barely audible: "Okay."

Mom, confirming: "Okay?"

"Yes, okay."

"No good-byes, Jimmy."

Dad, sobbing: "I'm sorry. God, I'm so, so very sorry, dear girl."

Robin sobbing.

Dad, plaintively: "I only wanted to be near you, to believe that you could—"

Mom: "Jimmy, stop. Leave her be now."

Dad: "Okay, okay. I'm sorry."

Mom: "Shhhhh."

Dad and Robin whimpering.

Then Mom again, so tenderly: "Time to go now, my love."

Robin: "I can't. I'm afraid."

Mom: "I know, my lovely girl. I know you're frightened, but don't be. You can do this. Do this for me. Go on with words . . . Go on with everything we started . . . You can."

More whimpering, shushing, her small body moving. The tape in her pocket, circling.

Robin, muffled: "Good-bye."

Mom, very close, kissing, an embrace: "Good-bye, darling."

Robin: "I love you."

A rustling separation, then Robin again, aside: "I don't . . . forgive you."

A pause. Nothing from Mom or Dad.

Shuffling, slow, light footsteps in the hall, the heavy, sucking front door opening, *swish*, closing, pause, *tat*. Closed.

Rhythmic walking, pocket fabric, breathing, soft shoes, and outside air.

Panic, moaning, deep croaking, throat-drying cry.

Fingers coursing, searching, finding, pressing.

Click.

I am startled by the click, still fogged in their good-byes, still listening. It cannot be over. It cannot. It will go on again. It will, I think, I plead. It must. Please, go on. Please.

I try her words.

Talk to me.

But it does not.

I feel abandoned. Absurdly, childishly, and—again, exactly as before in this house—impotently enraged. I think there must be, there has to be more. Not moving, I listen to the rest of the tape. I listen until it clicks, physically clicks itself off.

Nothing. There is nothing more.

Just a flood of my own questions trying to grab hold.

How much longer did it go on? How long did they wait? Did they watch her walk down the sidewalk and the drive and into her grandparents' house, just to make sure she was gone? And did she, lying in bed in the room above the garage where the nightlight goes on, did she stop her ears and wait? Or did she listen for the first shot, expecting it, knowing it would come, yet startled still when it did?

Or is that when she left, and why? That night, right from this room, left at their behest, and kept on going? Running as far as she could go, running so as not to hear the shots she knew were coming, not to see the bodies carried out under covers, not to hear the cries and see the gaping faces of her neighbors looking on in horror at what she—or so she thought—had done.

What had she done?

This morning, did she run across the street not *for* Iris, but *to* Gruber, hoping for the bullet, the bullet that she thought she deserved? It's what I did, she said. *What I did.* And what was it that she did? Telling? Was that the beginning of their deaths to her? Deaths, she thought, that should have been three and not two? Why? Because she told? Because she said something?

The loop of time coming back to the same place. Mrs. B. had said it. Running and running away until you are running back again and into the bullet. At last into the bullet that has been here all the time, waiting for you.

That is the worst of superstition.

The loop of time. The loop of tape.

For me?

Stop it.

Stop this now.

And don't listen. Don't think. Anymore.

Burn it.

This has not been deserved.

There is no significance for you.

In suffering.

I popped the tape out of the machine.

Don't think.

Don't think.

Don't answer the fear of what might be.

There is no prophecy in this.

No same place to come back to and die.

I eased a loop out of the cassette and pulled, right arm flinging to the right.

Again, again, again.

Until a pile of shining ribbon was lying on the table.

Scooped it in both hands, dropped it in the trash. Full circle.

The mesh trash where Robin had placed the first note.

All four notes were there on the desk. I threw them in on top of the tape.

And poured on some Jameson for closure.

I walked through the hall, through the kitchen, for matches, then the door.

Sliding out back.

Striking.

Slitch. Whoosh.

I dropped the bright gold match into the bin.

And a sickly blue-green flame leapt up.

Above a scar of melted black plastic bubbling, and the ash of a girl's diary expiring.

27

They had the service for Robin at Temple Israel. Same synagogue, same rabbi who buried John Bloom.

Mrs. B. greeted the mourners with her signature poise and salt of the earth. Most of them were people she hadn't seen in years or barely knew. They were there to be part of the history that they had heard, and sometimes said, so much about. The real estate agents and the classmates all grown up, the professionals who'd had some contact with the myth, or years ago maybe with Robin herself. Dr. Cunningham's widow was there with his surviving sister, Rose. Dorris and Jonathan Katz were there with the kids, chastened, looking like a family, remorseful over the good fortune they'd scorned.

Gruber and family were there, too, including, at Mrs. B.'s insistence, Jeff, who was ravaged with guilt and remorse over the accident and had thought it more seemly to stay away. But Mrs. B., being Mrs. B., took him aside and worked her magic, erasing all blame and the validity of self-torture. I can see her saying it: "Just come if it will make you feel better. If it won't, don't. But let it go, dear boy, let it go. This is not yours to carry." Or something like that. And I can see Jeff crumpling to the floor in relief and admiration, worshipping, as I did, the release in an old woman's words.

Jeff's case is still pending, natch, so no one knows for sure what's happening. My guess is he'll plead to involuntary and do a stint of probation/community service, or at the very most wear an ankle bracelet for a while. Definitely no time in juvie, even. He's a model kid despite his surroundings, and the lawyers involved will settle, no question, because there isn't a jury in four counties who'd convict an abuseling son of Gruber's for shooting at the oncoming ghost of Robin Bloom at five in the morning while having at it with the old man over his pistol collection.

Just a guess, but judging by the size and mood of the crowd at the funeral, the whole incident has been like a great collective sigh of relief for the community, as if someone—thank God it didn't have to be them or theirs—had finally slain the succubus and broken her curse.

Dave, Kitty, and Sylvia even showed up at the service, looking painfully related, like day-old sausages all gray in a row—same girth, same face, same hypertension. It's a testament to Mrs. B. again—a huge one—that they even let those three bears in the door, given Eggnacht, but then maybe everyone figured this was part of the purge. Tears of the neo-Naz wash away the stain? One Jew is very like another? Mourn one, absolve all.

God only fucking knows. Mrs. B. had way too much class to even notice, and—oh, I don't know—maybe she had a few other things on her mind just then. She wasn't likely to be concerned about whether Dave had completed his sensitivity training after all this time, or whether this was part of it. Every person there, including me, was an invader more or less. It didn't matter what your stripes were.

It made me sick. The whole service—being there, knowing all the dirty lines of contact that had run between the corpse and the crowd, and between the presiding and the lesser mourners—was like watching a lurking, slinking pack of scavengers circling a kill, waiting for the alpha to finish his meal.

At the mingle after the service, it got worse. Then it was like a receiving line for my spy self and his drunk infelicities, patching over or poking at all the shit that had gone down in recent weeks between my neighbors and me.

Katz offered me his hand and, with typically vulgar self-absorption and bad taste, said, "Did I do this?"

"How's that?" I said, not even looking at his face.

"Well, I don't know," he stammered, guiltily. "I guess I just thought I might have set this whole thing in motion."

I locked in on him coldly.

"Is that why you came?"

He looked away, embarrassed.

"God, no. I just feel so awful about all this, you know?"

"Yeah, I know," I said in a tone that was distinctly not understanding. "This is a funeral for everyone but Robin. I've never seen so many different people gathered to mourn themselves."

"I didn't mean it like that."

"Nobody means anything. That's the problem. You're all here wandering around as if you'd had a summons and you're waiting for your name to be called."

"Come on now," he said. "That's not really fair."

"Whatever."

I said this dismissively—conversation over—but he lingered, shifting his weight awkwardly and straightening his tie.

"Listen," he said, leaning in. His breath smelled of last night's booze and bad sleep. "What the hell happened with you and Simon?"

I chuckled dryly.

"See what I mean?"

"I'm just asking."

"Yeah. Of course you are. Pediatrics is a small world out here, right? Wouldn't want it getting around that you hastened one of your colleagues to his end."

"You really are a nasty piece of work," he said, squinting at my nasty face.

I ignored this.

"So, old Simon. You want to know, huh? Well, I'd say you definitely put the kibosh on that old man. Led me right in. He was waiting with his neck out, just as you said."

Katz looked as if I'd punched him in the stomach.

"Oh, relax," I said wearily. "I would have found him with or without you. Or he would have found me."

"What do you mean?"

"We had other business. It doesn't matter. Look—" I clapped him roughly on the shoulder. "All of this was already happening before you and I even had our first clue. Robin was a twisted bitch, okay? Sorry, but she was, and she'd have said it herself. This is what she wanted."

He was shocked.

"What, to die?"

"And to tie us all in knots in the end. Big-time . . . If she's anywhere now, I guarantee you, this conversation is making her laugh. Hard."

He looked at me with disgust.

"God, Nick."

"What? Am I ruining your orgy?"

"Have some res—"

"I knew her, okay?" I said angrily. "I knew her up to the last moments of her life, and I knew what she was doing all along. There's nothing you can tell me. Nothing. Got it? And I'm not going to give you a handshake and a smooth-over because you feel kinda sorta bad about all this and you've figured out that you were wrong about me."

It was his turn to balk.

"I wasn't wrong about you at all." He snorted, shouldering past me with a last glare. "You've made that clear enough."

He pointed his finger at me.

"I'm watching you."

"Well, that's something, anyway," I called after him.

He shuffled off without turning, huffing to himself and shaking his head. Within a few steps he ran into someone he needed to impress, and he pulled out his swooping, asskiss handshake again and the nauseating grin that went with it.

I was still gawking at him when Dorris touched me on the shoulder. She'd been trailing behind Jonathan with the kids, scrounging fistfuls of comfort from the cake table. She hadn't heard my exchange with the good doctor.

She was all sheepish pursed lips and motherish oh-isn't-it-just-awful, which softened me slightly, but only slightly. The rest of me wanted to nudge her into a pileup with Dave and kin, whom she was assiduously avoiding, and watch her squirm.

"I'm sorry, Nick," she said, surprising me.

I nodded stiffly. "Okay."

"No, really. I'm sorry about everything. I'm sorry for the accusations and the ugliness that happened between us. I had no right."

She looked down at Miriam, who was now standing between us, her needy thumb hanging loose in the gape of my trouser pocket.

"I'm really ashamed . . . I got so caught up." She shot a look across at Dave, who was huddled by the bar *sans famille*, sucking obscenely on a can of Coke. "I just lost all perspective on everything and I shouldn't—"

I felt again the old pathos of Dorris Katz sobbing in the mirror. I could see her face there up close in the glass, through the glass and through the dark glass of my TV, with all the furrows of grief gouging themselves deeper in the image of her face. I thought, too, of her ripping Miriam out of my grasp, or, rather, ripping me out of hers on my doorstep and marching her into the dungeon with Dave. I could see now, once again at close range, the copper-colored sideburns on her cheeks, poorly bleached, and the desperation they exposed. I thought of how hard I'd cried the first time I'd seen

Dorris sobbing and cutting herself at home, a mother like my own, lost in motherhood and afraid and angry at the diminishment of her person in the role that had been prescribed for her.

"He was punishment enough," I said, nodding at Dave. "And I really don't deserve an apology. I've treated you and a whole hell of a lot of people only marginally better than Dave treated you, and that's nothing to be proud of. I'm the one who should be sorry, and I am. I really am."

I smiled down at Miriam.

"Do you accept?"

She looked up, confused.

"Huh?" she said.

"Do you accept my apology," I said.

She frowned and shook her head.

"Unh-unh."

Dorris and I looked at each other and laughed.

"Yes," said Dorris. "I do. I do accept."

"Well, okay, then," I said.

She took Miriam's hand from my pocket and squeezed it.

"Well, okay, then," she repeated. "Good."

She kissed the tips of her fingers at me and slid into the crowd waving backward as she went. Miriam didn't even turn around.

Meanwhile, Dave had seen us watching him. He was still waiting to catch my eye. When I turned to him, he shrugged exaggeratedly, threw up his hands, and raised his eyebrows, as if to say, "So what now?" or "What's been has been, right?"

A nasty piece of work, I thought. Yeah, there. That Alders creature, she'd said. How strange to hear that, to think of it being on her mind and thrusting to the fore in the last argument. And now it is written here in these last transcripts, my long association with this emblem. Dave, the standing image of every base inclination I have ever hated in myself. This was the self that I was still being, or still capable of being in the company of my neighbors—hadn't Jonathan said or shown as much?—the self that I would always revert to with them, because they could provoke me like no one else. Like family.

Here was the front of the familiar, the mask that had been my face. All of these people, this place, this revolving grief and punishment growing out of this neighborhood and this ground, as surely as we had. Robin was right.

The knots you tie that make a net you cling to. With every turn the trap cuts deeper.

Get away, I said to myself then. Just get away. That's the message. That's the course. And as I said this, I believed it for the first time. I could move. A plan and motion conceived. You cannot stay here and change. Isn't this the proof of it, standing right there, courting liquored apathy with you as usual?

I looked across at Dave, and as kindly as I could, I shook my head. No, I just can't do it, fatso. Not anymore.

He cocked his head sideways, like a dog trying to get a tone of voice.

I shook my head again, more slowly. Just quit it.

Then his face fell, in surprise, I think, as much as anything else. He knew I meant for good. But he recovered quickly, sliding into that lazy, sleazy turn of mouth that I had come to know so well.

He would be fine. He would be Dave, eternally standing in line at the all-night drugstore buying Twizzlers and chew. He would slop over himself over the years, in great globular folds, a row of teats down his front, and he would shuffle to and from the bathroom with a cane by the time he was fifty, if he made it that far. And then, one day, they'd find him dead in his basement chair with his flesh fused to it.

Leave now, I said to myself, and someday you'll read about it in the paper.

And so I did. I turned and I went.

And as I was squirming through the crowd with my shiny, freeing resolution in mind, eyes down, avoiding, making my way purposefully for the first time in years toward an exit, it was then that I knew I was going to have to sell the house in absentia. Gut it, scrape it, clean it, and leave it. Right away. As in: now. A mission. Go out. Go home. Go quickly. There is nothing else to do but this.

I didn't even say anything to Mrs. B. on the way out. She was busy being gracious to the gawkers in a corner, and, anyway, she would understand. I had a plan for that, too.

I walked out in the automatic daze of my intentions, drove home, and started in.

I took the smashed video equipment first, eight heavy-duty garbage bags full, and ran it to the dump. And I can tell you, right from the overbearing heart of a boy who cried for elusive absolution, no confession to the parish priest ever felt that good. Watching those bags tumble down the embankment into that ripe, piled, rag-strewn midden, I felt high and soaked through with the shirking of it.

I made a dozen more trips to the dump this afternoon and evening, my car piled with bags full of everything detachable in the house, until all that was left was the furniture and a duffel bag full of my clothes.

I am writing this now sitting at my emptied desk, in this criminal room, for the last time. When I finish, I will take my duffel bag and my laptop and put them in the car. I will drive to the FedEx/Kinko's on Maple and Fourth, print these pages, bind them, and post them to Mrs. B.

Then she will understand everything.

And that is an end to our acquaintance. An exit. As quick in the making as it was slow in coming. A decision and change. An escape, which can happen only when the moment is right, and must happen in the moment. Now. A complete break, a run for the gate when the guard turns, when the guard and the prisoner are both me.

Flit. That's the way. Slip out and gone. Become someone else somewhere else, and you will know the story of names changing, and the hitch of people not quite changing, their pasts forever lost but never leaving.

See what happens.

I had a short-term girlfriend at boarding school senior year who said that to me all the time. It was her answer to everything. It was the way she lived her life. Just wait. Just hang around and see what happens. That's all you have to do.

It was the main reason I broke up with her. That, and the fact that her name was Sunny. No joke. Sunny. I told her right out: Look, I can't be with someone named Sunny. I just can't do it. It makes me want to punch you in the face, and I don't think that's very fair to you.

She agreed, and we went our separate ways. She wasn't in the business of changing anyone. She didn't think she had that much agency. Hence the mantra. She was a happy person. It was as simple as that. And after we broke up I'd see her around campus occasionally just being happy. Being happy with her friends, being happy in the library, in the cafeteria, in geology class, in the infirmary for a week with the flu—wherever. Just hanging around and breathing, taking what came and not getting angry or upset or even that excited about anything.

I envied her, of course. I still do. And now, of all times, after everything that's happened, I'm thinking mainly of her and the mind-blowing simplicity of those three words.

See what happens.

When I say that to myself now, I feel my bowels unclench and my shoulders drop and I am almost able to laugh aloud at how easy it could all be if I just stopped trying so hard.

I am at the far end of something that has gone on for all of my thirty-four years, the last thirteen of which have been excruciating. And for what? I have gained nothing. I have lost time.

I have thought, like a spoiled child, of wanting to die, because I was uncomfortable. I have put my toe in the riptide. I have put myself in danger and asked fate to intervene. I have tempted the violence and vengeance of others. Yet all of this has been a flying at life, not a relinquishment of it. You do not shake your fist at the world when you want to leave it. You cannot shake your fist at the world and be taken seriously as an adult.

I will never get this part right. How to be serious. How to say what's on my mind without reaching. I do not have the right circuitry for serious, or for musing or joking in earnest, either. I can hear it even now as I am saying this. The tone is wrong. The adolescent is still there protesting, making a show of his conscience and the big ideas that he has just discovered. Life, death, I don't have to take this anymore, and so on.

It's funny to look at myself this way. Genuinely funny, because I am laughing with kindness for the first time as I am looking in the mirror. This is friendly ridicule.

I accept that I have made a poor showing. I accept that this acceptance is still itself a poor showing, still self-conscious and posed and overly didactic. That's me. Here I am. The germ behind the clown in the polo shirt revealed as he has been throughout. I have been a baby *and* I have been through something unimaginable—as Mrs. Bloom would say, both are true.

Dr. Cunningham was wrong. Knowing has released me. I know what has been done, the awful things that were done by whom to whom and why. I have even heard some of my parents' last words, and contrary to everything I expected, they were banal. As banal as my father's poems and promises and threats on paper. As unimaginative as any fight between two married people dragging out the same old six or seven grievances, slurring the same dull insults back and forth.

I have seen Dorris and Jonathan do the same with a different ending. I have seen Ellie and Gruber not do it, because Ellie figured this out a long time ago and simply turned off the receiver. To think that all this time she has been the happiest, knowing the secret that fullness lies in silence. She must have practiced it. Or did she just know? Every time you feel the rope go taut, walk away. Every time you feel your feet slipping, let go.

Mrs. B., you have a way of doing this. But you learned it. You had to practice it, which meant that at the key moments you would always fail to embody it. You would put your hands to your mouth and scream when the news came. You would sit up in bed in the middle of the night, not able to help it. You would feel the hoofbeats on the ground from miles away, and cold worry would have its way with you.

We are alike in this. I will practice, and I will get pretty good at hanging around. At the easiest times, I will seem like a master, as you seemed to me that day I first rang your bell. I will even make wispier jokes and learn to speak in lassos that never cinch. Some days, you will be amazed by my equanimity. Others you will see me fighting myself and losing and breathing deeply to regain control, and you will rightly laugh at how neurotic I still am. I will have forgotten that control is not the point, and I will have to settle for gaining control of my need to control.

I will find a way to paste a laugh over all this, because I will concede that I can do only so much with who I am. I will change, but you will always know that I am there under the garment. There is a singular person in there after all, a man with qualities, though I cannot say what those qualities are, and neither really can you. But you will know them and smile to yourself and say, yes, there is the Nick Walsh I know, and I will smile, too, affectionately, having found that much forgiveness for myself.

But the verdict now is for life. Striding life. And I will do my sentence with joy and constant invention, because Denmark is not a prison after all.

As mad as I sometimes am, it really isn't.

But Hamlet is.

I know that now.

He *is* a prison.

And at the end of the tragedy—guess what?—Hamlet dies.

He dies along with everybody else.

Thump.

Everyone except Horatio, whose name itself sounds like a cheer and whose temperament is cool and light as a cloud and shaped like a scoop of ice cream.

Horatio, who passes up suicide.

Horatio, who is there at the beginning—did you notice?—*and* at the end, too, surrounded by soldiers and ghosts.

Horatio, who completes the circle, who persists and tells the story again. *See what happens.*

He is the hidden hero, the narrator, and the floating moral of the sleight of hand.

Hamlet is just the decoy.

So, in momentary contradiction of everything I have just said, and one last maudlin time, I say this.

Mom? Dad? Here's the thing, if you're listening. Take this as a conclusion. The baby's valediction that is not one, because the baby can never stop saying what the baby always says as long as he is speaking.

This is the best I can do for closure.

This testimony has been for you. My life up to this point has been for you. And every part of me that I have put down here in these pages has been a form of pleasing you, still, and a form of explaining and excusing myself for what I have become and what I have failed to become.

That is over now.

I exist, and in violation of all instruction on this matter, I do not have to justify myself to anyone. I am not your continuation. I am not your mistake, or the bright spot in it. I am just another person, and nothing that I have read or not read or achieved or failed to achieve has any bearing on that fact. Your conflicts have not made me, and your crimes, your deaths have not condemned me. Not anymore.

I have heard your voices and your judgments and your petty conceits, and how anticlimactically they ended your life together. I am not impressed by your complexity.

Now I am for living below the frequency of obsession. I am for the great defiant act of taking up space, of continuing simply.

I am not for death anymore, or half in love with it, even in quotation marks. I am not enamored of my pain. I am not sophisticated. There are no answers. There are not even any questions.

It is the noise that kills us.

So I am for bland as bread, Mommy. I am for the inadequacy of language, and I am against its very real power to do harm. I am against the cruelty of a little learning and the bludgeon of memory.

And, Daddy?

Finally.

Yes, finally. You.

I am for the limits of genes and influence, father to son. I am for reinvention. I am for burning paper and what is written on it: poor imitation to a despicable end.

And

lightly now,

shallow,

go,

I am

for

no

more

words.

I would like to thank my editor, Paul Slovak, for his belief, kindness, and support, as well as my agent, Eric Simonoff, for the same.